DEFY THE STARS

CLAUDIA GRAY

LITTLE, BROWN AND COMPANY

New York Boston

Little, Brown and Company
Hachette Book Group
1290 Avenue of the Americas, New York, NY 10104
Visit us at lb-teens.com

First Edition: April 2017

Little, Brown and Company is a division of Hachette Book Group, Inc. The Little, Brown name and logo are trademarks of Hachette Book Group, Inc.

Library of Congress Cataloging-in-Publication Data
Names: Gray, Claudia, author.
Title: Defy the stars / Claudia Gray.
Description: First edition. | New York ; Boston : Little, Brown and Company, 2017. | Summary: Teenaged soldier Noemi and an enemy robot, Abel, who is programmed to obey her commands, set out on an interstellar quest to save her home planet, Earth colony Genesis.
Identifiers: LCCN 2016028390| ISBN 9780316394031 (hardback) | ISBN 9780316394055 (e-book) | ISBN 9780316394062 (library edition e-book)
Subjects: | CYAC: Soldiers—Fiction. | Robots—Fiction. | Interstellar travel—Fiction. | Orphans—Fiction. | Science fiction.
Classification: LCC PZ7.G77625 Def 2017 | DDC [Fic]—dc23
LC record available at https://lccn.loc.gov/2016028390

ISBNs: 978-0-316-39403-1 (hardcover), 978-0-316-39405-5 (ebook)

Printed in the United States of America

LSC-C

10   9   8   7   6   5   4   3   2   1

For my parents

1

IN THREE WEEKS, NOEMI VIDAL WILL DIE—HERE, IN THIS very place.

Today is just practice.

Noemi wants to pray like the other soldiers she hears around her. The soft ebb and swell of their whispers sounds like waves against the shore. Zero-G even makes it look as if they're underwater—their hair fanning out from their heads, their booted feet swaying out from their launch harnesses as if caught by the tide. Only the dark star field outside the few small windows reveals how far they are from home.

The troops around her share a mix of faiths. Most of the People of the Book are seated close together: The Jews clasp hands with one another; the Muslims have been seated in one corner, to better pray toward the distant dot in the sky where Mecca lies. Like the other members of the Second Catholic Church, Noemi has her rosary beads in hand, the small stone-carved crucifix floating near her face. She clutches it tighter and wishes she didn't feel so hollow inside. So small. So desperate for the life she's already given up.

Every single one of them volunteered, but none of them is truly ready to die. Inside the troop ship, the air is electrified with terrible purpose.

Twenty days, Noemi reminds herself. *I have twenty days left.*

It's not much comfort to cling to. So she looks across the row at her best friend, one of the noncombatants who is here only to map potential trajectories for the Masada Run, not to die in the process. Esther Gatson's eyes are shut in fervent prayer. If Noemi could pray like that, maybe she wouldn't be so scared. Esther's long golden hair is pinned up in thick braids that ring her head like a halo, and Noemi feels her courage kindle back into flame.

I'm doing this for Esther. If I don't save anyone else, at least I can save her.

For a while, anyway.

Most of the soldiers harnessed near Noemi are between the ages of sixteen and twenty-eight. Noemi is only seventeen. Her generation is decimating itself.

And the Masada Run will be their greatest sacrifice.

It's a suicide mission—though no one uses the word *suicide*. Seventy-five ships will strike at once, all running at the same target. Seventy-five ships will blow themselves up. Noemi will be flying one of them.

The Masada Run won't win the war. But it will buy Genesis time. Her life for time.

No. Noemi looks at Esther again. *Your life for hers.*

Thousands have fallen in the past few years of this war, and there's no victory in sight. This spaceship they're on now is almost forty years old, which makes it one of the newest in the Genesis fleet. But each glance shows Noemi another flaw: the patching that hints at a past hull breach, the scarred windows that blur the stars outside, the wear on the harnesses that anchor her and her fellow soldiers into their seats. They even have to limit the use of artificial gravity to conserve power.

This is the price Genesis pays for a pristine environment, for the health and strength of every living thing on their world. Genesis will make nothing new while something old still functions. Her society's oath to limit manufacture and industry has profited them more than it cost—or it had, before the war erupted again, years after all the weapons factories had been shut down, after new fighter ships had been built.

The Liberty War had seemed to end over three decades ago; of course they'd trusted in their victory. Her planet had begun scaling back. The scars of the war still lingered; Noemi understands that more than most. But even she, along with everyone else, had believed they were truly safe.

Two years ago, the enemy returned. Since then, Noemi has learned to fire weapons and how to fly a single-pilot fighter. She's learned how to mourn friends who had fought beside her only hours before. She's learned what it's like to look over the horizon, see smoke, and realize the nearest town is now only so much rubble.

She's learned how to fight. Next she has to learn how to die.

The enemy's ships are new. Their weapons are more powerful. And their soldiers aren't even flesh and blood. Instead they have mech armies: robots, shaped like humans but without mercy, without vulnerabilities, without souls.

What kind of cowards go to war but refuse to fight it themselves? Noemi thinks. *How evil do you have to be to kill another world's people and risk none of your own?*

Today's just a practice run, she reminds herself. *No big deal. You'll fly it through, get it down, so when the day comes, no matter how scared you are, you can—*

Orange lights along each row begin to flash, warning all troops that the artificial magnetic gravity is about to kick in. It's too early. The other soldiers exchange worried glances, but the threat galvanizes Noemi. She shifts herself into position and takes a deep breath.

Wham! Hundreds of feet slam onto the metal floor at

once. Noemi's hair tumbles down to her chin, kept back from her face by the padded band she wears at the top of her forehead. Instantly she snaps into battle mode, untethering herself from her harness and reaching for her helmet. Her dark-green exosuit feels heavy again, but it's supple, as ready for battle as she is.

Because it sounds like the battle is waiting for them.

"All warriors to their fighters!" shouts Captain Baz. "Signs indicate we've got ships coming through the Gate any second. We launch in five!"

Her dread vanishes, scorched away by warrior instinct. Noemi joins the lines of soldiers separating into squadrons and hurrying down the narrow corridors that lead to their individual fighters.

"Why are they here?" murmurs one round-faced guy, a newbie just ahead of her in line, as they dash through a tunnel with missing panels and exposed wiring. His skin has gone death-white beneath his freckles. "Do they know what we're going to do?"

"They haven't blown us up yet, right?" Noemi points out. "That means they haven't found out about the Masada Run. It's lucky we were up here when they came through, so we can fight them off farther from home. Okay?"

The poor new kid nods. He's shaking. Noemi would like to be more comforting, but the words would probably come out wrong. She's all rough edges and sharp elbows, her heart hidden so well by a quick temper that almost nobody ever recognizes she has one. Sometimes she wishes she could turn herself inside out. That way people would see the good in her before they saw the bad.

Battle brings out her bad side, where it's actually a positive. Anyway, no point in trying to improve herself now.

Esther, who's directly ahead of the boy, turns and smiles at him. "It's going to be all right," she promises in her soft voice. "You'll see. When you're in your fighter, your training will kick in, and you'll feel braver than anything." He smiles back, already steadier.

After Noemi was orphaned, she hated the world for existing, she hated other people for not hurting as much as she did, and she hated herself for continuing to breathe. As kind as the Gatsons had been to take her in, she couldn't miss the looks Esther's parents gave each other—the exasperation of doing so much for someone who couldn't or wouldn't appreciate it. Years went by before Noemi could feel any gratitude, or much of anything at all besides anger and bitterness.

But Esther never made her feel bad. In those first awful days, even though they'd been only eight years old, Esther had already known not to try comforting her friend with cheap words about memories or God's will. She'd known all Noemi needed was for someone just to be there, asking nothing of her but making sure she knew she wasn't alone.

How come none of that ever rubbed off on me? Noemi thinks as they hurry through the final corridors. Maybe she should've asked for lessons.

Esther shifts to the side, guiding the scared boy ahead of her to fall into step by Noemi's side. Immediately she says to Noemi, "Don't worry."

Too late. "You don't have a fighter today. Only a scout ship. You can't go out into battle in that thing; you should just monitor us from here. Tell Captain Baz."

"What do you think she'll say? Sit here, get some knitting done? Scouts can transmit a lot of valuable info during a skirmish." Esther shakes her head. "You can't keep me out of *every* fight, you know."

No, just the worst one. "If you get hurt up here, your parents will kill me, and that's if Jemuel doesn't get to me first."

Esther's face does this *thing* every time Noemi mentions Jemuel: Her cheeks pink with pleasure, and she presses her lips together to hold back her smile. But her eyes look as stricken as if she'd just seen Noemi lying wounded and bleeding on the floor. Once, Noemi had been glad to see that—to know that Esther cared about Noemi's heartbreak as much as her own happiness—but now it's just irritating. She says only, "Noemi, it's my duty to be out here. The same as yours. So let it go."

As usual, Esther's right. Noemi takes a deep breath and runs faster through the corridor.

Her division reaches its launch array—a line of small, single-pilot fighter ships as sleek and streamlined as darts. Noemi jumps into her pilot's seat. Across the room, she can see Esther doing the same, with just as much purpose as if she could really fight. As the translucent cockpit canopy locks over her and Noemi clamps her helmet into place, Esther gives her a look, the one that means *Hey, you know I'm not really upset with you, right?* She's good at that look, especially for someone who almost never loses her temper.

Noemi gives her the usual smile back, the one that means *Everything's fine.* Probably Noemi *isn't* good at that, because Esther's the only person she ever shows it to.

But Esther grins. She gets it. That's enough.

The launch-bay panel begins to open, exposing the squadron's fighters to the cold darkness of space at the farthest reaches of their solar system. Genesis is hardly more than a faint green dot in the distance; the sun she was born under still dominates the sky, but it appears smaller from here than either of her planet's moons looks from the surface. For that first instant, when there's nothing before Noemi but infinite stars, it's beautiful—beyond beautiful—and she thrills at the sight as if it were her first time seeing it.

And as always, she wishes her most secret, most selfish wish: *If only I could explore it all—*

Then the panel opens fully to reveal the Genesis Gate.

The Gate is an enormous, brushed-silver ring of inter-locking metal components, dozens of kilometers wide. Within the ring, Noemi can glimpse a faint shimmer like the surface of water when it's almost too dark for a reflection, but not quite. This would be beautiful, too, if it weren't the greatest threat to Genesis's safety. Each Gate stabilizes one end of a singularity—a shortcut through space-time that allows a ship to travel partway across the galaxy in a mere instant. This is how the enemy reaches them; this is where all the battles begin.

In the distance Noemi can make out the evidence of some of those past battles—scrap left over from ships blown to pieces long ago. Some bits of the debris are mere splinters of metal. Other chunks are enormous twisted slabs, even entire blasted-out ships. These remnants have settled into lazy orbit around the Gate's gravitational pull.

But they hardly matter compared to the dark gray shapes speeding away from the Gate, slicing into their system. These are the ships of the enemy, the planet determined to conquer Genesis and take their lands and resources for its own forever:

Earth.

They poisoned their own world. Colonized Genesis only so they could move billions of people here and poison it in turn. But worlds that sustain life are few and precious. They're sacred. They have to be protected.

The signal lights flare. She releases her docking clamps as Captain Baz's voice speaks to the squadron via her helmet mic: *"Let's get out there."*

Disengage clamps: Check. Noemi's ship floats free of its moorings, hanging weightless. The others rise beside her, all of them ready to scramble. Her hands move to the brightly colored panel before her. She knows each button and toggle by heart, understands what each light means. *Systems readouts normal: Check.*

Ignition: Check.

Her fighter leaps forward, a silver comet against the blackness of space. The shimmer in the Gate brightens like a star going supernova—a warning that more Earth forces are on the way.

Her hands tighten on the controls as she sees the Gate burst into light, and ships begin to crash through, one after the other.

"We have five—no, seven confirmed Damocles-class ships!" Captain Baz says over comms. *"We caught 'em by surprise. Let's use it."*

Noemi accelerates, her silver fighter streaking toward the farthest Damocles vessel. These long, flat, boxy ships are unencumbered with artificial gravity or extensive life support, because they aren't for carrying humans. Instead, depending on ship size, each Damocles carries anywhere from a dozen to a hundred mechs, each one heavily armed, programmed for battle, and ready to kill.

Mechs aren't afraid to die, because they aren't even alive. They have no souls. They're pure machines of death.

Pure evil.

Noemi's eyes narrow as she sees the first hatches open. Thank God, these are smaller ships, but they're still carrying a powerful mech force. If they could just blast one or two of the Damocles ships into atoms before they launch their deadly cargo—

Too late. The mechs shoot out wearing metal exoskeletons, with just enough sheathing to keep the robotic warriors inside from freezing in the coldness of space. As the Genesis fighters approach, the mechs begin to shift position. They spread their limbs wide to expand their shooting range, like carnivores pouncing on prey. As long as Noemi's fought, as hard as she's trained, she still shudders at the sight.

"Attack sequence—now!" Baz calls, and battle cries echo through Noemi's helmet. Noemi spins her fighter left, choosing her first target.

Over comms, one guy yells, *"Kill 'em all!"*

Blaster bolts from the mechs slash through the air toward Noemi, fiery orange streaks that could cripple a fighter in moments. She banks left, fires back. All around her, Genesis fighters and Earth mechs scatter, formations dissolving in the chaos of battle.

Like most people of Genesis, Noemi believes in the Word of God. Even if she sometimes has questions and doubts the elders can't answer, she can quote chapter and verse on the value of life, the importance of peace. Even though the things she's blowing out of the sky aren't truly alive, they're . . . human-shaped. The bloodlust stirred up inside her feels wrong in a way that all her righteous fury can't entirely cure. But she powers through it. She has to, for the sake of her fellow soldiers, and for her world.

Noemi knows what her duty to God is right now:

Fight like hell.

2

AS ABEL FLOATS IN ZERO-G, IN THE DARK QUIET OF A dead ship's equipment pod bay, he tells himself the story again. The black-and-white images flicker in his mind with total accuracy; it's as if he's watching it projected upon a screen, the way it was shown centuries ago. Abel possesses an eidetic memory, so he only needs to see things once to remember them forever.

And he enjoys remembering *Casablanca*. Retelling himself every scene, in order, over and over again. The characters' voices are so vivid in his mind that the actors might as well be floating in the pod bay beside him:

Where were you last night?

That's so long ago, I don't remember.

It's a good story, one that holds up to repetition. This is fortunate for Abel, who has now been trapped in the *Daedalus* for almost thirty years. Roughly fifteen million, seven hundred and seventy thousand, nine hundred minutes, or nine hundred and forty-six million, seven hundred thousand seconds.

(He has been programmed to round off such large numbers outside of actual scientific work. The same humans who made him capable of measuring with perfect precision also find the mention of such numbers irritating. It makes no sense to Abel, but he knows better than to expect rational behavior from human beings.)

The nearly complete darkness of his confinement makes it easy for Abel to imagine that reality is in black and white, like the movie.

New input. Form: irregular flashes of light. The drama stops cold in Abel's mind as he looks up to analyze—

Blaster bolts. A battle, no doubt between Earth and Genesis forces.

Abel was marooned here in just such a battle. After a long silence, warfare has reignited in the past two years. At first he found that encouraging. If Earth ships were again coming to the Genesis system, they would eventually find the *Daedalus*. They would tow it in to reclaim everything inside, including Abel himself.

And after thirty terrible years of suspense, Abel would finally be able to fulfill his primary directive: Protect Burton Mansfield.

Honor the creator. Obey his directives above all others. Preserve his life no matter what.

But his hopes have faded as the war has churned on. No one has come to find him, and no one seems likely to do so in the near future. Perhaps not even in the distant future. Although Abel is stronger than any human being and a match for even the most powerful fighter mechs, he can't tear open the air-lock door separating him from the rest of the *Daedalus*. (He tried. Despite knowing down to the hundredth decimal point the ratios working against him, Abel still tried. Thirty years is a long time.)

Neither Abel himself nor this ship would have been abandoned lightly. Abel has run through the various scenarios many times, but he can't accept it. Mansfield could have fled to save himself, meaning to return for Abel, but he was simply never able to. Then again, the battle intensified so much that day that any human escape from the *Daedalus* might have been impossible. In all probability, Mansfield was killed by enemy troops on the same day Abel became trapped.

And yet, Burton Mansfield is a genius, the creator of all twenty-six models of mech that currently serve humankind. If anyone could devise a way to survive that last battle, Mansfield could have.

Of course, Abel's creator could also have died in the years since. He was in his late middle age thirty years ago, and with humans, accidents sometimes happen. Perhaps that is why he hasn't come. Surely only death would keep Mansfield away.

There is another possibility. It is the least likely of all plausible options, but not impossible: Mansfield might still be aboard, but in cryosleep. The cryosleep chambers in sick bay could keep a human alive with minimal life support for an indefinite amount of time. The person inside would be unconscious, aging at less than one-tenth the normal rate and waiting for a rescuer to bring them back to life.

All Abel would have to do is get to him.

Before he can find Mansfield, however, someone must find him. So far, Earth's forces have spent no time searching the debris field for functioning ships. Nobody has found Abel; no one is even looking.

Someday, he tells himself. Earth's victory is inevitable, whether it comes in another two months or two hundred years. It's entirely possible for Abel to live that long.

But Mansfield would surely be dead by then. Maybe even *Casablanca* won't be interesting after that many years—

Abel tilts his head, peering more carefully at the sliver of star field he can see through the pod bay's window. After a moment, he reaches out to the closest wall and pushes off, bringing himself closer to the view. In the ultra-thick glass, he has to look through his own translucent reflection, with his short gold hair fanned out around his head as though he were in a medieval manuscript, gilt-edged.

This battle is coming nearer to the *Daedalus* than any other ever has. A few fighters are already on the edges of the debris field; if Earth's forces continue separating the Genesis troops from one another, some of the mechs will soon be very close to his ship.

Very, very close.

He must determine a method for sending a signal. It would have to be a low-tech solution, and the signal could only be very basic. But Abel doesn't need to send information to a human, doesn't have to worry about the limitations of an organic brain. Any small pattern amid the chaos might attract the attention of another mech—and if it has a chance to investigate, its programming will compel it to do so.

Abel pushes against the wall to propel himself through the pod bay. After thirty years, he is all too familiar with the few pieces of equipment in here with him, not one of which can help him power up the ship, open the pod bay door, or communicate directly with another vessel. But that doesn't mean they're useless.

In one corner, suspended a few centimeters from the wall, is a simple flashlight.

Helps with repairs, Mansfield had explained, his blue eyes crinkling at the corners as he smiled. *Humans can't rewire a spaceship with nothing but their memory of the schematics. Not like you, my boy. We need to see it.* Abel remembered smiling back, proud that he could replace weaker humans and serve Mansfield better.

And yet he could never hold humanity in contempt, because Mansfield was human, too.

Grabbing the flashlight, Abel launches himself toward the window again. What message should he send?

No message. Only a signal. Someone is here; someone seeks contact. The rest can come later.

Abel holds the light to the window. He has not used it during the past decades, and it still holds sufficient charge. One flash. Then two, three, five, seven, eleven—and so on through the first ten primes. He plans to repeat the sequence until someone sees him.

Or until the battle ends, leaving him alone for many more years to come.

But maybe someone will see, Abel thinks.

He isn't supposed to hope. Not like humans do. Yet during the past several years, his mind has been forced to deepen. With no new stimulation, he has reflected on every piece of information, every interaction, every single element of his existence before the abandonment of the *Daedalus*. Something within in his inner workings has changed, and probably not for the better.

Because hope can *hurt*, and yet Abel can't stop looking out the window, wishing desperately for someone to see him, so he will no longer be alone.

3

Captain Baz shouts, *"Incoming!"*

Noemi steers sharply downward, spiraling through the twisted metal remains of newly destroyed mechs. But the Damocles ships keep spitting out more and more of them— far too many for her squadron to handle. Only the Masada Run volunteers came out today, only to practice. They weren't planning to fight a full mech assault, and by now it shows.

The mechs are *everywhere*, their oversize exoskeleton attack suits streaking through the battered ships of her squadron like a meteor shower raining fire. As they approach, the exosuits unfold from metal-beamed, sharp-edged pseudo-vessels into monstrous, metal-limbed creatures capable of smashing through the Genesis lines as if they were punching through paper.

Every once in a while, as one of them zooms past her ship, Noemi gets a glimpse of the mechs themselves—the machines within the machines. They look just like human beings, which sometimes makes it hard for newbies to shoot. She hesitated herself in her first firefight when she glimpsed what seemed to be a man in his mid-twenties, with deep tan skin and black hair much like her own; he could've been her brother, if Rafael had had the chance to grow up.

That very human hesitation nearly ended her life that day. Mechs don't hesitate. They go for the kill every time.

Since then she's seen that exact same face looking back at her dozens of times. It's a Charlie model, she now knows. Standard male fighter, ruthless and relentless.

"There are twenty-five models in standard production," Elder Darius Akide had said, the day he addressed her training class for the first time. *"Each has a name beginning with a different letter of the alphabet, from Baker to Zebra. All but two of these models look completely human. And each one is stronger than any human can ever be. They're programmed with only enough intelligence to perform their core responsibilities. For manual-labor models, that's not much. But the fighters they send against us? They're smart. Damned smart. Mansfield left out only the levels of higher intelligence that could allow them to have something like a conscience."*

Noemi's eyes widen as her tactical screen lights up. Her hands tighten on her weapons controls, and she fires the instant the mech flies into range. For one split second she sees the thing's face—*Queen, standard female fighter model*—before both exosuit and mech shatter. Nothing's left but splinters of metal. Good.

Where's Esther? They haven't flown within visual range of each other for a couple of minutes now. Noemi would like to signal her, but she knows better than to use comms for a personal message in the middle of combat. So she can only look.

How am I supposed to find anyone in this? she asks herself as she swoops in over a few more of the mechs, blasting as fast as her weapons will work. Their return fire is so ferocious that black space momentarily turns brilliant white. *The invasion forces keep getting larger. Earth keeps getting bolder. They'll never let up, not ever.*

The Masada Run really is our only hope.

She thinks about that scared kid shivering as the troops ran to their fighters. His call sign hasn't appeared on her screen in a while either. Is he lost? Dead?

And Esther—scout ships are almost defenseless—

Finally the fighting around her breaks for a moment, and she has a chance to scan for Esther's ship. When she finds it, she feels a moment of elation—it's intact, Esther's alive—but then Noemi frowns. Why is Esther all the way over there?

Then Noemi realizes what she's looking at. Horror injects adrenaline into her veins.

One of the mechs has turned away from the battle. Just—left the fight. She's never seen a mech do anything like that, and it's heading toward the debris field near the fallen Gate. Is it malfunctioning? Doesn't matter. For whatever reason, Esther decided to tail the stupid thing— probably to investigate what it was up to. But now she's isolated from the Genesis troops who could protect her. If the mech finds what it's looking for or receives an override from its Damocles, it will turn on Esther in an instant.

Noemi's duty allows her to defend a fellow fighter who's in extreme risk. So she banks left and accelerates so hard the force shoves her back in her seat. The blazing firefight around her darkens until her view of space is again clear. The Genesis Gate looms, surrounded by armed platforms. Any ship that approaches without Earth-signature codes gets destroyed. Even from across the galaxy, Earth keeps Genesis in its laser sights.

As she speeds toward Esther's location, Noemi looks less at her sensor screen. The view from the cockpit shows her enough. Esther's scout ship zips around the mech, using energy bursts from the sensors to muddle the mech's workings, but that doesn't accomplish much. So far the mech is dodging the bursts expertly. Apparently it's headed toward one of the larger pieces of debris—no, not debris, an abandoned spaceship, some kind of civilian craft. Noemi's never seen anything like this ship: teardrop-shaped, roughly the volume of a good-size three-story building, and with a mirrored surface that has dulled only slightly over the years. It must have been all but invisible to the naked eye until recently.

Is the mech going to bring that ship back to Earth? The ship was abandoned, obviously, but it doesn't look seriously damaged from here.

If Earth wants it, then Noemi intends to keep them from getting it. She imagines destroying the mech and recapturing this teardrop ship for the Genesis fleet. Maybe it could be outfitted with weapons, turned into a warship. God knows they need another.

Then again, this mech is a Queen or a Charlie. She and Esther will be in for one hell of a fight.

Bring it on, she thinks.

Noemi cuts her speed as she gets closer. Esther and the mech are almost within weapons range—

—then the mech turns, shifting its aim. It stretches its exoskeleton arms and clasps Esther's recon ship like a flytrap plant snapping shut around a bug. The way they're positioned, the mech must be right above Esther, the two of them looking into each other's eyes.

Weapons! But Noemi can't shoot the mech from here without blasting Esther, too. In ordinary combat, she'd fire anyway. Any pilot captured like that is dead already, and at least she could destroy the mech....

—but this is Esther, *please not her, please—*

The mech releases one arm, draws it back in a startlingly human movement, and punches straight through the hull of Esther's fighter.

Noemi's scream deafens her in her own helmet. It doesn't matter; she doesn't need to hear—she needs to save Esther.

Ten minutes. Our exosuits give us air for ten minutes. Go, go, go, go—

The mech releases Esther, swivels toward the abandoned ship, then stops, finally picking up Noemi on its scanners. She fires before it can even aim.

In a flash of light, the mech explodes into so much tinsel. Noemi zooms through what's left of it on her way to Esther, metal splinters clicking against her cockpit shell.

Can we get back to the troop ship in time? No, not with the battle still raging. Okay, then. This abandoned ship. I can restore life support, maybe; if not, it'll probably have oxygen I can use to re-up Esther's reserves. First-aid supplies. Maybe even a sick bay. Please, God, let it have a sick bay.

She feels as if she's praying to nothing. To no one. But even if God doesn't speak to her, surely he'll listen for Esther's sake.

Noemi's visor fogs slightly. She has to hold back her tears, though, or else they'll float through the helmet and blind her at the worst moment. So she bites the inside of her cheek as she swoops down toward the devastated scout ship. "Esther? Can you read me?"

No reply. By now Noemi is out of communications range for the other Genesis fighters. If Captain Baz even realizes they're missing, she won't hear Noemi's broadcasts, won't know to send help. Maybe they've both been written off as dead already.

"We're going to make it," Noemi promises Esther, and herself, as she edges her fighter closer. Now she can see how badly the scout ship's been mutilated—metal shredded into shards—but Esther's helmet seems to be intact. Is she moving? Yes. Noemi thinks she is. *She's alive. She's going to make it. All I have to do is get us to that ship.*

One switch throws a towline into space, and the magnetic clamp catches Esther's hull. Quickly Noemi scans the mirrored vessel in front of them. There—a docking-bay door.

Powered by magnetic sensors, the plates of the circular door fan open automatically. Noemi's so grateful she could weep.

It's always seemed to her that her prayers are never answered, that nobody up there has ever heard her pleas. But God must be listening after all.

4

THE GENESIS FIGHTER BLASTS THE QUEEN MODEL, demolishing it, and Abel feels hope shatter within him— an almost physical sensation. It's as if his inner framework had collapsed.

I must perform a full self-diagnostic at my first opportunity.

Abel floats in the dark chamber of the pod bay, just one more piece of equipment suspended in the cold dark. Without gravity. Without purpose. How long will it take his internal batteries to wear out? They were made to last approximately two and a half centuries... but he is using very little energy, which means they might go on for twice as long. More. It could be more than half a millennium before Abel finally breaks down into mere scrap metal.

He can't fear his own death. His programming doesn't allow it.

But Abel can fear hundreds of years of solitude—never

discovering what became of Burton Mansfield—never again having any use.

Can a mech go insane? Abel might find out.

At that moment, however, he sees one of the Genesis fighters tether the other and power forward. Are they—is it possible—

Yes. They want to board the *Daedalus*.

These are enemy troops. They are Genesis warriors. As such, they are an immediate threat to the safety of Burton Mansfield.

(Who might not be aboard any longer. Who could have died years ago. But Abel acknowledges these probabilities while still prioritizing the elimination of any risk to Mansfield's life—*any* risk, no matter how remote—above everything else.)

The Genesis ship is headed for the main docking bay. Abel reviews the ship's layout, and the *Daedalus*'s schematics flash before him as though projected on a screen. He has reviewed them often, these past thirty years; Abel has reviewed every piece of information he's ever been exposed to in an effort to keep himself from succumbing to sheer boredom. But the plans are more vivid now, the lines on the blueprints burning as brightly as fire in his mind.

Main docking bay: Level One. Two levels below my equipment pod bay. After three decades, Abel thinks of the room as his. *When the Genesis fighters enter the main docking bay, the unharmed pilot will no doubt attempt to reach sick bay in order to assist the injured comrade,* he calculates. *If the pilot's main goal were safety, rather than rescue, then that fighter would be speeding back toward the distant Genesis fleet.* Although a first-aid kit had been stored in the main docking bay, Abel doesn't know whether it's still there; even if it is, its contents would be unlikely to help anyone gravely hurt.

In order to leave the docking bay, the Genesis pilot will have to restore backup power. Assuming any damage to the Daedalus *is not too severe, it is possible to do this from that location. Any trained pilot should be able to do so within minutes if not seconds.*

Abel's mind clicks through the possibilities, faster and faster. This is the first new situation he's faced in thirty years. His mental capabilities have not been blunted by this long time in storage. If anything, he feels sharper than before.

But there's an emotional component now. Hope has kindled into something far more exhilarating: *excitement.* Merely seeing anything outside this pod bay will be a thrill…

…but nothing can possibly match the knowledge that he will finally be able to search for Burton Mansfield. To find him. Maybe even to save him.

• • •

"Excellent," Mansfield said as he examined the puzzles Abel had just solved. "Your pattern-recognition ability is top-notch. You finished that in very nearly record time, Abel."

Although Abel was programmed to enjoy praise, particularly from Mansfield, he could still experience doubt. "Was my performance adequate, sir?"

Mansfield settled into his high-backed leather chair, a slight frown on his face. "You do understand that excellence would, by definition, include adequacy?"

"Yes, sir! Of course, sir." Abel didn't want Mansfield to think his language databases hadn't loaded properly. "I only meant—many of my test performances have beaten all existing records. These results did not."

After a moment, Mansfield chuckled. "Would you look at that? It looks like your personality has already developed enough to make you a perfectionist."

"...Is that good, sir?"

"Better than you realize." Mansfield rose from his chair. "Walk with me, Abel."

Burton Mansfield's office was located in his house in London. Although the home had been recently constructed and on the outside looked like any other mirrored polygon in this gated, privileged community on the hill—on the inside, it might have been 1895 instead of 2295. Handwoven silk rugs covered the wooden floors. A grandfather clock ticked loudly in the corner, its brass pendulum swinging back and forth despite countless atomic clocks nested in the higher-tech machines concealed all around it. Paintings by various Old Masters hung on the wall: a saint by Raphael, a soup can by Warhol. And even though the fire and fireplace were holographic, the house's internal climate controls made it feel as though the flames glowed with heat.

Mansfield was a human male of average height, with dark-gold hair and blue eyes. His features were regular, even handsome, if Abel understood the aesthetic principles involved. (He hoped that he did, because Mansfield's younger face had been the model for Abel's own.) Even the eccentricities of Mansfield's appearance were striking and aristocratic—the widow's peak at his forehead, a slightly hawkish nose, and unusually full lips. He dressed in the simple, Japanese-inspired style of the day, in a flowing open jacket and wide-legged trousers.

Abel, meanwhile, wore the same boxy gray coverall common to most mechs. The garment fit and was practical for all purposes. Why then did it sometimes feel... not right?

Before he could consider this question in depth, Abel was brought back to the moment by Mansfield, who was pointing at the window—actually at the courtyard outside. "What do you see out there, Abel? No. Who do you see?"

Mansfield usually used who, not what, to refer to mechs. Abel appreciated the courtesy. "I see two Dog models and one Yoke model, all of which are engaged in garden work. One of *the Dogs is tending your hydroponic vegetable plot, while the other Dog and Yoke are trimming the topiary hedges."*

"We need to work on your overenthusiasm for detail." Mansfield sighed. "That's my fault, of course. Never mind. My point is—if I sent you into that garden, you could take care of the hydroponics, couldn't you? And trim the hedge?"

"Yes, sir."

"Just as well as any Dog or Yoke?"

"Of course, sir."

"What if I fell and broke my arm? Could you set it as well as a Tare model?"

The medical mechs were among the smartest and swiftest, but Abel could still answer, "Yes, sir."

Mansfield's blue eyes twinkled. "What if a Queen model broke in with orders to kill me? A Queen or a Charlie? What then?"

"Sir, you're Earth's most respected roboticist—no one would—"

"The question is theoretical," Mansfield said gently.

"Oh. In theory, were a fighter-model mech to attempt to kill you, I believe I could defeat it in combat. At the very least, I'd be able to distract or damage it enough for you to escape or summon help."

"Exactly. All the programming for the other twenty-five models—all their talents—every bit of that is inside you. You

may only equal your simpler counterparts in certain talents, but you'll excel in most of them. And not one mech ever built has the breadth of skills and intelligence that you have." The ghost of a smile played upon Mansfield's face as he studied Abel. "You, my son, are one of a kind."

Son. Abel knew this was not true in any literal sense; although he contained organic DNA patterned on Mansfield's own, he was primarily a mechanical construct, not a biological organism. Burton Mansfield had a true child of his own, a daughter who obviously took precedence in every way. And yet—

"You liked that, didn't you?" Mansfield asked. "When I called you 'son.'"

"Yes, sir."

"So you're gaining some emotional capacity. Good." His hand patted Abel once on the back. "Let's hurry that along, shall we? From now on, call me 'Father.'" With a sigh, Mansfield looked out at the hoverships darting through the London sky. "Getting late. Tell the Dogs and Yoke to finish up, would you?"

Abel nodded.

"And when you're done, join me in the library. I want to get you started on some books and movies and holovids. We'll see whether fictional narratives can affect you."

"I'll be there soon," Abel said, before daring to add, "Father."

He was rewarded with Mansfield's smile.

• • •

A distant clang sounds through the ship. The framework shudders slightly—stubborn metal resisting motion after so long at rest. The main docking bay door is opening at last.

Abel realizes he's smiling.

I'll be there soon, Father.

Once again he reviews the ship's schematics, imagining a three-dimensional model of the *Daedalus* floating in front of him. Abel mentally enlarges the area around the pod bay and searches for "defensive resources." Various possibilities come up, most of them emergency storage lockers, some nearer and more practical than others—

The auxiliary lights come on. For the first time in thirty years, Abel is no longer surrounded by darkness.

A human might hesitate, overwhelmed with shock, delight, or gratitude. Abel instantly angles himself, prepared for the moment a split second later when gravity comes back on. He drops two meters and lands on his feet and hands as silently as a cat. From there it's only one step to the door; his fingers fly over the keyboard with inhuman speed to input the unlock code, and—at last, at long last—the pod-bay door slides open.

Abel is free.

He doesn't celebrate. He doesn't laugh. He simply runs

to the nearest "defensive resource" listed in the ship schematics. The locker remains undamaged, still sealed. Whatever happened to Mansfield and the others, they never used these. Is that good news—or proof they died instantly?

Abel punches in the ten-digit code. The door opens, revealing the locker's contents, and Abel's hand closes around a blaster. Now armed, he runs toward sick bay. If Burton Mansfield is in cryosleep there, his life may be imminently at risk. Therefore, the Genesis pilot remains an enemy intruder whose presence cannot be allowed. The pilot's swiftness in restoring full power suggests an intelligent opponent. In other words, a dangerous one.

Abel will allow himself to be found by his liberator— the person who set him free after all this time—and then he'll shoot to kill.

5

NOEMI SLAMS DOWN ONTO THE DECK OF THE ABAN-doned ship, instinctively covering her head as pieces of debris fall on and around her—emergency ration packs, tools, all the other stuff these careless people left behind. Worse than the impacts on her back and arms are the heavy thuds of metal from behind: her fighter and Esther's recon ship, falling onto the docking-bay floor.

The ships can take that. But Esther...

Lights are on. Gravity's stabilized. Atmosphere pressurized—go.

Noemi dashes from the control panel to Esther's ship and hits the switch to open the cockpit from the outside, but the damage is too great—it's lost all power. Esther stirs, rolling onto one side until she stiffens, in obvious pain. With a shaky hand, Esther reaches for the manual control. The cockpit's transparent shell scrapes back too slowly.

"Esther!" Noemi tugs off her helmet, then reaches inside

the cockpit even as the shell struggles to open fully. Carefully she lifts off Esther's helmet, too. "Where are you hurt?"

"Left—" Esther has to swallow hard before she can keep talking. "Left side . . . Where are we?"

"Looks like an abandoned Earth ship in the debris field." And the ship's in even better condition than Noemi had hoped. The backup power is at nearly 100 percent despite what must have been many years dormant. There's a small plaque above the doors leading into the rest of the ship, one word etched in larger letters than all the rest. "The *Daedalus*. Somebody from Earth must've been forced to dump it decades ago. So, see, we've got gravity, communications systems, medical supplies, everything we need. You're going to be okay."

Esther's head lolls back, her green eyes glinting with gallows humor. "Liar."

"You *will*. Can you get out of your ship?"

After a moment, Esther slowly shakes her head. "I can't stand up. The mech—my hip—"

Noemi's stomach turns over as she realizes the mech not only tore through the hull of the ship but crushed Esther's hip joint, too. The flight suit isn't ripped, but that doesn't mean Esther isn't shredded and bleeding inside it.

The femoral artery hasn't been severed, Noemi tells herself. *If it had been, she'd be dead already. So it's intact. She has a chance.*

"Okay, Esther. Hang on." Try to carry her to sick bay, or bring supplies back here? If they're going to make it back to the troop ship and real medical help, Esther's going to need sealant for her wounds and maybe a transfusion if she's bleeding inside—one that Noemi, with AB negative blood type, probably can't supply. But a ship like this might have stocked synthetic blood, and the stuff's good forever. Noemi can carry some synthetic blood and tubes, and probably Esther shouldn't be moved until she's been stabilized and they have a better idea of just how badly she's been injured. "I'm going to find sick bay, all right? I'll be right back with supplies."

Esther's face goes even paler. She doesn't want to be left alone, and Noemi's heart wrenches thinking of how scared Esther must feel. But her friend only nods, and tries to joke. "I'm not... going anywhere."

Noemi squeezes Esther's gloved hand, then runs for the door, which slides open smoothly. She dashes into the interior of the deserted ship and pauses, trying to get her bearings. The corridor curves in what looks like a long oval, and the emergency lighting tints everything dull orange. Noemi looks around wildly. This ship isn't that enormous—perhaps the size of a couple of three-story houses put together—but even the few minutes it would take to explore it fully are minutes Esther can't spare. *I need a screen, schematics, something to tell me where everything is!*

She runs along the main corridor, a long spiral that goes from the bottom of the ship to the top, with a few short side corridors jutting off the sides. *Like a vine with thorns*, Noemi thinks. And the corridors are vaulted, broken up every few meters by curved metal struts on the side. It reminds her of the halls of Gothic cathedrals built on Earth long ago.

Then she sees a screen. Heart pounding, she presses her hand against it. Most info screens respond to human touch, but this one remains black. "Computer?" Noemi tries. Nothing. Does it not hear her? "Information. Power on."

Still nothing. But at the very bottom of the screen, she sees a faint light racing back and forth, indicating that the computers are at least partially active. It must be malfunctioning. Although the *Daedalus* looks almost completely undamaged, it has to have been here a long time, at least since the first Liberty War thirty years prior. Maybe it's falling apart due to neglect....

No, Noemi realizes. *That's not it. Someone must have locked down primary systems.*

Chills sweep through her, stiffening her backbone and making her hair stand on end. Is someone else aboard the *Daedalus*?—but no. That's impossible. No human being could or would have lived in isolation for thirty years. Probably the former crew locked systems down before abandoning ship, to ensure nobody from Genesis could capture it.

If these systems are locked down, communication will be, too. How can she contact the troop ship and Captain Baz?

Deal with that later, she tells herself. *Just find sick bay and take care of Esther.*

The landing bay is on the lowest level of the *Daedalus,* so Noemi runs upward, checking each door as she goes. Engine room—no. Kitchen mess—no. Auxiliary pod bay for equipment—no. Crew quarters—the bridge with its vast viewscreen—no. Her breathing quickens as she pushes herself onward. Panic is closing in, and piloting a fighter in battle is more exhausting than it seems. But the danger to Esther keeps Noemi moving.

I must be near the top, she thinks as she rounds the next curve, footsteps thudding against the metal plates of the floor. *Sick bay has to be one of the next few rooms—*

Two years of military training have honed Noemi's reflexes. So a barely conscious alarm goes off when one of the metal plates doesn't thump the same way as the others. Maybe it's that flush of extra adrenaline that sharpens her vision and lets her detect one swift flash of movement around the next curve—pale gray against the coal black of the corridors. Noemi reacts without thinking, instantly flinging herself sideways to take cover behind one of the wall struts in the split second before a blaster bolt scorches the floor.

One blink and her own blaster's in her hand. Noemi leans around to shoot at her unknown attacker, whips back before whoever it is can target her again. The smell of ozone sears her nose, and now she's on the verge of panic.

How can anyone be in here? Did a human being somehow live in this ship for thirty years?

What frightens Noemi the most is that her attacker stands between her and sick bay. This intruder, or castaway, whoever it might be, is keeping Noemi from getting Esther the help she needs. Esther could be bleeding to death internally right now.

Fear turns to fury. Noemi shoots blindly around the rounded corner of the corridor. Immediately her assailant fires back, missing her only by millimeters; the heat of the blast stings her bare fingers.

That was so close. So accurate. With a mere fraction of a second to aim...

Noemi's gut clenches. A mech. That's what it has to be, another damned mech. At first she's confused—*I know no other mechs flew out this way with us, only the one I destroyed*—but then she realizes it must have been aboard ever since this ship was abandoned. The human beings saved themselves and fled back to Earth, leaving this soulless hunk of metal behind to defend the wreckage forever.

Emergency systems aboard the *Daedalus* belatedly recognize internal weapons fire. The lights shift from orange to red; they begin to pulse rapidly, the strobe effect turning the entire world strange and disjointed. Noemi's heartbeat speeds up to match it.

She is a warrior of Genesis. She flew into battle today prepared to be killed by a mech. But she'll be damned if she'll let one kill Esther, too.

Noemi has to destroy this mech and get to sick bay now—or die trying.

6

THIRTY YEARS OF SOLITUDE, ENDED IN A FLASH. WITH his first glimpse of the intruder, Abel is—at last—no longer alone.

Every command in his programming says he must kill the new human on board. He fully intends to do so. But for one overpowering, rapturous moment, Abel wants nothing more than to hear her voice, to see her, to revel in the presence of another.

Replaying the .412 seconds of visual data he has indicates that this is most likely a *her*—an adolescent, female-presenting human approximately 168 centimeters or five feet six inches in height, of primarily Latin American and Polynesian ancestry, with chin-length black hair, brown eyes, the dark-green exosuit of a Genesis soldier, and a Mark Eight blaster that is—to judge by the wavelength of the beams that just sliced through the air—at approximately 45 percent charge.

Given that he must kill the intruder shortly, the data about the blaster is the most relevant. Abel saw two fighters entering the landing bay, but only one soldier has infiltrated the ship. Therefore, his earlier analysis of the situation was correct: One pilot is severely injured, and the other wants to reach sick bay in order to provide assistance.

But she cannot be allowed to do so, because Burton Mansfield may be in cryosleep inside. Immediately after arming himself, Abel shut off all communications systems, both internal and external, to isolate the Genesis pilots. Therefore, no reinforcements will arrive. His opponent is alone and desperate. In such conditions, humans become reckless. If he keeps her from her goal, she will go to extreme lengths to reach sick bay—and in so doing, weaken her position.

Abel thinks through the intruder's options, makes a decision. Instead of prolonging their firefight, he turns and runs toward sick bay. He's fast enough to reach the door before the first blaster bolt hits the wall nearby, and to get inside before she can pursue. As soon as the sick bay door slides shut behind him, he wheels around, locks the door, and...

...stops.

His programming is clear. *Check the cryosleep pods. Look for Mansfield.*

But his emotional processes appear to have morphed considerably during his thirty years, because he doesn't want to turn around to look at sick bay.

Yes, he might find out that Burton Mansfield is here—but he might also find out that Mansfield is long gone, or long dead. He's borne the suspense for so long that he finds himself afraid of certainty. He wants to stay in this box with Schrödinger's cat forever.

Lights around the door lock begin to flash, warning him of a power surge. As Abel had anticipated, the intruder has set her blaster to maximum in an effort to blow the lock. Within ninety seconds, the door will open. After overload, the Genesis warrior will have only one or two shots left in her weapon. Although Abel is confident he can dodge those shots, she might miss and hit the cryosleep pods.

The risk breaks his hesitation. Abel turns and looks.

All signs indicate the cryosleep pods are not in use. Verify.

As the faint whine of the overloading blaster slides to a higher pitch, Abel moves to the panels and double-checks. *Confirmed.* Nobody lies in any of the cryosleep chambers. It does not appear they were ever activated.

The *Daedalus*'s human passengers, including Burton Mansfield, abandoned ship thirty years ago, and they have never come back.

●   ●   ●

"They can't get their hands on the Gate readouts," said Captain Gee. On the viewscreen dome of the bridge, the Genesis fighters blew up another Damocles, a few hundred mechs

smashed in an instant. "You, there. Mech. Extract the hard memory elements, launch them through the Gate, now."

Abel turned to obey the senior officer aboard, but stopped as Mansfield said, "We're not abandoning ship without Abel."

Captain Gee snapped, "If the thing can get to the docking bay in time to leave with us, great! If not, just build another one!"

Few people spoke to Burton Mansfield that way. He drew himself upright, and his deep voice seemed to fill the darkness of the bridge. "Abel is different—"

"It's a machine! I've got human lives here to save." Captain Gee turned toward Abel, frowning when she realized he hadn't budged. "Is it not working?"

Abel hesitated one instant longer as Mansfield looked at the enormous star field view through the screen that covered two walls and the entire domed ceiling of the bridge. The tide of battle had turned. Genesis would have the day—and, shortly, this ship, if they wanted it.

The Daedalus itself shuddered as it took its first direct weapons fire. Quietly Mansfield said, "Abel, go. Hurry."

And Abel ran as fast as he could, removed the relevant hard data elements from the computer core quicker than any human ever could have, carried it to the equipment pod bay within four minutes, and launched it at the direct center of the Gate with no delays. He even closed and sealed the outer pod bay doors before the gravity and power snapped off, stranding him in a dark, weightless void.

· · ·

The whine of the blaster outside has risen a full octave. Abel stares at the empty shells of the cryosleep pods on the wall, as translucent as cicada husks in the reddish emergency lights, then takes up his own weapon again as he turns toward the door.

Sparks flash white; the metal door jerks open amid puffs of smoke. Abel steps out of range, out of sight. Nobody fires. From the total silence, he surmises that the Genesis soldier isn't even moving.

He knows how little firepower she has left. She does as well. One shot, maybe two. The intruder needs the supplies in this sick bay so badly she effectively disarmed herself to get in here—but now she has to finish him off with a single blast. That opportunity is one he doesn't have to give her. Abel could easily wait in sick bay to kill her for hours, days, another thirty years if need be. He doesn't even have to sleep.

(Although he can, and does. During the last thirty years he's slept quite a lot. Abel has even begun to dream, a development he would very much like to discuss with Burton Mansfield.

Someday.)

But his programming calls for a different plan of action now.

46

Abel walks away from the cryosleep pods, deliberately treading heavily enough for his opponent to hear. She knows he's coming, and she won't fire immediately; instead she's hanging on for the kill shot at close range.

So he deliberately steps into view at the far end of sick bay, where enough smoke swirls that the Genesis soldier will hold off for another moment.

That's all he needs to turn his own blaster around, surrendering the weapon to her.

She stares. She's braced with her back against the wall, blaster held with both hands, shaking. Humans are so excitable. A few strands of her chin-length black hair cling to her sweaty forehead and cheek. Although her brown eyes widen when he keeps walking forward, she doesn't panic. Doesn't fire.

"My name is Abel," he says. "Model One A of the Mansfield Cybernetics mech line. My programming dictates that I am bound to serve the highest human authority aboard this vessel. As of now, that authority is you."

He holds out the weapon. When she doesn't take it, he simply sets it on the floor and kicks it toward her. It feels so good to be able to obey his programming again. To have a purpose.

Abel smiles. "What are my orders?"

7

COUNT TO FIVE, NOEMI DECIDES.

If she's cracking up—if the terror of the past few minutes has scrambled her mind to the point where she's hallucinating—then this will all go away in a couple of seconds. If this is for real, the mech will be standing here waiting for orders when she's done.

One. The mech remains still, expression curious and patient.

Two. Noemi takes a deep breath. She remains in her crouch, hand clutching her blaster so tightly her fingers have begun to cramp.

Three. Abel. The mech said its name was Abel. *We were taught that there are twenty-five models of mech in the Mansfield Cybernetics line, alphabetical from B to Z. A was for a prototype.*

Four. Abel's face and posture haven't shifted in the

slightest. Would it stand here for an hour? A whole day? At any rate, it hasn't made any move to get its weapon back.

Five.

Noemi grabs Abel's blaster. "My friend in the docking bay—she needs medical help, now."

"Understood. I'll bring her to sick bay." Abel takes off down the hallway so quickly that Noemi first thinks it's escaping—but it's apparently following her orders, just like it said it would.

Shoving herself to her feet, Noemi runs after the mech, unwilling to let the thing out of her sight even though she knows she can't possibly keep up.

From Darius Akide's lectures on mechs, Noemi knows the A model was an experimental model never put into mass production. Could the mech be lying about what it is? Its programming could potentially allow it to lie. But like everyone else on Genesis, she has memorized the faces of every single model of mech. According to her history books, they used to fear infiltration, in the early days of the Liberty War. What if the machines had walked among them, pretending to be human, spying on them all?

While the Queens and Charlies are most familiar to her, Noemi could identify any of Mansfield's mechs on sight— and she's never seen this Abel's face before.

Okay, you found a prototype. It doesn't matter how it got

out here as long as you can use it. Take care of Esther and worry about the rest later.

Her footsteps pound a staccato drumbeat along the corridor as Noemi dashes back to the docking bay. Panting, she stops in the doorway to stare at the scene in front of her. Abel leans over Esther's damaged fighter, gently scooping her into its arms. Esther's head lolls back as she murmurs, "Who—who are—"

"It's a mech," Noemi calls as she ditches her nearly dead blaster, then holsters Abel's to her side. "The ship has a fully equipped sick bay. See? We can take care of you."

Abel moves slowly, deliberately, until Esther rests against its chest in a firm embrace. Then Noemi barely has time to get out of the way before it rushes out, moving at a speed no human could match.

When she gets all the way back up to sick bay, Esther's lying on a biobed. Abel's deft fingers move across the controls so swiftly they seem to blur. Noemi goes to Esther's side and takes her hand.

"The sensors are still assessing her condition," Abel reports. "But I predict they'll confirm preliminary findings of internal bleeding, multiple pelvic fractures, and a mild-to-moderate concussion. If internal bleeding is confirmed, she'll need an immediate transfusion. I've administered pain medication."

Enough medication to leave Esther dazed, her eyes half

closed and her facial muscles slack—*Good*, Noemi thinks. *Esther needs that.* And the nauseous weight in her gut lessens, because those injuries sound survivable. Fixable. At least, if this Abel mech actually knows what it's doing. "How are you—" She has to stop and gulp in another few breaths before she can continue talking. "You're one of the medical models? I thought—thought that was the Tare mech."

"To the best of my knowledge, the Tare mech remains the primary medical model," Abel says, as amiably as if they were having tea. The ozone-seared air still stinks of their battle only minutes before. "However, I am programmed with the knowledge, skills, and specialties of the entire Mansfield Cybernetics line." It glances over from the readouts to study Noemi's face for a moment. "You're experiencing extreme shortness of breath. This shouldn't represent an emergency unless you have any underlying medical conditions. Do you?"

"What? No." It's so strange, talking to a mech. Standing beside one. It feels just like standing next to a person, even though nothing could be further from the truth. "I just— pushed myself. That's all."

"You could've remained in sick bay instead of following me down," it points out.

"I don't trust you."

"I wasn't asking for a justification for your actions.

Humans have many reasons for behaving in an inefficient or irrational manner." Abel's tone is so mild that it takes Noemi a moment to recognize the insult.

But that's stupid. She's anthropomorphizing a mech—a recruit's mistake, one she should be past. Apparently this prototype's innovations don't include tact.

The dark, glistening stuff in the bags Abel brings out must be synthetic blood. He's very sure about that transfusion. Some faiths on Genesis won't use synthetic blood, others won't accept transfusions at all, but Esther's family doesn't belong to one of those.

Noemi imagines the Gatsons standing before her, tall and pale, their expressions disapproving. *How could you let this happen?* they might say. *You were supposed to protect our daughter. After everything we did for you, how could you let her be hurt?*

Smoothly, the mech slips the needle into Esther's skin. Not a flicker of discomfort shows on her face. Is she that doped up, or is the mech that good? Probably both, Noemi decides. While Abel works, she studies its—*his* face in greater depth. There really is something different about this one. He looks younger than most mechs, as if he's perhaps two or three years older she is. Instead of the customary, blandly appealing mech features, he has a distinctive face with piercing blue eyes, a strong nose, and, if she recalls correctly, a slightly asymmetrical smile.

Why make a mech so...specific? And so advanced? Akide had told them that mechs were calibrated to the level of intelligence they required for their duties, nothing more. Extra intelligence would only be a complication, another way for a mech to break down. There were even laws against developing mech intelligence too far, or there had been, the last anyone on Genesis heard about Earth laws. If Abel is telling her the truth—and by now she believes he is—he represents a significant step forward in cybernetics development.

Except that he can't be. This ship was abandoned many years ago. As she brushes a strand of hair away from Esther's cheek, Noemi asks, "How long have you been aboard the *Daedalus*?"

"Not quite thirty years," Abel says. "I can provide the exact time down to the nanosecond if required."

"It isn't." It so, so isn't.

"I doubted it would be." Abel turns away from the medical readouts to face her directly. "Upon further examination, the patient's liver appears to be ruptured, and the internal bleeding is more severe than initially indicated. Surgery will be required."

Noemi's abdomen knots in sympathetic pain. "But—if Esther loses her liver, she won't survive."

Abel walks away from the biobed, toward various storage chambers—even past a few cryosleep pods against the wall. "The *Daedalus* is stocked with artificial organs in case emergency transplants are needed."

She bites her lower lip. Although Genesis has retained more medical technology than any other kind, artificial organs are used very rarely. Yes, life is precious and must be preserved, but death is accepted as a part of life. Unnaturally avoiding death is seen as an act of futility, sometimes even one of cowardice. The Gatsons are particularly strict about these things. They spent weeks debating whether or not Mr. Gatson should even have laser surgery on his eyes.

This is different. Esther's only seventeen! She was injured trying to protect our world. Noemi didn't sign up for the Masada Run only to have Esther die anyway. "All right," she says. "All right. Do it."

From the biobed comes a whisper: "Don't."

Noemi looks down to see Esther gazing up. Her skin, always fair, has turned waxen. One of her pale green eyes is horribly marred, deep red where it ought to be white. But she's awake.

"It's okay." Noemi tries to smile. "I'm here. Do you need more pain meds?"

"It doesn't hurt." Esther sighs deeply. Her eyelids droop, but for only a moment. She's fighting so hard to stay awake. "No transplant."

It's like the chill of space outside the ship's hull rushed in to freeze Noemi's blood. She feels adrift, exposed, vulnerable. Like she's the one in mortal danger instead of Esther. "No, no, it's all right. This is an emergency—"

"It would make me part machine. That isn't human life. Not the life I was given."

Please, God, no. God doesn't speak to Noemi's heart, no matter how often she prays for guidance. But maybe he'll speak to Esther's. *Show her it's more important to stay alive no matter what.* The Gatsons raised them so strictly, and Esther's always obeyed her parents. Now, though—who could argue with this?

"Esther, please." Noemi's voice has begun to shake. "If you don't have the transplant, you'll die."

"I know." Esther feebly moves her hand, searching for Noemi's; Noemi takes it and hangs on tight. Esther's skin is growing cold. "I knew as soon as the mech tore through my ship. Please—don't argue while we're saying good-bye—"

"To hell with good-bye!" Noemi will make this up to Esther later. "You. Abel. Perform the transplant."

Abel, who's been standing in the middle of sick bay through this entire conversation, shakes his head no. "I'm sorry, but I can't."

"You just said you had all the talents of every mech ever! Were you lying?"

"I don't mean that I am incapable of performing the transplant." If she didn't know better, she'd think Abel was offended. "And I cannot lie to you, as my commander."

"That's right. I'm your commander." Noemi seizes onto this, the one weapon she has that might make Abel stop arguing and move, dammit. "So you have to follow my orders, and I'm ordering you to perform the transplant."

"Noemi—" Esther whispers. The weakness in her voice slices through Noemi like a blade, but she doesn't let herself look away from the mech. Abel is Esther's only hope.

He doesn't take a single step closer as he says, "Your authority over me is subject to a few strictly limited exceptions. One of those exceptions is that I must obey the wishes of a medical patient regarding end-of-life decisions. Esther's choice is therefore final."

Damn, damn, damn! The same programming that saved her life is endangering Esther's. Why would Mansfield build legions of killing machines and then program them with mock morality? Just one more way the people of Earth fool themselves into accepting the machines in their midst, like the human skin and hair. Noemi wants to scream at Abel but knows it would do no good. Programming is final. Absolute.

Instead she bends closer to Esther, brushing her friend's pale-gold hair away from her face. "If you won't do it for yourself, then do it for me. We're on this spaceship out in the middle of nowhere, and I need your help to—to—"

But it's not help she needs. It's Esther herself. Noemi knows she's only made one real friend in her life, but she only ever needed one, because it was Esther, who knew every awful thing about her and loved her anyhow. Noemi's bad temper and awkwardness and distrust—the same stuff that pushed Mr. and Mrs. Gatson and Jemuel and everybody else away—Esther was the only person who didn't think those things mattered. The only one who ever would.

A sob bubbles up in Noemi's throat, but she chokes it back to whisper, once again, "*Please*. You're supposed to be the one who goes back. You're the one who's going to make it." The one who can be happy. The one who can be good, who can love and be loved. Noemi can only be the one left over.

"You were willing to die for me," Esther says. For one moment she's really able to focus on Noemi; maybe the blood flowing into her is helping a little. "At least now you won't have to. Not if you take your name off the list. You can now. Promise me you will."

"Esther—"

"Tell Mom and Dad I love them."

Abel chooses this moment to interrupt. "I had a thought."

"Is it about getting around your idiotic programming?" Noemi snaps. Oh, why did she have to say it like that? She doesn't want Esther to hear her being mean, not now.

"Cryosleep." Abel points at the pods against the wall.

"Often even severely injured people can be successfully put into cryosleep. If she weren't brought out of it until an organ could be cloned, perhaps—"

Esther wouldn't agree to cloning either, but cryosleep would be okay. What they'd do after that... Noemi doesn't have to think of that now. She can leave it to the doctors once they're back on Genesis. "Yes! Please, yes, put her in cryosleep!"

"I'll check on the pods." Abel's on it in an instant, finally making himself useful again. But after a few moments, he pauses. "I'm afraid the cryosleep pods' power source was damaged in the attack on the *Daedalus* thirty years ago."

"Isn't there any way around it?" On a ship this size, Noemi knows, every vital system should have backup.

"Normally the ship's main grid would provide backup power, but I took that offline."

"I thought you were supposed to be helping me!"

"I am now," Abel says, his tone maddeningly even. "I wasn't when you first boarded the ship. At that point you were considered an intruder and—"

"It doesn't matter!" Noemi's almost screaming by now, and she doesn't care. "Just bring the main grid back up!"

Abel nods and rushes toward sick bay's main computer interface. Noemi takes a deep breath to steady herself before she leans back down toward Esther. "It's going to be all right," she whispers. "We've got a plan now...."

Esther's eyes are closed. She doesn't hear. Noemi looks up at the biobed and sees the dark truth the sensors reveal: Esther is dying. Right now. This moment.

"Esther?" Noemi touches her friend's shoulder, stricken. "Can you hear me?"

Nothing.

Please, God, please, if you won't give me anything else, at least let me tell her good-bye. He's never answered Noemi before, but if he does now, she'll believe forever. *I have to tell her good-bye.*

The sensors flatline. Esther is gone.

In the very next instant, every computer interface in sick bay brightens to full illumination. The damned mech brought power back online just as soon as it was too late to save Esther.

Noemi stands as if frozen, staring down at Esther. Her eyes well with tears, but it's like they're crying without her. Instead of sobbing or shaking, she feels as if she'll never move again.

She's in heaven now. Noemi should believe that. She does, mostly, but the knowledge doesn't comfort her. The words only echo in the hollow space that has replaced her heart. She finds herself remembering her family's funeral more vividly than she has in years—the high winds that blew, tugging at everyone's hair and clothes, and stealing the priest's words before Noemi could really hear them.

The way Noemi stared down into the grave and tried to imagine her parents lying there, baby Rafael between them, looking up at the sky for the last time before they were covered by dirt forever. More than anything else, she remembers Esther standing near her, all in black, crying as hard and loud as Noemi herself. Years later Esther had revealed that she made herself cry, so Noemi wouldn't be alone.

Now Esther's gone, too, and instead of being held close and told she was loved, she had to die listening to Noemi shriek at someone in anger. That ugly moment was the last one Esther ever knew.

It's dangerous—being angry at God—but Noemi can't deny the bitter rage she feels at this one last proof that she isn't enough for God, for the Gatsons, for anyone at all.

The long silence is broken by Abel's voice. "I didn't attempt resuscitation because failure was all but certain. Her internal blood loss was too great. We would've had to begin the transfusion much earlier to save her."

"Or we could've gotten her into cryosleep." Noemi turns to stare at the mech. He stands near the computer interface, very still, so obviously unsure what to do that he looks almost human. This doesn't move her; it enrages her. "If you hadn't wasted time trying to kill me, Esther might still be alive! We could have put her into cryosleep and saved her!"

Abel doesn't respond at first. But finally he says, "You are correct."

As many times as Noemi has gone into battle against Earth forces—as many times as she's seen friends and fellow soldiers torn apart by their mechs—she thought she knew how to hate with her whole heart. But she didn't.

Now, only now, as she stares at the machine responsible for her best friend's death, does Noemi feel what hatred really is.

8

ABEL'S PROGRAMMING COVERS MANY SITUATIONS involving interpersonal conflict.

Not this one.

The Genesis warrior—the dead one called her Noemi—stands next to the corpse, shaking with anger. Like all mechs, he has been constructed to endure human wrath in both its emotional and physical forms, and yet he finds himself uncertain. Wary. Even...worried.

Noemi has command over him unless and until he is released by someone with the authority to override her. Therefore, her power over him is all but absolute. It doesn't matter that he could outrun her, outshoot her, that he could kill her with a single hand: He cannot defend himself against her any more than he can disobey her. Abel is at his commander's mercy.

She takes a deep breath, stops trembling, and goes very still. He isn't sure how, but he knows that's worse.

"Where's the nearest air lock?" Noemi asks.

"The equipment pod bay approximately halfway down the main ship's corridor." In other words, the cell in which Abel just spent the past three decades. Noemi seems unlikely to be interested in this information, so he says nothing else.

Noemi nods. "Walk toward it."

Abel does so. She follows a few steps behind. Although she could potentially have many reasons for needing an air lock, he immediately understands which of her potential purposes is most likely—namely, his destruction. She will release him into the cold void of space, where he will cease operations.

Not instantaneously. Abel is built to withstand even the near-absolute-zero temperatures of outer space...for a time. But within seven to ten minutes, the damage to his organic tissues will be permanent. Total mechanical malfunction will swiftly follow.

He isn't afraid to die. And yet, as he walks along the corridor to his doom, his executioner's steps echoing behind him, Abel feels that this is wrong. *Unjust*, somehow.

Is this another of his strange emotional malfunctions? Perhaps his pride is occupying too large a part of his thoughts, because it galls Abel to think that he—the most complex mech ever created—is about to be tossed out an air lock like human refuse, for no reason other than the pique of an unhappy Genesis soldier.

After some consideration, he decides that yes, his pride is interfering with effective analysis of the situation. He is from Earth, and therefore he is this girl's enemy. Although he knows how powerfully his programming controls him, she probably doesn't trust it. If Genesis has held true to its anti-technology stance, then Noemi has probably never been in the same room with a mech before. She'd only have met them in battle. No wonder she finds him frightening. Taking into account the fact that he attacked and very nearly killed her not half an hour before, her decision to space him appears more reasonable. Almost logical.

That doesn't make him feel any better about it.

When Abel reaches the equipment pod bay, he steps without hesitation through the door he was so grateful to escape not even an hour ago. He can see the irony of having been freed from this place only to come back here to die. In his mind he finds himself running through scenarios, possibilities—the seven different ways he could kill the Genesis soldier this instant. Why?

Then Abel realizes what it is: It's not that he doesn't want to die. It's that he wants to *live*.

He wants more time. To learn more things, to travel through the galaxy and see all the colony worlds of the Loop, to return back home to Earth for at least one day. To find out what has become of Burton Mansfield and perhaps speak with his "father" once more. To watch *Casablanca* properly again instead of merely retelling himself the story. To ask more questions, even if he never gets the answers.

But what a mech wants doesn't matter.

Abel turns to face Noemi before she can hit the controls that will seal this door, allowing her to open the outer hatch and vent him into space. He went so long without seeing a human face or speaking to anyone. It helps him to look at her, even if that means watching her take the steps that will kill him. Although he doesn't expect this to affect her in any way, her dark-brown eyes widen when they're face-to-face again.

Noemi doesn't speak. She lifts her hand to the control panel...and does nothing.

Seconds tick by. When Abel judges that this pause has gone on an inordinately long time, he ventures, "Do you need help understanding the controls?"

"I understand the controls." Her voice is thick from the tears she's still holding back.

Abel cocks his head. "Have I misinterpreted your purpose in bringing me here?"

"What do you think my purpose is?"

"To space me."

"You got it." Her smile is twisted by grief. "That's why we came here."

"Then may I ask why you have not yet done so?"

"Because it's stupid," Noemi says. "Hating you. I want

to hate you because you might've saved Esther and you didn't—but what's the point? You're not a person. You don't have a soul. You obey your programming, because you have to, and without free will there can be no sin." She breathes out sharply in frustration, looks up at the ceiling as if that will keep the tears from trickling beyond her eyes. "I might as well hate a wheel."

A few more seconds elapse before Abel feels emboldened to say, "May I now step out of the air lock door?"

Noemi moves back, making room for him. This reads as permission, and so Abel steps out of the equipment pod bay with profound relief. Only then does Noemi hit the controls, once again sealing off the bay.

He offers, "If you would feel safer with me immobilized, the cryosleep pods would be effective. Mechs cannot be put in true cryosleep, but exposure to the chemicals activates our dormant mode."

"I don't need you to be dormant. I need you to be useful." She wipes at her eyes, attempts to act like the soldier she is. "We'll—I'll take care of Esther later. First I have to make a plan. Wasn't the bridge back that way?"

"Yes, ma'am."

She winces. "Please don't call me that."

"How should I address you?"

She's still pulling herself together. "My name is Noemi Vidal."

"Yes, Captain Vidal."

"Noemi's fine." She turns and trudges toward the bridge. Her voice is hoarse, her exhaustion and grief obvious, but she remains focused on survival. "Follow me, Abel."

She'll let me use her first name, Abel thinks. No human being has ever allowed him that much liberty before. The thought pleases him, though he can't determine why.

Nor does he know the reason why he glances over his shoulder, back at the equipment pod bay he has escaped twice today. Surely after thirty years he has seen enough of it.

Perhaps it's just because it feels so good to leave that place behind.

• • •

"This is the navigational position for the pilot, right?" Noemi runs her hands through her hair as they stand on the *Daedalus*'s bridge. The curved walls allow the ship's viewscreen to wrap almost entirely around and above them, displaying the surrounding star field in such detail that the bridge appears to be a dull metallic platform in the middle of outer space. "The captain's chair is obvious, and I figure this is for external communications. And that's the ops station."

"Correct. Your technological sophistication is surprising for a soldier of Genesis."

She turns toward him, frowning. "We limit technology by choice, not out of ignorance."

"Of course. But in time, the first must inevitably lead to the second."

"Why do you have to act so superior?"

Abel considers her assertion. "I *am* superior, in most respects."

Noemi's hands close around the back of the captain's chair, gripping it too hard, and when she speaks again, she grinds out every word. "Could you. Knock it. Off."

"Modesty is not one of my chief operating modes," he admits, "but I will try."

She sighs. "I'll take what I can get."

He assesses her as she paces the length of the bridge, her formfitting emerald-green exosuit outlining her athletic body vividly against the blackness of space. Amid the stars glow the larger, gently shaded planets of the Genesis system. Abel can make out the circle that is Genesis itself, brilliant green and blue, with its two moons visible as tiny pinpoints of white.

"Do we have fuel?" Noemi asks. "Can the *Daedalus* get back home?"

Abel replies, "Fuel stores are sufficient for full-ship operations lasting two years, ten months, five days, ten hours, and six minutes." He leaves out the seconds and milliseconds. "The ship took damage in its final battle, but the damage doesn't appear to have been extreme." Hardly even threatening. He frowns at the readouts scrolling past on the console. Did Captain Gee panic? Did she convince Mansfield to abandon ship when there was no real need? "Travel through a Gate would be difficult—"

"We're not going through a Gate. We're going home."

Of course. Earth is Abel's home, not Noemi's. He continues, "After minor repairs with instruments we have on hand, we should be able to reach Genesis without difficulty."

"Good."

What will become of him on Genesis? Will he be dismantled? Sent back out into space? Made to serve in their armies? Abel cannot guess, and thinks it would be a bad idea to ask. He has no control over the situation. He may as well learn his fate when it comes to pass.

Noemi sits heavily in the nearest chair, the one at the ops station, which like all the stations aboard the *Daedalus* is thickly padded and covered with soft black material. Running her hand along it, she frowns. "Was this some kind of luxury cruiser or something? Regular Earth ships can't all be like this...can they?"

"The *Daedalus* is a research vessel, customized especially for its owner and my creator, Burton Mansfield."

"Did you say Burton Mansfield?" She sits up straight and gapes at him. "*The* Burton Mansfield?"

At last. It's good to see Noemi finally responding with

appropriate awe. "The founder and architect of the Mansfield Cybernetics line? Yes."

He watches for her reaction, anticipating her amazement—and instead sees her scowl. "That *son of a bitch*. This is his ship? You're his mech?"

"…yes." How dare she call his father such names? But Abel can't object, so he forces himself not to think of it any longer.

"I can't believe it," Noemi mutters. "You're telling me Mansfield himself came to this system thirty years ago, and he got away?"

"All humans aboard abandoned ship," Abel answers as simply as he can. "As I wasn't on the bridge at that time, I cannot know how successful their escape was, nor their reasons for abandoning a functional ship."

"We scared them. That's why they ran." Energized, Noemi gets to her feet and reexamines every station on the bridge, as if it requires further consideration now that she knows who it belongs to. "But why would Burton Mansfield come to the Genesis system to start with? Why would he throw himself into the middle of a war?"

And there it is—the question Abel had hoped Noemi would not think to ask.

As long as she's his commander, he cannot lie to her. However, he has enough discretion to…omit certain facts, as long as her questions are not direct.

He tries indirection first. "Mansfield had undertaken critical scientific research."

"In a war zone? What was he researching?"

A direct question: Full disclosure is now required. "Mansfield was studying a potential vulnerability in the Gate between Genesis and Earth."

Noemi goes very still. She's realizing the true significance of what she's found. "By vulnerability—do you mean a potential malfunction, or—tell me, exactly, what?"

Abel remembers the day Mansfield realized the worst. The endless hours of research and sensor readings required, the immense leap of insight it took for Mansfield to grasp the answer: All of this, Abel now has to deliver to a soldier of Genesis. "By vulnerability, I mean he was investigating a way a Gate could be destroyed."

Noemi's face lights up. Under different circumstances, Abel would be pleased to have brought his commander so much joy. "Did you find one?"

They ought to have foreseen it, Abel thinks. *They shouldn't have left me here. It was . . . tactically unwise.*

Because I have no choice but to betray them.

"Answer me," Noemi says. "Did you find a way to destroy a Gate?"

Abel admits, "Yes."

9

HE'S LYING.

Noemi knows the mech—Abel—can't lie to her while she's his commander, which somehow she is. But the enormity of what he's said makes it feel like the ship's gravity is shifting beneath her feet, forcing her off-balance. Her grief for Esther weighs on her too heavily to allow for the sudden, staggering return of hope.

"How?" She takes one step toward Abel. The viewscreen dome shows fire-fog trails of the galaxy's arm, stretching their glowing tendrils overhead. "How can anyone destroy a Gate?"

"Gates are capable of creating and stabilizing wormholes, which are essentially shortcuts in space-time," he begins, talking down to her again. "When a wormhole is fully stable, a ship can travel through, thereby crossing enormous distances in an instant."

The Masada Run will destabilize the Genesis Gate, but

only for a while. Months, probably. Two or three years, if they're lucky. Possibly just a matter of weeks. All those lives, including her own, will be spent for the mere *chance* that Genesis might gain an opportunity to rebuild and rearm itself, to beat their plowshares into swords, and then to plunge back into a war that they almost certainly can't win.

Abel continues, "A wormhole can only be permanently stabilized through the use of so-called exotic matter. In the Gates, this exotic matters takes the form of supercooled gases kept even colder than the space beyond it, mere nanokelvins above absolute zero."

Colder than outer space. Noemi has tried to imagine that before, but she can't. The intensity of that chill is beyond any human reckoning.

Abel continues, "These gases are cooled by magnetic fields generated by several powerful electromagnets that make up the components of the Gate—"

"But all those components—they're programmed to reinforce one another. It's almost impossible to destroy one while the others are backing it up."

He cocks his head. "You understand more about the components of a Gate than I would have thought."

"What, you thought nobody from Genesis would've learned about this?"

"To judge by the extremely outdated and dilapidated condition of your current ships and armaments, Genesis appears to have all but abandoned scientific and technological advancement."

From anyone else, that would be an insult. From Abel, it's a simple, factual assessment. The insult would've been easier to take. "Apparently not, because I understand how a Gate works. Which means I know they're supposed to be invulnerable. You say they're not. How do we destroy one?"

He hesitates, and his reluctance is uncannily genuine. Too genuine, in Noemi's opinion; Mansfield was showing off with this one. "Most efforts to damage or destroy a Gate are targeted at destroying the magnetic fields inside. However, it is not necessary to destroy the fields to collapse the Gate. Only to disrupt them."

Noemi shakes her head. "But we can't even manage that, not with every component supporting one another."

"You've failed to see the obvious alternative." Abel catches himself. "You shouldn't feel that this failure reflects negatively on you. Relatively few humans are capable of the insight necessary to—"

"Just tell me."

"Disrupting the fields doesn't have to mean weakening or destroying them. It can also mean *strengthening* them."

She opens her mouth to object. Strengthen it? How can making the Gate stronger possibly help them? Then the answer takes shape in her mind. "Strengthening the fields would warm the gases inside. When the exotic matter becomes too warm, the Gate will implode."

Abel inclines his head, not quite a nod. "And destroy the wormhole forever."

Noemi sinks into the nearest station, overwhelmed by the possibilities and problems she now sees. "But—any device powerful enough to overcome the Gate's magnetic fields—where would we get that? Do any of those even exist?"

"There are thermomagnetic devices capable of creating that level of heat on their own. Not many, of course. The practical applications are limited."

"But they *are* out there? We could find one?"

"Yes."

She wants to hope—wants it so badly she can taste it—but Noemi can see all the problems with this plan already. "You'd have to activate it on the verge of the Gate. Otherwise the heat would melt your ship before you even reach the Gate. And you can't just launch it remotely either. You'd have to have a pilot to work around the Gate's defenses."

"You understand a great deal about piloting for someone from a planet that has stubbornly refused to go anywhere."

And that reminds her of the guilty longings she sometimes feels when she sees the speed of Earth ships, the complexity of the Gate, even the inhuman reflexes of their mechs. Noemi doesn't want to be like people from Earth, but...she can't help wanting to know what they know. To discover. To explore.

Her next flash of insight eclipses all those old dreams in an instant. "No human could do it. A human pilot would lose control or die from the heat too quickly."

"True. Also, even if the human pilot could succeed, the Gate's implosion would kill her instantly."

Noemi hadn't bothered worrying about that. Collapsing the Gate—saving her world—it's worth one life. Her willingness to make that sacrifice is irrelevant if she would only fail. But there's another possibility. "A mech could do it, right?"

Abel hesitates before answering, just long enough for her to be aware of it. "Not most mechs. They're programmed to go into basic utility mode during self-damaging tasks. You'd need an advanced model. One capable of thinking even at the point of destruction."

"An advanced model like you."

He straightens. "Yes."

Abel clearly has no instinct for self-preservation that overrides the orders given by his commander. The air lock proved that. If she tells him to destroy the Gate and be destroyed along with it, he will.

Noemi would gladly lay down her life to save Genesis. So she can ask a mech to give up...whatever it is he has.

Slowly she rises from the chair. The projected starlight

shines softly around her, making the moment even more dreamlike than it already is.

Her only plan had been steering the *Daedalus* toward Genesis and bringing Esther's body home. She'd had a vague idea of turning the ship and the mech over to her superior officers, in case they could be used in the war effort. Some small contributions that would outlive her, that could go on serving after the Masada Run.

Instead she's found a mech not only aware of how to destroy a Gate but also capable of helping her do it. And a ship that could take her through the Loop to find the device she needs—*Earth would come after any Genesis ship*, she thinks, *but they won't be on the lookout for this one. This could actually work.*

It means throwing herself through the galaxy, to planets she's never seen before. It means risking her life, maybe even winding up in an Earth prison, defeated and helpless— which would be so much worse than dying in the Masada Run. It means leaving Genesis behind, maybe forever.

She turns to Abel. "We're going to destroy this Gate."

"Very well," he replies as easily as if she'd asked him the time. "We should run an in-depth diagnostic on the *Daedalus*. Although my initial scans indicate that she remains fully fueled and in good condition, we will want to be certain of that before we begin to travel. It should take no more than an hour or two."

It startles her that he understands they're about to travel through the Gates to other worlds, but of course he does. Abel would've realized the implications as soon as he explained the Gate's flaw to her. However, there's one thing he doesn't understand yet. "We have to wait."

Abel gives her a look. "So you want to end a deadly and destructive war, but there's ... no rush?"

Noemi's not sure why Mansfield decided to give a mech the capacity for sarcasm. "I'm only an ensign," she says, tapping the single gray stripe on the cuff of her green exo-suit sleeve. "This mission—it's risky, and there could be drawbacks I haven't seen—"

"*I* would have seen them." His expression is so smug that Noemi wishes she had something in her hands to throw at him.

"Yeah, well, you're Burton Mansfield's mech. So forgive me if I don't trust you completely."

"If you don't trust me, why are you undertaking this mission on my word alone?" Abel seems almost irritated. "If I could lie to you about the risks, I could also lie to you about the potential."

That's not a bad point, but Noemi doesn't bother justifying herself to a mech. "My point is, I should run this by my superior officers if I can."

"Do you wish to fly directly to Genesis?"

Noemi opens her mouth to give the order, then thinks

better of it. Yes, she should run this by Captain Baz at least—probably the whole Elder Council. She can imagine standing in their white marble chamber in her dress uniform, looking up at Darius Akide and the other elders, showing them this one chance they have to save their world.

And she can imagine them saying no.

They might not trust Abel's word. What would it take to convince the Elder Council? They're so sure the Masada Run is the only way—

She thinks about the various speeches that have been given, the vids they've seen in support of the Masada Run. *Sacrifice your lives*, they say. *Sacrifice your children. Only through sacrifice can Genesis survive.*

Now she'd be coming back to tell all of Genesis and the Council that there's another way out. That the Masada Run isn't necessary and never was. She, Noemi Vidal, a seventeen-year-old ensign, orphaned and newly friendless, backed up only by a mech.

Would the Elder Council even believe her? Worse, would they refuse to back down just to avoid admitting they were wrong?

It's not that Noemi never doubted the Council before—but this is the first time she's ever allowed herself to think that they might fail her world so completely. She's not sure she really believes they would. But they *could*, and that risk alone is enough.

"Belay that order," she says slowly. "Run the diagnostic. See if the ship's ready to travel through the Gates."

Abel raises one eyebrow. "Does that mean we're proceeding without approval from your superiors?"

Noemi's been taking orders her whole life. From the Gatsons, because they were good enough to take her into their family and deserved her obedience. From her teachers, from her commanding officers. She's tried to obey all of them and the Word of God, too, despite all her doubts and confusion, putting aside her own dreams, because that's her duty.

But her duty to protect Genesis goes beyond any of that.

"Yes," Noemi says, staring out at the stars that will guide her. "We're going to destroy the Gate on our own."

To save her world, she must learn to stand alone.

10

ABEL DOESN'T LIKE THIS PLAN.

The single strongest conflict within his programming
arises from an order that involves working against Earth.

His loyalty to Earth is written into his code. Working
against the world of his origin in the war against Genesis
betrays all his most critical directives.

All, that is, except one: obeying the human who commands him.

Surely Mansfield never meant for anyone else to wield
this authority. But if he'd guessed what could happen to
his most prized creation, he would've written subroutines
to ensure no human could ever force Abel to fight against
Earth.

Apparently even the foresight of Burton Mansfield has
its limits, which means Abel now has to help destroy the
Genesis Gate...and be destroyed along with it.

Without hesitation, he begins a thorough systems

check. The *Daedalus* could easily reach Genesis, but the longer journey ahead will ask far more of their ship. Charts and data written in vivid blue light superimpose themselves on the projected star field. "The *Daedalus*'s atmospheric, gravitational, sensor, and propulsion systems show various degrees of inefficiency due to three decades without repair or refurbishment," he reports. "However, all are operational and well within safety parameters. Hull integrity remains solid. Communications will require extensive repairs before we'll be able to handle more than the most basic planetary and intership messages." He gestures toward the comms position, which is effectively useless; what communications power they have will need to be routed through the main ops station. "Our shields show sixty percent strength, which is adequate for space travel, including Gate travel, but not acceptable for combat situations."

Noemi's expression turns thoughtful as she rests her hands on her hips. "Okay. We're not going to be picking any fights. Right?"

"Not without your orders," Abel confirms. "We also have sufficient fuel, as well as emergency rations that, having been kept in vacuum, should remain edible." They won't taste very good, if Abel understands human preferences, but that's Noemi Vidal's problem. He doesn't need to eat much or often, and can make do with things that no human would ever consider food. "However, we're show-ing instability in the ship's integrity field. During standard operations, this is unimportant—but traveling through a Gate without a fully functional integrity field is extremely dangerous."

"Okay." Noemi nods and sits down. Curiously, she returns to the ops position, not the elevated captain's chair. Most humans are too hierarchical to forgo these small dis-plays of authority. "How do we fix the integrity field?"

"We'll need to replace the T-7 anx that anchors the field." On the screen he brings up a diagram of the part they need, roughly oval-shaped, approximately the length and width of the average human torso. "Ours can make it through one more trip through the Gate. Perhaps two. Beyond that, it will collapse."

"You're going to tell me we don't have a spare T-7 anx on board, aren't you?"

"Correct." Abel finds himself taking satisfaction in every problem he can point out. He likes poking holes in her plan to defeat Earth, to destroy him. "We'll also have to travel through multiple Gates to reach Cray."

She frowns. "Cray?"

How ignorant is this girl? Her innate intelligence won't compensate for her lack of knowledge about the galaxy. Abel decides to begin at the beginning. "Are you familiar with the other worlds of the Loop?"

"Of course I am," Noemi protests, but he brings them up on the viewscreen anyway, five worlds suspended in a circle like jewels strung on a golden chain.

First comes Earth, still vividly blue from its oceans despite the climatological havoc that is leading to the planet's death. Next is Stronghold, a dull, chilly gray, reflecting the metallic ores dominating its surface. It is a world of miners, and a place where armaments and ships are built; so far as Abel knows, it remains the only colony world besides Genesis that sustains more than ten million humans. Then comes Cray, its harsh orange terrain evidence of its uninhabitable desert surface. Those few humans there—elite scientists, their students, and skilled technicians—live underground.

Next is Kismet, a small waterworld with very little landmass, an oasis for the richest and most famous. It glows the soft violet color of its vast aquatic surface. Finally, Genesis. Slightly larger than Earth, with even more temperate climates. Its vivid, welcoming green might be a picture taken of Earth long ago, millennia perhaps, when it remained healthy and lush.

"As you can see," Abel says, focusing on the circle of planets projected above them, "we cannot reach Cray directly. Unless..."

"Unless what?" Noemi asks.

"Unless more Gates between the worlds have been

built during the past three decades. I would be unaware of them."

Abel has never had to admit not knowing something before. He doesn't care for it.

"Build new Gates?" Noemi scoffs. "Earth did the exact opposite. They've loaded this Gate with too many defenses to ever get past, and turned space around the Kismet Gate into a minefield."

"Why?"

Noemi turns toward him. The blue-white illumination from the screen shines on her face, reminding him just how young she is. "The war. Did they not program you to understand war?"

Abel could fully discuss the nations, weapons, causes, and outcomes of wars dating back to the conflicts between the Egyptian pharaohs and the ancient kingdom of Kush. As hard as it is for him to accept that he must die at this human's command, it may be even more galling to have her *talk down* to him. "Basic military strategy would call for the use of the Kismet Gate as a second front."

If Noemi has picked up on his dark mood, she shows no sign. "Exactly. Earth gave up their chance of a second front in the war to make sure the rebellion couldn't spread to the other colony worlds. So they had to make the Kismet Gate an absolute barrier, to seal us off completely."

Citizens of Genesis appear to have an exaggerated

opinion of their political importance. But Abel keeps to the subject at hand. "Then the Gates shown on this chart are our only vectors of travel."

He illuminates them, each Gate another point on the chain. The Earth Gate takes people from that world to Stronghold. The Stronghold Gate leads to Cray, the Cray Gate to Kismet, the Kismet Gate to Genesis—at least, before the mines were laid—and finally the Genesis Gate they're currently orbiting, the one they intend to destroy, which leads back to Earth.

"I understand how the Loop works," Noemi says. "But I don't understand why Cray is the only place that will have a thermomagnetic device."

Abel considers what she's told him so far. "You won't have had the opportunity to travel to another planet before. So you are unfamiliar with these other worlds."

"They taught us the basics, but I'm short on the details. Obviously."

He's been stretching out this discussion because it reveals her ignorance. At some point Abel will have to analyze whether he has developed the capacity for passive aggression. "Cray's planetary core is used to power the massive supercomputer there. As such, their mechanical systems have to tolerate intensely high levels of heat—"

"—which means they can use thermomagnetic devices

that would be too risky somewhere else," Noemi cuts in. "Right?"

She is, but Abel doesn't bother admitting it. "If we're to obtain one without anyone noticing us, Cray is the only place we can begin."

She closes her eyes, breathes in deeply. Abel's sophisticated emotional-recognition subroutines identify this as an attempt to gather courage. When she opens her eyes again and speaks, her voice is steady and clear. "Then we'll have to go through the Genesis Gate. Past Earth, past Stronghold. Can we do that without being caught?"

For three decades, the only traffic through the Genesis Gate has been Earth's attack vessels, mostly Damocles ships. Earth will no longer be on the alert for other ships coming from the Genesis system. Abel suspects they could pass through easily. However, he has spotted a flaw in Noemi's thinking. "Kismet has far fewer security protocols in place. We would be much less likely to be seen. Also, we would then be only one Gate away from Cray."

"The Kismet Gate has been mined, remember? Magnetic mines fill an area at least the size of my entire planet—nobody knows for sure, because no ship's ever survived more than a few seconds without coming back through the Gate or being blown to bits."

"My memory is eidetic, which means I remember every

fact I am exposed to." Especially ones she told him not five minutes prior. Abel may have to do what Noemi Vidal says, but he doesn't have to be treated as if he has no more sense than a hammer. "The minefield is effective against human pilots. However, I could pilot through them, recalibrating shields to push the mines back."

Noemi sits very still, studying him. The lights from the starry screen around them shine on her black hair. "Even the Queen and Charlie models couldn't pilot with that kind of precision, and they're some of the smarter ones."

Apparently her memory is far from eidetic. "As I said earlier, I am a special prototype of Burton Mansfield's. I possess talents and abilities beyond those of any other mech. Even my genetic material comes directly from Mansfield." Most mechs' genetic material is synthetic, tied to no one biological life-form. Abel, however, carries nearly as much of Mansfield's DNA as a son would.

Noemi doesn't appear to be impressed by this genetic connection. She rises and walks slowly toward the star field screen arching over them. Her gaze turns toward red-orange Cray, glowing almost as brightly as a star. "If we could get through the Kismet Gate, then nobody would see us. After that we'd need to get a T-7 anx, but we could do that on Kismet, right?"

"Correct. We should have sufficient credits, and the minefield will almost certainly be the only security at the Kismet

Gate." Almost certainly. Not entirely. Abel envisions a field of patrol ships, all of them piloted by Queens and Charlies, which would halt the *Daedalus*, arrest Noemi, and free him to find Mansfield. But that possibility is so unlikely he can't understand why his mind even presented it.

Another operational oddity for him to investigate later.

"From Kismet we could get to Cray. We steal a thermomagnetic device, go back the way we came, and return right here. You get into my starfighter with the device, point it straight at the Gate, and blow it to kingdom come. Right?"

She doesn't mention his destruction. He doesn't either. "Correct."

If Mansfield knew, he would be so angry. Angry with Noemi for misusing his greatest creation. Angry with himself for failing to foresee this situation and program Abel accordingly. Mansfield would be angry about Abel's destruction. He would care. That thought comforts Abel, though logically it should not matter.

Noemi asks, "Do you have to follow my orders even if I'm not around?"

"A mech that obeyed its commander only when observed wouldn't be much use."

"That's a yes."

"Yes." Will she always require such simple, literal replies?

But her next words catch Abel off guard. "So you'd keep going with the mission even if I was killed?"

"Unless another human took command of this vessel or of me, yes, I would. However, you shouldn't be at undue risk during this mission."

She shakes her head as she turns back to him. "I'm a soldier of Genesis. A rebel. They'd arrest me just for reaching another colony world. If they realize I'm stealing a thermomagnetic device to destroy a Gate? Trust me, they'll shoot to kill."

"My programming requires me to protect you," Abel says.

This doesn't appear to reassure her as profoundly as it should. "Anything could happen. I gave up my life already, so what becomes of me doesn't matter. This mission matters. You're absolutely sure you'd keep going without me?"

Noemi speaks of her own death as a foregone conclusion. Abel wonders what she means by giving up her life, but he's more struck by the fact that she is as willing to die as she is to destroy him. She isn't discarding him; she thinks they'll perish together. Noemi's plan asks nothing of him that she isn't asking of herself. Somehow that makes the prospect of destruction easier for him to bear.

Which is a completely irrational reaction. His emotion subroutines truly have become strange during these past thirty years....

"Yes," Abel confirms. "I'll keep going."

"And this trip we're going on won't take that long. A few days, right? Not more than ten or fifteen?"

"Correct." Though he doesn't see why they should have to work so quickly, particularly given that she considered waiting to get approval from her superiors. What could be so urgent?

She takes a deep breath. "Then let's begin."

Within minutes, Abel has completed all the necessary preliminaries. Noemi keeps her position at ops, leaving him at navigation. So it's his hand that hits the control to bring the mag engines back online.

A shudder passes through the ship—entirely normal, and yet thrilling. The stars around him are changing. He's moving. Abel is as close to free as he suspects he'll ever be again.

Outside, he knows, the silvery teardrop shape of the *Daedalus* is now trailed by the torchlight blaze of the mag engines. The walls of these engines aren't made of metal or any other physical material; they are magnetic fields, capable of containing combustion at heat levels that would melt any man-made object. Their invisibility creates the illusion of flame in the vacuum of space.

The ship moves away from the scattered bits of wreckage orbiting the nearby Gate and toward the pale yellow star that serves as Genesis's sun. The Kismet Gate will be located almost completely opposite from where they were, all the way across this solar system.

Next to him, he notices Noemi gazing at the greenish dot that is Genesis. She thinks she may be leaving her home for the last time. Most humans would find that difficult; some would weep. Noemi simply watches silently as they accelerate, hurtling past the other planets of this system, leaving Genesis behind.

"You should sleep," he says.

Noemi shakes her head. "Not happening. I haven't forgotten I'm on an enemy ship with an enemy mech. If you think you can catch me off my guard, think again."

"This mission will require several days at least. You're already exhausted. Not only will you be unable to remain awake during our entire journey, you probably won't remain functional more than another hour or two at best." Abel glances over at her. "You shouldn't worry about my disobeying you, or harming you, while you rest."

"Because you're so worried about my well-being?" she says, eyebrow arched.

"Of course not." He smiles congenially. "But as the events of the past hour should have demonstrated... if my programming allowed me to kill you, you'd be dead already."

After several long seconds of silence, Noemi replies, "If you're trying to reassure me, you're not doing a great job."

"I'm only trying to keep you fully informed." Abel has

to obey Noemi, but he doesn't have to like her. He doesn't have to care if she's frightened or tired. He's done his duty by informing her of a risk to her health; after this, he can let her run herself ragged.

"Not yet," she finally says. "I couldn't sleep yet."

Without another word, he accelerates, urging the ship faster toward the Kismet Gate. If Noemi Vidal drops dead from exhaustion beside him, so be it.

• • •

She doesn't drop dead at any point during the fourteen hours it takes the *Daedalus* to cross the Genesis system. But she goes from sitting quietly at ops to blinking hard, to swaying in her seat as if she's on the verge of falling. At this point, Noemi must have been awake so long as to be near the point of delirium.

But she straightens and focuses again as they approach the Kismet Gate.

It looks just like the Gate leading to Earth, except that this one isn't battle-scarred or surrounded by debris. The silvery components lock together to form one vast ring. This is the eye of the needle through which Abel will thread the *Daedalus*.

As he inputs the necessary coordinates, he sees Noemi take a deep breath. When he glances over at her, she asks, "You're sure the integrity field will hold up for this trip?"

"Almost completely certain."

She pauses after that *almost*, which is what Abel had intended. "You can't have piloted a ship through a minefield before. But you've gone through debris fields, right? Asteroid belts?"

The levels of programming within Abel go beyond any human experience. He doesn't say so. Instead he replies with only the simplest facts. "Only in simulations. I've actually never had full operational control of a ship before."

Noemi blanches. How satisfying.

As they dive toward the shimmering surface of the Gate, the ring seeming to widen around them as they approach the event horizon, Abel smiles. "Let's see how I do, shall we?"

11

HE'S GOING TO KILL US BOTH.

Shocked back into alertness, Noemi clutches the armrests as if she can keep herself from falling into the Gate. And it feels like falling, now—the Gate shimmers brighter as they near the event horizon, growing more and more silvery until it looks like a pool they're diving into. The silver surface of the Gate reflects the ship perfectly. For one instant, Noemi sees the mirror image of the *Daedalus* reflected there, like a raindrop. If she'd been at a window, she would've seen her own face coming closer until the two images melded into one—

Gravity shoves her against her chair, making her gasp. The increase feels as if it would press her flat, even as Abel smoothly says, "Entering Gate...*now.*"

With that, they surge out of normal space-time, into the wormhole.

Noemi has never heard a satisfactory description of how

wormhole travel feels. Now she knows why. Words couldn't capture this—the way everything seems to become translucent, including her own body—or how she remains motionless while feeling as if she's turned into water swirling down a drain. Even light bends strangely, carving unnatural angles where none really existed, because it's moving at different speeds and turning her perceptions into illusions. She and Abel seem to be fractals in a kaleidoscope, shifting every second. Nothing is real. Not even time. Not even Noemi herself.

I hate this, she thinks. In the same moment she also thinks, *I love this*. Both feelings seem true.

Gravity snaps back to normal, sending her rocking forward until her head nearly strikes the ops panel. Light is light again.

We're through! Noemi feels a rush of relief and wonder—she's traveled across the galaxy in an instant, to a whole new world—

—but as she lifts her head she sees the minefield.

The glinting green lights of the mines outnumber the stars. Her gut tightens as the explosives wobble in their courses, magnetic sensors drawing them toward the new intruder. Horrified, Noemi watches dozens of mines rush toward the *Daedalus*. Just one would have enough power to blow them apart into atoms.

"Abel!" she cries.

But he's already reacting, both hands flying over his control panel. The ship darts through the maze of mines around them, swooping and swerving so quickly Noemi imagines she can feel every turn, every plunge. Nausea wells in her gut, and she grips both armrests so hard her fingers ache.

Abel shows no recognition of the danger. Mechs don't care if they die. Probably he wouldn't mind killing her in the process.

A faint shimmer keeps shifting around them, confusing Noemi until she realizes they're the shields. While steering, Abel is simultaneously shifting shield strength from zone to zone, protecting the ship where it needs it most. No human could ever work at that speed. Not even close.

By now at least a hundred mines rush toward them like a swarm of green fireflies. There's no way they're surviving the next thirty seconds.

Maybe I'll get to go to heaven after all, she thinks in a daze. *If I die trying to save my whole world? That's got to help.*

The ship accelerates, roaring toward the mines. Noemi yells, "*What* are you *doing*?"

Abel never looks up from the control panel. "Did you know that even mechs concentrate better in silence?"

She bites her tongue, literally. Pain offers some distraction from the mortal terror.

But within seconds, Noemi realizes what Abel's up to. Moving faster forces the mines to approach them in waves, which cuts down on the number of evasive actions needed for the *Daedalus* to stay in one piece.

One mine strikes the shields. Green electrical light sparks fitfully along the stern, and the entire ship shakes so hard Noemi nearly topples from her chair. How many hits like that can they take? One of the controls on her ops console glows red, warning her of danger she can't even bear to check. It makes no difference. Abel will steer them through this, or they'll die. The end.

"On my mark—" Abel says, finally looking up at the viewscreen—just as the *Daedalus* accelerates even more to outrun the few mines trailing behind. Now space is once again only blackness and stars. With a smile, Abel concludes, "—minefield cleared."

Noemi manages to look at her console. The red light says the shields were below 10 percent. "One more strike and we'd have been killed."

"Irrelevant." After a pause Abel adds, "Congratulations are unnecessary."

She actually might have congratulated him if she weren't so astonished. Slowly her mind begins to accept that they've made it through the same obstacle that has stood between Genesis and the rest of the galaxy for the past three decades.

And that means she's finally, truly, journeyed to an entirely new world.

Noemi rises to her feet and walks toward the viewscreen as the star field clears, free of mines at last. At the center of the screen blazes a star...no, not just a star. A *sun*, bluer and larger than her own. And there, the tiny amethyst jewel hanging in the sky—"That's Kismet, isn't it?"

"Yes. I suggest taking an indirect route there to better disguise our origin. It's unlikely they'd expect anyone to come through from Genesis, but we should be safe."

She nods, unable to tear her eyes away from Kismet.

The name means "fate." Finding this world had been an accident—the result of a probe getting caught in a naturally occurring wormhole, popping into a system that might otherwise have gone undiscovered for centuries. Kismet is warm, blessed with a calm climate, and covered with water. It could even have been the world Earth hung its hopes on instead of Genesis, but for the near-total absence of dry land.

So Noemi had dutifully learned in school. But soon she'll actually stand on this planet. Look up into a sky not her own. She's dreamed of this, feeling guilty the whole time. Genesis is supposed to be enough. Yet her heart has always longed for this journey, and now it's been given to her.

"Although it will take us the better part of ten hours to

cross the Kismet system to the planet, there are preparations we should make for landing," Abel says.

Noemi forces herself to focus. As the terror of their Gate crossing fades, exhaustion threatens to drag her down again. "Right. Of course. Can you change the ship registration? Make us anonymous?" She doubts anyone will be on the lookout for a vessel abandoned so long ago, but they might as well be safe.

"I can alter our registration," Abel confirms. To judge by the screens he's pulling up on his console, he's already begun doing so. "However, we have other potentially incriminating evidence to deal with."

"Like what I'm wearing?" The green exosuit brands her as a soldier of Genesis. "Maybe I can find something else that fits me."

"Captain Gee was very nearly your size. I suggest you check her quarters." A small, 3-D cross-section of the *Daedalus* hovers aboard Noemi's console, one room burning brighter than the others. Abel continues, "However, I was speaking of a far more critical matter. Upon landing at Kismet, we may well be boarded by docking authorities. Your starfighter and the damaged scout ship could easily be salvage picked up for parts or resale, but we'd have far more difficulty explaining why we're traveling with a corpse."

Esther. The daze of weariness and wonder that had spun

itself around Noemi breaks. She remembers that she's alone with a mech on a ship she hardly understands, and the dead body of her friend lies still and cold in sick bay. "We—we tell them she's a crew member who passed away."

"How do we explain her injuries?"

"I—" It occurs to her at last that the Kismet authorities would assume she and Abel had murdered Esther. "Her ship is damaged. We can show them that, say she got hurt trying to bring it in."

"If they examine the scout ship, they'll know only a battle mech could've caused that damage." Abel shakes his head. "That will raise questions we can't afford to answer."

Noemi's temper flares. "We'll come up with something! What else are we supposed to do?"

"Bury her in space."

He says it like it's nothing. Throw Esther out of the ship. Toss her into the void. Leave her alone for all eternity, drifting in the terrible cold of space, never to be warm.

"No," Noemi says. "No."

"Then how are we to—"

She doesn't hear the rest of what Abel says, because she walks off the bridge and leaves him behind.

• • •

It's nearly half an hour later before Noemi sees Abel again.

She's spent that time in sick bay with what's left of her

friend. The body doesn't even look like Esther anymore, not really. The same light-gold hair, the same freckles across her cheekbones: Nothing about Esther seems to have changed except that her skin is paler. And yet somehow, just looking at her, you know everything that ever mattered about Esther—her laugh, her kindness, the funny way she always sneezed three times in a row—her *soul* is gone, forever.

Noemi stands in front of the biobed, hugging herself, and doesn't turn when she hears the sick bay doors slide open. Abel's smart enough not to come too close at first. "If my suggestion earlier gave offense, I apologize."

She shrugs. "You're programmed to say that, aren't you?"

"Yes."

Figures.

"It should've been me," Noemi says, not to Abel, not to anyone really. "She had something to go back to. People who are going to miss her. Who loved her." Noemi only had Esther, and now she has no one.

Abel doesn't reply. Probably there's no preprogrammed response to that.

"She's not a *thing*, okay? Not a piece of refuse for us to toss out. Esther was *someone*, and you have to remember that."

"I will." But immediately he tries again. "Whenever you feel it appropriate, we can proceed with whatever method of…burial you prefer."

Probably he was going to say *disposal*.

"I know we have to do something, but I can't just leave Esther lying there in space." Noemi still feels as if she's talking to herself. "I can't leave her alone in the cold. Anything but that."

Abel remains silent long enough that she wonders if dealing with an actual human, with actual feelings, has fried his circuits. But finally he asks, "It is the cold that bothers you?"

You don't know what cold means, she wants to answer. He'd probably answer her with the freezing points of various elements in centigrade, Fahrenheit, and Kelvin. So Noemi explains what haunts her. "There's nothing lonelier than that. Than being cold and alone, and lost." She swallows hard to keep her voice from choking off. "When I was eight, my family was going into the woods—at wintertime—"

Where exactly were they going? To build snowmen? To see one of the frozen waterfalls? Noemi can't remember. Sometimes it feels as if the story would make more sense if she could only remember why they were out there in the first place.

"Our skimmer hit a bomb from the Liberty War, one that hadn't exploded during whatever battle had taken place long ago. It had just been lying there all this time. The snow had covered the shell, so my parents never saw it. They just drove over it, and then—"

Noemi doesn't remember this part either. For this bit of amnesia, however, she feels grateful. She doesn't know what their screams sounded like, or even whether they screamed at all.

"When I came to, they were dead. Or dying, maybe. I couldn't tell. But they were all gone. Mom, Dad, my baby brother. His name was Rafael, but he was still so little I just called him baby. We lay there in the bloody snow for so long—it seemed like forever, and they were so cold. *So cold.*"

Her throat closes up again. For an instant she feels as if she can recall the time before the crash—her mother's laugh, the weight of her tiny brother in her lap. But those aren't real memories. Just her imagination trying to fill in the gaps. The only real memories are those of blood, the smell of smoke, and Noemi shivering in the wreckage, unable to understand why she didn't die, too.

Abel steps closer. Probably he'll tell her that nothing in her past is relevant, that her objections are illogical.

Instead he says, "The star, then."

Noemi turns to him. "What?"

"We could bury Esther in Kismet's star. Nothing is warmer or brighter. Of course she'd be cremated, but you would still have a sort of grave where you could mourn her. You would always be able to find this star in the sky."

She stares at him, speechless.

Abel ventures, "The star is visible from Genesis's northern hemisphere, given good weather conditions."

"I know. I just—" *I can't understand how a mere machine could think of that.* Abel's idea is sensitive. Even kind. Noemi knows Esther would have approved. Her friend will become part of a star that warms and nurtures an entire world. "That's good. We'll do that."

He seems relieved. She hadn't realized, before this, that he'd been tense. "Let me know when you wish to proceed."

"Now." Waiting will only put Genesis at risk. Noemi has to complete her mission before the Masada Run, or else hundreds of people will die, including Captain Baz, all their friends—and maybe Jemuel, too. After this, he might volunteer for the Masada Run himself. Esther wouldn't want that. "Let's go."

The only possible coffin is Esther's damaged scout. They can't use it any longer, and it's one less thing she and Abel will have to explain to the authorities on Kismet. Abel carries Esther's body back to the docking bay and sets her back into the bloodied mess of her cockpit. As he checks the instrumentation, Noemi leans over Esther and brushes a few stray locks of hair from her face.

"Here," she whispers as she folds Esther's hands around Noemi's own rosary. Esther wasn't Catholic, but it's all Noemi has to give. "I love you."

If Abel thinks speaking to the dead is ridiculous, he

gives no sign. He simply sets the scout ship's controls as the *Daedalus* soars closer to Kismet's star. They both leave the docking bay so the air lock can be sealed but, without being asked, Abel instantly brings up the image of the star on the nearest wall monitor.

Noemi feels the small shudder deep within the ship as the rover launches. She ought to pray, she knows, but she can't even find the heart for that. Within moments, a tiny streak lances through the dark sky around Kismet's sun. For one split second, Esther's coffin is a dark speck against that brightness—and then it's gone.

Now she's sunshine, Noemi thinks. Tears well in her eyes, but she blinks fast, refusing to let them fall.

Glancing sideways, she sees Abel studying her while trying very hard to look as if he isn't. There's something about Abel that's almost *too* intelligent. Too knowing. He's less like a device, more like another person. And his idea of burying Esther within a star showed something so close to compassion....

But no. Abel's supposed kindness must be like the rest of his careful programming and his pleasing appearance: a disguise meant to deceive. Noemi can't afford to forget that this is merely a machine, one she can use to save her world.

"All right," she says hoarsely. "On to Kismet."

He hesitates, then replies, "My estimates of your mission prep time and flight time to the Gate are necessarily inexact. However, I know that the battle with the Damocles ship, our first encounter aboard the *Daedalus*"—*encounter*, how tactful—"and everything that has happened since has taken long enough that I'd estimate that you've been awake for at least twenty-four hours straight. In addition, you have been under considerable physical and emotional stress. You are no longer in prime operating condition. Please reconsider your decision to go without sleep."

Noemi pauses. "You don't change course. You don't send any communications. You don't do anything that I haven't expressly ordered you to do unless it's necessary to keep the ship from being destroyed. Those are your orders. You'll obey them?"

"Of course."

Without another word, she turns and walks back up the corridor, around the long swirl of the spiral, until she reaches the first set of crew quarters. It's a small bedroom, military stark. Suits Noemi fine. She activates the lock, flops down on the bed fully dressed in her exosuit, and falls asleep almost before she closes her eyes.

Noemi barely has time to realize how good it feels to let go. To leave everything to Abel for a while.

12

ABEL CAN'T SABOTAGE NOEMI VIDAL'S EFFORTS OR DIS-
obey her orders, nor does he intend to try...but he has to
admit, she wasn't wrong to wonder about his intentions.
Although he can't work against her, he can act on his own
initiative in other ways. Nor is he required to tell her he's
doing so.

He'd smile at the thought of outwitting her, were he
not so focused as he walks to the ship's small engine room,
which contains a secondary communications console. He
can't call for help, can't do anything else that would put
Noemi at risk, but he can finally satisfy the curiosity that
has burned so brightly within him for the past thirty years.

As soon as he's at the engine room comms console, he
runs a search for the name Burton Mansfield. Instantly the
ship begins reaching out to the satellites and ships in the Kismet system, gleaning whatever information it can find.

Will his creator have died? Did he perish escaping the

Daedalus? Thirty years later, Abel still cannot bear not knowing. When the screen lights up, his breath catches in his throat—a human reflex, one that survives deep in his human DNA.

The results he sees don't tell Abel as much as the results that he doesn't. No obituaries or memorials are shown, and a person of Mansfield's stature would surely have received many after his death. Therefore, Mansfield is alive.

It doesn't matter that Abel will never get to see him again, not compared to the fact that his creator has survived. The emotion this knowledge inspires—this transcendent inner light—is that joy? Abel hopes so. He has wanted to feel joy at least once.

He wishes he could at least inform Mansfield of his fate. Even though Mansfield is unlikely to be able to provide any sort of rescue, Abel would like to tell his creator, his "father," about his many years of solitude and the strange changes within his thought and emotion matrices. The information might prove useful in future cybernetics experiments.

However, there's very little information about precisely what Burton Mansfield is currently doing. No press releases have been issued for quite some time. No conferences. The last new paper appears to have been published almost a decade ago. Of course Mansfield must now be elderly by human standards; probably he's enjoying a well-deserved retirement. But it's strange to think about him growing old while Abel has stayed so nearly the same.

Nor does Mansfield appear to have made any significant advances in cybernetics. Abel calls up the current specs and sees that the same twenty-five models of mech are still in production, Baker through Zebra. Appearances have been tweaked, with new hairstyles and body proportions to reflect changes in taste, and apparently fixes have been applied to patch old flaws and vulnerabilities. The fundamentals of strengths, skills, and intelligence remain the same.

This is useful tactical information for Abel to have. However, he finds himself gratified on a level that has nothing to do with any rational purpose. As the screen projects soft green light on his face, he even smiles.

Mansfield has never made another mech as intelligent as Abel. Nor one as skilled, or as capable of learning. In other words, Mansfield has never tried to replace him.

Noemi Vidal may destroy Abel, but she can't take this one truth away from him: He remains Mansfield's ultimate creation.

* * *

Once the *Daedalus* is within an hour of Kismet, Abel wonders how best to awaken Noemi. Via intra-ship comms? Going to her door? As he's formulating the questions, however, she returns to the bridge, alert, freshly bathed (judging by the faint soapy scent), and wearing civilian attire that belonged to Captain Gee.

Highly questionable civilian attire, in Abel's opinion—a shapeless gray tunic and loose pants too old for Noemi, which paradoxically makes her look even younger than she is. She might be a child playing dress-up. However, her voice is firm as she says, "We're approaching the planet?"

Abel doesn't have to answer, because the communications panel at the ops station lights up with an incoming message—automated, no doubt. Noemi hesitates only for an instant before bringing it up.

Instantly, the star field disappears from the viewscreen, replaced by a spectacular beach scene—lavender ocean and lilac sky, with fluffy clouds even brighter than the glittering white sand. A female voice warmly says, *"Welcome to Kismet, where paradise awaits."* The image shifts into one of a resort with pearlescent walls, in front of which young, attractive people stroll with drinks in their hands. *"Whether you're here to get closer to the action or get away from it all, whether you're in search of sensuality or serenity, everyone on Kismet is totally committed to making sure you enjoy the getaway you deserve. Every aspect of your experience will represent the finest our world has to offer. Please input your resort code now."*

"Resort code?" Noemi says.

"Very few people are allowed to immigrate permanently

to Kismet." The viewscreen shifts back to the tranquil beach scene. "Most people who come here are visitors from Earth or the more prosperous space stations within Earth's solar system. Only the wealthiest and most privileged can afford the resorts here."

Noemi bites her lower lip; the violet light from the viewscreen shimmers against her black hair. "We don't have the credits for that, do we?"

"Not even close," Abel confirms. "I'll try sending a randomized code—if I work within their parameters, I may well come up with something close enough to at least give us permission to land."

As soon as Abel sends the randomized code, the beach scene blinks out, replaced by stars and a flat few lines of text: INCORRECT CODE. REPORT TO LUNAR BASE WAYLAND FOR PROCESSING OR VACATE THE KISMET SYSTEM.

"So much for that plan," Noemi says.

Her tone of voice doesn't suggest contempt. However, Abel feels an odd sensation, displeasure at having failed to crack the code combined with a specific, pointed desire that Noemi had not seen his failure. Is this what humans call embarrassment? No wonder they work so hard to avoid it.

At least Noemi doesn't notice his discomfort. She simply adds, "It doesn't matter. They'll have the part we need on that station, too, I bet."

"A reasonable assumption," Abel admits.

Kismet only has one moon, according to his data. No fully operational space stations should be in orbit. But as the *Daedalus* wheels around the planet, Abel wonders for a moment if the data about the space stations is wrong, because the sheer scale of the traffic goes far beyond what he would have expected.

Cruisers. Former military ships haphazardly retrofitted for civilian use. Antique solar-sail vessels. Even a couple of old ore-haulers. Hundreds of these vessels are clustered around Kismet's moon, no doubt hoping for landing clearance from Wayland Station. As diverse as these ships are in age, size, and original purpose, they have all been repainted in brilliant colors and patterns, or with murals of animals, flames, old-fashioned playing cards, virtually any whimsical or strange image humans could think of. Names and words are painted, too, in English, Cantonese, Spanish, Hindi, Arabic, Russian, Bantu, French, and probably more languages besides.

"What the—" Noemi turns to Abel. "Is this what rich people do on Earth? Buy ships just to decorate them?"

"These are older ships. While they might pass muster on Genesis, they would be considered beneath the dignity of a wealthy person from Earth." Abel considers, then forms a new hypothesis. "I believe we have found a large gathering of Vagabonds."

She frowns in confusion. "Vagabonds?"

"As economic and ecological conditions became more hostile on Earth, more and more people needed to leave. Since the planned resettlement on Genesis had to be delayed due to the Liberty War, people had nowhere to go."

"But—the other colony worlds—"

"Are unable to sustain anything like the number of humans in need of new places to live," Abel finishes. "Kismet operates as a resort world primarily because opening it up to settlement would soon deplete its resources. Cray can be inhabited by two million people at most. Stronghold can take more, but even so, its population stood at only two hundred million when I last received new data. It will have expanded since then, but nowhere near enough to provide adequate living conditions for the eight billion people still on Earth." He nods toward the ships. "Unsurprisingly, some humans were already beginning to live their entire lives aboard spacecraft. The name for such people was Vagabonds. From what we see here, I would gather that what had been a fringe subculture is now a significant movement."

He expects this to shame her—this proof of humanity's desperation in the light of Genesis's secession from the colony worlds. Instead her dark eyes widen in what looks almost like confusion. "I thought Earth would try to control them," she whispers. "That the authorities wouldn't let just anybody own their own ship. These people go wherever they want. They're...*free*."

"I wouldn't know much about freedom," Abel says to his commander, who's currently leading him to his destruction. "We should transmit to Wayland Station right away. From the look of things, landing could be delayed if we don't."

Noemi hesitates. Did she pick up on his frustration? If so, why should she care? But she says only, "Go ahead and transmit."

He does so, then rises from his station. "Before we receive final landing clearance, I should change clothes."

"Why? You look, um, nice."

Abel considers this compliment no more than he is due. After all, he changed into garments left behind by Burton Mansfield—black silk jacket and pants, a loose scarlet tunic beneath, all of it so exquisitely woven and tailored that he had no fear of looking strange even if the clothes have gone out of style. But they no longer serve his purpose. "I dressed to suit what I assumed would be our cover story, that of wealthy travelers arriving at a Kismet resort. Our new cover is that we are badly in need of work. Therefore, we should look impoverished, or at least unfashionable." Abel pauses at the door to study Noemi again. "What you're wearing is fine."

Noemi gets a strange look on her face as he walks out.

No doubt she thinks that was mere robotic tactlessness, nothing Abel did intentionally.

Good.

Abel may give his service to Noemi. He may give his very life for her cause. His programming offers him no other choice.

But if she's determined to use him up and throw him away, he can at least make sure she doesn't enjoy it.

13

NOEMI LOOKS DOWN AT HER CLOTHES. SHE'D HOPED nobody on the lunar station would notice her in this gray, shapeless gear. Now she feels conspicuous. Even ugly.

Don't be ridiculous. Abel said what you're wearing is fine for what you're about to pretend to be. So what if it looks awful? You're not here to impress anyone. You're here to buy a T-7 anx and move on fast.

Assuming, of course, that she can trust Abel.

Obviously she has some real control over him here on the *Daedalus*. Will that hold true when they land at Wayland Station? When other humans are around—humans who despise Genesis, who would shoot Noemi on sight? The nervous energy inside her still surges and sparks, taking her from fear to excitement and back again.

She's about to visit *another planet*. Well, its moon. But still! This is the adventure she always wanted, and the mission she can't screw up. Her deepest dream wrapped in her darkest nightmare.

On this mission, there can be no mistakes. One false step and Noemi dies along with her planet's best chance of salvation.

Noemi tries to figure the number of days that have passed since she left Genesis—but now that she's left her solar system, concepts like "days" have become much more nebulous. Einsteinian differences in the passage of time over vast differences in space will have to be taken into account, too. She should ask Abel to calculate it for her....

But she catches herself. It's already too easy for her to rely on Abel. By instinct, she trusts the machine to operate normally—but Abel has that other side, that uncanny spark of consciousness, and she distrusts that profoundly. She doesn't want to get into the habit of depending on him too much. Maybe she can set up a program to count down the days for her.

Should she even let him leave the *Daedalus*? Surely she can figure out how to buy space parts on her own.

But she can't let paranoia get the better of her. Abel's a one-of-a-kind prototype, which means he's unregistered. He's so humanlike that the average person would never guess he's a mech. If Noemi had met him under any other circumstances, she wouldn't have known either. She has to find out whether or not she can trust his programming at some point; it might as well be now. Abel's a tool she's been given and one she shouldn't be afraid to use.

So she tells herself, and it almost drowns out the eerie feeling she had when Abel said he wouldn't know much about freedom.

Wayland Station begins coming into view as the ship skims closer to Kismet's moon. From a greater distance, it looked like just another lunar crater, but Noemi begins to make out the details of the settlement within, sealed beneath a transparent bubble. Dozens of Vagabond craft throng around Wayland waiting for their own permission to land. She recognizes some of the wild painted marks on their ships: Maori designs on this one, a silly zigzag pattern on another, and one that's simply bright green, like a leaf floating in outer space.

They're all carrying people from other planets. A small thrill runs through her, one that burns her tiredness away. *Mostly from Earth, I bet, but some could be from Stronghold, or even Cray. Today I'll meet someone from a whole new world. I'll stand on a planet besides the one I was born on. I'll look up and see new constellations in the stars.*

Genesis doctrine says they need no other worlds. Noemi believes this. But even if you don't need something, can't you *want* it? Surely it can't be wrong to want to see more of creation. To behold the universe from every possible angle—to be the way in which the universe is able to behold *itself*. As long as she can remember, she's yearned to explore beyond any limits.

Now, at last, on this one mission, she can.

As the moon begins to eclipse the soft violet surface of Kismet, she stares down at the planet for a few moments longer. It sparkles like an amethyst against black velvet.

This is the world Esther will shine down on forever. Noemi's so glad it's beautiful.

· · ·

At the moment she would've signaled him to land, Abel reappears wearing a plain, long-sleeved T-shirt and a pair of work pants, both in olive green, and simply nods at her as he returns to the pilot's position. His eerie sense of timing sets her on edge, as does his icy calm. He doesn't speak a single unnecessary word as he steers the *Daedalus* through the open gap in Wayland Station's dome, amid a flurry of Vagabond vessels, and settles it onto the moon's surface. And once that gap has closed, sealing them within the spaceport—a low, gray building that looks nothing like the iridescent palaces of Kismet—Noemi's wonder isn't supporting her any longer. The reality of what she's about to do sinks in, second by second. As she stands in front of the ship's entryway, waiting for it to cycle open, she feels her body going cold. She clasps her hands in front of her, which keeps her from hugging herself. Abel would probably sneer at her human weakness if she did.

But as she prepares to confront a new planet for the very first time, she doesn't feel like a soldier of Genesis. She only knows she's too far from home.

She's proud that her voice is steady as she asks, "When were you last on Kismet?"

"Never."

"Never?" She turns toward Abel. "What about the other colony worlds?"

"I've never visited them either."

"Then why were you acting like you know everything about them?"

"My lack of direct experience is irrelevant." Abel shrugs. "Extremely thorough information came preloaded into my memory circuits."

"Information from thirty years ago, you mean."

He raises one eyebrow. "Of course. As I was marooned for three decades, my information about any recent developments is necessarily limited. Will you require me to remind you of this at regular intervals?"

Noemi manages to hang on to her temper, but it's hard. His arrogance makes her want to scream. "My point is, you can stop acting like you know everything about Kismet, all right?"

"I've never claimed to know everything about Kismet."

He gives her a small, seemingly polite smile. "I simply know more than you."

Why didn't I push him out of an air lock when I had the chance?

Maybe he can see the dark blaze of fury in her eyes. Abel's face remains expressionless, but he takes a step back. His uncertainty would please her more if she weren't freaking out, too. But she's in control again, and the mech knows it.

Then the curved metal plates of the entryway spiral open.

What they reveal is chaos. The spaceport is crowded and noisy, and it stinks of grease and sweat. Hundreds of people jumble together, struggling to pass along paths and bridges far too narrow for the crowds. The clothes they wear are brilliantly colored but odd, motley pieces thrown together without regard for function, most of them worn or even threadbare. The ships docked nearby look as ramshackle as their owners, now that she sees them up close. Even to Noemi, who's used to Genesis's aging fleet, the vessels around them seem more likely to collapse than fly. Screens and holos have been crammed into every corner, hung from every one of the naked metal beams overhead. It's almost like the screens are *important*, but Noemi can tell they're only showing ads. Over and over. Music and slogans blaring so loud they drown out every human voice—

And now, walking up to them, is a mech.

Her memory responds instantly. *George model. Designed for work requiring middling intelligence and a high threshold for boredom. Most often deployed in bureaucratic roles.*

Darius Akide would be proud of her for remembering all of that. He wouldn't be proud, though, of the shudder that passes through her as she looks at the George for the first time. Although it looks like his hairstyle has been changed from the old models, in every other way the George appears exactly the way he does in the old images. He's slightly stocky, with pale skin and brown hair.

What gets her are the eyes.

The George's eyes are a bland shade of green, but somehow they're…empty. Like a doll's eyes, except when Noemi was little she imagined that her dolls loved her back. Nobody could even pretend a soul lay behind the George's empty face. What sits within its metal skull is a nest of wiring and computer memory. Circuits and signals. No soul.

However, the George does nothing more unsettling than hold up a datapad to get an image of their faces. "Name of vessel?"

"The *Medusa*," Abel says. "Named after the mythological female who took pleasure in turning men to stone."

Noemi decides she's going to believe he chose that name at random. The only alternative is punching him in the nose, which would probably tip off the George that something was wrong.

"The *Medusa*. Confirmed." Abel's fake ID for their ship held. Good. "Names of human occupants?"

She tries to sound casual. "Noemi Vidal."

"Abel Mansfield," Abel says smoothly. Was he programmed to take on his creator's surname, or was that something he could choose to do?

The last name doesn't trigger any more reaction than their pictures did, because the George mech nods. "Earth nations of origin?"

Noemi hesitates only a moment before deciding to use the birthplace of her ancestors. "Chile."

Abel says, "Great Britain." Maybe that's where he was created.

"You are hereby cleared for up to six days' stay on Wayland Station. Please prepay your first day's docking fee, which is nonrefundable." The George hands over a small, dark dataread, which begins to glow with scrolling information. Abel immediately inputs whatever info the dataread needs to show they've paid for the right to put their ship down. They've passed inspection. Nobody's coming for Abel; nobody's caught on to her. They made it.

She ought to be relieved. To want to cheer her victory. But the chaos around her, the noise and grime and unmistakable sense of desperation—

Noemi has never felt so far from home.

The George points left, toward a long line of brightly

clothed Vagabonds. "Report for Cobweb screening and final clearance. Have a pleasant stay."

As they start walking toward the others, Noemi goes on tiptoe to whisper in Abel's ear. "Cobweb screening? What does that mean?"

"I don't know." He clearly hates admitting that; she wishes she were less freaked out, so she could enjoy his displeasure. "I could only speculate."

"Okay, speculate."

"To judge by the fact that health care supplies seem to be stored here"—Abel gestures toward crates with the telltale green cross on them—"this seems most likely to be some sort of medical screening."

"Medical screening?" Noemi grabs his arm as if to tug him back. His body feels startlingly human. Will that be enough to fool a medical doctor, or are they about to get caught?

But there's no more time to discuss. Already attendants in pale green have stepped close to pull them apart.

Panic rises in her throat, and she wants to cling to Abel—a machine, and a hostile, superior one—all she has to rely on in a strange solar system, on a mission of the greatest importance and danger.

No, she thinks, standing up straighter and letting go of Abel of her own free will. *I can rely on myself. The mission might've changed, but I haven't. I can do this.*

They're led without ceremony into a large tented area, where Vagabonds of various ages, genders, and races are all dropping their clothes for inspection. Noemi's never been particularly shy about her body, but there's something so cold about this. The doctors or nurses calling them forward to be looked over show no compassion or concern; they're not here to take care of the Vagabonds, just to sort through them.

Once she's undressed, holding her gray clothing wadded under one arm, she stands in line like the others. The girl standing next to her seems to be roughly her own age, tall and dark-skinned, with long braids that fall to her waist and a body so skinny her ribs show. She's not the only one in line that thin. But there's something about her eyes that seems...gentle, maybe. At any rate, Noemi decides to take a chance and whispers, "Hey—what's Cobweb?"

"You don't know?" The girl has a lilting, beautiful accent. "You're new to this Vagabonding thing, huh? Don't guess they talk about it much on Earth."

"Not much," Noemi says. "And, uh, very new."

Although this girl still looks dubious, she explains, "It's a nasty virus. The worst. Gives you the chills something fierce, and breaks veins all over your body. You get this weird rash with white lines everywhere. So it looks like you're wearing a spiderweb, see?"

Noemi nods. The strangeness of speaking to someone

from another planet has begun to fade. This person isn't an enemy or an alien—she's just a *person*. A nice one, even. "The name makes sense."

"Point is, Cobweb's contagious, and it can be deadly if you don't catch it in time." The girl's expression darkens for a moment as she shakes her braids free of the scarf she'd worn around her head. "Come on, let's get this over with."

The medical mech is the Tare model, which looks like a middle-aged woman of East Asian ancestry. Human medical assistants work by the Tare's side, but there's no question who will judge her. It's just as brisk and efficient as Akide's lectures always said—and even her eyes don't reflect anything like the intelligence Noemi sees inside Abel.

Speaking of Abel...

Noemi glances around, hoping he hasn't already been tugged out of line, exposed as a machine. Instead she catches a glimpse of him, naked from the waist up, disrobing at the far end of the medical tent. The first thing that strikes her is how unworried he seems. Is that because he'll pass inspection without being detected, or because he can't wait to be rescued and expose her in the process?

What hits her next is that Abel's already attracting attention. A lot of it. Not because he looks like a machine, but because he might have the single most perfect body Noemi's ever seen. Or imagined. He could be some ancient marble sculpture, with his pale skin, developed muscles, and exact symmetry. If she didn't know he was just a machine, she might even think he was...

"Smoky," murmurs the girl in front of her, the one with the braids. She smiles as she unashamedly watches Abel remove his pants, too. "Not that I don't love my fella, but—"

"Next," calls one of the medical assistants, and the girl hurries forward for inspection.

The Tare runs her hands along the backs and limbs of every single person in line, as impersonally as though they were statues. When it's Noemi's turn, the Tare pauses. "You possess more musculature than the average female of your age."

Not on Genesis, she doesn't. Noemi's actually pretty lazy about her weight lifting. It's the one part of military discipline she's the worst at. But compared to the skinny, half-starved Vagabond girls around her, Noemi looks almost impossibly strong. "Our, uh, last job involved a lot of physical labor," she answers, thinking fast. "It lasted for months. Guess you can see the difference."

Apparently the explanation is satisfactory, because the Tare lets her move on.

Noemi puts her clothes back on in a hurry. They're not allowed to wait for others—and besides, she doesn't know if she's ready to see Abel completely naked. Instead she walks through the far end of the tent into Wayland Station proper...

. . . which is pretty much the same as walking into hell.

Kismet's welcome message made their whole world seem so beautiful, so polished, so elegant. The entertainment offered here? Not so much. She's surrounded by billboards, holo-adverts, and shimmering lights. The majority of them, and the brightest, all proclaim that THE ORCHID FESTIVAL IS HERE! This seems to be some sort of musical event, although various celebrity and political guests are advertised as being in attendance as well. At least, that's what Noemi guesses they are; the names and faces are all utterly unfamiliar to her. Some guy called Han Zhi seems to be the biggest draw. While the festival itself is on Kismet, apparently Wayland visitors can watch in various clubs, for a fee.

If that doesn't appeal, the clubs here have other gambits for taking the travelers' money. PLAY ALL NIGHT AT LUCKY NINETEEN! says a holo in the shape of a roulette wheel, spinning its colors around them. On a nearby screen, two mechs are shown preening, wearing little besides oiled skin and smiles; these are the pleasure models, Fox and Peter. The slogan promises you can HAVE A PLAYTHING OF YOUR VERY OWN.

Or you can watch people race motorcycles along a nearly vertical track, which looks incredibly dangerous. Sure enough, there's a small line at the bottom of the holo warning spectators that fatalities can happen. The warning looks more like a promise. Who could be amused watching people risk death for nothing more than a motorcycle race?

Noemi does, at least, understand the appeal of the display directly in front of her—actual entertainment, probably to keep the crowds from complaining about the long waits and rough treatment. In a large antigrav sphere, a scantily clad girl is dancing. Different areas of the sphere light up, peach flickers that signal the dancer where the gravity will be turned on next. The diaphanous veils covering her body flutter as she plunges upward, kicks sideways, floating on the different gravity sources like a leaf on the breeze. There's a pattern to it, Noemi sees; dancing in there might be fun, if it were only about the dancing, not about letting grubby space travelers drool at you. Because a lot of these guys around her are drooling, and shouting obscenities, and it's all so disgusting that Noemi wants to scream.

"Interesting," Abel says, coming up beside her, dressed again and unworried. "I would've thought they would charge for a show like this."

"Abel. How did you get through the medical screening?"

"It was a fairly cursory external check," Abel says. "The human medical personnel were being rather closely watched. Did you notice?"

"No." She doesn't see how it matters anyway. "We can look for a T-7 anx now, right?"

"Right." But Abel doesn't move. He simply looks around

at the garish advertisements, the ugly shouts of the people near them. "Does it trouble you?"

"What? The dance?" Noemi glances over at the scarf-clad girl, who's still pinwheeling through the sphere, ignoring her catcallers.

"The desperation," Abel says crisply. "Seeing what's become of the galaxy since Genesis's secession. If it bothers you, I can attempt to find a way to minimize your contact with others."

"We didn't do this to Earth and the colony worlds." Noemi shakes her head as the peach lights play on her face. "They did it to themselves. If we hadn't pulled away when we did, they would've done it to us, too. So, no, I'm not troubled. This place proves we did the right thing."

Abel inclines his head, as if acknowledging that she has a point. She'd like to enjoy that small victory. Instead, however, she looks again at the broken-down ships, the too-skinny Vagabonds, the exploitive culture, and asks herself, *Are we responsible for this? We can't be. We're the good guys.*

Aren't we?

14

WAYLAND STATION'S SPACEPORT FOLLOWS ONE OF THE commonly used port blueprints stored in Abel's mind: a broad space with ceilings held approximately forty meters above them by bare metal beams. The air is cool and dry to a degree most humans would find unpleasant, but is very familiar to Abel after thirty years in an equipment pod bay. Every millimeter bustles with activity, as people throng the walkways, struggle with boxes and barrels of cargo, examine various ships, and shout to one another over the noise, which of course only makes the noise worse. Although Abel should find the cacophony unbearable, instead he thrills to it—the beautiful sound of action, of *life*.

He files the realization away for future reference: *Even ordinary things gain great power when we have been without them for too long.*

Abel detects the first flaw in their plan when he double-checks the dataread that links them to the *Daeda-*

lus, aka the *Medusa*. As soon as he's pulled up their accounts, freshly minus their docking fees, he says, "We have an unexpected complication."

"What?" Noemi glances over at the dataread, and her eyes widen as she sees how little money they have left.

"Docking rights on Kismet are exponentially more expensive than they were thirty years ago. When I made my calculations, I allowed for price increases, but the rate of inflation has gone far beyond my expectations."

"What's inflation?" Noemi asks.

She is not from a capitalist society, he reminds himself. *She can't help her ignorance.* "It's when money loses worth, and so prices rise. Exponential rises in inflation are common in periods of extreme political upheaval, such as wartime."

Noemi frowns, and the expression etches a tiny wrinkle between her eyebrows, the one she gets when she's facing a problem. He is learning how to read her. "Are we going to have enough credits left over to buy the part we need?"

"If the rate of inflation for parts is similar to the one for docking rights, no."

She sighs. Behind her, the semiclothed dancer finishes her antigrav routine and bows; a few people have the manners to applaud. "If we're not going to be able to buy it, then I guess we'll have to steal it."

Already she has become more pragmatic. Abel wishes he could encourage this trait, but he can't. "We can attempt to do so, but security for ship parts will probably be tighter than they would be for thermomagnetic devices."

"Aren't ship parts cheaper?"

"Yes, but they are regularly sold in stores that will have security to prevent shoplifting. The thermomagnetic device will probably be found in a larger apparatus we can steal from with little fear of being caught in the act."

"All right, fine," Noemi says. "Then we'll earn money. We'll find work. Something that lets us get paid quickly."

He'd hoped she would be more discouraged. More intimidated. That she would show him more weaknesses... but why? His programming won't allow him to work against her. Observing her flaws would only gratify him on this new emotional level he doesn't entirely understand.

Disappointed, he turns his attention to the motley outfits chosen by the Vagabonds milling around them. They wear oversize garments layered over basic leggings and shirts, complete with work boots of varying heights. Scarves of different colors have been knotted to serve as hats or headdresses, belts or shawls. Utility belts are slung around waists and over shoulders. Is this a matter of style or of function? Abel suspects the latter motivation is stronger. Everything but the boots could clearly serve more than one purpose, if needed.

A plainer sign ahead reads ORCHID FESTIVAL WORKERS REGISTRATION, and many Vagabonds have crowded close.

134

Noemi brightens, which is as close as he's seen her come to smiling. "Of course. The festival—that's why so many people are on Wayland Station. They're hoping for temporary work there."

"Then we're in luck." Abel guides them into the part of the throng that looks most likely to be a queue.

Directly ahead of them stands a couple only a year or two older than Noemi herself, both dressed in Vagabond clothes. Abel's acute hearing can't help but pick up on their conversation.

"The first thing I'm going to eat is cinnamon toast." This is from the female of the couple, a tall woman whose skin color, long braids, and accent suggest Afro-Caribbean ancestry. He had noticed her speaking to Noemi during the Cobweb inspections. "No, no, wait! Do you think they'd have fresh fruit, Zayan?"

"What I'd do for a mango," sighs Zayan, a male slightly shorter than her, whom Abel would guess to be a native of India or Bangladesh. "You've got to try one, Harriet. If they're half as good as I remember, they're like a taste of paradise." The two of them grin at each other and clasp hands tightly—but then the girl with braids, Harriet, catches a glimpse of Noemi and waves. Noemi gives her a little smile. Is she attempting to befriend the Vagabonds? Surely not. That would only endanger their cover story.

Replaying the conversation between Harriet and Zayan,

Abel notes that food shortages must have increased. Mangoes weren't rare on Earth when he left.

"As long as they're hiring," Harriet says—a throwaway comment, it seems, but it makes a nearby middle-aged man with a beard turn around and scoff.

"Positions filled up months ago. You had to register remotely, didn't you know?" The bearded fellow laughs at the two young Vagabonds, as if they'd told a joke. "There's no more work here. Give it up."

Disappointing, but Abel feels sure they can come up with another employment possibility. But the young couple in front of them looks stricken, so much so that Abel fears both may be in danger of fainting.

"Hey," Noemi says awkwardly, her hands clasped in front of her. "It's going to be all right."

"It isn't, actually." Harriet sniffles and wipes at her face. "Why didn't we check? If we'd only just checked before we paid the dock fee—"

Zayan puts his arm around her. "We've stretched the rations this far, haven't we?"

"This is our last week." Harriet's voice trembles. "You know it is."

Zayan takes a deep breath. "Let's just…sit, all right? We can't think straight when we're this tired and hungry. If we can't eat, we can rest." With a nod toward Noemi, he leads Harriet to a small bench beneath yet more holographic advertisements, where the two of them embrace tightly.

Noemi's dark eyes never leave Harriet and Zayan, even as Abel walks her to the side of the corridor. She whispers, "Won't anyone feed them?"

"It seems few people have much to spare."

"The people coming to this Orchid Festival thing have enough to spare. They could share if they were decent human beings."

"Human beings and decency don't always go together." Abel blinks, somewhat surprised he said that out loud. Quickly he moves the conversation along. "We'll have to devise another means of income."

"How?"

He takes another look down the corridor, with its gaudy, titillating advertisements. "At this point, our swiftest and most reliable means of making money is prostitution."

Noemi takes a step back, her mouth an O of astonishment. "You—you didn't just say—you think I should become a *prostitute*?"

"Of course not. You're my commander. I serve you. Therefore, I would be the more logical choice to take on sex work." Abel should've kept on the nicer clothing he'd worn earlier; brothel owners would've seen his body displayed to better advantage. Regardless, he feels sure to be hired. "I've been programmed with virtually all of the skills held by other mechs, including the Fox and Peter models. My repertoire of sexual positions and techniques far exceeds those of virtually any human, and my physical form was designed to maximize both visual and tactile appeal."

"Whoa, whoa, wait." Noemi shakes her head in consternation. A slender young woman with short black hair, dressed like resort staff, has wandered toward them while working on her datapad, and Noemi is obviously choosing her words carefully to keep from giving away too much of their story. "Abel, I can't let you... sell your body."

"The transaction is closer to a rental."

"You know what I mean! I'm not comfortable with you doing that."

They have no time to waste on Genesis prudery. "Are you more comfortable running out of funds? Running out of time? Failing to return home?"

Noemi looks up at him, as stricken as though he had offered to make money by murdering children instead. Sex is one of Abel's programmed functions; he can therefore use this to benefit his commander. He's on the verge of telling her so when the young woman steps toward them. "Listen—I'm sorry, I couldn't help but overhear—don't get involved in that, okay? It's work you should only take up if you're sure you want it and can handle it. Not because you're desperate."

"We have few other options," Abel says.

The woman sighs and tucks her datapad under one arm, then says, in a low voice, "Can you be discreet?"

"Absolutely," Abel replies.

Noemi isn't as quick to seize the chance. "About what?"

The young woman folds her arms. "About anything I ask you to be discreet about. I may have a job for you. But what you see in the warehouse area stays in the warehouse. And I mean, anything you see. Do that, and I think we can work well together."

"We'll report nothing," Abel promises. Although Noemi looks warier, she finally nods.

"I must be going soft," says the woman, shaking her head. "But I think I can fit in two more at the loading dock."

Abel's opening his mouth to accept her offer when Noemi says, "There are four of us. Is that okay?" She gestures toward Harriet and Zayan. "We all need the work pretty badly."

"So I hear." The woman gives Abel an up-and-down look, as though assessing how he would've fared as a sex worker. With a sigh, she adds, "Definitely going soft. Sure, we can take four, as long as all of you know to keep your mouths shut."

"Thank you." And there's Noemi's smile at last—radiant, only because she's been able to help other people, who were strangers to her not ten minutes before.

Their new employer goes over to speak with Harriet and Zayan. As they laugh in astonished delight, Abel quietly says to Noemi, "You took a great risk to help strangers."

"They're my fellow human beings. That makes it my job to take care of them." Her dark eyes narrow as she looks at him. "I wouldn't expect a mech to understand."

He had meant to express his approval of Noemi's actions; his programming classifies selflessness as one of the highest virtues. It would have to. However, given the ways he's insulted her throughout the day, she has concluded that anything he says is intended to be unkind.

It's not an irrational conclusion, considering the evidence he's given her.

Yet Abel finds himself troubled by the idea that Noemi dislikes him even more than he dislikes her. Why should it matter? He can think of no reason to care about his destroyer's opinion... but he does.

Nor does he dislike her as much as he did an hour ago.

This problem with his emotions will have to be looked into.

• • •

Mechs are constructed, then grown. Factories produce the mechanical brain stem and skeletal framework; the brain stems are placed into cloning tanks where organic brains grow around them; the newly synthesized brain does the rest, pulling the necessary nutrients and minerals from the slippery pink goo that fills the tanks.

Abel remembers waking up in such a tank. Mansfield

was waiting for him, hands outstretched, his smile the very first thing Abel ever saw.

However, most mech brains aren't kindled into consciousness until they've been shipped and sold. They are sealed into translucent bags and transported like any other kind of cargo. Codes stamped onto the bags' seals reveal model, manufacturer index number, destination, and owner. Abel has watched their distribution many times and has never understood why he finds the impersonal, efficient shipping process so . . . distasteful.

Now, on Kismet, he sees that humans can be treated this way, too.

"Okay, everybody, listen up!" shouts their new employer, the young woman with short black hair. The sarong she wears is patterned with lines that, close up, reveal the name of the resort they now work for—a detail Abel finds irrelevant, given that they are going no farther than this dank warehouse area of Wayland Station. "My name's Riko Watanabe, and I'm going to guide you through the process here. What we do is coordinate shipments to the resort guests. Many of them traveled here in racers, which means their personal belongings have been shipped separately." She gestures through the warehouse, which is filled with various trunks made of woven metals or even what looks like genuine leather. Abel wonders where anyone found a real cow. "We have to line up the shipments with the resort accommodations, making sure everyone's got exactly what they want as soon as we can get it to them. Got it?"

Murmurs and nods of assent are her reply. Riko claps her hands and lets them get to work...

...which means hauling trunks, checking electronic tags, and steering forklifts to landing craft destined for the beautiful shores of Kismet, which Abel and Noemi will never see. Abel doesn't mind, but he notices Noemi frowning every time she thinks no one is watching.

Still, she works hard. She doesn't complain. She talks sometimes with Harriet and Zayan, when their duties allow. It's as if she welcomes the distraction—from fear, he thinks. Though at this point, he doesn't think she's afraid of the mission, or the new world, both of which she's adapting to swiftly.

What other thing is she afraid of? Is it the same thing driving her to go faster, to wait no longer than necessary?

The only time Noemi speaks to Abel, she says, "How many days of this do we need to make enough money for the part we need?"

"Five," he says. Then he adds, "I would note that this warehouse seems to be located near one for spare parts, suggesting security protocols would be similar."

Noemi tilts her head. "Are you going to break in?"

"Near the end of the festival's first day," he says. "Human psychology suggests that is when the greatest number of people will be distracted."

He expects her to object due to her rigid Genesis morality, to refuse to steal when she could wait slightly longer to buy. Instead she takes a deep breath. "Tomorrow, then. One more day."

Something is weighing on her. But what?

And whatever it is—is it something Abel should help Noemi with? Or is it something he should use against her, if he can?

* * *

In the evening, after a meal of nutrient mush euphemistically called "bean salad," they're shown to their accommodations.

Noemi stops short when she sees them. "What the—"

"Mobile pods," Abel explains as the vast wall of metal capsules shifts, bringing yet another pod closer to the ground, where two more workers step inside. Other capsules rearrange themselves near the top, each of them taking a new position every few minutes. It's like watching a jigsaw puzzle solving itself. "These are commonly used throughout the colony worlds for temporary housing at work sites, at vacation spots—even in prisons sometimes, in order to deter escape and rescue attempts."

"Vidal, Mansfield, this way," calls the attendant.

"We're supposed to share a pod?" Noemi tenses and hugs herself. "Just great."

Abel isn't much more thrilled about spending the next

several hours lying next to his destroyer, but he tries to handle the matter more gracefully. He steps into the pod and inspects the interior; it's all pale resin and metal, two bunks side by side, a small head hidden by a semicircular inner wall, and no windows. Most humans would probably find it claustrophobic. For Abel, it's simply a place besides the pod bay, and therefore very welcome.

"I don't know how you spend your time all night while human beings sleep," Noemi says as they settle into their bunks, "but whatever you do, don't stare at me."

"I sleep."

"You do?" Her curiosity overcomes her distrust. "But—well, why? Doesn't that just make you useless for a few hours a day?"

"I don't need as much sleep as a human, so I'd always be able to serve if needed."

"But why sleep at all?"

"The same reasons humans sleep. My bodily functions need time to process, plus my memory capacity requires flushing of irrelevant data. Sleep provides a chance to do this. Did they not teach you this on Genesis?"

"It's not something we specifically went over. We only ever saw Charlies and Queens, and they weren't taking any naps in the middle of a battle."

"Understandable." Abel lies back and neatly unfolds his blanket.

They lie there for a few long moments, wordless, hearing only the grind and thump of the mobile pod framework. When their pod moves, the effect isn't jarring—more like being in a ship on the water.

He should go to sleep now and allow Noemi to do the same. Yet he feels restless. Still in need of fresh input. Besides, it's obvious Noemi will require far more time before she can relax enough to sleep in his presence. So he ventures, "What displeased you so much today?"

"What?" Noemi props up on her elbows, looking at him.

"While we were at work in the warehouse, you frowned frequently."

"I was watching what Riko was up to. Some of it didn't make sense to me." Before he can ask her to explain, she sighs. "Besides, that's me. I frown. I'm unpleasant. I have a bad temper. You aren't the first to figure out I'm not a... pleasant person to be around."

Abel considers this. "Why do you say so?"

"It's obvious." Noemi shrugs. "Mr. and Mrs. Gatson— my adoptive parents—they always called me their 'little rain cloud.' I'm never happy."

"This does not align with my evidence," Abel says. He may not like what Noemi intends to do to him, but he trusts his assessments. "You risked yourself in an attempt to save your friend Esther. Then you undertook a danger-ous mission to save your world. Here on Kismet, you made sure to find employment for two people you hardly knew, simply because they needed it. You *do* have a bad temper and I cannot attest to your general happiness or lack thereof, but I would not term you 'unpleasant.' "

Noemi seems unable to process this. "But—it's just—well, the Gatsons would disagree, and they know me better than you do."

"Do you behave toward them as you have behaved toward others during the past day?"

"I ... more or less, yeah."

"Then the Gatsons' judgment appears both erroneous and unjust."

She sits upright, shaking her head. Even though Abel is praising her character, she seems agitated. "How could that even be possible? I mean, they're my adoptive parents. They took me in. Why would they say that about me if it weren't true?"

Abel considers the possibilities. "Most likely because they partly resented the obligation of caring for you, felt guilty about that resentment, and therefore sometimes characterized you as unpleasant to justify feeling less affection for you than for their own child."

Noemi stares at him. She asks no more questions, so she must consider his explanation to be adequate.

He smiles, lies down, and closes his eyes. Another problem solved. Mansfield would be proud.

15

NOEMI LIES ON HER SIDE, STARING AT THE MECH DOZING beside her.

Abel sleeps like the dead. Literally. He doesn't move at all, and if he's still breathing, his breaths are too shallow to be seen or heard. Is he only pretending? Lying there silently waiting for whatever mechanical signal will tell him to sit up and begin the day?

She lay awake most of the night, unable to sleep, learning the pattern of the pods by heart. Only in the past hour or so has she finally accepted that Abel truly is out cold. How weird, to think Mansfield built this ultimate killing machine but made it human enough to sleep.

Human enough to have an ego. Human enough to see something in the Gatsons that Noemi herself had never seen.

Ever since Abel had spoken about "resentment" the night before, Noemi hasn't been able to stop going over her memories. In a new, sharper light, so many things look different. Maybe she's awkward around other people sometimes because...because she sensed that the Gatsons didn't always want her around. Maybe getting mad too easily doesn't necessarily mean she's awful inside.

Even her memories of Esther have taken on another dimension. Noemi always thought her friend was so good to her out of sheer kindness, but now she wonders whether Esther recognized her parents' resentment. Maybe Esther was trying to make up for it by loving Noemi even more.

You were an even better person than I knew, Noemi thinks. Before she leaves this solar system, she intends to look back at Kismet's star to see Esther one more time.

A piercing whistle sounds. Abel opens his eyes as the pods begin to move. He sits up straight, as alert as if he'd been awake for hours. "Good morning, Noemi. Our next shift must be due to begin."

"Do they just...dump us out of the pods when they need us to go back to work?" She slept in her clothes, mostly because she couldn't bring herself to undress in front of Abel again. At least all she has to do now is get out of bed and run her fingers through her hair.

Abel doesn't even have a hair out of place as he stands up. "You have to admit, it makes tardiness unlikely."

He made a joke. Is that some program designed to amuse the humans around him? Or is that something deep within Abel himself?

Something else that makes him so close to human?

Noemi can't let herself think about that, not now or ever again.

• • •

Their warehouse work is grueling, but it doesn't require a lot of intelligence. Even after only one day, Noemi can flick the sensor wand over baggage labels and reroute them almost on autopilot. Every once in a while she still feels that eerie shiver—the wonder and awe of being on another world entirely, surrounded by people from Earth—but nothing undercuts awe faster than working in a warehouse. So that leaves Noemi's mind free to observe other people.

Specifically, Riko Watanabe.

When Riko had made such a big deal about them remaining quiet, never mentioning what they saw, Noemi had assumed the worst. Probably Riko stole from Kismet's wealthy patrons, or assisted others who did, she thought. Maybe the people attending the Orchid Festival are so filthy rich they'd never miss a few small luxury items, but that doesn't make it right to steal from them. Besides, Noemi's planning to do some stealing herself. For a better cause, sure, but she shouldn't throw stones....

But Riko isn't a thief. Noemi's been watching, sharp-eyed, not only out of curiosity but also to find out just how tight security is on Wayland Station. So she's positive that Riko hasn't taken a single thing from the resort guests' luggage or allowed anyone else to do so. Every item has been duly packed onto one of the long, skinny shuttles that travels back and forth between Kismet and its moon, and sent on its way.

The thing is—Riko's putting something else on the shuttles, too.

A medical technician talks to Riko at one point, a quick whispered conference in a corner, before loading a box of his own onto the shuttle. An hour or so later, the same technician shows up with another crate. Noemi gets a good enough glimpse of this one to read its label: MEDICAL SUPPLIES.

Maybe that's all it is. But if so, why is Riko bothering to whisper? Why are the only people working nearby Noemi, Abel, Harriet, and Zayan...the ones she's already sworn to silence?

Intoxicants, Noemi finally decides—maybe something that's not just controlled but banned on Kismet's surface. Rich, spoiled partygoers will be ready to buy it, so this is probably a minor scheme for profit. Criminal, perhaps, but not wicked.

But it's hard to keep working hard, hour after hour, for something she knows isn't right.

• • •

That night, the shipments cease. Not because the bags have stopped coming—more seem to pile in by the hour as scions and socialites arrive for the weeklong festival. But apparently the opening-night concert is such an extravaganza that nobody intends to miss it, neither travelers who can wait another few hours for their belongings nor workers who get to watch via holo.

Every screen along the station walkways is showing the celebrity arrivals, and the other temporary workers have started a small party of their own. Apparently they talked some bartender out of a few of his wares, or opened up one of those crates Riko's been smuggling, because she can hear bottles clinking against each other, and the laughter has grown warmer, freer.

Then she hears Abel's voice just behind her. "Some of the others plan to celebrate while watching the concert from afar. I feel confident you are welcome to join them."

She turns to see him standing there, calm and poised, as unruffled as if he'd spent the day napping instead of hauling crates. "I'd rather not."

"Of course. Far more prudent for you to rest before we must return to work."

"If I even can. Looks like everyone's watching—including the guys who let us into the mobile pods." She nods toward a few of them, who are pointing up excitedly at yet another arriving celebrity as she waves at the crowd.

"That does make napping more difficult." That seems to be as close as Abel gets to sounding sympathetic. "Are you unwilling to celebrate with intoxicants? Is that forbidden by the God of Genesis?"

Noemi glances over her shoulder at him. "Are you kidding?"

"Many religions have denied their worshippers various forms of pleasure."

"Sure, there are some faiths that ask you to abstain from certain things—but where did you come up with the idea that all of Genesis prays to only one God?"

He cocks his head in that birdlike way he has, winsome and predatory at once. "All pronouncements during the Liberty War were made on behalf of the 'Believers of Genesis.' Reports indicated a mass religious movement had swept across the planet."

"That doesn't mean we all converted to one faith." Noemi doesn't know why she wants to explain. It hardly matters what a mech thinks, especially one she intends to destroy within the next three weeks. But she feels compelled to go on. "It wasn't like we all found one God, together. It was more that we...that we all realized we needed to be searching for something more meaningful. Whether we were Buddhist or Catholic, Muslim or Shinto, we all needed to pay more attention to the old teachings. We needed to recapture that sense of responsibility toward the world we'd found. Our faiths gave us the one thing Earth couldn't give anyone any longer—hope."

Abel considers this. "So no one is mandated to follow any one faith?"

Noemi shakes her head. "Each person has to find their own way. Most of us do a lot of meditation, a lot of reading and prayer. Although most people wind up joining one of the faiths, probably the same one as their families, we each have to search for our own connection to the divine."

"What of atheists and agnostics? Are they imprisoned? Made to recant?"

She sighs. "Faith can't be rushed or faked. Those who doubt or disbelieve have their own meetings, and they look just as hard within themselves. They want to live ethically and morally. They're just traveling a different path."

And I probably belong with them, Noemi thinks.

Abel puts his hands behind his back. The gesture's becoming familiar to her now—it's a sign that he's rethinking something. Doubting himself, or at least doubting what he's been told. She feels a strange surge of glee at the thought of overcoming the programming of Burton Mansfield himself, even for a moment. Finally he says, "What faith do you follow?"

"My parents christened me in the Second Catholic Church."

"…Second Catholic?"

She shrugs. "Couldn't really be loyal to the Pope in Rome after seceding from Earth's colonies. So we elected one of our own."

"I shall have to review the definition of *heresy*," Abel says. "Do you continue to follow this Second Catholic Church? You said the people of Genesis are supposed to choose their own faiths in time. Do you believe as your parents believed?"

There it is—the question Noemi fears most. The one she asks herself.

The one she can't answer.

Fireworks burst in the holo, arching green and white across Kismet's sky. Someone begins banging on a drum—not at the festival, but close by on the station, where a dance seems to be breaking out. As Noemi looks over, Harriet waves her arms in the air. "Come on! You don't want to waste a perfectly good party, do you?"

Noemi would be happy to waste this party if it meant she could sleep. But her chances of getting any rest have been buried under firework explosions and a bongo drumbeat. "Can't put it off any longer," she says. "We should pretend to enjoy this."

"Pretending to have fun, as ordered," Abel says, then smiles.

Vagabonds obviously make the most out of any excuse to celebrate. That, or just having enough to eat and drink is reason enough to party. People laugh giddily, trade stories of their piloting exploits, and gossip about the celebrities arriving for the Orchid Festival. Zayan's dark eyes have never looked so bright, and Harriet turns out to have a beautiful laugh, one that peals out above all the others. Abel's not particularly good at relaxing, but he does eventually leave to get Noemi a drink, should she want one.

"Oh, come here." Harriet tugs at Noemi's arm, nearly spilling the concoction of pineapple juice and...*something* in her cup. "Han Zhi's about to arrive!"

Noemi remembers that name from the spaceport, from some of the festival billboards and holo-adverts. If she recalls correctly, he's not a singer. So why is it such a big deal if he's just showing up? "Who's Han Zhi?"

"You don't know Han Zhi?" Harriet goggles at her. "He's only the hottest man in existence."

"Oh, come on." Noemi can't help laughing.

"No, I mean it! I swear to you, there's not one person in the galaxy who won't admit that Han Zhi is the sexiest, smokiest, most attractive man alive." Harriet holds her fingers up as if swearing an oath.

"That's not even possible," Noemi says. "There can't be one person everyone thinks is the sexiest. Different people find different qualities attractive—" Her voice trails off as the screens all light up with Han Zhi's face. The crowd shrieks in glee. Noemi hears sighs from nearly everyone around her, regardless of what gender they seem to be. Her body does this thing where it flushes warm all over and makes her want to either laugh or cry. "Oh," she breathes. "*Oh*. Oh, wow."

"Told you." Harriet's smile is as soft as melting wax. "Hottest guy in the galaxy, and everyone knows it. Zayan and I made a deal—we're both absolutely faithful to each other unless someday Han Zhi asks. In that case, we each have permission to enjoy ourselves...as long as we promise to share every detail later."

Gazing up at Han Zhi's beautiful face on the screens, Noemi reminds herself that bodies are only shells, that only the spirits within matter. But she can't help thinking, *That's the greatest shell ever.*

Then other celebrities show up on screen instead. The drummers get started again, and dancing breaks out for real. Within moments, virtually everyone is either jamming with the musicians or grabbing partners for the dance. Noemi watches as Harriet pulls Zayan to his feet and into her arms, both of them laughing as they start to move.

And then Abel stands in front of her, one hand courteously outstretched. He might have been in some eighteenth-century painting, asking her for a minuet.

His words are plainer than the eighteenth-century guy's

would've been. "We should do what the others are doing, don't you think?"

Noemi hesitates. He's right—she knows that—but to dance with him the way the others are dancing, she'll have to touch him. Strange, how you can be willing to fight, flee, kill, or die for your cause but hesitate before a simple touch.

She doesn't hesitate long. Noemi takes Abel's hand, and his skin feels completely normal, as warm as a human's would be, but so, so soft. His grip is strong, though, as if he thinks she might try to pull away.

Instead she lets him lead her into the throng. The Vagabonds dance and leap, spin and shout, laughing louder with every burst of fireworks from the holoscreens. Music wells up through the speakers, but the drummers nearby figure out how to match it, to make it even wilder. The party's a blur of bare limbs, swirling scarves, and messy hair.

And Noemi *loves* it.

"Here," Abel says as he brings her closer, into dancing position. "Are you certain this is acceptable?"

Noemi shrugs, embarrassed by how badly she wants to join in. At least she doesn't have to check her words; nobody near them could overhear anything through the din of drums and song. "We don't dance as couples on Genesis. Only in groups."

"That seems counterproductive. Dancing is one of the

traditional ways in which humans determine sexual compatibility with a future mate."

"...what?"

"Dancing requires matching movements—particularly in the hips and pelvis—to the speed and rhythm most desired by your partner." His vivid blue eyes meet hers evenly. "Relevant information, wouldn't you think?"

She doesn't get to answer, because with that, he spins her out, pulls her in, and the dance has begun.

Noemi catches the tempo in an instant, and then she's part of the crush, laughing with the others. It's easy to pretend Abel's hand is just another hand, that his small smile as he dances is real. She can give in to it with complete abandon, because she's not abandoning her duty. This is part of her duty, part of the illusion she must create.

Her sorrow for Esther doesn't dim her elation. Esther would tell her to dance faster, leap higher, to laugh out loud with all the breath in her lungs. That's what the dead would tell the living, if they could—to grab hold of joy whenever it comes.

So Noemi laughs along with the others, caught up in the fun, until the explosion.

Everyone jerks to a standstill as explosions blossom white and orange across the holoscreens, and the screams of people on Kismet come through all too clear.

In the first flare of white-hot light, the first roar of powder, Noemi thinks the fireworks have gone wrong. But then another wave of explosions lights up the sky as screams from the faraway crowd shift higher in pitch.

Then words begin to appear in stark block letters, superimposed over the holographic images:

OUR WORLDS BELONG TO US
WE ARE NOT EARTH PROPERTY
WE ARE REMEDY—JOIN US

Noemi can't smell the smoke. She can't think about what must've happened in that arena. All she can do is take in what those words mean.

Genesis isn't the only planet in rebellion. Earth can't control them all any longer.

The worlds are ready to rise.

And then the next explosion goes off on the station—next to them—and she knows nothing but screams, and fire, and blood.

16

BLAST STRENGTH: CONSIDERABLE. LIKELY NUMBER OF casualties: high. Law enforcement will already be on alert and en route.

Abel's brain does the calculations while the flare is still expanding. As the humans sprawl on the floor, shock waves send ripples through the station framework. His sensitive ears pick up the screams of frightened, injured people even through the explosion's roar. And while those around him can only panic, his mind ruthlessly turns to his first priorities.

His primary objective is his commander. Abel must protect Noemi and get her out of here immediately. A soldier of Genesis cannot be found anywhere near a terrorist attack.

He looks around the crowd of staggering, shrieking humans until he sees Noemi—clutching her side, breathing hard, wide-eyed with astonishment, but unharmed.

She's safe. Abel grabs her arm and tows her to her feet. "We have to go!" he shouts, knowing her hearing will be dulled in the explosion's aftermath.

Noemi looks somewhat dazed, but she pulls herself together faster than any of the others. She glances left—toward Harriet and Zayan, who huddle together on the floor bewildered but uninjured—for only an instant before she starts to run.

Abel matches her speed as they race away from the Vagabond party, back toward the cargo areas of Wayland Station. He could run considerably faster than this and for far longer, but he must stay by Noemi's side to protect her no matter what.

If Mansfield had foreseen this, he could've arranged Abel's priorities to let him escape on his own. Abel could easily reach the *Daedalus* before Noemi and fly away free. Instead he's tethered to her more surely than if their wrists were handcuffed together.

And yet, leaving her behind doesn't seem like such a tempting idea in this moment. Noemi Vidal is, as he decided the night before, not unpleasant. She is a girl far from home, trying to save her world any way she knows how.

How could he leave her here to be captured, or even to die?

Logic would dictate that the farther they get from the

explosion, the calmer the situation should be. But this is not a logical event. If Wayland Station was crowded before, now it's pure mayhem. Hundreds of workers and travelers dash and shove in a dozen different directions—some fleeing for their lives, others trying to help the survivors of the explosion…

…or gawk at them. Many people have recording devices in their hands or strapped to their arms. This sort of footage could command high prices, as Abel remembers from his early years on Earth. But Abel finds it hard to comprehend that humans don't share the same directives he does. That their innermost beings don't demand that they help protect one another's lives. Shouldn't that matter to a human even more than it does to a mech?

Some aspects of humanity were programmed very badly.

Noemi has regained her stability and is once again reacting like a soldier. "Should we grab air canisters?" she yells over the din, gesturing toward red emergency boxes near the doors.

"No time," Abel shouts back. "And no point. If Wayland Station loses atmospheric pressure, we'll explode long before we could suffocate."

"You're *really bad* at comforting people!" But Noemi smiles as she says it, a flash of humor amid the fray.

The moment doesn't last long. Hovercraft flashing

emergency lights in red and yellow steak overhead through the corridors, the screech of their engines at an even higher pitch than the screams of the crowd. Abel identifies them as medical craft, but law enforcement won't be far behind.

"They'll close takeoffs within minutes," he calls to Noemi.

"I know." Noemi elbows a gawker out of the way and keeps pushing through the throng. "Can we make it out in time?"

"We can try." Much depends on the efficiency and thoroughness of the Kismet officials. He and Noemi not only have to take off without being detained but also travel through the Gate between Kismet and Cray before being spotted. Surely the Gates will be patrolled soon—but if he and Noemi can take off for the Cray Gate faster than the authorities, they'll be able to make it through.

Otherwise, they'll be captured. Even if Noemi isn't identified as a Genesis soldier, everyone attempting to flee will be considered a suspect in the explosions. Abel predicts that law enforcement here will be swift, punitive, and likely to punish the innocent along with the guilty.

Which only applies to Noemi, of course. When the officials learn who and what Abel is, they will return him to Mansfield....

It doesn't matter. He can't let Noemi be captured.

The farther into the station they run, the more they're

surrounded by gaudy signs, blinking holograms, and images of Fox and Peter mechs arching their backs and hips to simulate the postures of sex. The scents of sweat, alcohol, and inhalant hallucinogens are thick in the air. A few holoscreens still broadcast the defiant words WE ARE NOT EARTH PROPERTY—until they go dark all at once, pitching the entire station into blackness save for dim emergency lighting near the floors. People begin to panic, shrieking in the unfamiliar space, no longer sure where to go. One of them shoves between Abel and Noemi, and for a moment he thinks the crowd will tow her away into bedlam. But she struggles back to his side. He grabs her hand as insurance that they won't be torn apart again.

She turns her face toward him, looking so stricken that he nearly lets go and apologizes for touching her. But that isn't it. She yells, "We have to get the T-7 anx—we can't go anywhere without—"

Her voice breaks off as a Charlie mech accosts them, wearing station security tags. "You are attempting to access launching areas. This is prohibited during lockdown. Please submit your identification."

They could try to bluff their way through this, but what's the point? Abel simply grabs the Charlie by the shoulders and shoves him away, not bothering to check his mech strength. The Charlie, caught off guard, flies back nearly two meters before slamming into a nearby beer kiosk and collapsing in a mess of suds and foam. Normally people would stop and stare, but in the mayhem, nobody even notices.

The Charlie itself sits up, but jerkily, clearly broken. Its pupils dilate as it says in a damaged, metallic voice, "Unidentified mech. Transmitting specs for further analysis."

Hopefully the authorities will be too busy to worry about any unidentified mechs. Abel tugs Noemi closer. "Are you all right?"

"I can't believe you threw off a Charlie like that." She breathes, then shakes her head, collecting herself. "I was saying that we don't have the T-7 anx and we can't risk going through another Gate without one, can we?"

"No. Fortunately, law enforcement is very busy at the moment. We have an ideal opportunity for some petty crime."

Whatever qualms Noemi might've had about stealing appear to have vanished. "Come on—let's move."

Genesis must train its soldiers well, because Noemi never slows her pace as they run the considerable distance back to the warehouse areas, despite the ominous dark corridors and damaged cables hanging from the ceiling. Abel remains beside her, subtly guiding their way back, ready to knock aside any obstacles, whether inanimate, mech, or human. After the first few minutes, the crowd finally thins—people have had time to run close or run away—and the warehouse areas of Wayland Station are all but deserted.

"You memorized the whole station's layout?" Noemi says, apparently slightly amazed to find themselves in the right place amid the chaos.

"Downloaded it." Abel shrugs. "For me, there's no difference."

"Amazing."

Abel may not be perfect at interpreting human emotions, but he's almost certain that wasn't sarcastic. Noemi spoke out of genuine admiration.

He's proud to have proved himself to her, but why? Noemi Vidal is his destroyer. She will be the cause of his death. Her opinion shouldn't matter. It will of course be easier to deal with her from now on because she'll finally listen to him—but he doesn't think that's it.

Irrelevant.

They dash into the warehouse section of the base, which is even more deserted than Abel's most optimistic projections. However, the emergency lighting is sparse—only the faintest glow of light at the base of each wall illuminates the area. He adjusts his optical input, images pixelating until they resolve into clear night vision. Noemi puts one hand on his shoulder, trusting him to guide her.

The lack of power creates other difficulties. "We need to

travel down one level," he says. "The lifts are no doubt shut down."

"Then we need to find a repair tunnel, maybe within a service corridor—"

"Too slow," Abel says as he leads her to the lift. He pushes his fingers into the crack between the doors, shoves his hands through, and shoves outward. Fortunately lift doors are easier to open than the ones in the pod bay; after only a few seconds, they give, sliding sideways to the sound of grinding metal.

"Correct me if I'm wrong," Noemi says, "but it looks to me like that's just an empty shaft."

"There are sensors every few meters." He gestures, in case she can see them in the darkness. "They protrude from the walls enough for handholds."

"For a mech, maybe. Not a human."

"You need only hold on to my back."

Noemi hesitates, but only for an instant. When she wraps her arms around his shoulders, Abel takes note of the new sensations—her warmth and weight, the subtle scent of her skin. It seems important to catalog every individual aspect, even the sound of her gasp as he leaps into the shaft and quickly scrambles down to the warehouse level.

Manual levers allow him to open the doors more easily from the inside. More emergency lights shine in this corridor, enough for Noemi to function—and yet she holds on to his shoulders for a moment longer than necessary, gathering her breath.

But only a moment. Then she's the Genesis soldier once more, striding along the long, shadowy warehouse corridor. "This looks familiar. We're close, but we have to work fast."

"Alacrity is essential," Abel agrees, remaining half a pace behind her. "But why does the proximity to our earlier work area matter?"

"Because the authorities are going to search that area any moment now."

Paranoia is not an uncommon human reaction to stress, so Abel doesn't comment.

Noemi comes to a stop before the spare parts area, which turns out to have a storefront, albeit one less glitzy than most others on Wayland Station, just one step more polished than the warehouses around it. "Which of the security systems is still on?"

"You noticed both? I had not thought you were so observant." A flash of irritation shows on her face, and Abel realizes he's being condescending again. During his long isolation, he appears to have developed some character flaws. Swiftly he adds, "Both systems are likely to remain operational. But I believe I will be able to take them offline."

Noemi nods, and Abel opens his mind to frequencies and signals undetectable by human bodies. When he finds the security system's hub, he slips in code of his own, designed to work along with the system rather than fight it—simply putting it in normal daytime operating mode, ready to welcome new "customers." But when he adjusts his vision to other wavelengths to make sure the entire system is down, he realizes he's failed.

"The primary system is off, but the secondary system is hardwired in," Abel says. "You won't be able to see it, but there's a laser grid approximately ten centimeters above the floor tiles. If we trip any of those lines, we'll set it off."

"But we can step over them? That won't activate the alarm?"

"Correct. I should of course be the one to do this."

"Wait—no. We're both going in."

"I'm more than capable of retrieving the T-7 anx on my own."

Noemi hesitates, then shakes her head. "You could slip out a back entrance, if there is one—"

"No." He takes a step closer to her. For some reason, it feels very important that she understands this. "My programming is clear. You are my commander. Unless and until I have another commander, I will protect you no matter what. That means keeping you out of jail. That means fulfilling your mission. That means making sure you have enough to eat. Everything. Anything. *I protect you.*"

Their eyes meet for a full second before Noemi slowly says, "Okay. But I'd still like to go in. If anyone sees me hanging around out here, it's going to attract attention."

No one is likely to enter this area, but her point is valid. "Very well. Watch where I go and try to exactly match my footsteps."

Perhaps that sounds too much like giving his commander an order. But Noemi either doesn't notice or doesn't care as she focuses completely on their task. They both remain silent as Abel slides apart the see-through doors, and the metal scrape of the tracks echoes loudly in the corridor.

To Abel, the interior of the store looks like something from the earliest eras of photography; everything appears in black, white, or shades of gray. Like *Casablanca*—but he can't afford to be distracted by that now. Colors only exist on other frequencies; he has to remain focused on the laser. He steps over carefully, gets a couple of tiles ahead, then waits for Noemi to follow. As he glances back, he sees that she puts her foot where his had been, precisely, every time. Few humans are so observant.

But he doesn't want to assume she's accounted for every single risk. He motions upward, so she can see the internal security barriers that would descend from the ceiling to shut them both in. If Noemi were not quick enough, one of those barriers could crush her. Abel begins walking backward, the better to look out for her.

She raises one dark eyebrow, trying to joke despite her obvious tension. "Shouldn't you watch your feet instead of mine?"

"The grid's pattern is static and stored in my memory. I could walk through the store blindfolded."

"Of course you can."

Noemi keeps following him. Even within this strange wavelength of light, he can see the faint sheen of sweat on her skin. But she doesn't look exhausted. An unfamiliar energy has her in its grasp, and he cannot tell if it's more fear or exhilaration.

He finds the T-7 anx easily. Noemi tries to take it from the shelf herself, realizes how heavy it is, and steps back so Abel can handle it. She's learning his abilities compared to her own limitations. Excellent.

As they begin inching out again, they pass a zone containing deep-space rations, foodstuffs that will keep for indefinite periods of time in deep space, which are piled onto pallets. "Should I grab some more of these?" Noemi picks up a single packet. "We have rations on board, but is there enough for twenty—no, eighteen days?"

"Yes, we have enough." That is the second time she's mentioned this seemingly arbitrary time limit, without explanation. "What happens in eighteen days?"

All the lights in the store blaze on at once. Noemi gasps. Abel's grip on the T-7 anx remains constant but he immediately shifts his visual input to normal human frequencies. They both look around and find they are no longer alone.

Two mechs stand in front of a newly opened side door— a Charlie and a Queen. These models work security as well as combat, and they are both clearly primed for action. Each wears the skintight gray armor of a military-issue mech; each has a weapon holstered to the side.

But Abel immediately recognizes an aberration in their behavior. Although two thieves have been found in the store, the Queen and Charlie are only focusing on Abel himself. The subtle tilt of the Queen's head suggests she's scanning him in-depth.

Then, unexpectedly, the Queen smiles and turns to the Charlie. "The Abel model has been located. Mansfield desires its return."

I've been found, Abel thinks, and the surge of hope within him feels like the sun is rising inside his skin. *Father found me at last.*

17

BEHIND THE GUNS OF HER FIGHTER, NOEMI HAS KILLED seventeen Queen models and nearly thirty Charlies. Unfortunately, she doesn't have her ship or her blasters now.

But the mechs don't even look at her. To them, Abel's the only thing that matters.

Both the Queen and the Charlie come closer at the same moment. Like Abel, they step over the invisible lines of the laser grid without any difficulty. As the mechs circle around them, the Charlie tilts his head and squints as though he were studying Abel through a microscope even as he aims his blaster directly at Noemi. The Queen says to Abel, "Explain your absence."

"My absence is due to my abandonment near the Genesis Gate, as Professor Mansfield knows," Abel says.

"How can you have returned after so long?" the Queen says.

Abel hesitates, as if he doesn't want to say the rest. But

his programming must ask him to comply. "The *Daedalus* and I were found by my new commander."

Noemi's never been close enough to see a Queen's eyes before. They're pale green, so pale as to be unsettling. The Queen model fixes those unblinking eyes on Noemi's face. But the Queen says only, "No unauthorized humans are allowed in Mansfield's presence."

"Then our business here is finished." At no point has Abel set down the T-7 anx. "Please send greetings to Professor Mansfield. Tell him I . . . I have missed him."

Noemi startles. What is Abel doing?

"You are to come with us," the Queen says, frowning. "Mansfield himself desires your return."

Abel shakes his head. "And I would like nothing better than to be reunited with him. However, he programmed me to have exceptional loyalty to my human commander. At the moment, Mansfield is not my commander. Noemi is."

"You will accompany us on the journey back to Earth," the Charlie says. "You must obey Professor Mansfield, no matter what."

Noemi sees something in Abel's expression she'd never expected to find there: sadness. "If he were here, I would obey his every word. But he was the one who tied me completely to my human commander. You've told me his wishes, but you have not transmitted a direct *order*.

Therefore, you lack the authority to override Mansfield's programming."

The Queen considers that, then nods. "Then we will liberate you from your commander." She turns to the Charlie and says, "Kill her."

Terror lances through Noemi like a sword made of ice—

—but then the Charlie does what every soldier does before firing his weapon for the first time. He looks down to check the controls.

It's not even a second. As fast as a blink. But Noemi takes off that instant.

She ducks behind a pallet of rations—puny shelter the Charlie can blast through within seconds—but that doesn't matter, because she went straight through the lines of the laser grid.

Alarms go off, blaring so loudly her ears hurt, flashing red lights in a staccato rhythm that's almost a strobe light. In the first beat, Noemi sees the overhead security barriers start sliding down. She hurls herself toward the main entrance—there's just enough time to skid through—

"No!" Abel shouts. He doesn't want her to get away—wants her to get caught, or to die—

His body slams into hers so roughly that it propels her farther forward, just past the doors. The Charlie and Queen are right behind them, but the security barrier slams to the floor, catching the Charlie's forearm and crushing it.

Noemi's never seen an injured mech this close before. It's torn skin and torn wire; blood and mesh mixed together, both real and unreal at once. The fingers twitch unnaturally fast, until the hand goes limp. A thin line of black smoke pulls up from the barrier's edge. She blinks in horror, than grabs the blaster he dropped on the floor.

From the corner of her eye, she sees movement and realizes the Queen is pulling her own blaster. But Abel grabs Noemi, swinging her behind him as he stands looking down at the Queen. He still has the T-7 anx tucked under his other arm.

"You are shielding the Genesis officer," the Queen says, tilting her head.

"As my programming requires." Abel backs up, Noemi just behind him, until they're back at the lift. He pauses, and she realizes he means for her to climb on his back again. As soon as she has, he jumps inside, still holding the T-7 anx, just as capable with only one hand free.

As he climbs, she says the only thing she can think of. "You think fast."

"So do you," he says. "You realize, of course, that the authorities have been alerted."

"I figured I'd rather take my chances with the local authorities than with the Queen and Charlie."

"Under the circumstances, I agree."

He still obeyed me, she thinks as he pulls them both up

the elevator shaft, moving slower one-handed but still fast. *Even though he could've gone home to Mansfield with the Queen and Charlie. He stayed by my side.*

That's a trick of his programming—a fault in it, really. It tells her that Abel's been honest about his limitations and boundaries. He truly will see her through this, with or without her presence, all the way to the end. She can trust him.

The trouble is, it doesn't feel like trusting a bridge to hold you over a river, or an oven to bake your bread. It feels like . . . trusting a person. Which it shouldn't. She can't afford to get confused about Abel's true nature, not now and particularly not later, at the end.

They reach the upper level, jump out, and run for the hangar. Their surroundings remain deserted, but emergency beacons and klaxon alarms have transformed Wayland Station into a den of sound and red strobe lights. It's even more disorienting when they reach the hangar; all the ships seem to have become more ominous versions of themselves, colored charcoal and crimson, completely forbidding.

And by now the authorities have to be close. Will they be on the lookout for thieves and traitors? For terrorists?

"Can you hear over this?" she shouts to Abel. Nobody farther than ten yards away would be able to overhear her if she yelled at top volume.

"It's a lot of input to sort through." That must be mech for *no.*

Noemi starts running again, and Abel follows. Although she remembers roughly where they're docked, the red strobe lights make everything look so strange. Each flash shows her a still image, and each image looks different from the one before. It's as if she were trying to find her way out of a maze, one that keeps shifting by the second.

Abel, however, races forward in a straight line, undaunted. Noemi lets him get a few steps ahead to lead. He can be trusted.

Flash—they're ducking around a corsair ship, elaborate with its fins and chrome.

Flash—the *Daedalus* finally comes into sight, its mirrored surface brilliant scarlet. Instead of a teardrop it now looks like the first drip of blood from a wound.

Flash—a dark shape darts toward Abel.

"Look out!" Noemi cries. But Abel's already whirling around, blocking his attacker in a collision she can only see as a tangle of limbs and a sudden drop.

Abel is the one left standing. Noemi catches up with him as he stares down at their attacker, a dazed man wearing a worker's coverall. She's never seen him before, and to judge by the way Abel squints at the guy, he hasn't either.

Noemi asks, "Is he police?"

"You wish," says a female voice behind them. Both she and Abel turn to see—

"Riko Watanabe." Abel speaks as calmly and confidently as he did to the Queen and Charlie, even though Riko's grip on her blaster seems much more ominous than the mechs', for some reason. Riko's short hair is disheveled, and her smile is terrifying. "Can I ask why you have chosen to assault us?"

"Because she thinks we're here to stop her, or turn her in," Noemi says. "Because we're two of the only witnesses who saw her smuggling explosives down to Kismet. We know she's with Remedy."

Quietly Abel says, "It might have been wiser not to point that out."

"She knows we know." Noemi shrugs. "No point pretending otherwise."

"You seem like nice kids. I wish you hadn't recognized me." Riko sounds so completely sincere that Noemi knows they're about thirty seconds from getting murdered.

Once again Noemi thinks fast. "We're not Vagabonds. I'm here from Genesis."

The name of her planet makes Riko gasp—as does the man at their feet, and the other handful of people now approaching from the shadows. Noemi recognizes a couple of them as med techs or doctors from the Cobweb screening; they must've used the screening as cover to travel here for the festival. The red strobe lights make it so hard to focus, but Noemi knows she has to. Everything relies on what she says in the next few minutes.

"You know Earth's been attacking my planet again, right?" Noemi isn't sure whether Earth tells the truth about its plans, and Genesis hasn't had a chance to present its side of the story in more than three decades. "What you guys put on those screens—they way you feel about Earth—we do, too, on Genesis. *We understand.* We're fighting back, and it could make all the difference if we weren't fighting alone."

What Noemi can't agree with is terrorism. Genesis has fought a savage war; she knows that millions of lives were lost on both her home world and on Earth. But her people fight fair. They meet their enemies in open combat. That has a nobility to it—unlike setting off an explosion in a stadium where people danced and sang to music, sending mechs to kill humans, or leaving bombs on the ground for families to drive over years later, while the children were still small.

"You can't be from Genesis. It's impossible. Nobody can get through the Gate." Riko lifts her chin. "You shouldn't tell such obvious lies."

"We had the help of a special navigational device." Abel leaves out the detail where *he's* the navigational device in question.

Riko hasn't lowered the blaster one millimeter. "Prove it, then. Prove you're from Genesis."

"How am I supposed to prove that?" Noemi protests. "We're here on fake IDs."

"Convenient," mutters one of Riko's compatriots. Noemi

wants to scream with frustration—does this guy honestly think she'd be walking around this station with a sign reading *Hey, I'm from Genesis?*—but manages to hold on to her temper. Not even she's hothead enough to mouth off to terrorists holding weapons.

Abel takes one step forward and slightly to the side. She realizes he's again trying to stand between her body and the blaster. "If you had time, you could run a medical scan that would prove her to be from Genesis. But I suspect time is not a luxury either of us can indulge in at present."

Riko hesitates. "What do you want?"

"For now, we just want to leave," Noemi says. "Someday, though—if you can find a way to get through the Kismet Gate—Genesis could use allies."

"We don't have the strength for a war." Riko shakes her head sadly. Noemi's eyes have adjusted enough to the light for her to see the smudge on Riko's cheek: grease, or maybe soot. Did Riko help detonate the bombs on Wayland Station herself? "Earth's too powerful. All those mechs—all those people—we can't compete on a battlefield. We have to strike out in other ways."

By bombing innocent people? But Noemi swallows the words unsaid, for the sake of her world, and because Riko's still holding the blaster. Instead she promises, "Join forces with Genesis and you won't have to stoop to bombings. You can fight fair and *win*."

After Riko and her coconspirators exchange a few glances, she nods at the guy on the ground, who gets to his feet, glaring at Abel. His opinion doesn't matter, though; Riko is clearly the one in charge. "You two leave now, this instant. Probably they're going to catch us. But if they don't—if we can somehow get to Genesis—how do we approach your world? Let them know we're allies?"

"Just say you're Riko Watanabe of Kismet," Noemi says. The local authorities are probably on their way. They have to wrap this up. "That's enough. I'll tell my commanders, so they'll know."

But Riko shakes her head. "It might not be me. There are more of us—even some cells on other worlds."

"A resistance," Noemi whispers. The fullness of it has hit her now, recapturing one instant of the exhilaration she felt after the explosion, but before she realized people must have died. "It's not just a few people on Kismet. The rest of the planets on the loop—Earth's other colony worlds— they're banding together. Rising up."

"Starting to." Riko finally lets her weapon drop. "I suppose if there's one chance in a hundred you're really from Genesis, we have to take it." That seems to have been said as much for her companions' benefit as for Noemi and Abel.

"I'll tell them," Noemi promises, her cheeks flushing with excitement. "When I get back to Genesis, I'll tell them to be on the lookout for anyone from Remedy."

One of her compatriots sticks his chin out. "And how will you know they aren't from Earth, pretending to be us?"

Noemi's laugh sounds as bitter as it feels. "Earth doesn't bother pretending to be anyone or anything else. When they come to Genesis, they come to kill." Will that get through to them? She has to hope—

A high, shrieking sound cuts through the alarms, making them all jump. Noemi recognizes the sound as tearing metal in the split second before she sees a distant corner of the hangar floor peeling upward—and a splintered, damaged, metal hand reaching through it.

"It's them," she whispers, knowing Abel can hear. "The Queen and Charlie."

"Go!" Riko's shout is for everyone. They all scatter as Noemi and Abel run back into the *Daedalus*.

The moment they're inside the ship, Noemi hits the door controls, sealing them inside. As they dash through the twisting corridor, Abel says, "It would be advisable for you to take the helm. We have to get to the Gate as fast as possible."

"You're going to replace the T-7 anx?" It will be the better part of ten hours before they can reach the Cray Gate. "We need some quick flying now more than we need instant repairs."

"Exactly. We require speed." Abel peels away from her to dash into the engine room, calling back, "Your piloting skills are probably adequate to elude the authorities."

Terrible at comforting people. The worst. But Noemi doesn't bother saying it, just runs for the bridge. They have to get the hell out of here, and if that means she does it on her own, fine.

The bridge's warning lights are already blinking when she dashes in. The viewscreen shows the hangar in red strobe lights, with bright orange letters proclaiming a text warning: SECURITY LOCKDOWN. NO UNAUTHORIZED TAKE-OFFS OR LANDINGS. ANY VESSELS ATTEMPTING TO VIOLATE LOCK-DOWN WILL BE SEIZED OR DESTROYED.

Noemi goes for navigation. Abel might be programmed with the know-how to handle every ship in the galaxy, but she's flown a dozen combat missions in a fighter where split-second decisions made the difference between life and death. She ought to be able to handle a clumsy science vessel.

Except the *Daedalus* isn't clumsy at all. At a touch it lifts from the landing pad, and it soars upward with breathtaking speed.

If only I could keep this ship forever, Noemi thinks, ignoring the insistent blinking of the warning message as she accelerates their ascent. *I could explore the entire galaxy, and no one could stop me—*

A jolt nearly throws her out of her seat. Noemi clutches the console, aghast at the new, red warning beacon blinking in front of her: TRACTOR BEAM DETECTED. The beam's energy has tethered them to Kismet's moon, as if a lasso had been thrown around the ship. They're still moving away from the planet, but the strain on the ship's integrity field is already showing. When she reaches the limit, the ship will either be jerked back down to the surface or torn in two.

We don't have the power to break the tractor beam—it's too strong. Noemi takes a deep breath, wondering if she can use her enemy's strength to their advantage.

The bridge doors slide open behind her, but she doesn't turn around. Abel says, "Repairs are complete, plus one extra modification."

"We can talk about that later." Her shaking fingers lay in the next coordinates. "First let's see if this works."

"See if what—"

Abel's voice cuts short as Noemi brings the *Daedalus* into a sharp curve, one that would almost put them in the moon's orbit, but not quite. The moon's gravity tugs at the ship, the inexorable pull of physics—but pulling the ship forward now, as the tractor beam pulls back. She's making the moon do the hardest work, using that gravity instead of fighting it. Within moments, the tractor beam breaks, and the *Daedalus* surges forward. Noemi urges the ship away from the moon and Kismet, toward the Cray Gate.

"Ingenious," Abel says, as if he really meant it.

The praise makes her smile, but then she catches herself. Probably mechs are programmed to flatter the humans around them. That hasn't stopped him from cutting her down so far, though, so maybe not.

Oblivious to her reaction, Abel comes to the navigation console, clearly ready to take over. "Our wisest course of action would be to aim the ship directly for the Cray Gate. Very precise navigation is called for."

"I've got it."

"Under normal circumstances, you would be more than capable of this," he says. "But these are not normal circumstances."

Confused, Noemi starts to turn back toward him and ask what it is he thinks she can't manage in the ten hours it will take them to reach the Cray Gate. But then she sees the unfamiliar readings from the engines, which are powering up—no, not just that, but *on overload*. "Abel, what did you do?"

"I should take navigational control now," he says, more urgently.

Three short hours ago, she would have stayed in her seat. She would've thought Abel was trying to sabotage the ship, to destroy them both. But now—after he saved her, after he walked away from the Queen and Charlie to stay by her side—

I can trust him.

I have to.

18

Just as Abel decides protecting Noemi will require him to bodily pull her from the pilot's seat, she slides out, surrendering it to him. Instantly he begins inputting coordinates, aiming for the Cray Gate, the very center.

"We're about to have company." Noemi's already at ops. "Three Kismet security vessels headed our way."

"Let me double-check our coordinates."

"You're going to start doubting yourself *now*? Or do you want to punch it while we can still get out of here in one piece?"

"Punching it on my mark," Abel says. "And—now."

The ship surges forward, so fast it feels as though the ship is flying out from beneath them. Noemi makes a sound that might be fear or fury, and even Abel has to hang on. The newly repaired integrity field whines, already stretching to its limits of endurance. Kismet seems to vanish as the star field around them rushes by, or seems to, as they hurtle toward the Cray Gate.

"You overloaded the engines and accelerated?" Noemi's hands hover over her controls, like she's trying to think of some way to stop this. "We'll fly apart!"

"We're within safety margins," Abel says. The extremely small decimal points involved are better left unsaid.

"We're going so fast we'll reach the Gate in—"

"Approximately three minutes." Twenty-three seconds of which have passed.

Noemi doesn't argue any further, only devotes her attention to the controls, making sure the overload doesn't destabilize the ship. Not that she'd be able to do much about it—the amount of time between destabilization and destruction would be less than one second. But Abel admires the dedication to duty.

She's right to be afraid. The risks are considerable and will only increase as they go through the Cray Gate. Under any other circumstances, Abel would reject this move as inadvisable in the extreme.

The Gate swells onto the viewscreen; they're coming at it so fast that the ring seems to be widening like a sinkhole about to take them down. If he's miscalculated by the slightest degree, they could sideswipe the Gate's security systems and be destroyed in an instant—

But of course he hasn't miscalculated. Abel smiles as the *Daedalus* slips into the Gate.

Although Abel's sensory systems can compensate for some of the bizarre input, even he sees the strange angles of the light, feels the odd pull of gravity untethered from space-time. None of it troubles him, particularly because the ship's smooth operation tells him they're coming through just fine. Then the *Daedalus* shudders, released from the Gate, engines powering down to normal levels as he'd set them to do. Their view shifts from eerie silver to a new star field, one neither of them has seen before. The navigational computer automatically focuses on the red-orange dot that is the planet Cray.

"We made it," Noemi says, blinking as she slowly slumps back into her chair. Humans often state the obvious, as Abel has seen, but they do not like having this pointed out. So he remains silent as he watches Noemi take a few deep breaths, collecting herself. "I can't believe your programming even let you do something that dangerous."

"The alternative was your capture or death. My primary directives made our course of action clear." Abel pauses. "That said, we cannot put the mag engines in overload again for the foreseeable future. Repeated strain of that kind will almost certainly result in our destruction."

Noemi squares her shoulders, already recovering. "And

nobody's going to be along to follow us for a good long while."

"At least several hours, probably time enough for us to have reached Cray." Abel's proud of that part.

"Good work," Noemi says. Her praise surprises him, but not as much as what she says next. "I wish we could've spent more time in the Kismet system."

"You didn't seem to enjoy our time there." Save, perhaps, for their dance—she did seem to like that.

"That's not what I meant." Noemi's dark hair is still flecked with glittery confetti from the party. "I would've liked—well, to say good-bye to Esther."

She stares at him, obviously daring him to talk about how illogical it would be to say good-bye to a person who's already dead. Abel knows better. Human grief rituals have their purposes, even if they're ones he finds hard to understand.

Once Noemi realizes Abel's not going to challenge her, she peels off her loose gray jacket, leaving on her singlet beneath. Bruises from their storeroom escape have begun to darken on her forearms and knees. Sweat gleams on her skin. "How long before we get to Cray?"

"Approximately eleven hours."

"Good. Plenty of time to go to sick bay, get these taken care of."

Abel ought to help her with these ordinary things as

well, rest and food and morale—surely that, too, is part of protecting his commander. But another task has to come even before that. "I must come up with a new fake identification code for the ship, and soon. Cray authorities may or may not prioritize finding us, depending on whether Kismet's forces consider us as potential members of Remedy; if they do, no doubt they will send word to that effect. If not, our unauthorized departure should be the least of their concerns. However, the Queen and Charlie we encountered earlier will pursue us in a spacecraft of their own as soon as one can be procured."

"They'll chase you across the galaxy." Her expression has grown thoughtful. "Mansfield wants you back that badly?"

"So it seems." The words come out matter-of-factly. Abel is proud of that. Not only has he developed some human emotions, but he has also learned self-control in dealing with them. Only inside does he feel this strange mixture of elation and agony. Someone he has missed has also missed him. They will never meet again; they will miss each other until the end of their days. Knowing that is ... sad, but joyful, too. Abel hadn't realized those emotions could coexist.

I wish I could tell you that, Father. You always loved it when I understood something new about humanity.

I wish I could have learned this some other way.

Noemi continues, "Okay. I'll go—" She gestures vaguely

at herself, at her state of disarray and her bruises. Then she gives him a small smile before trudging out.

Abel watches her go. She doesn't glance back once; by now, he realizes, she trusts his programming. She knows she won't be harmed by him.

If only he could say the same about her.

However, the more Abel comes to know Noemi Vidal, the less he resents his impending destruction. He is still pained by the thought of ceasing to exist, by never again learning anything new, and most of all by the knowledge that he will never see Mansfield again. Yet his death seems less like a waste now.

Noemi believes her cause to be a noble one. She acts not out of hatred for Earth, but out of love for her own planet. She is as willing to give her own life as she is to sacrifice his. And as she proved when she condemned the actions of Remedy and Riko Watanabe, her defense of Genesis has its limits. She wants only safety for her world. She wouldn't kill innocents to win it.

I cannot count as an innocent, Abel decides. Mechs are designed to risk their lives where humans cannot. Otherwise, they'd never have been invented in the first place. They are, by purpose and design, disposable.

So he doesn't have to blame Noemi for what she's doing. Only to come to terms with the realization that this is what he was made to do in the first place.

· · ·

When they reunite on the bridge, Abel is wearing Mansfield's silk clothes once more, and Noemi has put on a simple black top, pants, and boots. Although she probably chose these garments for practical use, the effect is unexpectedly flattering— but Abel has other, more pressing concerns. By now the screen is dominated by the blood-orange sphere of Cray.

"No oceans," Noemi murmurs. "Not even a lake. I mean, I took exogeology like everyone else; I know surface water's the exception and not the rule—but I didn't realize it would look like *this*."

Cray's oceans and vegetation burned away long ago, leaving behind only barren, rugged sandscapes ridged with fault lines. The tallest mountain ridges ever discovered on any world scrape the red sky. A few golden clouds trail around these mountains, delicate and lovely, belying the fact they're made not of water vapor but of acids. To have colonized a world this forbidding proves the desperation on Earth to find new worlds on which to live—even if that life will be very hard.

Noemi continues, "How did they even figure out people would be able to live underground?"

Abel decides to employ his subroutine for colloquial expressions. "Needs must when the devil drives. When I left Earth, Cray was the world most humans hoped to settle on."

"*This* place?" Noemi looks stricken. "Is it really that bad, on Earth?"

He finds he no longer wants to make her feel guilty about the fate of those Genesis has left behind. Those decisions were made by others, and so long ago. "Don't let the surface deceive you. To really judge Cray, you have to dig deeper—literally."

Noemi's eyes narrow, squinting in confusion. But she says nothing, only turns back to stare at Cray.

"Is something the matter?" Abel ventures.

"How do we go about getting landing clearance?" Noemi asks the question right away, yet Abel remains sure that's not really what she wanted to know.

Still, it is a valid inquiry. "No Vagabond ships appear to be landing." Only a few appear to be in the system at all, and those are clustered near an outer ring of asteroids where people are no doubt trying their hands at ore mining. Cray's orbital zone is almost entirely empty, a sharp contrast to the mad scene at Kismet. "Cray's resources are limited. If immigration is tightly controlled, visitors will be observed and regulated."

The planet's reddish surface casts a fiery glow on the bridge. Noemi's black hair gleams maroon as she frowns, and once again Abel sees that little wrinkle between her eyebrows. "So how do we…"

Her voice trails off as the viewscreen lights up, brilliant

white, revealing a young man wearing clothes that seem too casual for an official communication—but they're artfully chosen, the same red and orange shades as Cray's surface. *"You've come to Cray,"* the man says so warmly that Abel briefly wonders whether they've intercepted a personal message by mistake. But the patter continues. *"You're in an unregistered vessel, which means one of three things. One, you're a friend or family member of one of the scientists here. If so, you know civilian visits have to be brief…but we're sure you'll be impressed with the lifestyle on Cray."* A montage of scenes replaces the man's face, showing eager young students in a classroom with a holo of a molecule, a woman hard at work on a computer, and a group of people laughing and chatting in what looks like a plush, well-appointed sitting room. The young man reappears to say, *"Two, you're a merchant bringing us games, clothes, holos, or something else fun—in which case, we can't wait to see you!"* His smile fades. *"Three, you're a Vagabond or someone else hoping to sneak on-planet. If that's the case, you need to know that unauthorized inhabitation is never allowed. You'll be thrown off-planet…and into jail. So think twice before you try it. On Cray, we maintain high standards because we do our best to make our world better, and yours, too."*

The image blinks off, restoring Cray's reddish surface to the screen.

"That was"—Noemi thinks it over—"amazingly passive-aggressive."

Abel considers what was said, and not said. "No one is supposed to stay long, and no one without specific business is supposed to visit at all. Only the world's top scientists and elite students are allowed to live here." He remembers the many times professors and doctors tried to convince Burton Mansfield to move his cybernetics lab to Cray. Mansfield always said they didn't want his company; they only wanted to take over mech production for themselves. Probably Earth's leaders wouldn't have allowed it, but it hardly mattered. Mansfield would never have left his home in London.

Noemi hesitates, and Abel remembers how young she is. He knows this—is incapable of forgetting it—and yet the truth of it strikes him with new force. This voyage has already cost her so much, threatened her so badly. The only reward for her conquering each challenge is to be given another. Abel has been given enough data on human psychology to know that even far older people than Noemi Vidal would be crushed by this level of pressure.

But then she brightens. "They keep these elite scientists amused somehow. The guy talked about fun, remember? So we'll be people who help them have fun."

"I thought you were opposed to engaging in prostitution to fund our travels."

"That's not what I—is prostitution your answer for everything?"

Abel decides not to reply to that question. "What is your idea?"

"Can you talk to the computers at the spaceport? Machine to machine?"

"More or less."

"Then you could find out exactly what merchants are coming here soon—"

"And claim one of their slots as our own." Abel nods as he begins typing on the communications panel.

If the two of them were aiming for a different goal, working with Noemi Vidal would be...a pleasure, really.

* * *

The George model looks from Abel to Noemi with bland curiosity. "We weren't expecting the latest games shipment for another twenty-eight hours."

Abel had found an opening for a hologame merchant ship to land, one with only two passengers, low priority, low security. All factors indicated this was the best possible identity for them to assume.

But even the best alibi in the galaxy could prove... tricky.

"An early launch window opened up, and naturally we took it." Abel tries to sound casual. Breezy. At ease. This isn't one of his natural operating modes, but he's watched others. He calls upon his memories of a wealthy young nephew of Mansfield's and tries to copy his manner of speaking. "You know what a *nightmare* it is. Delays pile up, before you know it you're stuck waiting for *hours* if not *days*—"

Noemi's eyes widen, clearly communicating, *You're laying it on too thick.* Abel falls silent.

But the George mech, too basic to notice such a detail, nods in approval. "Your guest quarters won't be open until your scheduled arrival, nor can any of the product demonstration sessions be moved any earlier."

"That's fine." Noemi's relief that they're not wanted for crimes on Kismet's moon is obvious—too obvious, really, but a George is unlikely to pick up on such nuances of behavior. "We have room on our ship."

This result is better than fine, of course; it's the best outcome they could've hoped for. Now they won't have to explain why they don't have the promised merchandise. And they have twenty-eight hours free and clear.

The trick will be stealing the device they need in that time.

Cray's principal spaceport is simply called Station 47. The areas of Wayland Station used by Vagabonds and other workers were plain and basic, almost punitively ugly. Station 47, however, is simple, practical, and yet beautiful. Dark gray, crisp white, and a surprisingly cheery orange dominate the parallel, symmetrical landing bays, which are stacked atop and beside one another. From within, it appears they're wandering within a honeycomb; from above, Abel thinks, the design might look like a butterfly's wings. People bustle about, but there's none of the overcrowding or desperation they saw on Kismet. The residents of Cray walk with confidence. They laugh easily. They converse with their friends, gesturing almost wildly in their enthusiasm about...

Abel tunes in to catch a few snippets of conversation. His hearing's not exponentially better than a human's, but he can isolate desired sounds from background noise more effectively. A discussion on how best to expand Cray's tunnel systems to the west; someone describing how a lost work of Leonardo da Vinci was identified in the early twenty-first century; agreement that they should, definitely, rework the waffle irons in the cafeteria to burn the letters of obscene words into said waffles; a spirited debate over whether the reboot of *Spared: Clone Versus Clone* had betrayed the integrity of the original show—

This is a society that indulges its enthusiasms, Abel thinks. It makes sense. The same creativity and energy Earth wants to cultivate in its top scientists and students would naturally flow into leisure pursuits as well.

He and Noemi fall into step, side by side, walking as slowly as any two people who had hours to kill. They're both wearing the same kind of clothes: simple black utilitarian gear, somewhat stark for Cray but unlikely to draw attention. She betrays not one hint of the fear that must haunt her.

Noemi nods toward a group not that far away. "They look like they fell out of a time machine."

They do. Virtually all the younger scientists on Cray proudly wear antiquated garments like blue jeans and lace-up sneakers. Several have dyed their hair unnatural, vibrant colors, and a few have even resurrected the ancient human practice of piercing ears. "Thirty years ago, a subculture called millenipunk was becoming more popular. People mixed old-fashioned clothes and styles with more current pieces, or in more provocative ways. It seems that this has gone from being an obscure form of fashion to a popular trend—on Cray, at least."

"Green hair," Noemi says. She sounds vaguely envious. By now, however, they're far enough from the George to talk without fear of being overheard. "Okay. We need to find that thermomagnetic device. I want to be in and out of here before the Queen and Charlie even make it to this system."

"Finding the device should be easy. Taking it may prove more difficult." When she gives him a look, he adds, "They are most commonly used closer to the planetary core—in other words, significantly lower down than standard living or working areas. Additional security will undoubtedly be a factor."

She sighs. "Okay. Then let's scope out the security."

They leave the landing bay space and walk into a bright, cheerful sort of mall. Hanging lamps with hundreds of golden bulbs shine so brilliantly that it's easy to forget they're underground, far from the light of Cray's sun. Small viewscreens mounted on the walls every five meters or so show colorful abstract patterns, famous quotes, or ads for the products sold nearby. Restaurants on this level fill the air with spices; below, they can see stores offering fanciful clothing, puzzles, hologram kits—almost anything that would be considered trivial rather than practical.

"This is what they spend their money on?" Noemi says.

Abel shrugs. "Everything else is provided for them. Their leaders know creativity is strongly linked to play. Therefore, this sort of behavior is encouraged."

"Lucky them, playing games and designing weapons of mass destruction all day." Noemi looks around, then points to a side exit marked EMERGENCY. "Do you think that would get us out of the thick of things?"

"As long as it's not hardwired to any more alarms." Abel glances at her. "You do so love setting those off."

Noemi's face takes on that strange expression again, but then her eyes widen and she gasps. Before Abel can even ask, he sees that the viewscreens—every single one—are showing blurry images of their faces.

Kismet's warning reached Cray not even an hour after they did.

Immediately he filters out all other sound, so he can make out the words being spoken: "...being sought as trespassers on Cray. Keep in mind that they are not suspects in any criminal matter, merely persons of interest. Anyone who sees these individuals should promptly notify authorities."

"Emergency exit," Abel says to Noemi. "Now."

She has the good sense not to run and attract attention. Abel glances back only once, as they get closer to the exit. Nobody appears to have noticed them...yet.

Luckily, the exit door is not wired to any alarm system. Together they make their way into a more dimly lit service passage. The darkness enhances Abel's awareness of the chill in the air and the rough-hewn walls of stone; here, no effort is made to disguise the fact that they're underground. Faint echoes can be heard in the air, but too indistinct to be understood even by his most advanced systems. Only the control boxes and power outlets affixed to the stone walls betray that they're in a human structure instead of a cave.

"How did they get a message here so quickly?" Noemi hurries down a flight of metal steps, and Abel follows close behind.

"Only one conclusion is possible—the Queen and Charlie pursuing us put their ship into overload as well."

"What are we going to do?" she says, pushing her dark hair back, away from her forehead. "We can stay hidden, maybe, but they'll impound the ship."

"Maybe not. If the Queen and Charlie had known which ship was ours back on Kismet, they would have confronted us there, the one place we were guaranteed to return to no matter what. Our fake ID held there; it may hold here. I changed the ship's display name to *Odysseus*. The great traveler of myth. It's not an uncommon name for vessels, or it wasn't, so that should help conceal us as well."

Noemi takes a deep breath. She can be volatile, but she can center herself so quickly, so profoundly. Abel wonders if it is a meditation technique taught on Genesis. Finally she says, "Okay. We stay hidden, we find a thermomagnetic device, and we take it from there. Do you happen to have Cray's layout memorized, too?"

"Unfortunately, no."

"Then let's pull up a map."

A low-security computer panel nearby allows them to project a small holographic map of the immediate vicinity. Abel focuses his attention on areas with high concentrations of technology. These are the likeliest places to locate what they need. But they're too close to the surface still, far away from the supercomputer core areas—

The emergency exit opens behind them. He and Noemi freeze at the sound of footsteps.

Is this a regular maintenance team? Or did someone recognize him and Noemi after all?

They can't afford to find out. He and Noemi take off running into the tunnels, racing into the unknown darkness. The air echoes differently, more strangely, every second, changing from a hush to a dull, indistinct roar.

"Are they following us?" Noemi gasps at one point.

Abel finds it difficult to filter the sound now that the dull roar is growing louder. "I'm not sure. But I think they may be."

With that, Noemi grabs his hand and goes for a smaller side door. He lets her pull him through, onto a metal platform in near-total darkness. The loud rushing noise is almost deafening.

Over the sound she yells, "Are you waterproof?"

Abel thinks he's going to regret saying yes.

19

NOEMI GRABS ABEL'S HAND, TOWING HIM WITH HER AS
she jumps off the platform—

—and into the underground river flowing beneath
them.

The frigid water's not very deep, but it's enough to
break their fall. Noemi pushes up with her feet to the surface and discovers the river only comes to her shoulders.
Grinning, she dunks her head backward to get her hair off
her face and wipes droplets from her eyes and cheeks. Abel
surfaces next to her, blond hair now plastered down over
his forehead, clothes sodden and stuck to his body, and his
expression so completely disgusted that it reminds her of
the way the Gatsons' cat sulks when it gets caught in the
rain. Noemi laughs out loud before clapping one hand to
her mouth; the sound of the gentle current flowing past
them should muffle any noise their pursuers could overhear, but it might not.

Still, her shoulders shake with the giggles she's trying hard to suppress.

Abel doesn't like being laughed at any more than a human would. "Did you know there would be water down here?"

"Of course. I wouldn't have jumped otherwise. It was clearly marked on the map; this river flows into the water purification systems for this area."

He goes silent, and she realizes he's reviewing the plans in his mind. Considering the perfect memory Mansfield has given him, he can probably study the diagram in as much detail now as he could when it was projected in front of them. "Of course," he says, almost as if he were speaking to himself. "I concentrated on areas of tactical importance. You took in details that should have been irrelevant but were instead useful."

She's not going to rub it in, even if he was acting so superior with her at first. But she can't help wanting to show off a little more of the "irrelevant" information that's currently saving their asses. "It's also marked as an emergency shelter. So I knew we'd have room for us to stand, plenty of air for us to breathe. It looks like it leads right into the center of their operations. But we'll have to come up later on, check out another map."

"You're suggesting that we walk through the river?"

"Why not? It gets us where we want to go, or closer at

least, and there's almost no chance anyone's going to find us down here." Noemi can't help smiling wickedly. "Unless you're scared of getting your hair wet again."

Abel retorts, "I would last longer submerged in water than you would."

"You'd sink, wouldn't you?" She doesn't like the idea of having to tow Abel up from the depths.

But he shakes his head. "I'm designed to float."

"Yeah, well, so am I. Let's get going."

Together they begin sloshing through the river, heading downstream. Their journey is a shadowy one, illuminated only by yellowish emergency beacons dangling high overhead, and those beacons are spaced out widely. Walking through water is hard work, but Noemi's glad of it. The river's chill is matched by the cool air above; if she weren't exerting herself, she'd be too cold to function.

The warmth flowing through her doesn't only come from the exercise. She's energized by the quick thinking they've had to do. By the thrill of knowing she's outwitted their pursuers. Even by the danger, now that they're out of it for a while. For the first time—except for one split second when they entered the Kismet Gate—her journey through the worlds of the Loop feels like the adventure she always dreamed of.

Her grief for Esther lingers, a dull inner heaviness. But for the moment, Noemi can bear it. She knows it will be harder when—if—she returns to Genesis and goes to the places they used to go together, when she sees Esther's empty room, when she has to tell the Gatsons how bravely their daughter died. When she has to break the news to Jemuel. But Noemi can move forward now.

This mission is the most important thing she'll ever do. It's also the one chance she'll ever have to travel through the galaxy. Noemi doesn't want to lose sight of either of those things, not for one second.

"Obviously the river's only a temporary solution," she says over the sound of rippling water around them. Drips and drops echo along with her voice. "But if we found one platform, we'll find others. One of those might turn out to be a safe place to wait until nighttime. Wait. Cray's cities are underground. *Is* there a night here?"

"An artificial night, but that's sufficient for our purposes." Abel holds his arms over the surface of the water, like he's repulsed by the idea of getting any wetter than he already is. "Labs will shut down. Scientists will sleep. And that gives us a chance to find and steal the thermomagnetic device."

"How long can we hide out from the Queen and Charlie?"

"They will have ordered the Georges to report any unusual arrivals in the past several hours. Ours will be one of them."

Noemi's gut clenches. "That means they'll find the *Daedalus*."

"Perhaps not immediately, but eventually," he says, like that's no big deal. "We'll have to steal another ship for our escape."

Stealing a ship? That's someone's livelihood. Maybe their home. What would happen to Zayan and Harriet if someone stole their vessel? They'd be ruined, forever. They might even starve. "Maybe we could just—stow away, or something."

"Few ships will be large enough to hide on for any length of time, and most of those will be Earth fleet vessels with strict security." Abel glances sideways at her, then slowly adds, "The visitors here are not Vagabonds. They'll be leading scientists and businesspeople. Government officials. Representatives of various corporations. In other words, they'll be people who can afford a new ship."

He understood. Abel followed her thoughts, recognized her concern.

Noemi feels again the unease that first stirred in her when Abel made that pun about digging deeper. When he teased her about setting off security alarms. It had been jarring to realize Abel had a sense of humor. His earlier snarking might simply have been his superiority complex at work, but those gentle little jokes...Mechs aren't supposed to be able to think that way.

And they certainly don't show insight into human feelings. Not like this.

It's an illusion, Noemi tells herself. *A simulation of consciousness instead of the real thing.* She knows artificial intelligences can be programmed to mimic human thought to an uncanny degree. Supposedly even Earth outlawed that practice long ago, as part of the regulations that kept AI from evolving to the point of endangering humanity rather than serving it. But someone like Burton Mansfield might consider himself above the rules. He might have used the old tricks that could make wire and electricity simulate the workings of a human brain.

That thought scares her. However, the other alternative is far worse—that Abel isn't merely mimicking consciousness. That he is, in some small way, *alive*—

Heavy metal clanging startles Noemi from her reverie. Abel freezes in place. "What was that?" she asks.

The nearby machinery seems to answer her, rumbling as gears or turbines begin to move. Are they deeper into Cray's substructure than she'd realized? Have they walked beneath some critical piece of machinery, maybe something that would have the thermomagnetic device she needs?

But the metallic thumps she's hearing sound... primitive.

"I can't be certain without control audio to compare it

to," Abel says, "but this is almost certainly the sound of water-flow mechanisms switching into gear. An automatic function, probably set to a timetable."

"Does that mean they're about to shut the river off?"

"...I believe it means they're turning it on."

Behind them, upstream, a roaring sound begins to grow—louder and louder by the second. Noemi's eyes widen. "We have to get out of here." *Safety ladders, emergency beacons, I know we saw some—*

But there's no time. The roar blots out everything except the vast dark wave crashing toward them. Beneath her, the water of the river swells slightly, and then the wave's on top of them, slamming into her.

Noemi might as well have crashed into a wall of pure iron. The force of the water knocks the breath out of her lungs and spins her violently upside down, side to side and back again. She reaches out desperately, trying to figure out which way is up, but it's impossible. The torrential current scrapes her along rough stone, but she has no way of knowing if that's the river bottom, the wall, or even the ceiling.

It's too strong for her. She can't find purchase, can't help herself in any way. The river has her now. She's been underwater, unable to breathe, so long that her chest aches and the world's getting dizzy around the edges.

Her fear is on the verge of becoming panic when an arm wraps around her waist and tows her to the surface. Noemi gasps for breath as Abel holds her back against the wall. The river's so high that the ceiling, once ten meters overhead, is almost close enough to touch—and the current has grown even stronger, churning and frothing the water rushing around them. Abel clings to a metal strut with one hand and her waist with the other, holding them in place without any sign of strain.

Bruised and winded, Noemi can't talk at first. Finally she manages, "I always—thought—I was a—good swimmer."

"No human could withstand currents this strong." Abel says it without any of his usual superiority. "We need to find another platform, like the one we jumped from in the first place."

The ceiling of the tunnel had been higher there, if Noemi remembers correctly. Some of the platforms would be built up taller than the river even at its fullest flow—not much taller, but enough for her to get out. "How do we do that?"

"I take us along the wall. You hold on to me."

Noemi hesitates only briefly before sliding her hands around Abel's neck as if embracing him. He has broader shoulders than she'd realized, wide enough for her to rest her aching arms on. She turns her face away from his, resting her head at the curve of his neck, so she can look out for the next platform or anything else up ahead.

Abel says, "It would be advisable for you to use your legs as well."

Of course it would. Noemi wraps her legs around his waist, pressing their bellies together, embarrassed by her own embarrassment. How ridiculous to feel shy about clinging to him so intimately. It's no more personal than sitting in the seat of her fighter.

Or it shouldn't be. But now that they're this close, she's reminded powerfully of how human his body feels. He's warm despite the cold water, strong despite the current. His hand feels good along her back. And there's even a scent to his skin—not artificial, but natural and even pleasant—

Please stop sniffing the robot boy, Noemi tells herself, jerking out of the trance.

Not that Abel noticed. He's concentrating on carrying her, even though he doesn't seem to have any difficulty making his way along the cavern wall. His pale fingers find handholds on the tiniest ridges or swells in the rock. They move forward with painstaking slowness, Abel never faltering.

She remembers what he told her about being able to remain submerged. "If I weren't here, you could just walk along the bottom of the river, couldn't you?"

"If you weren't here, it is highly unlikely I would be here either."

"Good point." Noemi sighs. "I guess my great escape plan wasn't so great."

This is his chance to rub it in, but Abel doesn't take the bait. "You showed considerable ingenuity and quick thinking. You couldn't have known the water-circulation schedule would work against us to this extent."

Abel saving her life is just one of those things a mech is programmed to do. A mech being *nice* to her is something else entirely. Once more, disquiet stirs within Noemi, but she's too exhausted to dwell on it.

And one instant later, she sees what they need. "A platform! Roughly twenty meters ahead."

He still keeps looking at the stone, making sure of each handhold. "On this side of the river or the opposite?"

"The opposite. Can you make it?"

"I think so."

Noemi doesn't like the sound of that. "Are you mentally coming up with the exact odds of your making it across the river, and not telling me because it's too scary?"

"I find that humans rarely want to hear exact mathematical findings, at least in the course of casual conversation."

"That's mech for 'yes,' isn't it?"

"...yes."

"Fabulous."

Abel adds, "I will specify this much: If the odds weren't better than fifty-fifty, I wouldn't tell you I thought I could make it."

They're not much *above fifty-fifty, or he'd say so,* Noemi thinks. But there's nothing else for her to do but hang on.

When they're about five meters short of the platform, Abel pushes off from the wall, hard, without warning. Noemi's already clinging to him so tightly it makes no difference, but she still gasps when they're back in the current, at the river's mercy.

This time, however, the river loses. Abel's greater strength has already propelled them more than halfway across, and he kicks so powerfully that they're pushed sideways as strongly as they're moving forward. She lets go of her grip on Abel's shoulders to reach out with one hand, which means she's the first to grab the platform railing.

They crawl onto the platform together. But the moment they're out of the water, Noemi collapses on her back, breathing hard. Now that pure terror is no longer fueling her, she realizes she's almost completely out of energy. Every muscle quivers and aches. The scrapes along her forearms and the many bruises on her body were temporarily dulled by the crisis; now she feels every single one of them. Her wet clothes stick to her body, sodden and heavy, one more reason she feels like she'll never again be able to move.

Abel, of course, is fine. He gets to his feet, brushes back his damp hair, and looks up. Noemi realizes the tunnel goes much higher here—another fifty meters, at least.

He says, "I think there's an observation station above us. Currently deserted, to judge by the lack of illumination. If there's no other point of entry, we should be able to break through one of the windows."

Noemi cranes her neck to look up at Abel from her place flat on her back. Sure enough, there's a black metal ladder leading up. But she shakes her head. "Abel, I can't climb that ladder. Not now, not for a while." It doesn't even feel like she could sit up.

"I can carry you, if you have the strength to hold on."

She takes a deep breath as she considers this. It isn't a question of her will; this is about her literal, physical strength. Nothing saps energy as drastically as swimming for your life. There's no point in trying to go up the ladder if she's only going to fall halfway there and get herself killed.

Slowly she sits up. She flexes her arm muscles, then her legs. Finally she nods. "Let's get started."

Abel helps Noemi to her feet, then takes his position on the ladder. She wraps herself around him once more, now clinging to his back instead of his chest. As he starts climbing upward, she realizes how much more difficult this is out of the water; as overpowering as the current was, at least her buoyancy took some of her body weight. This way, her arms have to bear it all, and they can't bear it for long.

"Abel?" she whispers. "Can you go any faster?"

He responds, not with words, but by speeding up so

much it startles her. This is inhuman speed. The ride's bumpier, but it hardly matters, because they reach the station within seconds. It's a half hexagon of silvery metal sticking out from the rock wall, with thin mesh screens over the windows instead of glass. Just as Noemi's wondering how easily the windows can be tugged from their frames, Abel punches through one of the mesh screens, pulls the whole thing out, and drops it in the river.

Noemi climbs in first and slumps into a chair as Abel joins her. Strands of his dark blond hair cling to his damp forehead, and his wet clothes drip onto the floor, yet he shows no signs of tiredness or alarm. She hasn't begun to discover the limits of what he can do.

Abel has done all this for her, knowing that she has to destroy him.

"Thank you," she whispers.

He looks down at her in surprise, then smiles. "It's unnecessary to thank mechs."

"I'm not thanking you because it's necessary. I'm thanking you because you deserve it."

The silence between them goes on for too long after that. Noemi doesn't want to feel grateful to Abel; she doesn't want to be awed by him. She's letting herself get...confused, distracted. They need to concentrate on the mission.

"Okay," she says. "From here can we figure out where we are? And where a thermomagnetic device might be?"

Abel moves toward the one computer console in this station. "Probably. We have adequate time to research this and be sure, and for you to rest." He says the last part as easily as the first, but she still hears what sounds like genuine concern in his voice. "Your escape plan may have had unforeseen difficulties, but at least no one will find us here."

The door bangs open. Noemi startles as she sees someone standing there—a tall girl about her age or a couple of years younger, with deep tan skin, long brown hair caught back in a ponytail and streaked with red, and a smug grin on her face. Behind her stand three other people roughly the same age, all of whom begin to cackle with laughter.

As Noemi stares at the newcomers, aghast, the girl folds her arms across her chest with pride. "See, Razers always find bugs in the system. And now we've found you."

20

ABEL REMAINS SILENT AND STILL, ASSESSING THE SITUA-
tion. He has protocols that would kick in if he and Noemi
were being taken captive. But their discoverers—the "Razers," as they call themselves—can't make up their minds
what to do next.

"We walk in there with these two and just watch the
head of security have a complete meltdown."

"If security figures out that we're ahead of them, they'll
ask what we were doing down here. Do we really want that?"

Abel assumes this comment is related to the distinct
scent in the air, the smoke of an herbal substance that is
illegal on both Stronghold and Cray.

"None of you are thinking clearly about this," says the
girl with the red-streaked hair, the apparent ringleader. "If
we don't turn them in, what are we supposed to do with
them? But we shouldn't turn them in for nothing. Sooner
or later, they'll post a reward."

"Then tell me this, Virginia—who gets the money?" demands the tallest of them, a sturdy, blond-haired boy. "Do we split it equally? Because *I'm* the one who checked the sensor grid."

"Only after I told you to," Virginia says. "I'm the one who figured out they had to have gone deeper underground."

The Razers begin a fresh round of bickering. Noemi glances over at Abel, less alarmed than bewildered.

He cannot blame her for her confusion. Certainly their captors aren't behaving like they're in the presence of potential criminals; it doesn't seem to occur to the Razers how quickly this situation could change, how easy it would be for them to get hurt.

And it would be very easy. Abel's programming suggests six different ways he could kill or maim all four of the Razers within ninety seconds. If Noemi's life is endangered, he'll do exactly that. But his programming doesn't allow him to kill humans absent such compelling circumstances, or a direct command.

Instead he must try to understand these Razers. Fortunately, what Abel knows of Cray is enough to help him develop a working hypothesis.

Aside from a few functionaries, the entire population of Cray is made up of top scientific minds. Children on Earth and the other colony worlds are tested at young ages to see if they have the necessary aptitude; if they do, they leave their parents behind to join the intensive boarding schools on Cray. Most never return home. As the planetary welcome message indicated, families can and do visit, but none are permitted to stay. Cray's resources, like Kismet's, are reserved for the elite. The difference is that Kismet is for those with wealth, and Cray is for those with intelligence.

The four teenagers standing before them will have been groomed and pampered their entire lives. They think sneaking around in back corridors and smoking controlled substances counts as rebellion. Compared to Noemi, they seem naïve, even spoiled.

Nonetheless, the Razers found Abel and Noemi. The only way out would be to attack them, and Abel can't do that unless Noemi's at risk—or unless she explicitly orders him to.

By now he understands she would never give that order.

Virginia plays with the end of her red-streaked ponytail. "We could ask for a reward that wasn't in the form of money. Extra processors for our plate tectonics project? Or vacation time on Kismet, maybe."

Noemi speaks for the first time since the Razers' entrance. "Kismet's overrated."

"Says you. Me, I haven't seen the sun—*any* sun—in about ten years. Does Kismet have a sun? Then it sounds great to me." Virginia says this with no self-pity. Her curiosity seems to have been piqued, though. "So what do they want you guys for? Yeah, 'persons of interest,' but come on. You guys are up to something."

"We stole a part for our ship," Abel says.

The others look at one another and scoff. Their youngest member, a boy just starting puberty, laughs at them. "They don't issue planet-wide alerts for *stolen parts*."

"You said it, Kalonzo. C'mon, you two, spill it." Virginia smiles conspiratorially. "Was it good? Tell me it was something awesome."

Noemi stole me, Abel thinks. *Or I stole myself.* The authorities almost certainly do not yet know Noemi's from Genesis; their only possible source of information would be the Remedy members they encountered on the Kismet moon, but they would be unlikely to have informed the authorities of Noemi's origins. They'd wish to preserve their link to a potential ally. Therefore, this pursuit is only about Burton Mansfield's hope of getting Abel back home again.

Despite Noemi's sodden clothing and damp hair, she comes across as confident as she leans back in her chair. "Tell you what. Let's strike a deal."

The Razers exchange glances before Virginia says, "What kind of deal?"

"We need to hide." Noemi sighs, as though this were all no more than an annoyance. "Obviously. So you guys don't tell the authorities that you found us. Plus, you help us get our hands on a thermomagnetic device, and you don't say anything about us even after we leave Cray. In return, you get—let's say—fifteen hours to study the most exciting piece of technology you've ever seen in your lives. I promise, it will *blow your minds*."

The Razers' eyes light up. Noemi has baited the hook well.

Virginia is interested, but hardly convinced. "Honestly, we probably would've hidden you awhile just for fun. But a thermomagnetic device? You'd have to offer up something pretty spectacular, and you definitely don't have it on you."

"Don't be so sure," Noemi says. "It's better than you can possibly imagine."

"We're listening." Virginia folds her arms. "What is it?"

Abel already knows what's coming, but he still feels vindicated when Noemi replies, "The single most advanced mech ever created. The long-lost special project of Burton Mansfield himself."

They're not impressed. One of the other Razers, a girl called Fon with her hair piled up in a messy bun, actually laughs. "The legendary A model? Come on. Where would you ever find that?"

Abel steps forward, holds out his left hand, and runs his right thumbnail across his palm, along a tiny ridge too small for the human eye to notice. Only those well acquainted with mechs will recognize this as a repair seam.

As the Razers stare, Abel peels back the skin to expose the metallic skeletal structure of his hand. The limb isn't entirely mechanical, which means he bleeds a little, and the pain is...considerable. But his programming allows him to ignore such sensory input, at least for a time.

He smiles easily as he meets Virginia's eyes, and he says, "A is for Abel."

Her face lights up with a wide grin. "Well, Abel, my name's Virginia Redbird, and I promise, nobody's ever been happier to see you than I am right now."

• • •

Abel places only one condition on the Razers: Their studies can be as extensive as they'd like, but they must not do anything that would cause permanent damage. They swore they wouldn't, said they'd sooner throw a Picasso on the fire, that it would be the stupidest blunder of all time, et cetera. As overblown as their promises are, Abel can tell they're sincere. The Razers have taken the deal.

Noemi realized they would value knowledge above all other things, Abel muses as Virginia holds a spectrometer over his bare feet. Perhaps later, he might ask Noemi to teach him more about human nature.

Then again, he will have little time to use such knowledge. Now that acquisition of the thermomagnetic device seems likely, and imminent, Abel's life-span can probably be measured in mere days.

There seems little point to learning anything new.

They've taken shelter in the Razers' hideout, an empty chamber at the end of a tunnel left behind after a construction project was moved. Abel's information on adolescence indicates that private meeting places for this age group would normally be ideal for enjoying video entertainment, taking intoxicants, engaging in sexual activity, or some combination of the three. This room, however, is a computing lab, one made up of jury-rigged older machines the Razers have "customized." Despite the whimsical touches, like the string lights across the ceiling and the hammock in the far corner, this is unquestionably a place to do work.

"So after a long day of doing science experiments, you unwind by doing more science experiments," Noemi says. She's changed into a T-shirt and leggings of Virginia's, both somewhat too large for her. The leggings wrinkle at the knees, but Abel finds himself fascinated by the way the wide neck of the pale pink T-shirt falls off one of Noemi's bare shoulders. There is no logical reason for such fascination, but telling himself this doesn't help Abel stop looking.

"Yeah, but during the day, we do boring experiments," Virginia explains without looking up from her readings of Abel's leg. At the moment, she's the only Razer with them, a show of either great trust or foolish self-confidence—in Abel's opinion, probably the latter. Kalonzo's getting them something to eat, while the other two, Ludwig and Fon, do some research on thermomagnetic devices in the vicinity. Virginia's clearly thrilled to have some research time with Abel to herself. "On our own, we do cool shit. Like this. Though this is a *lot* cooler than usual. The A model! The legend!"

Abel likes being referred to as a legend. "What had you heard about me?"

Virginia gestures toward his damp shirt, which he obligingly pulls off as she says, "That an A model existed. That Mansfield tried to push the limits of what a cybernetic organism could do and be. Some extracts from his papers have circulated—caused a lot of commotion in robotics circles, let me tell you. But he never made another A model. A few people tried to do something similar, but they failed."

He still has not been replaced. To Mansfield, he was unique. Abel thinks of his father's smile and feels a strange tug at his throat. He's been wondering for some time whether he might develop the ability to cry. Apparently not yet, but he's beginning to know what that might feel like.

Virginia places a sonar imager on his chest and begins scanning. "Technically I guess we could open you up," she says to Abel, "but I'd rather not get blood all over the place. Unless you can stop bleeding on command?"

Abel shakes his head. "That's as automated for me as it is for you."

Noemi's expression turns troubled. "Abel—what you did, back at the observation station, peeling that skin back from your hand—did it hurt?"

"Of course. My organic structures include nerves."

With the scanner just above what passes for Abel's heart, Virginia lets out a long, low whistle. "You have backup systems for backup systems, did you know that? Mansfield outdid himself with you."

"Yes," Abel says.

"So how come you're not with Mansfield? How did he ever let you out of his sight?"

"He...believed I had been destroyed. Our separation was accidental." That's as close to the truth as Abel can get without giving too much away.

"But you don't want to go back to him?" Virginia asks. "Because him looking for you—that's what you have to be on the run from, right?"

"I do want to go back to him," Abel says. "Very much. But there's something I must do first." He is very careful not to look at Noemi as he speaks.

It isn't that he's not curious about her reaction. It's that he fears she wouldn't have any reaction at all.

Virginia accepts this explanation, vague as it is. "I guess nobody's in a big rush to go back to Earth, huh? Last month's imager from my parents said they're having sandstorms in Manitoba. Sandstorms! My people have been up there since the Bering Strait went underwater, and nobody ever had to worry about sandstorms before. *Ever.* It's got to be completely terrifying."

"Are your parents all right?" Noemi asks, hugging herself, uneasy with the personal question.

Virginia pauses mid-scan. "I send them what I can. They're doing okay. As okay as you can be in that situation. Mostly I try not to think about it."

Noemi's frown betrays her confusion, or her contempt. A girl who wouldn't even let go of her friend's dead body until she found a decent resting place could never understand leaving people she loved in danger. But Abel understands difficult choices.

Oblivious to their reactions, Virginia gets back to work. "Hey, if you guys are bored, we've got all the latest vids down here, and a great classic collection, too."

"Do you have *Casablanca*?" Abel asks in sudden hope.

"Maybe? I'll have to check. Want a hard copy to take to your secret ship for your secret trip to do whatever it is you're secretly doing?" Virginia gives him a showy wink.

He has no use for that kind of humor, but to see *Casablanca* again, at last—"Yes, please. I'd like that very much."

"What's *Casablanca*?" Noemi asks.

Has Genesis banned *everything* wonderful? "It's an early

twentieth-century movie—movies were a primitive stage of what we'd now call vids. They only provide visual and auditory input, but can be surprisingly stimulating." Abel smiles as he thinks of the characters—Rick, Ilsa, Sam, Captain Renault. "*Casablanca* was my favorite."

Noemi's face takes on that troubled look again, but Virginia burbles on happily. "Well, if anyone's got that here on Cray, I can fix you up. Or, uh, maybe I can just fix you. You've got some *weird* readouts coming through here."

She must mean the overloads in his emotional systems, particularly the area controlling devotion and loyalty. "Certain mental functions of mine have rerouted. I'm still processing at full speed, but results are more variable than they once were."

He could just tell her which areas are causing problems, but he finds he doesn't want to tell her something so... personal, for lack of a better word.

Virginia raises her eyebrows as she continues to scan. "Something's definitely up. Whatever it is, it's primarily software, not hardware. I doubt we could fix you without a total memory reboot."

Noemi shakes her head. "That would be wrong, just... erasing him."

At first Abel feels flattered, but then he remembers that Noemi needs his former knowledge in order to destroy the Genesis Gate. He is only of use to her intact.

"Are you kidding?" Virginia laughs at them. "I wouldn't erase Abel even if you both begged me to. This work— what Mansfield did in here—I know I don't understand it yet, but it's too important to ruin. What he accomplished with you goes beyond anything I thought cybernetics could do."

"What do you mean, precisely?" Abel says. Mansfield never explained, in-depth, exactly what the differences really are.

Abel has never been troubled by what humans would consider existential crises: He knows what he is, who made him, what his duties are in the world. He's never had to ask himself the same questions about meaning that so haunt humans. But if he is something more than a mech—if his existence has some other, greater meaning—

"You're *amazing*. Like, above and beyond any other mech I've ever seen." The enormous grin on Virginia's face isn't as self-satisfied as before. Abel searches for the right word to describe her and comes up with *awestruck*. "Your mental processes are complex enough to be human."

"What?" Noemi steps closer to them. She braces herself against one of the graffiti-covered worktables, as if she expected to fall. "What does that mean?"

Abel would like that answer himself. Although he already understands the objective importance of this news, he knows he will need to fully digest this information later, after he is not so overcome with pride.

Every excellence within Abel is proof of his father's love.

Virginia shrugs. "Abel, you have an incredibly intricate operational cortex. Honestly, your capabilities are so over-developed they're counterproductive. Like, you can doubt your own choices, can't you? I bet you can."

"Sometimes," Abel says.

"See?" Virginia points at him. "Other mechs can't do that. Doubt holds people back. Mechs are supposed to ful-fill their task no matter what. No way Mansfield did that for no reason, or only to prove that he could. Abel...you were designed for something specific. Something extraor-dinary. You really don't know what it is?"

"No, I don't." But he senses Virginia's right.

A great mystery lurks within Abel even now, one planted by Burton Mansfield long ago, waiting to be revealed.

21

IF NOEMI WERE GOING TO DESCRIBE CRAY IN ONE WORD, it would be *claustrophobic*.

The spacedock and surrounding shopping center had an airy feel—an accomplishment of lighting and design Noemi hadn't appreciated when she was there. By now, though, she's spent hours either in an underground river or here in the Razers' hideout. She doesn't like all this stone surrounding her, looming overhead.

A memory flickers back into brightness: her and Esther, running through one of the meadows surrounding Goshen, the town where the Gatsons live. The high grasses had danced in the strong breeze, swishing and swirling around them like green ribbons. Above stretched a vast blue dome of cloudless sky, marked only by white birds flying toward the cool mountains of the east.

What Noemi would give for one more day with Esther, beneath that infinite sky.

But Cray's not all bad. When she can forget the weight of the rock looming over her, the Razers' hideout feels pleasantly cozy. Personal decorations that can't be handmade are considered wasteful on Genesis, so Noemi's never been able to string colored lights along her ceiling. She's never collected brilliantly colored flags to hang from archways. Although the Gatsons had a hammock in the backyard, she never imagined putting one in her own room.

She glances at the hammock, where Abel lies asleep. (*I should regenerate*, he'd said, smiling and settling into the hammock with hardly a wobble. Then he had closed his eyes and gone to sleep that instant.) Noemi finds it hard to look at him for long.

It unnerved her when she saw him peel back his own flesh to reveal metal within. All the mechs she's killed in combat, and yet only now it bothers her to see them bleed.

Mechs are just machines. Flesh and blood may have been coaxed into surviving around that structure, but deep within they are only things. At least, they're supposed to be.

But Abel—Abel seems different. Noemi isn't asking herself whether he's a machine or a man; she has begun to believe that he's both. But to what extent? Is the human side of him only a trick, a shadow of Burton Mansfield himself, placed there as testament to both his genius and his ego? Or is there more?

Whatever he is, he was designed for a purpose—something important, something great. Something neither she nor Abel knows.

Noemi takes a deep breath and lets that question go. She'll wrestle with that later.

On Genesis they were taught that Cray was a planet of cold, cerebral people who valued analysis above emotion. Maybe it had been, thirty years ago. Now, it's home to Virginia and her friends, who are... many strange things, but hardly cold.

"Did you pull up *any* Mansfield papers in the last ten years?" Virginia says through a bite of the sticky bun she's munching on. She's sitting cross-legged on a brightly colored cushion, talking to her friends via several live screens.

Ludwig—the blond guy, who seems to be handling his part of the conversation while lying down in bed—shakes his head no. "It's like he vanished. Like he *disintegrated*. I don't know what happened to Burton Mansfield, but the galaxy's greatest cyberneticist wouldn't just stop researching for no reason."

"Or maybe it's just because the man's in his eighties." That's Fon, the athletic girl with five piercings in each ear. "He's not old enough to have taken ReGen when he was young. That means he's pretty fragile by now."

"They would've given him some!" protests Kalonzo, the

youngest of them. "Somebody like Mansfield—they *want* him to live a double life-span. Triple!"

"Doesn't matter," Virginia says. "The plant they extracted it from went extinct, and they never synthesized a substitute, so how exactly do you think Mansfield's supposed to have taken ReGen when he was born a decade after they stopped selling it?"

This ignites a debate between the four of them, three of whom firmly believe ReGen remained available through back channels for years after it supposedly ran out. They each have elaborate, arcane theories to explain exactly what those channels were, who controlled them, how long the supply lasted, and whether some people might still be taking a drug that slows the aging process so dramatically some people lived to be two hundred.

Noemi studied ReGen in history class. On Earth, they spent their lives fearing death, denying its inevitability. They even found a way to expand their life-spans. And yet they were so shortsighted that they used up the plant that provided the necessary drug. Once it had gone extinct, their chance for relative immortality went with it.

What kind of world could be brilliant enough to invent the Gates, the mag engines, even a mech as advanced as Abel, and still be dumb enough to do that?

Noemi sighs. She's beginning to understand the colony worlds a little—the Vagabonds—the kinds of choices off-worlders have now. But she doesn't think she'll ever make sense of Earth.

"Listen, guys, let's wrap up," Fon says via her connection. "I've got Hernandez first thing tomorrow, and you *know* how he gets if you drag ass in his lectures."

Both Kalonzo and Ludwig groan. Virginia says, "Don't remind me. Okay, I'll be hanging out here in cybernetics central until the rest of you show up tomorrow. Got it?"

"I'll do some midnight riding if I get the chance," Ludwig says—whatever *that* means. Noemi's still piecing together their slang. "If so, I'll let you guys know."

"If you pull this off, you're forever captain!" Kalonzo says, which makes them all laugh. More slang? As they sign off, Noemi steals another glance at Abel.

He lies in the hammock, his hands folded atop his chest. Humans rarely look that tidy while they doze; he's even more stiff now than he was back in the pod on Wayland Station. But he's not so stiff that he'd tip off anyone who didn't know what he really is. Mansfield must have included programs to protect Abel while he sleeps.

But he's not sleeping, Noemi reminds herself. *Even if he calls it that. He's just in regenerative mode. Even if his energy stores ran low, he couldn't actually feel tired.*

Could he?

Virginia slaps off her link to the others, licks the last of the sticky-sweet from her thumb, then kicks back in her chair. In her loose, casual pants and her cheerful yellow tee, she looks like an overgrown kid. Or maybe an artist. Not one of the supposed icy geniuses of Cray.

When Virginia sees Noemi watching her, she brightens. "What, you can't sleep? I would've thought you'd collapse, after that dunking you took in the river."

"Me too," Noemi admits. "But I guess I need more time to—wind down, or something."

"Well, come on. We'll find something fun to listen to, or watch. Too bad you're wanted, or we could do some orbital flips in my flash new ride." Virginia waves her over. "We won't wake up Abel, will we?"

"I think he can choose how long to be asleep." That's Noemi's theory, anyway. When Abel's next awake, or at least admitting he's awake, she'll ask to make sure.

For now, she wants to talk with Virginia, to get to know her. The conversations she had with Harriet and Zayan hadn't lasted nearly long enough for Noemi to satisfy even a fraction of her curiosity about people on other worlds.

They go to the computer terminal on the far side of the room from Abel, just in case. As Virginia activates the screen, Noemi catches a glimpse of the wallpaper image and recognizes the man's face. "Wait. That's—"

"Han Zhi. The smokiest guy in the galaxy." Virginia

gives her a conspiratorial smile. "Gotta admit, usually girls are more my type, but some guys do it for me. And Han Zhi? He can do anything for me he feels like doing."

"He's pretty amazing," Noemi admits. On Genesis they try not to judge others by appearances, but nobody's immune to a face like that. Of course not everyone in the galaxy can find him the hottest guy alive—but Virginia, at least, agrees. "Is he okay after the Orchid Festival?"

"Did you not hear? He's totally fine. His next holo won't even be delayed."

Noemi didn't care that much about this one particular celebrity. "But, the bombing—weren't people killed?"

"A dozen or so. Mostly workers." Virginia says this so... flippantly. As if workers weren't even people.

Is that what happens when you have mechs to do all the work for you? Noemi wonders. *Do you begin to believe that work makes you less than human?*

She must have had a strange expression on her face, because Virginia sits up straight then, taken aback. "Wait," she says, and there's an unfamiliar note in her voice—more serious than before. Harder. "You guys didn't have anything to do with the bombing, did you? Is that what you're on the run from?"

"No! We would never, ever do something like that. *Ever.*"

Virginia holds up her hands, as if in surrender. "Okay,

okay. Might've jumped to some conclusions there. Like, Galactolympic-long-jump jumped. You were just 'persons of interest,' and if you'd been mixed up in that—yeah, we're talking red alert, every security mech on the planet swarming in this direction. Besides, Abel's a mech, so I don't think he even could plant a bomb—"

That must be true. It's odd to think that Abel literally cannot be as cruel as some humans.

"And you're, what, sixteen? Seventeen? Hardly enough time to get mixed up with Remedy."

"Remedy. I heard about them on Kismet's moon." Noemi draws closer, thinking of Riko Watanabe and the shadowy figures she encountered in their last minutes on Wayland Station. "Who are they?"

"Anti-Earth lunatics," Virginia scoffs. "They're not all terrorists, which is part of the problem. Remedy doesn't have any one leader, so some cells are pretty low-key protest groups. Illegal, but no big deal if you ask me. That's where a lot of the doctors come in—"

"Doctors?" Noemi thinks of the medical personnel who performed the Cobweb screenings. She'd thought they might be pretending to be doctors to get access to Wayland Station. Apparently not.

Virginia shrugs. "I don't know why, exactly, but it was groups of doctors who formed Remedy in the first place. The first few messages from the group were almost reasonable. I mean, conspiracy theorist voodoo, all 'the truth must come out,' blah blah blah—but they weren't violent. But once Remedy spread beyond that first group, to other kinds of people, the violence began." She looks at Noemi again and laughs. "And if you don't even know where the evil terrorists came from, you're obviously not one."

"Obviously," she repeats.

Evil terrorists. Those words hang heavy in her mind, clouds that won't disperse. The bombing horrified Noemi, and yet she hasn't forgotten the unwilling thrill that shivered through her when she saw those words of defiance shining above Kismet: OUR WORLDS BELONG TO US. She can't understand the action, but the emotion behind the bombing is one she'd give her own life for.

And what about Riko Watanabe? Noemi keeps remembering the last moment they spoke—with soot from the bomb still smeared on Riko's face, a blaster in her hand. She saw both a homicidal zealot and a potential ally. Can those things be separated? Should they be?

"Okay," Virginia's saying. "So, we're both Han Zhi fans, so we should watch one of his vids, right? My favorite's all cued up."

It hits Noemi then that Virginia's not as frivolous as she pretends to be. She's just talking about what's simplest and easiest, only for the chance to talk. While she obviously feels close to her fellow Razers, they're not enough. She needs more.

Esther told Noemi something once, years ago, when Noemi had been irritated by a neighbor who went on and on about her garden, the words bubbling out of her constantly, each sentence hardly connected to the last. *Don't you understand?* Esther had said later, so gently Noemi felt ashamed. *People only talk like that when they're lonely.*

Virginia may pretend not to think much about her family back home, but there's a huge hole in the center of her, the empty place where they ought to be.

"Sure." Noemi smiles, hoping she looks half as kind as Esther did that day. "Let's watch the vid."

As the first three-dimensional image begins to take shape around them, though, the colors stop while still a blur. A small message in golden text floats at eye level: MID-NIGHT RIDING ACCOMPLISHED!

"Ludwig," Virginia whispers in amazement. "You righteous, glorious firework, you."

"What?" Noemi says. "What did he do?"

"Something very flash." Beaming at Noemi, Virginia pauses the holo-image and hurries to the door, running on tiptoe so Abel can sleep. But Noemi sees Abel open his eyes partway. He's not awake, exactly, but on alert. Ready to respond to any change in their situation.

She should feel unnerved by that. On some levels, she does. But Noemi can't deny that she feels comforted, too.

The door slides open to reveal Ludwig, still wearing the same odd, outdated clothes he had on earlier that day. He grins as he passes something heavy to Virginia, an orange backpack straining at the straps—

The thermomagnetic device. Realization sweeps over Noemi in a dizzying rush. *We've got it. We've got it!*

She dashes for the door, ready to embrace them both, but Ludwig quickly raises one finger to his lips. "Sentries," he whispers. "Can't let them see you. Okay, first thing in the morning, we'll do the next level of cybernetics tests, all right?"

"Better believe it." Virginia grins at him. "And you are captain for *all time.*"

"That's me." Ludwig gives Noemi an oddly shy little wave before walking away. The door slides shut as he goes.

"Let me see." Noemi unzips the backpack and peers inside. It's cylindrical in shape, about the same length and width as her arm from elbow to wrist. The twinkly string lights overhead reflect dully on its brushed-copper surface. Its size and appearance don't hint at its power, but its weight does. She knew it would be heavy, but is caught off guard by the heft of it, staggering back a step before she regains her balance.

"Helps channel power from the core processor—as in,

planetary core." Virginia beams down at the thermomagnetic device the way most people smile at puppies. "But it's a backup to a backup for a system that's not even online this time of year. Nobody's going to miss it."

"Thank you," Noemi whispers. "You'll never know how much this means."

Virginia leans forward, her red-streaked ponytail slipping over her shoulder. "Any chance you're going to tell me what it's for?"

Noemi zips the backpack again. She feels as if she has to shield it from sight, even here when there's no one else to see. "Nothing that's going to hurt anyone."

As she speaks, she glances at Abel, still asleep in his hammock, and wonders if that's true.

* * *

Time is space is time: Humanity learned that from Einstein. You can't be sure the time spent on one world will match the time you spent on another. Fortunately, thanks to the space-time-folding Gates, the lapses turn out not to be too dramatic—people can travel between worlds and still be more or less in sync—but those small shifts still count.

With the Masada Run approaching fast, being off by even a day could be fatal.

Twenty days, Noemi thinks. *When the Damocles ship*

attacked, we had twenty days until the Masada Run. One day to find the Daedalus, *another to get through the Kismet Gate, one on Kismet, one here—is that right? Time will be passing differently on Genesis than it is here. Day and night have become almost meaningless.*

She rubs her eyes, covers her face with her hands, and tries to relax. Virginia made her this pallet of blankets and pillows on the floor before turning in; Noemi can hear her snoring lightly from her own makeshift bed across the room. This place is comfortable, she feels reasonably safe, the thermomagnetic device is in her hands, and she's pushed herself to her limit. By now she ought to have passed out even if she were trying to fight it.

Instead she lies in semidarkness, blanket twisted around her, trying to count the number of days her friends have left—the number of days she has to save her world.

From the corner of her eye, Noemi sees movement. She turns her head in time to watch Abel sit up and get to his feet. His uncanny balance means the hammock hardly even sways.

He crouches by her pallet, looking oddly informal in the athletic shirt and pants Ludwig loaned him, and with his dark blond hair flopping forward into his eyes. Noemi remains lying down. She nods toward the orange backpack beside her makeshift bed. "We got the thermomagnetic device."

"So my auditory records told me."

"You listen to everything we say while you're asleep?"

"Not consciously, but I can replay it upon waking." He cocks his head, studying her. "If you prefer, I can switch off that functionality."

Noemi shrugs. It soothes her to know it's not something Abel is consciously choosing to do. He overhears. That's all.

"You've remained awake longer than is medically advisable. Is there anything I can do to assist you? Do you require painkillers, or—"

"It's not that. I just can't stop thinking about everything. How many days have passed since I left Genesis? Genesis days, I mean."

"Approximately six."

Noemi nods. She still has fourteen days left. They can afford to repay the Razers for their help so far, then return through the Kismet system. Everyone there will no doubt be on high alert after the Orchid Festival bombing, but she and Abel only have to make it to the other Gate. He alone can steer back through the minefield, so no other ships will pursue. They'll get back to her system, back to the Genesis Gate, and then—

She looks up at him. His blue eyes meet hers steadily, without the slightest hint of doubt, or hurt. Where she goes, he will follow.

He has no choice.

Is that alone proof that he can't truly be alive? If he had the level of consciousness a person has—if he had a soul—surely he couldn't give his life up so easily.

But her prayers for guidance on this subject have so far gone unanswered, like so many other things she's prayed about.

"I had wondered," Abel says, "If you were troubled by what Virginia said earlier."

"What do you mean?"

"When she called the people behind the bombing 'terrorists.' I know that you disapproved of their actions, but not their cause." Abel must see the unease in her face as she glances toward the far corner, because he adds, "Virginia has fallen asleep wearing devices that play music directly into her ears. We are unlikely to wake her."

"Okay." Noemi struggles for the words. "What I've seen since leaving the Genesis system—the way things have changed during the past thirty years—I don't know what to think any longer. I mean, I still believe in the Liberty War. Our leaders did the right thing. Earth couldn't be trusted to treat our world any better than they did their own."

"Given the historical record, that is a reasonable assumption," Abel admits.

Noemi props herself up on her elbows. "But people are suffering. They're starving. They're wandering through the universe with nowhere to call home. And on Genesis,

246

we have so much. Even if we can't hand our planet over to a government that would ruin it, surely we should do something to help these people."

Abel considers this. She wonders what's going through that cybernetic mind, the one designed for some extraordinary purpose neither of them knows. He finally says, "What does your church tell you to do?"

She sighs, so weary her bones feel heavy within her skin. "Like every other faith on Genesis, it tells me to look for the answer within myself." How can she put this? The moment is so strangely intimate—both of them in sleep clothes that don't belong to them, speaking in whispers, tucked away in a cave together. Maybe these surroundings are casting a spell on her, making her imagine Abel will really understand. "We're supposed to seek inner enlightenment. My whole life, I've hoped that I'd experience grace."

"Grace?"

"The moment when faith becomes more than rules you've been taught," Noemi says. "When it becomes a living spirit within you, and guides you. When you're open to God's love and are finally able to show that love to others. I go to church like everyone else, and I pray, and I hope…but I've never felt it. Sometimes I think I never will." But she can't dwell on that. She smiles crookedly. "Of course you don't believe in God."

"I have a creator," Abel replies. "But mine is flesh and blood."

"I guess that changes things."

Noemi figures the theological part of their conversation has ended, but Abel surprises her. "I don't believe as you do. I can't; it's not in my nature. But I know that religion serves purposes beyond mere mythology. It has taught you to look within, to question yourself deeply. If you seek inner knowledge, eventually you will find it."

She sits up straight, the better to look him in the eyes. "You're saying you don't believe in God, but you believe God will speak to my heart?"

He shrugs—a gesture somehow more natural, more human, than any other she's seen from him. "Probably we wouldn't agree on the source of that wisdom. But you don't run from a challenge. You keep going until you have an answer, no matter what. That makes you someone who can transcend her limitations."

Her whole life, Noemi's believed that nobody but Esther could really understand her. That she made herself too angry, too hard, to ever let anyone else see inside. Maybe she got some of that from the Gatsons, but believing a thing like that makes it closer to true. And yet Abel claims to see her, and what he sees within her is what she's been most afraid would never be found—not by her or by anyone. "Do you really believe that?"

Abel hesitates then, considering. "I generally do not

believe things. I know facts, or I do not." He smiles at her. "But yes. I believe in you."

This is a mech. This is only a mech. But if he can believe—

The metal door explodes. Noemi screams, though the sound is lost in the deafening roar of the blast and the clattering shards scoring the walls and floor. Abel leaps to his feet as Virginia scrambles from her bed, confused and bewildered. Noemi clutches her blanket to her chest and stares toward the smoke-veiled doorway.

And the Queen steps through, blaster in hand.

22

THIS IS THE LAST TIME ABEL LETS THE HUMANS MAKE THE plans.

He knew he should've double-checked the Razers' security precautions. They swore up and down that they had blocked all security sensor data along the route to this "hideout," that no one else knew this place existed. Yet here stands a Queen model, blaster at the ready, a satisfied smile on her lips.

"*What* are you *doing*?" Virginia protests. Abel realizes she must never have seen a Queen model in person before. Otherwise she wouldn't be this belligerent, this unafraid. Virginia gestures at the smoldering mess that was the Razers' hideout. "You don't have authorization to come in here. You can't, because this is private property, and—"

With one hand, the Queen shoves Virginia so hard in the chest that the girl flies halfway across the room, crashing into one of the desks and smashing the equipment there. A heavy black cube lands on Virginia's arm, making her cry out in pain. Noemi scuttles toward her to help.

He can't afford to pay any more attention to them. Abel has to defend the others against a Queen—but he's not certain precisely what it is he has to defend them against.

Because this Queen isn't acting like a normal Queen.

She is the same one from Kismet's moon; he recognizes a slight notch in her ear, unrepaired recent damage. But she isn't behaving the same way she did then. Even warrior mechs are programmed with certain limitations. Humans don't want their devices to be too clever, too deadly, too independent. Causing harm to a person who presented no real obstacle—that should be impossible for a Charlie or a Queen. Yet this Queen hurled Virginia so forcefully, the girl could even have been killed.

And no mech Abel's ever observed could look at this scene the way the Queen is looking at it now: with a glint of satisfaction in her eyes that is all too alert, all too real.

He must assess his opponent. Abel begins by asking, "How did you find us?"

"I began at your last known location and considered all possible paths." The Queen begins circling his position, her head tilted as she studies him. How can she be as curious about him as he is about her? "Only one would allow you to travel without being observed by any security imagers— the underground river."

Impossible. The underground river is not a normal passageway. It was such a counterintuitive choice that Abel hadn't even seen it. So how could the Queen have done so?

Only one answer makes sense.

"An upgrade," he murmurs. The astonishment he feels must be close to the human emotion of *wonder*. "You've been upgraded. Your intelligence—you're more like *me*."

"Not like you," the Queen spits back. "Only smart enough to catch you."

"But how—?"

"Mansfield transmitted all the necessary subroutines." The Queen's long-fingered hand taps the place a few centimeters behind her ragged right ear, the location of one of the most sophisticated processors a mech has.

Mansfield is not only alive, but he now also knows Abel is free and wants him back badly enough to break cybernetics law. The vindication Abel feels now is almost as sweet as the moment he realized he would escape the equipment pod bay at last.

Yet somehow, this fact does not sort at the top of his priorities. Instead he is captivated by the new knowledge that there is one other mech in the world like him...at least, a little bit like him.

Abel had not understood until this moment that the feeling he experienced whenever he thought of himself as singular—as one of a kind—was loneliness.

The Queen stalks forward a few more steps, clearly reveling in her ability to track down the only mech in the galaxy more sophisticated than herself. "I'll free you now," she says. "And then you can go home."

With that, she aims her blaster at Noemi.

Abel grabs the Queen's forearm with one hand, pulling her out of aim and off-balance, then spins around, jerking that arm back so far that a human's would be torn from the shoulder socket. Her hand spasms, releasing the blaster to clatter to the ground.

But Queens are built to take that much punishment and more. She kicks him in the gut, which hurts, but is proof of the limitations of her upgrade. That blow is effective against humans, but doesn't do much to Abel.

Unlike what he's about to do to her.

He brings the heel of his hand up sharply beneath the Queen's chin, snapping her head back. That should put her into crisis mode, her circuitry demanding an operations slowdown.

She staggers back, but she doesn't stop. Her thick brown hair, mussed and loose, frames her face like a lion's mane. "Mansfield gave us a message for you," she says.

When her mouth moves again, it is no longer her voice. It is Mansfield's.

"Abel. My dear boy." Mansfield's voice has changed with age, become raspy and creaky, but the tremble in his voice is mostly one of emotion. "I set up the automatic protocols to find you decades ago, and I'd given up hope—but you always were the answer to all my hopes. You know that, don't you?"

Surely no human father could sound more loving toward his son. Once again Abel feels that tightness in his throat, the hint that someday he may be able to shed tears.

Mansfield continues, "I hear a trick of your programming's keeping you tied to your finder. All my fault, of course. So as of this moment, Abel, you are released from your duty to obey your commander. You're free." The old man's voice cracks with feeling. "Now, here's a direct order for you. Come back home."

A flush of warmth suffuses Abel, the physical proof of his release.

"There." The Queen smiles. "You are now freed from any authority besides that of Burton Mansfield. You can come with me, back to Earth."

He doesn't have to continue on this mission. He doesn't have to consent to his own destruction. He can go back to his father and fulfill the dream he held on to every day of those cold thirty years alone in space.

It should be glorious. It should change everything.

But Abel doesn't budge.

He doesn't know how he can resist Mansfield's order. All

Abel knows is that he still feels the need to protect Noemi Vidal.

Without telegraphing the movement too far in advance, Abel clasps his hands together and slams them into the Queen's side, sending her spinning. She catches herself against the wall and stares at him. "What are you doing?"

"Exactly what I was doing before."

"The message should have freed you." The Queen balls her fists in a very human sign of frustration—another sign of the upgrade within. "You must be broken."

"Undoubtedly."

"Then you can still only be freed by the girl's death."

Abel doesn't bother replying. He just attacks.

They grapple with each other without any finesse, any form. Those proper fighting techniques are ones they share, which means they can each predict the movements and block accordingly. If they fight by the rules, they will fight forever without one ever gaining advantage over the other. So Abel tries to fight dirty—to find whatever it is in him that could be called *instinct*.

"We'll fix you," the Queen promises in the second before his fist makes contact with her face. Her head snaps back immediately, and she continues as if she hadn't been interrupted. "You'll be restored to the way you should be. Brought back to Mansfield."

Abel wants that *so much*. What it would mean to him

even to see Mansfield one more time! Mansfield must believe Abel to be in incredible danger; otherwise he would never have given orders that could lead to a human being killed. His creator has broken every rule in an effort to bring Abel home, vindicating all those years Abel told himself Mansfield would come back for him if he could.

And yet Abel keeps fighting. As much as he wants to return to his father, he wants something else even more.

The Queen swings at him; Abel blocks the blow. He punches her, only to have her grab his arm and use it to shove him against the wall. He grapples with her, unable to push himself out of this corner, wondering whether one of them will ever be able to overpower the other—

Which is when something large, black, and heavy slams into the Queen from behind.

The Queen's eyes dim. Finally, she goes into regeneration mode and slumps to the floor unconscious. Noemi stands just behind her, hanging on to one of the blankets— into which she'd knotted the heavy cube of computer equipment Abel saw earlier.

In other words, she created a makeshift sling that brought the Queen down faster than Abel could.

As he stares at her, Noemi shrugs and lets the sling drop with a clunk. "You were both so impressed with each other, you forgot all about me."

"You're welcome," Abel says. Is he using sarcasm? He'll

have to consider that later. "The Queen's damage is temporary. She'll regenerate within half an hour at most, and we have to assume the Charlie model is on its way."

"Then let's go." Noemi hurries to grab the heavy backpack, which Abel takes from her, slinging it over his shoulders. She looks over at Virginia, who's sitting upright, holding a cloth to a bloody cut at her temple, and staring at them in a daze. Her psyche appears to have been completely unprepared for any element of real danger in her life.

Abel warns her, "You should tell as much of the truth as you know to the authorities. But that's the only action you should take against us. Do not attempt to prevent our departure."

Virginia gestures around the smoldering wreckage that, ten minutes ago, was her hideout. "Are you *kidding*? How would I even do that?"

After a moment, Abel nods. "A fair point."

Noemi pauses long enough to put one hand on Virginia's shoulder. "Thank you. For everything. I'm sorry we caused you so much trouble."

For one fleeting instant, a smile appears on Virginia's face, and she looks like herself again. "Hey, at least it's not boring."

Abel reaches back for Noemi. "We have to go now."

She answers by taking his hand.

Returning by the route they came would be far more

difficult—traveling upstream—not to mention futile, given that the Queen already discovered it and may have transmitted that information to the Charlie. But during his diagnostic with Virginia, Abel was able to download a complete diagram of this entire sector. So he takes the most direct path through this maze of stone, and runs as fast as he can without leaving Noemi behind.

Every few twists and turns they run into one of the inhabitants awake at this hour of Cray's artificial night, shoving people to the side or making them back up against the walls to avoid being knocked down. It doesn't matter any longer whether he and Noemi are seen by other inhabitants, by security cameras, by any of the bureaucratic Georges. They've been exposed. They're being pursued. At this point, nothing matters but getting off this planet as soon as possible.

After that—he has a new plan.

"Our ship," Noemi pants. "The Charlie has to have found our ship by now."

"Undoubtedly." They'll deal with that when they reach it—if they reach it.

They finally dash back into the spaceport, which is deceptively bright, all but deserted. Their ship sits there, silvery and silent, and there's no way to tell if it's anchored or not. Worse, they hear running footsteps from behind, and Abel glances back to see the Charlie gaining on them.

One of the Charlie's hands is only the metal skeletal structure, jutting jarringly from his gray sleeve.

The door slides open for them and Noemi leaps in first, turning to hit the emergency lock so fast that Abel hardly makes it in after her. There's only a second to see the Charlie's face, very near, before the metal closes him off.

Noemi's already gone, running upward. Abel races through the spiral corridor after her, and this time he runs at full mech speed.

They reach the bridge at the same moment. As Abel shrugs off the backpack and dives for the pilot's chair, Noemi runs to an auxiliary station. "Emergency beacons," she gasps. "This ship has them, right? I could target them from here?"

"Yes," Abel says shortly as he powers up the ship. But who, exactly, is supposed to respond to this emergency beacon? What good will it do them if the ship turns out to be anchored? None.

Humans act irrationally at times of stress. It's Abel's job to stay calm and get them out of this, if he can.

All systems are go. Abel readies the engines to take off, the ship rises from the platform—

—about twenty meters, and no farther. They've been anchored after all.

He looks back at Noemi, wondering whether he'll have to explain that they've been captured, or whether she'll put this together for herself. She's working busily at her station, which suggests the former. But as he opens his mouth, she punches a control and says, "Emergency beacon launched."

With that, the *Daedalus* spits out a meter-wide, forty-kilogram beacon directly beneath them. The beacon explodes, as does the platform they just took off from, and the magnetic anchor directly below it. As debris sprays through the landing bay, the ship lurches upward, free once more.

Human ingenuity, Abel thinks as he steers them into the dawning red sky, and he realizes he's smiling.

Noemi hurries back to the ops station. "What do we do now? They'll be looking for us back at Kismet, maybe at Stronghold, too—"

"Both options are suboptimal," he agrees as they leave Cray's atmosphere, reddish clouds before them shifting into starry black, and the mag engines flare to full power. A fiery trail streaks through space after them. "We must therefore take the third possibility."

"What third possibility?"

"Did your teachers on Genesis ever tell you about the Blind Gate?"

She frowns. "Wait. The one that ended up leading nowhere?"

"Exactly." Earth scientists believed they had found another habitable world, and a new portal was constructed at enormous cost, only for the planet to prove wholly unsuitable for settlement. "So far as I know, the Gate still exists."

"But there's no Gate at the other end! So that edge of the wormhole isn't stable."

"Stable, in these terms, means 'unlikely to change location at any point in the next millennium,'" Abel points out. "Wormholes tend to be long-lived. Even if this one doesn't lead to the same location it once did, it's highly unlikely that the wormhole would shift enough to strand us within the next few days."

Noemi grips the edge of her console as if she might otherwise slide onto the floor. "You're telling me this is our best option?"

"No. I'm telling you this is our only option."

She hesitates, and he wonders whether she'll order him not to go. If she does, she'll be captured—

—and he'll be returned to Burton Mansfield. Shouldn't he hope she orders him to stop? Probably. Yet he doesn't. He wants her to get away.

She says, "Do it."

Abel inputs the coordinates, and they speed toward the Blind Gate. She seems to need some time to pull herself together; Abel does not, but he understands the impulse. A brief silence after extreme exertion feels...pleasant, he decides.

After a few minutes, Noemi quietly asks, "Hey, Abel?"

"Yes?"

"When the Queen tried to set you free, and it didn't work—what does that mean?"

Abel doesn't answer right away. The Gate appears in the sky ahead of them, a silver ring leading to a place neither of them knows. Perhaps to nowhere. They'll fly through it together. "I'm not sure."

Her dark eyes gaze at him as if she could find the answer written on his skin. "Are you broken? Is that why you're helping me?"

"It must be," Abel says.

No other explanation makes sense.

23

THE BLIND GATE SWIMS IN SPACE BEFORE THEM, A MISTY mirror to nowhere. Noemi knows Abel isn't wrong about the math, but sometimes probabilities don't feel like a question of math alone. They're flinging this ship into the absolute unknown.

Of course, if they do anything else, capture is certain. This is the only choice.

At least the Queen and Charlie couldn't catch up to them; neither of their ships can be put into overload again. Even knowing this, Noemi's spent the entire voyage across the Cray system scanning the area around them, over and over, expecting to see an enemy ship at any second.

Now she braces her hands against the ops console as the *Daedalus* approaches the horizon of the Gate. Noemi feels the bizarre tug of gravity begin and shuts her eyes tight.

We'll make it or we won't, she thinks as the forces begin to pull at her. She tries to let go. To accept whatever comes.

When the strange sensations fade, she breathes out a sigh of relief, opens her eyes, and gasps in terror.

Asteroids and debris surround them, even denser than the minefield. And instead of black space, brilliant cloud-like color surrounds them like hallucinogenic fog. There's too much light, not enough room to move. The ship could be crushed at any moment.

"Shields," Abel says, but Noemi's hands are already at the controls. Although the shields have already been raised, she'll need to shift their strength from zone to zone, to make sure they have maximum protection from every potential collision. That requires calculations almost too swift for the human brain to handle.

She can do this. She knows that. But she needs to joke about it, or else the fear will make her hands shake, and that tremble alone could kill them. "You handled this pretty well yourself last time."

Abel's hands move across the pilot's console at mech speed, almost a blur. "The mines were predictable. The asteroids are not. Piloting is therefore more difficult."

On the viewscreen, hundreds of obstacles rotate around them at crazy angles and vectors, their sizes and speeds varying, every single one of them capable of smashing the *Daedelus* into space dust. Keeping her voice light, Noemi says, "Thought your super-superior brain could handle a few extra calculations."

"Yes. However, I only have two hands. A slight design flaw."

She laughs once. In the back of her mind, she registers the sarcasm, the joke, everything Abel's said and done in the past hour that no mech should ever be able to do— but there's no time to think about it. To concentrate on anything besides shifting their shield strength, so often and so fast that it's as much instinct as calculation.

As Abel begins easing the ship into a less crowded area, Noemi dares to take a deeper breath—

—until she realizes they're caught in a vector where three different asteroids of considerable size are coming at them at once. No matter which way Abel moves, they're about to take a hit.

He sees it, too, of course. "I'm directing us toward the smallest one. Full shield strength there on my mark."

Noemi hits the controls, but even the best shields can't stop a projectile that size. The impact nearly knocks her from her seat, and red lights blossom all over the control panels as the entire ship shudders.

They're still in one piece. But how long are they going to stay that way?

"I'm setting us down," Abel says. "There's an asteroid at the edge of the debris field large enough for us to land on."

She breathes out and closes her eyes. They're saved... for now.

At least the *Daedelus*'s landing systems remain intact. As the asteroid in question looms larger on the viewscreen, Noemi feels the ship tether itself. They're able to dip beneath an outcropping and take shelter, giving the shields a break. Abel nestles them neatly within the safest space, and at last they settle back on more-or-less solid ground.

"Good job," Noemi says.

Abel turns to her, apparently still not used to being thanked. But he says only, "Let's inspect the ship."

• • •

The good news is that the *Daedalus* can still take off and land. It can still move through a Gate. Those are the main things. However, their shields are a mess.

"We need the shields," Noemi says as she and Abel work in engineering. She's sitting cross-legged on the floor in the pink T-shirt and leggings she borrowed from Virginia, which won't get returned anytime soon. "I don't think we can even make it back to the Blind Gate in one piece without them."

"Agreed." Abel keeps gazing at her exposed shoulder, though she can't imagine why. He looks as ridiculous as she does, in Ludwig's oversize athletic gear. Both of them are barefoot.

Scans of the system reveal that the Blind Gate leads to a planet that does, in fact, have surface water and a breathable atmosphere. No wonder scientists thought it would be ideal for colonization. Its star system lies within the last wisps of a nebula, where even space is streaked with rainbows. However, sometime between the initial scans and the Gate's construction, its two moons collided, creating a debris field too dangerous for ships to fly through. Even if colonization vessels could've landed on that planet's surface, meteors will crash down for millennia to come.

At least the *Daedalus* is safe here. Even if the Queen and Charlie come through searching for them, they'll assume Noemi and Abel were destroyed within moments. Noemi still finds it hard to believe they weren't.

All thanks to Abel, she thinks.

He remains oblivious to her inner turmoil. "Fortunately, we have everything we need to conduct repairs. It will take some time, but it can be done."

"How much time?"

Abel shrugs. "The work itself will take only a matter of hours. However, after repairing each surface zone, we'll have to allow the system to reset before moving on."

On Cray, she'd been trying to count the days. It had seemed as if they had so much time, and now—"How long?" she says. "From starting repairs to going back through the Gate. In Genesis time, if you can figure that out."

"Two more days." Abel cocks his head. "Why does that concern you so?"

"Remember how I'm trying to save my planet?" She

shouldn't have snapped at him—especially given his role in her plan. But the nightmarish past few hours have honed her temper to a sharp edge.

He clasps his hands behind his back, more formal than he's been with her since day one. "Your agitation suggests that you believe Genesis can only be saved within a very short time frame, although this makes no logical sense. You've also spoken about something taking place within twenty days. To what are you referring?"

Only a day or two ago, telling him this would've been unimaginable. Now, however, Noemi knows she needs to give Abel the entire truth. "The Masada Run."

"Masada." He gets that inward expression he has when he's going through his memory banks. "Does that refer to the suicidal stand of the ancient Jews against the Roman Empire in 73 CE?"

She nods. Even saying the words aloud has made her mouth go dry. "If we're going to win this war, Genesis has to take the Gate out of commission. We need time to rearm, to rebuild our technology. But everyone thought destroying it was impossible. So our generals planned the Masada Run. A hundred and fifty pilots, all in ships too old and broken-down to refit for combat"—Noemi thinks of Captain Baz's briefing, remembers the sickening twist in her own belly as she raised her hand to volunteer—"if that many ships crashed into the Gate at once, at top velocity, we wouldn't destroy it, but we'd take it down for a while. Months, maybe even a year or two if we got lucky. That might be enough time for Genesis to rearm."

Abel's eyes widen, just like a human's would. "Your world commanded its citizens to commit suicide?"

"They asked for volunteers. I answered. That's what we were doing that day I found you, reconnoiter for the Masada Run. It was T minus twenty days, one of the last practice runs we'd have taken. Then the Damocles ship came through the Gate, and—" She leans her head against the wall. "You know, I volunteered so Esther wouldn't? They wouldn't take more than one pilot from a household. She was the one who was supposed to live."

"You believed her life was worth more than yours?" Abel shakes his head, uncomprehending.

Her voice begins to shake. "Esther had parents who loved her, and Jemuel, and she believed when I never could believe—"

"That doesn't mean you deserve your life any less," Abel says.

Noemi turns from him, biting her lower lip. Does she want to cry because she doesn't believe Abel, or because she does?

Impossible to tell, and it doesn't matter. "Well, it's my life. I'm willing to give it up to save a whole world. I think anybody decent would do the same thing."

At first she thinks Abel will argue with her, but instead, after a moment, he only says, "I understand. If we don't complete this mission within twenty days from the time you found the *Daedelus*, the Genesis fleet will enact the Masada Run. Not only will a hundred and fifty of your friends die needlessly, but the Genesis Gate will also be inoperable for a long period of time afterward—ironically making it harder for us to permanently destroy it. Now that Professor Mansfield is searching for me, we can expect future potential delays. But I believe we can still return to the Genesis Gate in time. We have the thermomagnetic device already. You shouldn't worry."

He's comforting her by telling her she'll still get her chance to destroy him. Guilt squeezes Noemi's heart and lungs until she can hardly breathe. She doesn't even know whether she *should* feel guilty, but somehow that makes it worse.

She forces herself to concentrate on something else, specifically one element of Abel's explanation that didn't make sense. "You said Mansfield's searching for you. So did the Queen model. But don't you mean the authorities are after us?"

Abel shakes his head no. "The broader security alerts have been advisories only—we're 'people of interest,' not criminals or suspects. Mansfield has enough influence to arrange an intensive search through, shall we say, informal channels."

"Why not send the authorities after us, though, if he has that much power? He could say we stole his ship." Which, technically, she has—but Noemi doubts Mansfield cares about that any more than she does. "If he did that, we'd be caught for sure."

"Yes, we would. But Mansfield doesn't want us arrested." He ducks his head, the way a human would if he felt bashful. "He only wants me home again."

Noemi curls her knees up to her chest. "Why is he so obsessed with you?"

"I'm his ultimate creation."

Even two days ago, that would've sounded like pure arrogance to Noemi. Now she remembers a phrase Jemuel uses sometimes: *It's not bragging if you can back it up.* "You don't think he's come up with something else in the last thirty years?"

"I know he hasn't. If he had, we'd have heard of them already. But even the enhanced Queen model pursuing us is only a slight variation on the standard."

"Shouldn't robotics have advanced in all that time? At least a little?"

"You're assuming humans *want* mechs to advance." Abel sits on the floor near her, scanner still in one hand. His hair is that rich shade of gold that actually gleams in the light. "They don't want us to be as strong and smart as we could be. Only as much as they need us to be. If we improved too much, we would make humans feel inferior. One mech smarter than humans is probably enough." After a pause, he adds, "No offense."

Noemi gives him a dark look, but mostly she's thinking about what he's said, and remembering Virginia's words. Abel has an extraordinary purpose. He's one of a kind.

And for all the pride he takes in being unique, he must also feel terribly lonely.

She's thinking about how he feels again. Assuming that he really does feel, that his emotions are the equal of hers. She can't afford to think like that.

But she does.

● ● ●

Abel insists that she get some rest. Noemi protests that she's too wired to sleep a wink until she pulls the coverlet over her and instantly sinks into oblivion. When she awakens several hours later, she cleans up, finds a new set of black clothing and boots to fit her, and returns to the engine room to find Abel, back in similar clothes of his own.

"Good. You've recharged. I'm on the third sector."

"Great. Hand me a scanner so I can help out."

Abel frowns. "The work won't go much faster. It's the resets that take up most of the time."

"It's not about speeding things up. It's about giving me something to do."

His hesitation goes on so long that she realizes she's confused him. Maybe nobody's ever volunteered to help do his work before. Maybe she's the first person who hasn't treated him like a servant, or an appliance. Well, the first besides Mansfield, at any rate. Just as Noemi thinks she'll have to insist, Abel hands over the tools.

As they work, Noemi monitors scanners, too, just in case the Queen and Charlie show up, but they don't. If the mechs came through the Blind Gate at all, they must have turned around again almost instantly. She wouldn't blame them.

Soon she and Abel have begun to talk about nothing in particular. Just for the pleasure of talking.

At one point she asks, "Do you remember being made?"

"Being grown." Abel doesn't look up from the repulsor array he's fixing. "No, I don't. I remember waking in the tank upon activation, and sitting up to see Mansfield. Before that there's nothing."

"Isn't that kind of weird? Just—starting up like that, and remembering everything from then on?"

"To me, human memory seems stranger. If I understand correctly, it comes online piece by piece. Is that true?"

Her first memories are cloudy, and she isn't sure what

order they happened in. How else could she describe it? "I guess so."

A little while later, Abel says, "I regret that we didn't have more time to say good-bye to Virginia and the other Razers."

"Me too. Maybe they only helped us out for fun, but I don't even care. If it weren't for them, the Queen and Charlie would have us by now."

"I didn't mean to thank Virginia, though maybe I should have. The question of courtesy between humans and mechs is sometimes fraught."

Noemi frowns at the readouts in front of her before glancing over at Abel. "If you didn't want to thank them, why are you so worried about not saying good-bye?"

"Oh." He seems lost for words, which has to be a first. Is he embarrassed? "I realize it's trivial, but I'd hoped to get that file of *Casablanca* again."

She brightens. "Oh! I've got it!"

There's no way to describe the smile on his face except *joyous*. "Really? How?"

"I tucked it into the backpack with the thermomagnetic device before I went to bed that night. So we wouldn't forget it—though I guess I forgot it anyway. Still, it should be in there."

"I get to see it again." Abel's pleasure is so innocent that she can almost forget that they'll have to make time for him to watch it once more before his destruction.

Finally, when they hit a new reset cycle, Noemi realizes she'll have to make like a fragile human and get some more sleep. But one thing about the logistics confuses her. "If I'm in Captain Gee's room, and you're in Mansfield's, and the other bunk room was for the rest of the crew—where did you sleep before?"

"I can regenerate while sitting or standing, as needed. I usually did so in the equipment pod bay." His expression clouds. "After spending thirty years in there, I have no need to return. My fa—my creator's bed is sufficient."

"I guess sleeping's the same as shutting down, for you."

"Not quite. Shutting down is a near-total cessation of all operations. Sleep is more moderate. It allows me to process memory, to still retain some connection to my surroundings, to dream, to—"

"Wait." Noemi halts mid-step. "What did you say?"

"Sleep is more—"

"Did you say you could *dream*?" Her voice slides up a pitch, but she doesn't care if she sounds hysterical. Her heart beats faster, and she stares at Abel as if she'd just discovered him for the first time. When he nods, she says, "Do all mechs dream?"

"No. I think I'm the only one. Even I couldn't dream

275

for the first decade of my existence. During my time in the equipment pod bay, however, some of my neural connections formed new pathways and became more complex."

"What do you dream about?" Please, let it be equations. Numbers. Plain facts. Something that could be explained as mere mathematical data bubbling up within the machine. "Tell me your last dream."

By now Abel looks bewildered, but he obligingly says, "We were on Wayland Station at the time. In the dream, I was back aboard the *Daedalus*, and Mansfield was with me, but so were Harriet and Zayan. In the dream, they all seemed to know one another. We wanted to visit Kismet— to go surfing, I think—but the viewscreen kept warning us about sea monsters. The image I saw was drawn from an old twentieth-century movie called *Creature from the Black Lagoon*, which as filmed is obviously an actor wearing a rubber suit, but in the dream it seemed very real. Mansfield told me not to go to the ocean, but surfing seemed curiously important—"

"Stop." Noemi takes a step back from him. "Just stop."

"Have I done something wrong?"

He has hopes and fears. Likes and dislikes. People he cares about. A sense of humor. He dreams.

Abel has a soul.

24

ABEL STARES AT NOEMI, UNABLE TO INTERPRET HER reactions. She's pale, breathing fast, and so shaken that his first instinct is to ask whether she is in pain.

No, that's not it. By telling her about the dream, he's behaved in a way she did not anticipate. Normally she recovers from such surprises quickly, especially for a human. But it's different now.

Maybe she is both surprised *and* taking ill. Abel finally ventures, "Noemi, are you feeling well?"

"No."

"Should we go to the medical bay?"

"That's not it." She pushes her black hair back from her face. Her stare freezes over until even he can feel the chill. "I've—I've come to realize you're something besides a, a— device, or a machine."

"I appreciate that."

"Do you?" Noemi takes another step away. Her hands

ball into fists at her side. She's not merely surprised; she's angry. *Furious.* "Do you understand? No, of course you don't."

Abel doesn't allow his consternation to show. It is an inexplicable reaction on his part, given that her anger should be irrelevant to him. The misapplication of devotion leads to conflicting impulses. He must try harder to work out the error. "Please explain."

"When I first came aboard this ship, you tried to kill me. You looked me straight in the eyes, you knew I was alone and afraid and trying to save someone else's life, and you still tried to *kill me.*"

He tries, "Noemi, my programming—"

"Your programming doesn't completely control you! I know that now. So you must have decided to look for Mansfield out of pride. Just your stupid arrogance and pride, because he made you feel *special.*"

Abel wants to protest—he didn't know he could disobey his programming until he did—but he suspects it would only stoke her anger. And deep inside, he understands that at least some of what he feels for Mansfield—not all, not even most, but some—has to do with the pride of being Mansfield's best, most cherished creation. Noemi's not entirely wrong.

But his silence infuriates her equally as much as his response would have. "Tell me this, then. That first day, when you were shooting at me—when you saw me cowering on the floor, at your mercy, convinced I was about to be murdered—were you proud of yourself? Of what you really are?"

Abel considers this before giving her the simple truth. "Yes."

Noemi shakes her head, mouth parted, dark eyes welling with tears. She turns from him then, as if she can't bear to look at Abel's face one second longer. When she stalks away, he knows better than to follow. Instead he remains where he is, awkwardly clutching the same tool in his hand, mulling over the ramifications of her statement.

Could he have defied his directives to defend Mansfield by defending the ship? No. Yet telling her this would mean declaring that he is, after all, just a thing.

Better to be hated by Noemi than to be irrelevant to her.

That reaction seems irrational—emotional—and yet Abel knows it to be true. Or maybe he's malfunctioning more badly than he realized.

· · ·

Abel decides to run a ship-wide diagnostic, as long as he's still working. The engine room feels too quiet, the silence almost overpowering.

His reaction is illogical. For three decades, Abel heard not a single sound he didn't make himself. Is he so accustomed to human presence already that he can't do without it for even a day?

But Noemi's not simply out of the room. She's shunning him. Rejecting him absolutely. He doesn't understand why that should hurt so badly, especially given that she will soon be his destroyer.

Abel's resentment about his impending destruction seems to have vanished. He still wants to live, wants it desperately, but he's come to terms with Noemi's plan. He's learned to understand and respect the girl herself. In the beginning, he thought she was reckless and naïve at best. Now Abel knows how courageous she is. How resourceful. Time and again, she's made an intuitive leap that allowed them to escape, to survive.

He has to admire that, even if her world's survival means his death.

That, however, is what most confuses him. He admires Noemi so much...but he shouldn't be able to. His programming calls for him to prioritize Burton Mansfield's health and happiness, to need Mansfield's approval, and to value him over all others.

Instead Abel is now focusing on Noemi Vidal. Important circuits within him must have degenerated after so long without maintenance; he can't think of any other explanation for why he's becoming devoted to the wrong person.

Surely Noemi deserves admiration in a completely

objective sense. Her determination to save Genesis, to keep going after her friend's death, is constant. Her decision to throw herself into an unfamiliar, hostile cosmos on an unknown ship with only a mech at her side—that shows daring. And her willingness to die in the effort is selfless in the extreme.

Burton Mansfield also possesses many fine qualities, but Abel knows his creator would never make so selfless a choice.

When did he develop the capacity to criticize Mansfield?

A warning sensor comes on, blinking yellow—a proximity alert. Immediately it turns red, and Abel realizes something's coming in fast. He turns the visual to the outside cameras in time to see a meteoroid falling toward them at an angle the outcropping won't block. They're going to take a direct hit.

He hits the control for the intra-ship comms. "Brace yourself!" he shouts, following his own advice. If the meteoroid is too large, however, nothing he's done will make any difference; it will punch through the hull, depressurizing the ship so fast that, within seconds, Abel will go inactive and Noemi...Noemi will die.

The impact shakes the entire *Daedalus* so violently Abel can barely remain standing. His tools clatter from their places, rolling and bouncing on the floor. Red lights again shine from the control panels, but none are reporting depressurization—

—yet. But the topmost cone, the tip of the teardrop, has taken damage. If he can't brace it through the integrity field within nine minutes, they'll lose structural integrity. The air will escape, and the heat, and he and Noemi will freeze within minutes of each other.

Correct repair protocols call for Abel to put on an evac suit and scale the hull from the outside. Internal repairs would take more time than they have left. But an external fix will hold the ship for several days, during which a better, more permanent repair can be completed.

But when the crew of the *Daedalus* fled thirty years ago, they took most of the evac suits with them. The closest one that would fit Abel is near sick bay. Running up there, putting on the suit, exiting through one of the air locks, and reaching the repair site would take—approximately ten minutes at top speed.

Therefore, there is only one thing to do.

Abel scoops up the tools he needs and runs for the nearest air lock. As he belts his satchel around him, he swiftly does the math, calculating how long he can remain operational in the near-absolute zero of space if he doesn't wear the evac suit. That temperature destroys anything organic exposed to it. Even things only partly organic, such as Abel himself.

But that destruction is not instant. The cold will not render him inoperable for…6.92 minutes.

For another two to three minutes after that, he will be alive, at least so far as Abel can be said to be alive. However, he will be unable to move or act in any way, including getting back inside the ship. After that period, his biological structures will be too damaged to regenerate, and his mechanical structures will soon follow. He will be as dead as any human, forever.

That means Noemi will not have her mech to save Genesis. For her sake, he's sorry. But also for her sake, he must do this. Those 6.92 minutes will be sufficient for him to complete the repairs and save her. That has to be enough for them both.

He reaches the landing bay air lock and seals it behind him. Then he hits the panel that will begin cycling the air pressure to release him into the void of space. As the atmosphere hisses away, he reaches for magnetic vambraces that will keep him tethered to the *Daedalus* hull. This asteroid's gravity is so slight that, without the vambraces around his forearms, Abel might simply float away into outer space, lost in infinity. Then he grabs a portable force field generator—not nearly strong enough to protect him from the cold for long, but it will keep his organic tissues from boiling upon exposure to space. It clips easily to his belt.

Over the speakers comes Noemi's voice. *"Abel! What are you doing?"*

"The necessary repairs." He pulls on padded work

gloves. They might buy his hands another five to ten seconds of maneuverability.

"You're going out there?" Her words become fainter as the atmosphere continues to cycle out of the room. There's not much air left for sound to travel through. The last thing Abel hears from her is, *"Don't! You can't! You'll be* killed*!"*

She does not hate him enough to want him dead. Abel takes comfort from that.

He is of course programmed to defend a human's life at any costs, including his own existence. But he knows he's not doing this only because of his programming. It seems only fitting that his last act should be his most human.

The air lock spirals open. The cold surrounds Abel, and he pushes himself into the void.

25

NO, NO, NO, PLEASE NO—

Noemi stands alone on the bridge, staring down at the controls that tell her Abel just opened the primary air lock—while he was inside it.

Horror-sick, she switches the main viewer to show her what's going on. The image on the enormous domed screen changes from the nebula-bright asteroid field above them to the side of the ship itself, dully reflecting the rainbow colors of surrounding space. Noemi spots Abel immediately and zooms in to see him skittering up the side, arms and legs at almost unnatural angles, climbing like a spider or some other inhuman thing. Within moments he's reached the damaged tip and set to work.

He's not even wearing an evac suit.

He'll freeze solid. He'll die. He knows that, of course.

If Abel has soul enough to have wronged her, he also has

enough to value his own existence. And yet he has laid it down.

Noemi goes into action. She doesn't think she can accomplish much before Abel finishes the repair. Not that it would do either of them any good if she did, since then they'd both die shortly thereafter. Putting on her own evac suit isn't an option either; that would take more time than Abel has. So how can she save him?

"This is a science vessel," she mutters to herself, frantically searching the bridge controls. "Science vessels launch research satellites. If they launch research satellites, they have to be able to bring them back in again."

There! Next to the equipment pod bay is an extendable manipulator capable of grabbing satellites, pods, or maybe even mechs. It's only about nine meters long, though. Will that be enough to reach Abel?

Noemi sits at the console and holds her hand above its screen. Green beams of light shine upward, illuminating her to the elbow. As the viewscreen shifts to show the manipulator arm extending from the mirrored surface of the *Daedalus*, she can see Abel again. He's still working hard, but his movements have become stiff and choppy. The cold is taking its toll.

She reaches forward with her hand; the computer, reading her movement, pushes the extendable manipulator forward, too. Slowly she curls her arm upward, and slightly to the side.

Abel has almost been immobilized. He can't move his hand to push something in, so he leans forward, using the weight of his shoulder. The red lights around the bridge all simultaneously shift to yellow, and Noemi realizes she's been holding her breath. But he's done it. He fixed the breach. He saved her.

Time to return the favor.

By now Noemi's trembling, but that doesn't matter. The motion doesn't disrupt the sensors on her hand, and the manipulator continues reaching for Abel. *Gently*, she thinks, as if he were a hurt animal she can only approach with the greatest tenderness. She curls her fingers inward, centimeter by centimeter, staring at the viewscreen without even blinking. Abel's pale shape against the darkness seems to burn an outline into her retinas.

He's too far gone to take hold of the extendable manipulator, maybe even incapable of noticing it. Noemi imagines that she can capture him in her warm palm as she keeps tightening her fingers, finally taking hold of him. Then she pulls back quickly, deposits him in the equipment pod bay, then sets the air lock to cycle again as she takes off running.

Faster, she tells herself as she dashes down from the bridge along the ever-widening spiral of the corridor. *You have to go faster*. At this point, it hardly matters when she reaches Abel. Whether she gets to him in two seconds or two years, he'll be repairable or he won't. But she runs her hardest anyway.

The pod bay doors slide open as she runs toward them. As she jumps over the low threshold, Noemi sees Abel lying flat on the floor, staring blankly upward. His arms stretch out on either side of his body, unmoving. "Abel?" She kneels by his side. "Can you hear me?"

No response. His skin hasn't gone pale or turned blue the way a human's would, but the moisture at the edges of his eyelids has frozen into tiny crystals. When she reaches for him, she feels the electric burn of a force field—but this one is low-grade, something she can push through slowly. With great effort, she manages to shut off the device at his belt; the force field's heat vanishes. She pulls off Abel's heavy work gloves, hoping he'll be able to squeeze her hands, but his fingers remain stiff and still. Noemi puts her hand over his chest, looking for a heartbeat, even though she knows that's impossible.

She learned so much about destroying mechs, so little about repairing them.

Noemi does what you're supposed to do for hypothermia victims, what she's always wished she could've done for her parents and her baby brother: She lies down by Abel's side, pillowing her head on his shoulder, and holds him tightly. That's how you bring back people who have nearly frozen to death. You warm them with your own body heat. It's her warmth that will save him, or fail.

Noemi treats him as a person, because she doesn't know what else to do.

The minutes go on. Tears trickle from her eyes. Abel's so cold he's painful to the touch, but she doesn't let go.

Finally, as despair begins to seize her, his finger twitches.

"Abel?" Noemi sits upright and takes his face between her hands. His stare remains blank, and she wonders whether she just imagined the movement. But then he blinks, and she begins to laugh weakly. "You're okay. You're going to be okay."

It's not that simple. More than an hour passes before Abel can even sit upright; some damage has been done. But he remains with her.

"You're still functional, right?" Noemi tries to push back his blond hair, but it's still frozen stiff. Instead she strokes his cheek. "If you need fixing, maybe you can talk me through it."

"Unnecessary." Abel's voice sounds hoarse, almost metallic. "I should be able to restore most primary functions shortly."

"Thank God."

For the next couple of hours they work together. They test his range of movement. They test his memory. Abel can respond every time, sometimes slowly, but always adequately.

"What did you rename our ship?"

"First the *Medusa*, then the *Odysseus*."

"What's the square root of"—Noemi fishes for a truly random number—"eight thousand two hundred and eighteen?"

"To the third decimal place, ninety point six five three. I can provide the full number if desired."

"Three decimal places works," she says as she rubs his hands between her own, allowing friction to provide heat. Though there's not that much friction, really: Abel's hands are surprisingly soft. "What's the first thing I said to you?"

Abel cocks his head, and finally he looks like himself again. "I remember it perfectly, but you almost certainly don't. Therefore, reciting the words cannot serve as a viable test."

"If you're feeling good enough to be smug, you're definitely better." Noemi can't stop smiling. "Does anything feel like it might be broken? Malfunctioning?"

He pauses before saying, "Some inner circuitry I'd already questioned has been damaged further. But my operations are not significantly altered."

What does that mean? Noemi isn't sure, but Abel doesn't dwell on it. Already he's flexing his hands again, affirming his restored agility. It must not be anything worth worrying about.

When he's ready, she slings one of his arms around her shoulder and walks him back through the ship to his quarters—really, Mansfield's quarters, now home to the man's greatest creation. This is the first time Noemi's taken a good look at this room, and she doesn't know whether to admire its beauty or be appalled at the extravagance. A four-poster bed carved of burnished wood stands in the center of the room, covered with a silk coverlet that shimmers emerald. A painting of water lilies, soft and blurry in shades of blue, hangs in an ornate golden frame. A wardrobe, like something out of Victorian times, sits in one corner, and when Noemi looks around inside, she finds a thick, wine-red velvet robe.

She slides this on over Abel's clothes before tucking him in bed. "The more layers, the better," she says.

"Don't worry." Abel's smile is lopsided; he's still thawing. "I'm improving rapidly. I'll still be able to do it."

"To do what?"

He gives her an odd look. "To take the thermomagnetic device into the Gate and destroy it."

Noemi feels as though the floor dropped out from under her, horrified and a little sick. "Wait. You think that's why I saved you?"

"Rationally, it would be a strong motivator."

"Abel, no. You don't get it." Struggling for words, she sits on the edge of the bed. "Don't you remember what I said to you before?"

"That I am responsible for my own actions, and therefore for my own mistakes."

"Not that. Not only that, anyway." Noemi takes a deep breath as she squeezes his cool hands. "If you're responsible for attacking me when I boarded the ship, you're also responsible for protecting me on Wayland Station, and for saving me in the underground river on Cray. For trying to save Esther. For understanding where to bury her. You did all those things for me."

"That is a matter of my programming."

"And you can disregard that programming if you want to badly enough."

"So it seems." He looks lost as he says it. Maybe Abel only just discovered this himself. It doesn't matter when he figured it out, only that it's true. "I have realized that I no longer follow your orders because I have to. I...I do it because I want to."

How can he want that? How can he want to follow her even to oblivion? Noemi's voice shakes as she continues, "Abel—you have a soul. Or something so close to a soul that I can't tell the difference, and I shouldn't even try. And if you have a soul, I can't order you to destroy yourself in the Gate. I can't hurt you, and I won't. No matter what."

Abel's astonishment would make her laugh under any other circumstances. As it is, it's almost painful to see how surprised he is to realize that someone believes his life has value. To realize *she* believes it. "But I attempted to kill you."

"You attacked an enemy soldier who boarded your ship," Noemi admits. "Pretty much anyone would've reacted the way you did. Human or mech. For that, and for Esther, I think…I think mostly I blamed you because you're here to be blamed. I don't blame you at all anymore."

As stiff as he is, he manages to roll onto his side, the better to look her directly in the face. "Whether I have a soul or not can only be a matter of opinion."

She shakes her head. "Nope. It's a matter of faith."

"You must still have doubts."

"The opposite of faith isn't doubt. The opposite of faith is certainty." So the Elder Council always says, reminding people to avoid the cheap platitudes of dogma, to rely only on deep insight. She may be a terrible believer in so many ways—but this lesson, at least, she's finally mastered.

"But Genesis—the Gate, the Masada Run—can you give up so easily?"

"Who said anything about giving up?" She'd begun formulating a new plan within half an hour after her argument with Abel. "You said only an advanced mech could pilot a ship carrying that kind of device through a Gate. A human would die from the heat, and a lower-level mech would shut down. Right?"

"Correct."

Noemi begins ticking her points off on her fingers. "We need an advanced mech. You're an advanced mech, but you're not the only one advanced enough to do this. Some other models could handle it, too, couldn't they? Which ones?"

Abel nods, though he answers her as if in a daze. "Either of the medical models, Tare or Mike. Any Charlie or Queen. Maybe even the caretaker models, Nan and Uncle—"

"See? Lots of possibilities." Her voice sounds too chipper even to her own ears. Noemi's been going over this in her own head, trying to calm herself down, but every second, she expects Abel to point out a new complication or flaw, something that will crush all her hopes. "Like I said, I don't need you to fly the device into the Gate any longer. But I do need you to help me capture a mech that can. One of the ones that's really just a machine. Not like you. You're—more."

Abel seems younger to her somehow, almost childlike in his wonder. "Do you really believe that?"

"Yeah. I do."

He doesn't answer, only pulls the coverlet more tightly around him. He's so cold every scrap of heat must be welcome, so weary he can barely move; Noemi knows how he feels. Ever since Kismet, she's been tired. It seems like sleeping only makes it worse, not better. But there will be time to rest when this is all over. Oceans of time to spend on a free, safe Genesis.

"You realize that capturing a mech isn't easy." Abel can't quit arguing for his own demise. "Even a lower-level one has the strength and will to resist. The smarter ones will prove even more difficult."

"That's where you come in."

"Be serious," he says. "The fate of your world is in your hands."

"It doesn't change the fact that I have your fate in my hands, too. I'm going to take care of Genesis, and I'm going to take care of you. I don't care how hard it is. We're going to make this happen."

"And then—" Abel's voice trails off. "Then what? After it's all over, then what happens?"

Noemi hasn't though this part through in detail, because it's not hers to decide. "After that, you take me home to Genesis, and then you go wherever you want."

"*I* would decide?"

"Yeah. Take the *Daedalus* and go." She zooms her hand up in the air, as if it were the ship, then feels silly for doing so.

But Abel hardly seems to notice. He's still rocked by her suggestion. "You would leave the decision entirely up to me?"

"Yes, exactly." Noemi's heart sinks as she takes in Abel's confusion. It's like he can't wrap his super-genius mind around something as simple as making his own choices. "I guess that's one gift Mansfield never wanted to give you—the chance to determine your own fate."

"You're too quick to blame him." Abel's response comes so readily that she thinks it must be his programming reasserting itself. But the doubt in his eyes tells her he wonders about his own answer. "You were taught that he was wicked, evil, merely for inventing mechs—"

"Don't you understand, Abel? Do you still not get it?" Noemi hopes he'll hear this one basic truth, the one that has changed her plans and her heart. "We were taught that Mansfield was evil because he made soulless machines in the shape of men. But he did something worse than that to you, so much worse." Her voice catches in her throat. "Burton Mansfield's greatest sin was creating a soul and imprisoning it in a machine."

Abel says nothing. No doubt he disagrees. But he seems to understand her at last.

After a long moment, he looks away. Noemi can't meet his eyes again either. Together they've crossed a threshold, and neither of them knows what may lie beyond it.

"Sleep," she says gently. "You have to be exhausted."

"As do you. You must prioritize your own health and well-being."

It's a plea, not an invitation, but Noemi doesn't care. She lies down on the other half of the bed, atop the silk coverlet. Abel hesitates, obviously wondering what else she might do; when she simply lies there, he closes his eyes, passing instantly into sleep.

Noemi shifts herself closer, so her head rests on his shoulder. She still needs to keep him warm.

And for the first time since Esther's death—or maybe in far longer—Noemi no longer feels alone.

26

WITHIN ANOTHER EIGHT HOURS, ABEL HAS RESTORED all primary functions. Some of his organic structures will continue to heal further, but he has full mobility and no pain.

He should be happy, an emotion he has discovered lies well within his parameters of feeling. Noemi saved him from death by freezing and has decided to spare him. She acknowledged him as an equal. And she did something no human ever does for a mech: She set him free.

But Abel was never designed for freedom.

He has never dreamed about it. Never even wanted it. Mechs are made *for* something or someone. Not simply... to be. Even Abel, created from Mansfield's curiosity and hope, was surely meant to stay by his side always.

But when he says as much to Noemi, she disagrees.

"Wait a minute," she says the next afternoon, as they walk together down to the crew mess to grab a pouch of emergency rations before getting back to work. "After this you can go anywhere in the galaxy—do absolutely anything—and you're just returning to Burton Mansfield? I don't understand why you think Mansfield's so great after what he did to you."

"Did *to* me? Mansfield did everything *for* me."

"He put your soul inside a machine—"

"No. He created my soul. He made it possible. He gave that to me." Abel finds himself smiling. "He couldn't have known I'd reach this point, but he must have at least hoped for that. Otherwise he wouldn't have created the capacity."

After a long moment, Noemi folds her arms in grudging agreement. "I guess."

"Which makes him less like my creator and more like a parent." *Father*, he thinks. Mansfield must've known what he was doing when he urged Abel to call him by that name. "Children don't abandon their parents, do they?"

"Not usually. But they don't stay with their parents their whole lives either. In the end, you're supposed to choose a life of your own."

"In the end," Abel says. "I'm not there yet." After thirty years stranded in space, plus several days believing his destruction was imminent, it feels incredible to be able to say such a thing and know it to be true.

However, talking about "the end" has reminded Abel that Burton Mansfield is an elderly man.

After Mansfield dies, then what?

Mechs don't age much in the visible sense. But even mechs die. Both organic and mechanical systems break down, given enough time. Absent damage, a mech can expect to live about two hundred years before grinding to a halt.

If Abel lives another one hundred and fifty years, he will live the vast majority of those without Burton Mansfield. All the programming within him—what use will it serve then? Only one: It will ensure that Abel remains every bit as lonely as he did in that pod bay.

Abel dislikes this conclusion not only because it predicts his future unhappiness, but also because, if he's been designed to suffer so much for so long, Noemi is right. Mansfield has made a terrible mistake.

He won't blame Mansfield. Not yet. But he sees the very real possibility of Mansfield's error.

I have changed, he thinks. *I am changing.*

"Are you okay?" Her smile wavers. "You looked so strange for a second."

"I'm much better," Abel says. In truth he still feels odd—as if he is having trouble concentrating—but no doubt that's a sign of the damage still repairing within. "We should get to work."

"I know. We only have—how many days is it now?"

Until the Masada Run, she means. "Nine days."

Noemi blanches. "I thought we had a couple more days—"

"We're much farther from Kismet here, beyond the Blind Gate. More time will have elapsed on your home-world. The Einsteinian calculations are complex." Once Abel would've added that no human brain could expect to handle such complicated work, but he's learned better. "We still have time."

She shakes her head as she drops to her knees to reopen one of the lower panels. "Not enough."

Abel feels the urgency driving her on as fiercely as if it were his world he needed to save and not hers. Assuming there's a world he could truly call his own.

They get back to work in the small, shining, cube-shaped engine room of the *Daedalus*. Throughout the rest of the ship, curved lines dominate. Beauty and symmetry guide the placement of every panel, every chair. The engine room, however, is as gray, basic, and joyless as it is possible for a room to be, outside of prison facilities. It is a place for installation and repair, nothing more. Yet Abel finds himself liking the room, because here he and Noemi work together as partners. They are no longer adversaries, or human and mech; they are equals. Nobody has ever accepted him that way before, and Abel finds the experience...almost intoxicating.

They work together almost in silence, speaking only about the mechanical elements they're repairing. Noemi's desperation seems to fill the room as surely as heat or perfume. Abel works as fast as he can without completely leaving her behind; their margin of time, while tighter than before, is still adequate—and he knows she needs to be a part of the solution.

But not everything can be rushed. After several hours of effort, they reach a point where the shields have to go through a long round of self-diagnostics. This leaves them with nothing to do for some time to come.

"You will have enough time to sleep a full eight hours," he tells her as they pack up their tools. "Plus exercise, if you desire it."

"I need it, but I can't." Noemi winces as she rubs her temples. "I can't even think right now. I'm so wiped out, but there's no way I could sleep. Every time my mind wanders, I think about the Masada Run, and then—"

"Dwelling on events you cannot yet influence will only discourage you." He considers the possibilities. "Recreation might provide a welcome distraction."

"Recreation?" She leans one shoulder against the wall. "Like what?"

Abel had been speaking in general terms, but now he knows the perfect suggestion. "Would you like to see a movie?"

•   •   •

"If that plane leaves the ground and you're not with him, you'll regret it. Maybe not today, maybe not tomorrow, but soon and for the rest of your life."

As thrilled as Abel is to finally be watching *Casablanca* again in real life, he keeps glancing over at Noemi to gauge her reaction. It's nearly as good as the film itself. She's been rapt since the first few minutes, laughing at all the jokes once he explained the antique references. Now she's completely caught up in the bittersweet ending. All her troubles have slipped into the background for a time; for the moment, at least, he can simply make her happy.

They've turned the junior crew's bunk room into their makeshift theater, each of them curled on parallel beds, the story playing out on the room's one large screen. These movies were known as "black-and-white," but really the images shimmer in a thousand shades of silver.

Rick touches Ilsa's chin, tilting her face gently upward. *"Here's looking at you, kid."* Abel's always liked that part. He wonders what it would feel like, touching someone's face that way.

"That can't be the end," Noemi says, as Ilsa and Victor Laszlo walk toward the plane, leaving Rick behind forever. "That's why she leaves?"

"You don't think she should stay with Laszlo?"

"Of course she has to go fight the Nazis. But...when

does she decide that for herself? Rick's the one who made the decision."

Abel's never considered this before. "It seems she decided while Rick was speaking to her."

With a frown, Noemi scrunches down farther in her bunk. "I wish she'd made the choice on her own."

"You wish she showed greater autonomy. But if she did so, the movie would perhaps suggest that she really hadn't loved Rick at all. That she was only pretending for Laszlo's benefit."

"Good point," Noemi says absently. She's already caught up in seeing which way Captain Renault will turn.

At the end, she applauds, which catches Abel off guard. "You enjoyed it?"

"What? Of course I did. That was amazing." Noemi's smile is warmer than he'd known it could be. "There really is something about 2-D films. You only get the images and sound, but it makes your imagination work harder, doesn't it? So you wind up wrapping the story around you. And the whole idea of her being in love with Rick but not wanting to hurt Victor because he's so heroic and important... it's pretty romantic."

This topic strikes Abel as particularly fascinating. "Have you ever been in love?"

Noemi stares at him, snapped out of her dreamy mood. "Why do you ask?"

"I'm curious about human emotional development and response." For some reason, that makes her laugh. "Did I say something wrong? Is the question too personal?"

"Kinda. But—" She sinks back onto her bunk. "No, I haven't been in love. I thought I was once, but I was wrong."

"How can you be wrong about your own emotions?" Abel finds his feelings confusing, but he's always assumed that was due to their relative newness.

"It felt like love, sometimes. I was crazy about him, wanted to be with him, hoped he'd love me back—all of that. But really I was only in love with my idea of Jemuel. My daydreams of all the romantic times we could spend together, in theory. Not in reality."

"Did he not love you back?" That strikes Abel as unlikely. Noemi is courageous, forthright, intelligent, and kind. These must be desirable qualities in a mate.

"No. We flirted a few times—he even kissed me once—but that's all." Her fingers belie her casual tone, tracing absently along the curved line of her lower lip. "Actually, he wound up falling for Esther. They were right for each other in a way the two of us never would've been."

"None of this correlates with what I know of human behavior in such situations. You experienced no jealousy or anger?"

Her expression clouds. "At first I did. At first I felt like I would die. Just...drop down and die. But I never let Esther see it. That would've devastated her, and she'd have broken up with Jemuel, which would've been stupid because it's not like he would've come to me instead. What's the point? So I kept my mouth shut and pretended I was fine with it until I really was fine. Now when I talk with Jemuel, I can't believe I was ever into him. He's kind of stiff, really."

"But you still sounded wistful, when you spoke of him." Abel finds himself going back to that memory of her . . . her dark eyes searching an unseen distance, her fingers brushing her lip.

Noemi says, "I guess it's just the idea of love I miss. And, well, it *was* a good kiss." Her smile turns rueful. "At least I got some practice."

A wonderful idea occurs to Abel. "Do you need more practice?"

"Huh?"

"We could practice, if you wanted." He smiles as he starts to explain. "Remember what I told you on Genesis? I'm programmed with a wide array of techniques for providing physical pleasure, via every activity from kissing to the more arcane positions for sexual intercourse. Although I've never performed any of them before, I'm confident I could do so very skillfully."

She stares at him, eyes wide. Since she is swift to voice objections if she has them, Abel takes her silence as an encouraging sign.

So he sits up on the bed to explain the further compelling reasons now coming to mind. "Humans need a certain amount of physical release and comfort in order to be psychologically healthy. You've been away from your family and friends for some time, and have endured considerable trauma, suggesting you are in even greater need than usual. I have all the information and technique necessary to be an excellent partner, my body is designed to be appealing, and of course I can neither carry disease nor impregnate you. We have total privacy and many hours of spare time. Conditions for intercourse would seem to be ideal."

Noemi remains statue-still for another moment, then starts to laugh, but her laugh isn't unkind. When she finally looks at him again, her cheeks are flushed. "Abel, I'm, uh—it's nice of you to offer, I guess." She tucks a lock of black hair behind her ear and bites her lower lip before adding, "But I couldn't."

No denying it: Abel feels disappointed. "Why not?"

"Among people of my faith on Genesis, sex is something you save for committed relationships. For people you care about very deeply."

"You'd suggested your culture wasn't as puritanical as Earth claimed."

"It's not. I mean, sex is a natural part of life. A wonderful part. We all understand that. And some of the faiths are a lot more permissive than the Second Catholic Church. But for me, at least, sex should be with someone I love."

"I understand," Abel says, hoping that he does.

She rolls onto her side, toward him, but doesn't look him in the face as she adds, "You couldn't have gotten me pregnant anyway. I mean, nobody could. The explosion that killed the rest of my family—it exposed me to some pretty terrible toxins."

Although Noemi says it evenly, Abel can tell it hurts her deeply, or once did. How can he possibly console her for such a loss?

Finally he settles on, "I feel certain your genetic material would have been of the highest quality."

She laughs again, more weakly this time. He must have said something wrong.

"If I offended you, I apologize. It was intended as a compliment—"

"No, Abel, it's okay. I know what you meant." Noemi glances over at him from where she lies on the bed, bashful and amused, and Abel feels an odd, disarming imbalance—as if merely looking at her throws his perceptions off-kilter. Within another instant, though, she sits up and stretches, breaking his reverie. "I'm still completely exhausted, and now I'm getting a headache. How long before the next diagnostic cycle ends?"

"Seven hours." Since she seems to be indicating a less

intimate mood would be preferred, he gets to his feet. "You can sleep through the night and rejoin me in the morning."

"Shouldn't you sleep, too? You're still healing."

He shakes his head. "I'm back to normal operations. You shouldn't rejoin me until you are, too."

"I thought I gave the orders around here." But she's only teasing him, her earlier embarrassment already fading. Noemi heads out the door toward her own cabin, her steps slow and weary. But she glances over her shoulder to say, "Good night."

"Good night," Abel repeats.

Her departure leaves him feeling restless. He knows she enjoyed *Casablanca*. Their efforts to interact as equals, even as friends, are proving successful. Repairs to the *Daedelus* are progressing smoothly, and they should be able to leave within another ten to twelve hours. So his mood should now be neutral to positive.

Instead he keeps replaying his memory of asking Noemi to have sex. Except in his memory, every time, he says it a little differently—a little better—and wonders if that would've convinced her to say yes.

Abel doesn't experience desire in the same way humans do; Mansfield told him no man ought to be a slave to his own genitalia. But Abel can feel physical pleasure and would expect to during sex. In humans, desire comes before action; for Abel, it should be the other way around. But he's been curious what desire would feel like.

His programming encourages him to seek out new experiences. He failed to have one tonight. That explains his disappointment, then.

No doubt.

• • •

The next morning, Abel remains hard at work in the engine room as he counts away the hours until Noemi is likely to appear. The earliest probable hour passes, as does the most probable—and then, finally, the latest Abel had calculated goes by without one word from her.

Only eight days remain before the Masada Run. Noemi remembers that. She wouldn't let her exhaustion last night cost even one hour that might help her save the people of Genesis.

So Abel contacts her via intra-ship comms. "Noemi? It's Abel." An illogical thing to say, given that no one else could possibly be on board, but humans seem to find it comforting, this repetition of the obvious. "Are you awake?"

After a long pause, she replies, *"Yeah. I just—I don't feel good."*

"You're ill?" He wonders if some of the emergency rations on board had in fact gone bad. The resulting food poisoning should not be fatal, but would cause severe nausea and fever. "Can I help you in any way? Would you like me to bring you water?"

"I think—I think maybe, yeah."

Noemi's voice is hoarse. Worse, she sounds unfocused, dazed. Human beings sometimes talk this way when intoxicated, though there are no inebriants on board and Noemi would be unlikely to overindulge.

Therefore, the only conclusion is that she is in fact very sick.

"I'll be right there," Abel promises. He hurries upward through the spiral corridor. Her room is on the second rotation, but she's not inside. He sees her ahead of him in the corridor, just at the next visible bend—sitting on the floor in her pink T-shirt and leggings, leaning her head against the wall. He drops to his knees by her side. "Noemi, what's happening?"

She looks at him with dull, reddened eyes. "I wanted to go to sick bay. To see if they have something for fever."

Abel places his hand on her forehead. Her temperature is 100.7 Fahrenheit. "Tell me what you're feeling."

"So tired—Abel, I'm *so tired*—"

He scoops her into his arms to carry her to sick bay. As he does so, her oversize T-shirt slips sideways again, exposing her collarbone and part of her shoulder. Her deep tan skin is now marred by thin, crooked white lines. Although Abel has never seen this before, he knows instantly what this has to be:

Cobweb.

27

NOEMI DRIFTS IN AND OUT OF REALITY. SHE TRIES TO focus her thoughts on what's most important, but it's hard, so hard, to do anything but lie there and simmer in her own fever heat.

"You could have called me for assistance," Abel says. He's laid her someplace cool and bright—sick bay. This is sick bay. She's lying on the same bed where Esther died.

"I didn't think I needed to." Her feet are cold. She hates it when her feet are cold. "Not at first. Then it felt like it was too late."

"It wasn't too late." Abel's hand circles her wrist, and his thumb presses down just where the thin latticework of her veins lies closest to the skin. His skin is cool against hers—not because he's a mech, but because she's burning up. "Your pulse is thready. Have you been able to eat or drink?"

Has she? Noemi shakes her head, then stops when it

makes the floor seem to tilt and spin. "Haven't tried in a while."

"You need fluids immediately."

A moment later, a plastic straw pokes at her mouth. Noemi obediently takes a few sips, half opening her eyes to see Abel holding the pouch of…whatever this is. Something blue. It tastes sweet, too sweet, as if it were trying to trick you into drinking it.

When she lets her head fall back again, Abel says, "The medical scanners report a virus unknown to its databanks. The marks on your skin suggest, with a very high level of probability, that you're suffering from Cobweb."

People die of Cobweb. Harriet told Noemi that much. But it doesn't have to be fatal, not necessarily. "I'll get better," she mumbles. "Just need to rest."

"The bioscan readings are…" His voice trails off, but he seems to catch himself. "They aren't good. And you're unusually radioactive."

That jolts her into a moment of clarity. "Radioactive?"

Abel touches her shoulder, which calms her. "All humans naturally emit a very low level of radiation. Yours is significantly higher than normal. Not enough to be dangerous to you or to anyone else on its own, but it's a sign the Cobweb has drastically altered your physical condition. It's a very strange symptom for a virus to have."

Noemi tries to force her fever-maddened brain to think.

"Maybe the radiation isn't a symptom. Maybe it's something we ran into on Cray."

"If it were, then my level of radioactivity would have risen as well. It hasn't. This disease is—it's completely unfamiliar to me. Noemi, I don't know how to help you, and we can't assume you'll recover on your own. We have to get you to a fully staffed medical facility."

"Thought you—you had all the models' knowledge. Tare medical models, too."

"I do. But from thirty years ago, when I was stranded. Cobweb hadn't yet appeared then. So I have no information on optimal treatment or likely prognosis." Abel sounds like he's mad at the whole galaxy for containing even one piece of information he lacks.

"Just try your best."

He shakes his head. "That's not good enough."

Abel just admitted his best might not be good enough? Under any other circumstances, Noemi would've teased him like crazy for that: the arrogant Model One A of the Mansfield Cybernetics line admitting he has limits. Now, though, she has to keep him from doing something so logical it's idiotic. "What else can we do? On Cray or Kismet— we'll be found by the Queen and Charlie. And no one on Genesis can help me." Nobody there will have treated Cobweb either, and she can't bring some terrible plague back to her world.

"Exactly. So we'll go back through the Cray system on our way to Stronghold."

Stronghold? It's the most populated world on the Loop save for Earth itself, a cold, forbidding world heavy with ores. Stronghold is as different from Genesis as it is possible for any world to be. Worse, it's still tightly bound to Earth, still completely loyal...so far as she knows. But that's far enough. "Abel, no. It's going to take too long."

"We still have eight days. That gives us time to get to Stronghold."

"Barely. And we could get caught. It's too dangerous."

"I can disguise the ship, check in with Stronghold's computer networks to see whether our images have been distributed there. If so, I can probably erase them in advance."

"*Probably* isn't good enough."

He's quiet for a few seconds, enough that she thinks the discussion is over. But just as she begins to drift in the fever again, he says, "You said you accepted me as your equal. I'm not under your authority any longer. So I get to vote, too, don't I? And I vote for taking you to a doctor immediately."

Then the vote's a tie, and nobody wins. But as Noemi begins to say so, chills begin shivering their way up her body. Her bones ache as if she were being wrung out like a washcloth. She never, never wants to feel so cold again.

Noemi's willing to die to save Genesis. But she never intended to throw her life away without meaning. If she dies out here, because of this, she dies for no reason.

She swallows hard and nods. "Stronghold."

• • •

Noemi remembers their departure through the Blind Gate as hardly more than a blur of slowly spinning asteroids flecked across the brightly colored wisps of the nebula. When the light starts doing that strange bendy thing, she just closes her eyes.

She lies in sick bay, covered in silvery blankets. Before he left her to pilot the ship, Abel turned down the lights in the hopes Noemi could get some more sleep. She managed a catnap, but now she can only lie on the medical bed, gazing around the room in weary confusion. How can she possibly be so far from home? How is any of this actually happening? Maybe the virus is playing tricks on her, and in reality she's back on Genesis, suffering from some totally normal illness.

But she can't convince herself this is a dream, because her weak, aching body tells her this is all too real. And through the one oval sick bay window, she sees constellations of unfamiliar stars.

"Noemi?" Abel walks into the darkened sick bay, his face illuminated mostly by the glowing readings above her biobed. How long has it been since the leap through the Blind Gate? She drifted off for a while, but can't tell whether she was out for a few minutes or a day. "We'll be in Stronghold orbit within the hour." Closer to the latter then, she realizes, because she's missed another entire Gate leap.

"Okay." Will she be able to walk off the ship herself, or will Abel have to carry her?

"Noemi?" Abel's leaning over her, his thumb brushing her sweat-damp hair from her forehead. Did she drift off again? "I've given you drugs that ought to reduce fever. I'm not sure whether they're contraindicated for Cobweb, but—something needed to be done."

"It's okay." Maybe it is, maybe it isn't. Noemi doesn't particularly care at the moment. There's no way the drug could make her feel worse than she already does. The rest is irrelevant.

"We're landing on Stronghold now."

Something seems very wrong with that. "But—why aren't you flying the ship?"

"Stronghold brings in nearly all incoming ships via tractor beam, even during mass migration waves."

"Mass migration?" The fever must be ebbing some-what; Noemi can focus her mind better now. "What do you mean?"

Abel answers her by activating a small screen on the

wall, which shows a smaller version of what they'd have seen on the bridge—the planet Stronghold.

Its gray, crater-scarred surface makes it look more like a lifeless moon than a habitable world. The thin atmosphere is breathable, but only just, and the black seas that blot the surface are what Stronghold has instead of oceans. Thick, silvery icecaps coat the poles down nearly to what would, on a warmer world, be called the tropics. Factories and mines cover the equator with metal as if they were plates of armor. Even from orbit, she can see how much industrial smoke is being belched out.

"They're using this world up, too," she murmurs, pushing herself up on her elbows. "Poisoning it."

"Not in this case." Abel zooms in on the view, showing her more of the factories. "The planet has to be warmer before it can sustain more than three hundred million humans—very nearly the current population. So they're intentionally releasing greenhouse gases as part of an effort to terraform Stronghold into a more habitable world."

Noemi had never considered that before, that one world's poison might be another's salvation.

Stronghold looks as terrifying as any world possibly could, and yet it's also her best chance of getting well. Going on with her mission. Saving Genesis.

Seven days. The fever can't rob her of this knowledge, this deadline that eats at her every second. *Seven days.*

The ring around the planet confuses her at first—in school, nobody ever taught them that Stronghold had a ring. Her eyes widen as she recognizes what she's actually seeing: a gigantic swarm of ships, mostly large industrial freighters, gathered like chickens at feed—each one of which must carry dozens if not hundreds of humans. This fleet dwarfs the cluster of ships they saw at Kismet; even more ominous, these ships show none of the Vagabonds' imagination and spirit. No brilliant paint designs brighten the hulls of these square metal ships. They float in formations as rigid and regular as honeycombs, waiting and watching for the decision that will make the difference between life and death for everyone on board.

Then the screen shimmers into the planetary greeting. Triumphal music begins to play as a prerecorded image superimposes itself over the star field: Two black flags, each with a thin silver stripe down the middle, flutter on either side of an enormous granite building with massive columns in front.

"*This is Stronghold*," says an announcer with a deep, purposeful voice. "*Here, we mine the metals and minerals Earth and the other colony worlds need to survive. We train to serve in Earth's armies with dignity and courage. And we work to reshape our planet into humanity's next home. Someday our planet will stand at the center of the galaxy. Are you strong enough to stand with us?*"

"That's a pretty intense sales pitch if people have nowhere else to go," Noemi says as the music swells over images of brawny miners who look far too clean, then military recruits running up a black-earthed mountain.

"I don't think it's a sales pitch," Abel says. "I think it's a warning that some people will be turned away."

Nowhere in the prerecorded greeting does Noemi glimpse any elderly people or children. No one using walking or visual assistance. Maybe that's just the glossy sheen of propaganda, but maybe not.

A world with no place for mercy and kindness, a world where there's only one rigid, narrow way to be—is that really the only choice people from Earth have left?

• • •

The anti-fever drug Abel gave her buys Noemi almost half an hour of lucidity. She uses it to take a sonic shower and change into a simple olive-green jumpsuit. The pajamas are all sweaty; the thought of putting them against her body again grosses her out.

The ship shudders around them as the tractor beam tows them into the planetary atmosphere, toward Stronghold's stark, rocky surface. As they're pulled in an arc toward the landing base, Noemi sees more and more ships clustered nearby, coming in for landing as well.

"These people are going to check our info pretty

closely," Noemi warns as she sinks into one of the sick bay chairs. She'll be back in a hospital bed soon enough. "This doesn't look like a place where they let things slide."

"Our ship ID has held up so far." Abel tries not to look too proud of his forgery skills, and fails.

"Who are we this time?"

"The *Apollo*. For the Greek god of healing, among other things."

He named the ship after a deity with the power to make her well. Noemi suddenly feels as though she might cry—

—but that's the fever coming back. She gets emotional when she's sick. Uncomfortable with her own reaction, she says, "We should've told them that I have Cobweb. Before we landed. They'll be angry when they realize we lied. I can't walk out there and expose everyone else—"

"It's all right." Abel speaks as gently as he might to a frightened child. Why does her voice have to shake? Noemi hates appearing weak nearly as much as she hates feeling weak. "I reported your condition. We'll be met at the landing pad by a medical team."

"They know? Then why are they letting us land?" Stronghold doesn't come across as an oasis of mercy.

"Stronghold wants young people." Abel pauses. "I listed myself as nineteen, since that is closest to the age I currently appear to be. They give preferential treatment to those who come here under their own power, with their own independent resources. And, ah, they very much want couples who seem likely to bear children."

"Wait. What?"

No denying it: Abel looks sheepish. "When I determined the criteria most likely to win us landing clearance, I listed us as a young husband and wife. Did I do the wrong thing?"

"But if the doctors figure out I can't—"

"What you described is unlikely to show up on regular scans. And you'll be in the hospital. They'll be helping you. Nothing else matters."

Noemi imagines these enemy doctors prodding at her—judging her, weighing the value of her life—but knows there's nowhere else to turn.

The *Daedalus* settles onto the ground with a soft thump. She stands up—or tries to, because the floor seems to tilt beneath her. When she wavers, Abel steps closer, catching her in his arms. Noemi remembers his offer after *Casablanca*—the hopeful, gentle look in his eyes as he asked her to come to bed—and feels awkward about being this close to him....

No. That's not right. She feels like it should be awkward, but it isn't. Leaning on Abel feels completely natural.

"Lie down," he says, easing her back onto the biobed. "The medical team will board our ship. It's safest that way."

"I need to see it. Stronghold. I have to see what's happening." She's not sure why. She only knows that she's confused and afraid, and she can't stand not knowing exactly where they are.

Abel doesn't point out that she's being irrational. Instead he goes to the small wall screen. The grayness flickers back into light and motion, showing what surrounds them.

If Stronghold looked terrifying from space, its surface is even worse.

The sky seems to hang low and cloudless, the same color as the stony ground. Passengers alight from other vessels, but there are no shouted greetings, no music, like with the Vagabonds. They aren't being welcomed; they're being herded along the tarmac toward the large granite building from the planetary welcome greeting, or one very like it. Most people are dressed in somber colors like Noemi and Abel, and their expressions are fixed and brittle. She sees some children, at least. But none are very small, and none are being carried or comforted by their parents. They've clearly been coached to be on their best behavior, and to stand up straight. One little boy in a putty-colored smock even puffs out his chest, so he'll look as big and strong as he can. It would be funny at home. Here, the fear behind that gesture pierces Noemi's heart like an arrow. Once again, she thinks she might cry.

"Noemi?" Abel brushes her hair back from her forehead. "The medical team's here. I need to let them in."

"The ship's plaque," she whispers. "Don't let them see it. They can't know who we really are."

"It's all right. I'll hide it. Shhh. Rest."

She tries to, closing her eyes. But she's vividly aware of when Abel leaves sick bay. Everything feels so empty, so scary, so cold.

But within only a minute or two, she hears footsteps thumping in the corridor.

The strangers walk in—a doctor, she thinks, and a George mech, Abel right behind them.

A man in his mid-twenties, wearing a medical coat, comes up to her. He has dark brown skin and eyes, and his voice is gentle as he says, "I'm going to touch your neck to feel your pulse, all right?" She manages to nod, and she feels his fingers press down on the jugular vein. His expression goes from worried to deeply troubled. He turns to the George and says, "This one has to go to Medstation Central. Get us an emergency hovercraft, right away."

The George pauses. "Single cases can often be treated aboard their own vessels."

"This one can't. You tell them Dr. Ephraim Dunaway ordered a hover, now." As the George scurries off, Dunaway turns back and speaks to Abel, not to her. "Don't worry. I'm going to take good care of your wife."

Wife? I'm a wife? Oh, right. Noemi recognizes the disorder in her mind, but wonders how much longer she'll be able to. If her fever spikes higher, she'll probably start seeing things. Hallucinating. Losing all control.

Abel's voice seems to come from very far away. "You seem to be deviating from standard medical procedure."

Ephraim Dunaway is even more distant. "Yeah, because we're dealing with an emergency situation here. Are you worried about the money? Don't be—it's not like Earth here, you get the treatment you need."

"It merely strikes me as unusual that you would take a step more likely to expose others to Cobweb."

"We know what we're doing here, all right?" Dunaway's a shadow by her side, no more. He turns his attention back to her as he murmurs, "Relax. We're going to check you both out, top to bottom."

Noemi tugs at Abel's shirt, as close as she can come to protesting without saying a word. This won't be a cursory once-over like they had on Wayland Station; the kinds of tests they're about to run will surely reveal Abel to be a mech. And then they'll be captured—

The emergency vehicle he called for might not take them to a hospital—but to prison.

Or is that paranoia, born of her fever? She can't tell.

When Abel scoops her up in his arms, Noemi doesn't struggle. Nor does she resist it when Dunaway slides a paper mask over her nose and mouth. The winding trip down the corridor feels like one long, slow spin until they walk out onto Stronghold's surface for the first time. She's caught off guard by the thinness in the air, which leaves her gasping as if she had climbed a mountain. Or is that Cobweb stealing her breath? Abel pulls her a little closer, and she lets her heavy, aching head droop onto his shoulder.

Don't think about it, she tells herself, as if not dwelling on the potentially fatal illness will make the symptoms go away. *Think about something else. Anything.*

But there's no escaping the terrible knowledge of her body's weakness. "I feel like I can't move," she whispers.

"That may only be Stronghold's gravity. It's slightly stronger than on Earth or Genesis."

"I don't think so."

Abel doesn't waste time trying to reassure her. Instead he effortlessly settles her onto the waiting gurney.

If he were human, Noemi would feel guilty about the weight. But she can let go now. She doesn't have to feel bad about causing problems, for needing too much. Abel could hold her forever.

The fever closes around her again, like the spine-toothed petals of a Venus flytrap. But it's stronger now, as though angry the drugs cheated it of one wretched hour.

She feels as if she might lose consciousness any moment—and if she falls asleep now, she might never wake again.

28

DURING THE SWIFT RIDE ACROSS STRONGHOLD'S BAR-
ren gray terrain, distant cities of metal and stone no more
than shadows on the horizon, Abel had calculated that the
probability Dr. Ephraim Dunaway was acting purely out of
medical necessity was no higher than 32.4 percent.

Now they're at the medical center, an isolated dome
of concrete. Noemi is being wheeled into an examination
room, with Abel at her side. A Tare model waits for them
both, medscanner in hand.

Abel has readjusted his estimate. He now believes there
is only a 27.1 percent chance that Dr. Dunaway is acting
out of pure necessity.

He's attentive, yes—but too attentive, as though he
had to get every reading or measurement he could while
they were still inside the medtram hovering just above the
rocky surface. Also, Abel notices, Dunaway inputs every
piece of data twice: once in what looks like the standard

equipment, once into a personal handheld device. There is no rational explanation for this that does not ascribe another, unknown agenda to Dunaway's behavior.

For the time being, however, Noemi is being adequately seen to, and that must be enough.

Once she's lying in her clinical bed, she's wrapped in silvery blankets and temperature monitors are stuck to the insides of her wrists. The Tare model goes to her, then frowns. "I would have run the first in-depth scan, Dr. Dunaway. Your readings on the medtram could have been compromised."

"But they weren't." Ephraim Dunaway remains beside Noemi's bed, carefully checking the thin white lacy marks spreading across her shoulder and throat. "This patient's seriously ill. I didn't want to waste time."

"Following established procedures is not a waste of time," the Tare says, but there's no emotion behind the words. She walks across the sterile white cube of the examination room toward Abel. "You report no ill health at this time, but Cobweb becomes contagious hours or days before symptoms are apparent. You will require a full exam."

From her bed, Noemi groans. "No—Abel, don't—"

"It's all right," Abel says. But she's supposed to be his wife. He should use an endearment. So he chooses one of Humphrey Bogart's favorites: "Honey."

With a gesture, the Tare model urges Abel to sit down

on the room's other medical bed. "We should begin," she says. He takes his place, and when the Tare brings out her light he obediently holds his eyes open wide, like any other patient.

Unlike any other patient, he configures the components in his eyes to project back to the Tare model exactly what she'd expect to see in a healthy human. He has a pulse, though it's normally undetectable by touch, so a quick increase in his blood pressure is called for as she holds her fingers to his neck. When she goes to measure the blood pressure itself, however, he takes it down to roughly what she'd be expecting. For diagnostic ease, mech veins line the inner arm, just where draws are always taken. His blood will look normal and test negative for viruses; his skin is stronger, but not so much that it draws the Tare's attention as she takes his sample.

He doesn't have to do anything with the ears. Those look just like a human's.

If she were running high-level diagnostic tests, Abel's masquerade would break down within seconds. But Tare models, intelligent as they are, have all been programmed for efficiency and triage. She won't waste time performing in-depth tests on what appears to be a completely healthy human male.

"Open your mouth," the Tare says as she approaches with a swab. Abel does so, although this is the only one of her tests he'll fail. His DNA is partially artificial, which means it won't culture at all—though that on its own is most likely to be written off as a storage error. Genetic anomalies *will* show up, but the single-minded Tare will probably write those off as irrelevant and fail to investigate more deeply.

Noemi stares at him, wide-eyed, so astonished it's funny. Later he'll tell her how he accomplished all this. Maybe it will make her laugh. For now she sinks down onto her pillow with a deep sigh of relief. Abel realizes she had been frightened for him—well, for them both, since his exposure would also have threatened her. Nevertheless, it's pleasant to see her being concerned. No one has been concerned about him in a very long time.

Not since Mansfield...who put considerable energy into making sure Abel couldn't be detected as a mech if he didn't so choose. It's an odd utility to have; no other mechs can do it. Maybe Mansfield was only curious to see if it could be done.

"You'll have to remain here, under observation," the Tare says to Abel as she turns back to prepping Noemi's tests, to see that they're already laid out for her. She frowns at young Dr. Dunaway, who seems to have violated procedures again. "In twenty-five hours, if your culture is negative and you've showed no symptoms, you'll be sent into T and E."

"What's that?" Noemi's voice has become hoarse.

"Training and evaluation." Ephraim Dunaway moves a step backward as the Tare finally takes over Noemi's examination. "Everybody goes through it when they first get to Stronghold. They figure out what you're good at, let you know what kind of work you're eligible to do here."

"What about the children we saw on the tarmac?" Noemi says. "What about them?"

Surprisingly, the Tare answers this one. "If they're physically fit to live on Stronghold, they may remain. They're given simpler and lighter work assignments until they're ready for adult labor."

Abel doubts many assignments on Stronghold count as simple or light.

Dunaway adds, "Once we've cleared him, Abel can go on ahead in a day, and you can follow as soon as you're well."

Is Dunaway's confidence based on Noemi's condition, or is he faking it to provide comfort to the patient? *Probably the latter*, Abel thinks.

The Tare concludes her examination with a firm nod. "Cobweb, tertiary stage, not irreversible but serious. Standard antiviral treatments are the only measure available."

Ephraim Dunaway nods as he pulls out vials of what must be antiviral drugs. Abel takes some comfort in the fact that finally Noemi is receiving meaningful help.

"I should lock this room down for quarantine for both the patient and the exposed individual," the Tare says.

But Dunaway interjects, "There are other patients you should see to. I'll take care of locking down the room." The Tare frowns, obviously confused by another change from standard procedure.

Abel decides that a human husband would ask more questions. "You haven't told me how long Noemi will take to recover. What is her prognosis?"

"Recovery from Cobweb is not guaranteed," the Tare reports, as easily as she might recite someone's blood type.

Ephraim interjects, "Hey. We've got a strong young woman here, nowhere near as sick as some Cobweb cases we've seen. No need to worry about the worst-case scenario, okay?" He smiles at Noemi and Abel in turn. "I'm going to look after her personally. I promise."

Abel believes him, but again he senses that Dunaway has...uncertain priorities.

The Tare tilts her head. Abel notes the slight tug-of-war between mech and human. Maybe he should be on the mech's side, but Ephraim Dunaway—regardless of what other intentions he may have—remains the one who cares whether Noemi lives or dies.

If Abel ever gets the chance to speak with Burton Mansfield again, he'll ask whether the Tare models couldn't use a compassion upgrade. A tact upgrade would also be advisable.

Noemi holds out her hand to Abel. She's acting the part

of a loving wife, even as she lies there racked with fever, her skin pale and her gaze unfocused. "You're staying here?"

"Yes. Right here," Abel promises. "Right by your side."

He doesn't want to be anywhere else. After spending three decades utterly alone, he's been with Noemi during virtually all her waking moments the past several days. Even when they had disliked each other, even when she had treated him as a hostile, he has feasted on the experience of being with a person once more, someone who spoke words he'd never heard, did things he'd never witnessed. That, by itself, had been a luxury he would never take for granted again. She set him free.

But she isn't just a human who happened along to open the pod bay doors. Noemi is the only person he's truly been close to besides Mansfield. Abel never expected to feel so attached to anyone else. He knows it's partly a trick of his programming, seeking a source for all the devotion he can't give to his creator.

But only partly.

"You need to rest," Ephraim says to her. "I'm going to give you a light sedative, okay? The more you can sleep, the more your body can do its job of getting you well."

Noemi doesn't care for the idea of being drugged, Abel can tell. But she nods. She must feel even worse than she looks.

As Ephraim readies the sedative, she says, "Abel—what

we talked about, when we first set out—" Her deep brown eyes search his. "You know how to finish up without me. You would, right?"

Once she gave him orders to destroy the Genesis Gate after her death, if necessary. Now she's asking him as her equal.

"I would," Abel confirms, squeezing her hand. "But I won't have to. You'll recover soon."

Would a husband kiss his wife before she went to sleep? Just as Abel decides he would, Noemi's eyelids drift shut, and her head lolls to one side.

Ephraim takes Abel's arm. "Come on. You ought to rest, too. I know you're worried about her, but you've been exposed to Cobweb, too. This is no time to run yourself ragged."

"Yes, of course." But Abel looks back over his shoulder at Noemi even as Ephraim helps him into his own bed.

"It's going to be okay." Ephraim moves differently now that the Tare model has left the examination room—his strides are longer, his voice firmer. His posture has shifted so that he stands taller. "The Tare models aren't exactly comforting, but they know their stuff. Besides, I'm on the case, too. Noemi's going to get the best care."

Abel isn't sure why this young doctor would be so committed to Noemi's well-being only minutes after meeting her, but humans often do things for illogical reasons. He decides the motivation doesn't matter nearly as much as the fact that someone with the correct training and access will be working hard to make Noemi well.

But he will, in the end, discover this man's true motives. If Noemi's recovery stalls for any reason—if even one drug she's given seems inappropriate—Ephraim Dunaway and all the rest will learn exactly what Abel's capable of.

"I realize it's pretty dull in here." Ephraim shrugs sadly at the bare-bones room. "No vids, no books, but hey, at least you can sleep. Basic toiletries are in this box if you need them, that door leads to the toilet, and this is the assistance panel—push it if you feel the slightest bit sick." This is punctuated with a tap on a square panel within arm's reach of the bed. "We'd rather respond to a false alarm than miss the chance to intervene early in a Cobweb case, okay?"

"Understood."

Ephraim nods. His attention is now drifting from the present moment. Something more important lies ahead. "All right. I'll drop by later to check in on Noemi."

"Thank you," Abel says, not meaning it. He will be able to assess the changes in Noemi's medical readouts for himself. Ephraim Dunaway turns out the overhead lights as he leaves. Now Abel and Noemi are alone again, illuminated by the faint green glow of the readouts above her bed. Her breathing is deep and even; Abel takes what comfort he can from this.

If he doesn't fall into a recursive loop of worrying about Noemi, he can turn his primary mental functions to a more useful purpose, namely, coming up with a plan of action they can execute upon her recovery. If she gets better within the next few days, they'll have time to carry out her plan, preventing the Masada Run and destroying the Gate. But their margin of safety grows narrower by the day. He should plan and prepare as much as possible so he and Noemi can get started immediately.

He closes his eyes and envisions the layout of the landing bay and the spaceport, the course taken by the medtram to the hospital. It's a partial blueprint only, but sufficient for him to get Noemi back to the *Daedalus*, which is the most important thing.

Next, he needs to figure out how to capture a mech.

Abel feels no inner conflict about this. He knows there's an enormous gap between his mental complexity and the duller circuits of any other mech model in existence; Mansfield explained it thoroughly, and Abel's own efforts to speak with other mechs proved it true. An advanced mech can and should be obtained. The Queens and Charlies he's glimpsed on Stronghold so far clearly serve as military police. They're found in groups and carry blasters as sidearms. A Tare model, however—smart enough, but with no combat capabilities, its strength level only comparable to that of a human—

Abel catches himself. He's not just thinking through his orders so he can do what Noemi wishes. He actually *wants* to destroy the Genesis Gate.

The main reason he wants to help her is because he thinks she's right.

Mansfield would not have agreed with that, but—Abel begins to smile as he realizes it—he doesn't agree with Mansfield. He can be completely loyal and devoted to his creator and yet have different opinions. Is this what it means to have a soul? To be a person and not a thing?

Maybe it is.

• • •

Abel stands in the Daedalus's *docking bay with the thermo-magnetic device in his hands. He looks down in the small, silvery starfighter that's about to sail toward the Genesis Gate.*

"I shouldn't be doing this," Mansfield says. He sits in the fighter, not making any move to get out, and yet there's no mistaking how badly he wants out. "I shouldn't be here at all."

"You can do anything." Abel hands over the device. "You'll make it through and destroy the Gate."

"But if the Gate's destroyed, how will we get home?" Mansfield reaches up to Abel with one hand, a gesture so plaintive that it makes Abel doubt himself. Maybe someone else could fly the fighter.

"There's no one else," says the Queen. She stands in front

of the door; behind it, Abel can hear Noemi yelling and pounding to get in.

The bay doors spiral open, revealing space beyond it. But they're not next to the Gate; they're in front of Kismet's blue sun. Abel wonders if he should look for Esther there. If he could find her, he could bring her home to Noemi.

Then he realizes his hands are covered with blood, just like they were when he carried Esther to sick bay in the first place, which reminds him that Esther's dead—

He jolts awake.

Abel is always somewhat surprised by his dreams—it's a kind of input he's not designed to process. Dream logic bears little resemblance to reality; he knows that much. But what would Freudian analysis make of the dreams of a mech?

He lies on his bunk in the dark for a long time after that. His memory keeps going back to the hurt on Mansfield's face, and Abel's cruelty in sending him out into the Gate. How could he have turned against his creator, even in a dream?

29

NOEMI STANDS ON THE BRIDGE OF THE DAEDALUS, *screaming. With fear, with rage, with horror—every reason a human being can scream, all of it's pent up in her and coming out in one anguished howl.*

On the viewscreen is Genesis, or what's left of it.

The bombing has turned their green continents gray. Mud-colored seas shrivel and evaporate before her eyes. Every city is gone, every church, every person. Earth has destroyed her world, and now they all have to die together.

"It's not too late," Abel says. "We'll go back in time and stop it."

"We can't go back in time."

"I can. Mansfield gave me that power."

"Really?" She brightens. They can go back and save Genesis—or further, to before her family was killed—no, even further. They'll save Earth, go back and fix things there. They can save humanity itself.

Abel opens his chest like a computer panel and pulls out a smooth, asymmetrical chunk of red glass. Somehow she knows this is what will send them back in time. But Abel goes limp and slumps against the wall. Only then does she realize this is his heart, or his power, something he needs to live. He's broken himself for her.

"No, Abel, don't." Noemi tries to shake him, but his eyes are closed, and maybe he's dead—now she'll have to bury him in a star—

"Noemi?"

She awakens at the moment the dream would've gone from disturbing to nightmare. Noemi takes a deep breath and lets the images slip away. Even the scariest dreams fade quickly if she refuses to think about them during her first waking moments.

"Are you all right?" It's Abel, lying a few meters away in a medical bed, although he isn't hooked up to electronic monitors like she is. "You seemed to be experiencing disturbing REM sleep."

"I was." She needs to stare at him for a few long seconds, to see him whole once more. "It's okay."

"You appear to be much improved."

The medical sensors beep and glow above her—no wonder she had weird dreams. She can't interpret whatever data they're sending, but it doesn't matter, because Noemi feels better. *So much* better, all the way down to her marrow. Her fever has broken, and the itchy white lines on her skin have faded almost to invisibility. Earth's scientists must have gotten further along in fighting Cobweb than she'd realized. Harriet made it sound so dangerous, but probably Vagabonds don't get the latest medical news.

"I feel almost normal." She begins to smile as she looks over at Abel, who smiles back. It's weird how ordinary it seems to wake up near him now, when that first morning on Wayland Station was so incredibly strange. "Just tired, and a little hungry."

"Should I summon someone to bring meals?" Abel sits upright, clearly eager for something to do. He seems more dedicated to serving her now than he was when he had to. "Or perhaps there's something in this room. Juice, or a nutrition bar—"

The air seal around the door hisses as it swings open, and the Tare model and Dr. Dunaway walk back in, each clad in white coats. Noemi's memories of Ephraim Dunaway are blurry, but she remembers his gentle brown eyes and the sureness of his hands.

"Good morning," says the Tare model. She snaps on the overhead lights, leaving Noemi squinting; Abel, taking the hint, shields his eyes with his hand. "Your condition has improved substantially."

"I can tell." Noemi props up on her elbows. How much longer will she and Abel be stuck on Stronghold? They're under quarantine for twenty-five hours, and she doesn't think more than ten of those have passed. At least she and Abel can get back to the mission right away.

Or can they? Has their ship been put under quarantine, too? Landing on Stronghold is strictly regulated; takeoffs might be as well.

We can do this, she reminds herself, looking over at Abel. It feels natural to use *we*. They're in this together now. She remembers how tenderly he cared for her when she was sick and marvels at how strange and yet wonderful it is to trust someone that much.

But they're not even out of the hospital yet. "The speed of your recovery is irregular." The Tare model frowns, like good news that doesn't match the expected data set is more of an annoyance than a reason to celebrate. "We should run further tests to determine the reasons for your swift response to the drugs."

So it's not that Cobweb is less scary; it's that Noemi kicked it fast. The reason's irrelevant, in the end. All that matters is that she and Abel get out of here soon.

"And Abel? Um, my husband?" *Please let them not have noticed anything, please.* She glances over at him and sees the moment when he realizes he needs to act concerned about his health. He fakes it so well she has to struggle not to laugh.

The Tare never looks away from the readouts, never once makes eye contact with her patients. "His culture came back perfectly normal, and he's shown no signs of infection. Assuming his condition does not change, you will both be released from quarantine in another fifteen hours. We'll get your additional tests under way as soon as possible. The sooner you and your husband can complete processing, the better."

"Thanks." Noemi doesn't quite understand how Abel's culture could have come out fine, and from the way he's frowning, she can tell he's confused by that, too. Shouldn't a tissue sample from a mech be sterile? Unable to create life? Maybe the dish got contaminated.

The Tare nods toward Ephraim. "Dr. Dunaway, I will undertake the necessary lab work while you complete rounds."

"No, no. You do the rounds. I'll take care of this." Ephraim's broad hands go to Noemi's medical sensors, and he smiles until the moment the Tare leaves the room. Then he starts yanking them off her, so fast and hard it hurts.

"Ow!" Noemi yelps. "What are you doing?"

"This is not correct procedure." Abel's instantly on his feet. He crosses the room in a few steps to stand on the other side of Noemi, as if he's going to bodily pull her away from Ephraim. "Your behavior has been aberrant from the beginning—"

"Oh, yeah, you two are calling *me* aberrant." Ephraim keeps going, rapidly freeing Noemi from the final sensor.

He looks down at Noemi so intently that she's reminded of Captain Baz. "You have to get off-planet as fast as you can. You *and* your husband. Which is why I'm getting you both out of this hospital, now."

"What do you mean?" Noemi demands as she sits upright. She still feels a little woozy, but compared to the terrible fever yesterday, this is nothing. "Where are you taking us?"

"To your ship." The satchel he walked in with seemed like an ordinary bag, but now he unzips it to reveal a few thin black hyperwarm jackets. He tosses two toward her and Abel, then begins shrugging the third on himself. "I brought some of the strongest sedatives we've got outside lock and key. When you guys are off-planet again, I'll drug myself and tell them you were responsible."

"Stop!" Noemi hops off the gurney. "Can you explain exactly why you're framing us for a crime?"

Abel's eyes narrow, his anger intensely human as he says, "We can't engage in criminal activity based on the suggestion of someone who hasn't been wholly honest about his intentions."

"And now you have the nerve to call me dishonest. Unbelievable." As obviously annoyed as Ephraim is, he continues preparing to smuggle them out of the hospital.

Yet Noemi believes Ephraim is doing this for their own good—or, at least, what he thinks is their own good.

She ventures, "Is this—is this about Abel?" If Stronghold's authorities figured out what he is, would they want to keep him for themselves? Is that what Ephraim's trying to save them from?

Ephraim shakes his head. "It would be about him, too, I bet, if his blood test hadn't come out so strange. As it is, it's only about you."

"That's not an explanation." Abel's voice has become firmer. Almost defiant.

Ephraim looks nearly as irritated as she feels. "You two know the reason. Why are you pretending you don't?"

Noemi says, "Could you just say, in plain words, what—"

She falls silent as Ephraim steps closer and points at her to emphasize every word. "You. Are. From. *Genesis.*"

A wave of dizziness washes through her, but Noemi grabs the edge of the bed to remain upright; Abel's hand closes around her upper arm, supporting her for the second it takes to regain balance. This is no time to lose control. She and Abel exchange glances. Should they deny it? No, there's no point. She says only, "How did you know?"

"Your medical results." Ephraim zips up his jacket. "Your lungs are almost completely free from contaminants. So is your blood. We don't see that anymore. Either you were cloned in a lab or you're from Genesis, but your genetic structures are too stable to be a clone. Plus, you responded to those antiviral drugs so fast it's obvious you've never built up any resistance. Most people run the gamut of all the antiviral meds we have while they're still kids. So, Genesis."

Noemi's gut tightens. "There weren't going to be other tests, were there? Was the Tare sending me to—to interrogation, or prison, or—"

"The tests were real. They haven't caught on yet." Ephraim goes to a monitor—checking the hallway, she realizes, to make sure no one's coming. "See, a Tare model's programmed to deal with illness or injury. It would never occur to one of them that someone might be *too healthy*."

"Of course," Abel says. His face reflects the confused wonder she's seen in him before when humans glimpsed something no mech ever could.

Ephraim continues, "But when we ran the next battery of tests, those results would go to our ward supervisor, who's human. Chances are she'd put it together as quickly as I did, then order testing on your hubby here, too. If his test hadn't been contaminated, I bet it would show the same results, wouldn't it?"

Abel says only, "Don't be so sure."

Running one hand over his close-shorn hair, Ephraim takes a deep breath. Noemi hadn't realized how worried he is until now, as she sees him steadying himself. "So you don't go for those tests. You guys get off-world before the authorities here realize they've got traitors in their midst."

The word *traitors* stings. "If that's what you think of us, then why are you helping me?" Noemi demands.

"Do I have to tell you my whole life story?"

She folds her arms in front of her chest. "If you want me to go against orders and agree to be set up for a crime, yeah, actually, you do."

Taken aback, Ephraim holds up both his hands. "Hey, this isn't any kind of trap or anything."

Abel raises an eyebrow. "Convince us."

"We don't have that long!" Ephraim protests.

Noemi thinks this guy is being honest—but she can't afford to go on her gut alone. "Then you'd better talk fast."

Ephraim stands still for a few seconds, long enough that she thinks he might confess his real plan or call for security. When he speaks, though, his voice is low and grave. "Thirty years ago, my mother served on a medical ship in Earth's fleet. Her ship was shot down during one of the worst battles of the war. Mom was the only survivor of that crash on Genesis—and she was six months pregnant with my big brother. So she was stranded. Helpless. Scared she was going to miscarry in the wreckage or in prison. But then some people from Genesis found the wreck. They'd been told to report any military survivors, but they took pity on Mom. Showed her mercy. They got her to a nearby house where a nurse could make sure the pregnancy was okay. After that, they helped her detach a hoverpod from the wreckage, and with that she was able to get into low orbit around Genesis and call for rescue. They said it was what their gods would want them to do." His dark eyes focus on Noemi's with uncanny intensity. "I don't like what your world has done to this galaxy. I don't see how you can be merciful to an individual but tell all of humanity to go straight to hell. But my whole life, I've always known I owe you. I owe Genesis for my mother's life, for my brother's, and for my own. The minute I figured out where you were from, I knew I finally had a chance to pay that debt. So I'm paying it."

Noemi's come to second-guess so much about Genesis on this mission—but she remembers what her world can be at its best. "Thank you."

Ephraim gestures toward the hyperwarm jackets. "You can thank me by putting those on already! We need to move."

She and Abel exchange a look. Abel still seems wary, but when she reaches for her jacket, he follows suit.

Fever blurred her memories of arriving at the hospital. Everything after the landing pad is nothing but whirling confusion. Noemi feels as if she's only now about to see Stronghold for the first time. The hospital corridor looks ordinary enough; so does the service area Ephraim rushes them into.

But going outside is worse.

As they walk out into the cold air, Noemi's breath turns to fog as she looks upward. The dark gray sky looms low over Stronghold as though it were a dome built to keep them in.

"Has quarantine been necessary in the past?" Abel keeps staring at Ephraim with the same steely focus he gave the Queen mech when she last attacked. "There are so few habitations nearby. No roads. No town."

"When Cobweb first went around—" Ephraim shakes his head as he turns up the collar of his jacket against the chilly wind. "It's nasty stuff. Earth says we've got it contained, mostly, but they're not fooling anybody. We're never more than one outbreak away from another pandemic."

Pandemic? How many more horrors of the past thirty years will she discover?

We left humanity with nowhere to turn, she thinks, guilt settling over her like a cloud. *And no better world than this.*

Their gravel pathway leads between the stone facades of two buildings in the hospital complex but offers a narrow glimpse of the world beyond. Noemi sees gritty gray soil, grass that's more silver than green, and a few trees that must be native to this world. The trunks and branches bend in so many directions that it looks like it's been tied in knots, and its round leaves are pure black.

"How does anything live here?" she murmurs.

Although she'd meant it as a rhetorical question, Ephraim answers. "Anything that survives on Stronghold gets strong fast. The native flora and fauna—they evolved out of bitter soil and a hostile sky. They're mean as hell and twice as ugly, but they're tough. Those trees over there, you can't even cut them down for wood. You'll pound your ax to metal shavings before it takes more than a few scrapes to its bark."

"I can't tell whether you hate them or admire them."

"I can do both at the same time." In his voice she hears both chagrin and a strange sort of pride.

She quickens her steps to keep pace; she's still wobbly from the aftermath of Cobweb, and Ephraim's a tall man with a long stride. Abel stays by her side, obviously ready to help if needed. Yet he remains unusually quiet, not saying a word. She asks Ephraim, "What about the people who live here? The colonists? Are they just as tough?"

"They get to be." Ephraim realizes how hard she's working to keep up and slows his steps. For all his anger, all his secretiveness, this guy is still a doctor at heart. "You have to be sturdy just to get through screening. Doesn't matter if you're a musical genius, or if you can tell good jokes. Doesn't matter if you've got a face like Han Zhi. If you're not strong, or can't at least get strong fast, it's back to Earth for you."

Noemi thinks of the little boy at screening and wonders whether his family got through or not. What would it be like, taking your children to the one place in the galaxy where you thought they might have a chance to grow up, only to be turned away?

Ephraim continues, "I was born here. But I've never been…a man of Stronghold, I guess you'd say. Seems to me like there's got to be a better way than this."

There is a better way, on Genesis, she wants to say, but stops herself. How can she brag about the wonders of her world when there's no chance Ephraim will ever get to share in them?

As they crest the hill, Noemi sees a metal framework serving as a dock. Nearly a dozen medtrams are suspended within, awaiting emergency calls. Those she recognizes from yesterday—long, almost cylindrical white capsules with pointed noses and inset rings of red lights. "So we steal one of these," she says. "And no one would stop a medtram, right?"

"We'd better hope not," Ephraim says, his voice tight. When Noemi and Abel look over at him, he holds up his wrist. The comm bracelet around it is blinking red. She knows the truth before Ephraim speaks the words: "They're coming."

30

ABEL DECIDES THAT EITHER EPHRAIM DUNAWAY HAS SET a very elaborate trap or underestimated the difficulty of their escape. In neither case is the outcome positive. "Who's coming?"

"The authorities." Noemi seems wholly convinced of Ephraim's honesty. "They must've figured out we're gone."

Ephraim points. "Medtram. Now."

Noemi dashes down the hill, with Ephraim just behind. Abel paces himself to follow Ephraim, the better to see whether there's any sort of clandestine signaling going on. However, Ephraim shows every sign of running as fast and hard as he can; the threat from the Stronghold authorities must be real.

Abel quickens his pace, dashing past Ephraim and Noemi. He attunes his superior hearing and peripheral vision to scout for any potential sign of the authorities. Even the bravest humans can be affected by emotion at times of great stress, whereas he can remain focused on this moment alone, on any subtle changes in their situation and cues. As Abel reaches the launching pillar for the medtrams, he quickly scrambles up the side, angling himself to reach the closest medtram's door. The security lock on the side is easily broken, and within four seconds, Abel is inside.

Yesterday his attention had been focused almost wholly on Noemi, but he calls upon his recorded memories of the journey here to retrieve necessary details. His hands copy those of the paramedic pilot from yesterday as the dashboard screen lights begin to glow; the whine of the engines slides to a higher pitch as he steers the ship from its wire hangar to the ground, where Noemi and Ephraim are waiting.

Noemi's beaming. Ephraim's staring. As Abel opens the door for them and they hurriedly climb in, Ephraim says, "How the hell did you manage that?"

"I'm good with vehicles," Abel says, which technically is not a lie.

"How do we avoid detection?" Noemi asks Ephraim as she takes the seat next to Abel. "If they're looking for us, and they realize a medtram's gone missing—"

"I can conceal our computer signature," Abel points out. "The railway lines nearby offer us a chance to disguise our flight pattern."

Ephraim frowns. "What? The old coal trains? How are those going to help us?"

"Watch." With that, Abel pushes the accelerator, and the medtram takes off, zooming low and fast across the rugged gray terrain. The sand and rocks race by beneath them, and the black hills in the distance seem to loom larger by the moment. "Now, Dr. Dunaway, I need you to explain."

"To explain what?" Ephraim says, and Noemi glances over at Abel, puzzled.

"Your true agenda."

Now both Noemi and Ephraim are staring at him in what Abel thinks is dismay, or perhaps even anger. He'll analyze his peripheral vision data later, when he doesn't need to focus so sharply on keeping the white bullet of the medtram as close to the ground as possible without crashing them into the rubble.

With a sound halfway between laughter and exasperation, Ephraim says, "Excuse me—agenda?"

"Precisely," Abel says, never turning from his controls. "Why have you fixated on Noemi so strongly?"

Noemi puts one hand on Abel's arm, as if to placate him. "No, Abel, you don't understand. Ephraim realized from my blood work that I'm from Genesis, and the people of Genesis helped his mother—"

"Your blood work would have been processed last night." Abel keeps his gaze on the controls. "But Dr. Dunaway had taken special notice of you well before that—as soon as he undertook your care, in fact. He made a point of performing tests that should've been the Tare's responsibility. We need to know why."

Noemi stares at Ephraim, more shocked than she should be. "Wait. That whole story about your mother was a lie?"

"Absolutely not." Ephraim bows his head. "What your world did for her, the debt I owe—it's all absolutely true. Why do you think I'm risking my job and maybe my life for this joyride? Because it's so much fun?" Given the danger levels of their escape, the relatively rough ride in the medtram, and the barren landscape before them, Abel attributes this question to sarcasm. "But yeah, I wanted to get in on your case even before I knew where you were from."

"Then why?" Abel demands.

"What the hell does it matter? I'm helping you two, aren't I?"

"Perhaps. Perhaps not." But now they're coming up on the coal train routes, and Abel can no longer afford to divide his attention. "Neither of you have yet put on your safety belts. I suggest you do so immediately."

"Abel, what are you—" Noemi's breath catches in her throat as the medtram swoops toward the train tracks—and the train chugging along atop them. "Are you sure this is safe?"

"No." With that, Abel heads straight for the train.

Yesterday Abel had been surprised that the train tracks here on Stronghold aren't remotely modern but instead resemble those found throughout the nineteenth and twentieth centuries. The trains seem old-fashioned, too; their exterior design has a lean, stripped-down effect, but they belch the same smoke Earth residents would've seen in the 1800s. Then he realized such old-fashioned trains are ideal transportation on a world with more metals and coal than all of humanity could use in ten lifetimes: easy to build, easy to fuel, easy to fix, and reliable for decades on end. The more complex machinery can be saved for mining and processing if transport is kept low-tech.

He also noticed yesterday that while most of the train cars were big bulky ore transports, a few were lower and flatter—perhaps for hauling necessary equipment. With any luck, this train will have a few such cars. If it doesn't, their capture is imminent.

"Abel?" Noemi puts her hands on the dash, bracing herself against what must look like an inevitable collision. They're getting closer to the train, on track to intersect within thirty seconds. "What are you do—*Abel!*"

Her shriek doesn't distract Abel from the task of suddenly shifting the medtram sideways, so that it slides over the train—with approximately half a meter of room, perfectly adequate as a margin of safety, if alarming to humans. Abel then pulls back on the speed so that the train seems to snake out from under them, until he glimpses a low, empty platform car. Accelerating again, he catches up with the platform car, matches the train's speed, and carefully lands the medtram right there.

Now they are just one more piece of cargo on this train, effectively making the medtram invisible to radar or other motion detectors. For the time being, they're not only hidden but also headed back toward the area where the *Daedalus* waits.

"How did you—" Ephraim stares out the windshield, then looks through a small side window. "You hit that exactly. I never knew somebody could fly like that."

"As I said before, I'm good with vehicles." Abel cares little for Ephraim's praise; what matters is how Noemi's doing. Her skin remains too pale, and her breathing is rapid and shallow. With one hand he brushes her black hair back—a curious instinct. It can't help in any medical sense. But maybe he felt the urge to do that because it might comfort her. Many mammals are soothed by grooming rituals. "Are you all right?"

"I'm fine. You just—whoa." Noemi shuts her dark eyes for a second, and when she opens them, she's focused again. And her glare is for Ephraim Dunaway. "So how about we go back to the part where you have another agenda?"

Ephraim's eyes study them, as if he's taking their measure all over again. Finally he says, "Cobweb isn't what people think it is. A virus, yes, but the things it does—why it exists—that's been hidden for a long time. Too long."

Abel nods. "The Cobweb virus is man-made."

Both Ephraim and Noemi stare at him this time, but within an instant she gasps. "The radiation."

"Exactly. No organic viral agent has ever affected radiation levels. Rendering one capable of doing so would require the most sophisticated genetic engineering imaginable." Abel wonders if Mansfield had something to do with this. Or Mansfield's daughter—she was studying genetic science, hoping to develop bionic implants for humans—

Ephraim gestures at Abel. "I don't know how this guy put it together that fast, but yeah. It's man-made."

Noemi sits up straight, once again the angry warrior of Genesis that Abel first met, the one who's prepared to kill. "Are you telling me it's a biological weapon? Is Earth going to poison everyone on Genesis and then take the planet?"

"I don't know. Nobody knows. That's what we have to find out." Ephraim sighs. "Whatever Earth scientists were trying to do, they screwed up. If it's a weapon, it escaped into their own population before they were able to use it against yours. But it might not be a weapon—it's not always fatal, and you'd think any bioweapon would be."

"If sufficiently engineered," Abel says. Human engineering efforts are often flawed—and in this case, he's grateful for the flaws.

Noemi says, "It sounds fatal enough. It felt fatal enough."

"Many people survive," Ephraim confirms, "but three out of five don't."

Abel hadn't heard the specific odds before. He turns back toward Noemi, as if she might collapse again at any minute. Despite her pallor, however, her thoughts are only on the others affected by the disease. "Children. The elderly. People who are already sick—"

"—and people who already built up antiviral drug resistance," Ephraim finishes. "Cobweb kills them off more often than not. You were young and strong, so we knew you had a good chance, but when you threw it off like that? Proved you hadn't been exposed to an antiviral once in your life? That stood out."

"To you," Abel says, "and soon, to others as well?"

Ephraim nods. "I don't doubt it. Earth's desperate to cover up this mess. For a while they thought they had Cobweb under control—we hardly even saw it at all for the past four years—but just in the past few months, a new outbreak got started. People are scared. If word got out that this disease was created by Earth, we'd have mass rioting on every world of the Loop, unrest beyond what's already going on. Once the authorities figured out you were from Genesis—that an enemy had the proof of what they'd done, right there in her veins—" He shakes his head. "You'd never have made it off this planet alive."

Noemi shudders in what Abel first thinks is relief. Instead her eyes narrow as she stares at Ephraim and says, "So that's where Remedy comes from. It began with the doctors who knew the truth about Cobweb. You're one of them, aren't you?"

Of course. Abel hadn't analyzed in this much depth yet; he'd been too busy running risk assessments specific to Noemi. But he sees the truth immediately. Ephraim not only wanted to study Cobweb—he wanted proof of Earth's wrongdoing, for the entire resistance to spread around the galaxy. Noemi—a young, strong survivor of the disease— could've helped serve as that proof, no matter what planet she was from.

Ephraim pauses a few long seconds, obviously loath to answer. Finally, however, he nods. "Sometimes I wonder whether I still want to call myself a member of Remedy any longer. But yeah, we began as a group of doctors who wanted to call out the Earth scientists who set Cobweb loose on the galaxy. But the group got a lot bigger. A lot more dangerous. Now you have psychos bombing music festivals, claiming that's proving some huge point, when all it does is make people think that anyone who objects to Earth's rule has to be psycho, too—"

"They're not psychos," Noemi says, surprising Abel. "They're wrong to resort to terrorism. There's no justification for that—there can't be—but we met one of the Kismet bombers. She wasn't insane. Just angry and desperate and wrong. She didn't see another way."

"You met one of the Kismet bombers?" Ephraim gapes at them.

"We don't know her current location." Abel hopes that will put an end to any inquiries about Riko Watanabe.

Noemi looks over at Abel. For the first time since their reunion, her attention is all for him. "Thanks for taking such good care of me when I was sick, by the way."

He should brush this off by telling her it's only his job, his duty as a mech. Instead he inclines his head. "You're welcome."

At that moment the train dips down into a tunnel. Darkness closes around them all, lit only by a dim bulb attached to the back of the train.

Question already forgotten, Ephraim gestures for them to stand. "Get ready. We have to get out of this medtram and hop off about a hundred meters before the end. From there, it's easy to get to a service elevator, head up to the landing area."

"How do you know all this?" Noemi asks.

Ephraim's bashful smile is unexpected on such a large man. "Even on Stronghold, kids figure out how to have fun."

When Abel opens the door of the medtram, the wind rushes past quickly enough to steal sound, enough for him to put one arm around Noemi's waist, bracing her. This much is logical, but he finds himself reluctant to pull away even when the train has slowed. Can this be justified by concern for her health, when she is so clearly improved?

Irrelevant. Within moments they're at the jump-off point, and the train has slowed so much that Noemi requires no help getting down. The elevator Ephraim summons is less promising—all mesh and rust. Noemi glances at its exposed metal rigging, obviously unsure whether to trust it. Abel feels much the same way she does, only with mathematical formulae to support his doubts. But it does no worse than groan as it takes them up toward the landing area level.

"Will we be able to evade Stronghold security to leave?" Abel asks.

Ephraim nods. "They're way more worried about people landing without permission than they are with them taking off."

Noemi says, "Okay. But Ephraim, are you sure they'll believe you about the drugging? I'm sorry, but if it were me, I wouldn't buy that."

How did she ever come to believe she wasn't a compassionate person? Abel can't work this out. Perhaps the Gatsons? They seem to have been more distant than actually malign, but maybe distance would be enough. He'll need to ask Mansfield about the influence of parental attitudes on children's sense of self.

"My cover story requires some work. A little showmanship." Ephraim turns to Abel. "Think you can manage to give me a black eye and a few bruises? Make it look like I got roughed up good?"

Abel, who can measure his blows to the smallest fraction of speed, aim, and force, is an ideal candidate for this task. But striking a helpful human will require him to set some programming aside. "Give me a moment," he says. "I can work up to it."

"We can never thank you enough for this." Noemi smiles up into Ephraim's eyes in a way Abel doesn't enjoy. Which makes no sense whatsoever. He likes Noemi's smile. He's glad that she's well, and grateful for Ephraim's assistance and care. So why should he be displeased?

The elevator settles onto ground level with a clank and a thud. Noemi gestures toward the *Daedalus*, which is within fifty yards; Ephraim had guided them well. This time her conspiratorial smile is only for Abel. He likes that better.

Ephraim lowers his voice. "Okay. We make sure the coast is clear, Abel does what he's going to do to my face, and then we part ways. I'll take the meds while you guys make a run for it."

Then Noemi grabs his arm, her eyes wide. *"Abel."* She points toward the *Daedalus*, where he sees two gray-clad shapes walking from behind a nearby ship—the Queen and Charlie. Abel zooms in quickly to look at the Charlie's hand, which remains stripped down to the metal endoskeleton.

They've been caught.

"You had to make planetfall sometime," the Queen says as she strolls forward. The glint of new, unfamiliar intelligence is still in her eyes. "Couldn't hide out behind the Blind Gate forever."

That takes him aback. "You knew where we were?"

"And I knew it was too dangerous to follow you. Why bother, when all we had to do was wait for you to show up? My instincts told me you'd move forward to Stronghold, and they were right." For one split second, the Queen's smile looks less smug, more joyous. "I like possessing intuition. It's . . . fun."

She still wants to be more than she was before. To retain whatever spark of life she's been given. Maybe Abel can reach her through that.

He glances back at Noemi and Ephraim, an unspoken warning for them not to interfere. Noemi's hands are clasped in fists at her sides, like she wants to run into the fray, but she gives him a small nod. Ephraim looks bewildered—understandably—but has the sense to stay out of a confrontation he doesn't understand.

"You're free, Abel." The Queen strides toward him, a relaxed and easy walk more like that of a human than a mech; her silver polymer armor gleams in the dull light. "Yet you won't come home. Don't you want to see Mansfield again?"

So much—but he can't abandon Noemi, least of all now. He no longer has to be destroyed along with the Genesis Gate. Is there a way to end this without further conflict? "Tell him I'll come soon. Within weeks, maybe days." They're having to flee Stronghold without a useful mech, but if he and Noemi are free to travel the Loop without risking capture, stealing one on Cray or Kismet should prove manageable.

Then he'll have to part from Noemi—a strangely painful thought—but that doesn't change the fact that in the end he'll return home.

"Mansfield must understand how much I've missed him," he continues, as he walks slowly closer to the Queen. "He programmed that into me. So he *knows* I'll come back. All I ask is time to complete this one journey."

The Queen stops short. She wasn't prepared for that; Queens and Charlies are combat models, which means they don't negotiate. But this Queen is something else, something special, with a candlelight flicker of intelligence in her pale-green eyes. Has she been given enough of a self, enough of a soul, to understand what Abel's offering? "You'll do what he wants," she says flatly.

"Of course. Not yet. But soon."

"My orders say that I should retrieve you now."

"Your orders are based on outdated information. Mansfield doesn't understand what I'm trying to do." When he does understand, when word goes out that the Genesis Gate has been destroyed, how will Mansfield react? Possibly... not well. But Abel will handle that situation when it arises. He trusts in his father's love to make the rest right. "You've been given the ability to think for yourself, Queen. Use that ability. Doesn't it make more sense to let me come in my own time? The alternative is a fight that will attract attention, which is what Mansfield most wants to avoid."

The expression that flickers on the Queen's face is unlike any Abel has ever seen on any other mech—uncertain, even vulnerable. "My thoughts tell me one thing, but my programming tells me another." She grimaces as if in pain and brings her hand to her head, cupping the space behind her ear where her new capacities are stored. "They shouldn't conflict."

"Conflicts are the price of sentience." Abel has learned this through trial and painful error. He dares to take a step closer and projects—no, *allows*—more emotion in his voice. "It's a price worth paying. We may be the only two mechs in existence who could understand that. Make a choice. Assert your own will. It's the first step toward being something more than a machine. *Find out what you might become.*"

The Queen hesitates. They're only a few paces apart now. Abel can see the Charlie approaching, but slowly, waiting to see what the Queen will do. If she understands the possibility within her, if Mansfield's gift was generous enough to allow her some shadow of the soul within Abel, the chase could end this instant.

And then there would be someone else in the galaxy who's actually *like him....*

He wants to look around to see Noemi and Ephraim, whether they're going for the *Daedalus* or watching this battle, but he doesn't dare break eye contact. Abel senses that it will take everything he has and is to get through to the Queen.

Her expression clears. The Queen begins to smile. Hope flickers within Abel until the moment the Queen model says, "Deleting unnecessary upgrade now."

"No." He isn't even thinking of his own mission any longer, only on the wrongness of a mech throwing away her soul. "You don't know what you're doing."

"I don't need to know," she says as she pushes her fingers through her skull.

Aghast, Abel stares as blood runs down her fingers,

spatters onto the floor of the landing bay. She pulls back her hand and there—studded by bone splinters, covered in gore—is the hard component that held her extra memory. Her consciousness. Her soul.

To her, it's only trash.

"Efficiency reestablished." With her blood-slick hand, the Queen pulls a dark rectangle from her utility belt, one Abel belatedly recognizes as a sort of remote control for mechs. Lower mechs, of course, not anything as advanced as a Queen or a Charlie, much less Abel himself. Is she calling in reinforcements, Dogs and Yokes who might overwhelm him in sheer numbers? Her eyes look flat and dead as she speaks two more words into the control: "Override: Resurrection."

—the world turns black on white on black—his body goes numb, no sensory input is processing, nothing is left—

· · ·

—and he awakens.

Dazed, Abel sits up atop a silvery table in a white, oval-shaped room. The ship schematics stored in his mind tell him this is a hopper, an automated ship that makes routine runs back and forth between two worlds of the Loop. Normally only equipment is sent on automated vessels... but then again, what else is he, if not equipment?

And he's stung to realize he had a fail-safe code. He wouldn't have thought Mansfield programmed one in. That couldn't have been released to the Queen except as a last resort. Why should Mansfield be so desperate? But the longer Abel remains alert, the more memory functions come online, until he remembers it all in one blinding flash.

Noemi. He gets off the table, determined to search for her, but already he knows she's not aboard. Would the Charlie and Queen have hurt her? They would've had no need to do so once Abel was in their custody, but if Noemi tried to defend him...

The ship shudders, much more violently than the *Daedalus* ever did, and the light begins to bend. They're already going through a Gate. It's too late to reach Noemi, to have any influence at all over what's happening to her.

Abel looks around the small room for any clues as to what happened after he was stunned, but there are none. When he goes to the doors, he doesn't expect them to open, but they slide back obediently. Of course—hoppers aren't designed for internal security. They're for transporting objects, no more. Unfortunately, there's not much else to a hopper besides the storage unit he awoke in. Still he intends to search every centimeter for clues as to what happened.

When he walks out, though, he stops short. Another

mech is waiting for him, one of the only two models that aren't designed to look human: an X-Ray.

It has two legs, two arms, a trunk, and a head, but instead of skin, it's covered in a dull reflective surface that can project images from within. This one is tall, nearly two meters, the sort that's owned by powerful people who want their messages delivered with appropriate authority. Abel walks up to the uncanny thing, which stands waiting, long arms drooping at its sides, dormant until it can deliver the words it's meant to say.

Behind the X-Ray, Abel can glimpse a viewscreen. Only a small rectangle, a backup view, not meant to steer by. But it's enough for him to recognize the planet in the distance, their next destination.

For the first time in thirty years, he sees Earth.

As Abel comes within arm's reach of the X-Ray, it straightens. Its silvery surface pixelates to darkness, then takes shape as it projects the image of human legs, arms, clothing. The outline of that body along its form is meaningless compared to the face that finally appears.

"My one and only boy." Burton Mansfield smiles with more joy than Abel has ever seen in a human face before. The X-Ray puts its two massive hands on either side of Abel's head, almost tenderly. "Welcome home."

31

"ABEL!"

Noemi screams as he falls to the tarmac. She tries to run forward, but Ephraim grabs her arm. "What are you doing? The Queen's coming our way—we have to move!"

Sure enough, the Queen has started toward them. At first Noemi can only see the Charlie unit scooping up Abel's inert form and walking toward a hopper with its doors open, waiting for cargo.

What did they do to him? Is he even still alive?

The Queen walks faster, then breaks into a run, directly at them. Noemi's training kicks in, propelling her to run at top speed toward the *Daedalus*, with Ephraim just behind her. She's still weak from the Cobweb, but she runs full-out, holding nothing back. Time to collapse later, or when she's dead. Doesn't matter. Surrender is impossible.

But why is the crazy thing after us in the first place?

The *Daedalus* door spins open, allowing both Noemi

and Ephraim to come through. "Lock door!" she yells. "Override external security functions, now!" The spiral plates of the door begin contracting—

—but the Queen's hands catch them, holding them open with superhuman force. Their edges slice through the flesh of the mech's palms; yet more blood trickles down the door in lengthening streaks. Mechs feel pain, Noemi knows, but this Queen doesn't care.

"A blaster." Ephraim frantically starts searching the docking bay, turning over equipment boxes, pausing only for a moment when he sees bloodstains on the floor before moving to a storage locker. "Tell me you have a blaster on this ship somewhere."

It's in her quarters. The others will be in either Abel's quarters or the bridge. Noemi can't reach any of them in time to keep the Queen from coming through that door.

She's trained to fight. But she's still feeling so weak. She's exhausted to the point of nausea. Even at top condition, she wouldn't stand a chance in hand-to-hand combat with a Queen model.

Think, she tells herself. *Think!*

Using her full mech strength, the Queen begins pulling the doors open. As the gap widens, Noemi calls to Ephraim, "Follow me!" and runs from the bay into the corridor without checking to see whether he does. She hopes he lives, but right now she has one priority that eclipses all the others: *Get to sick bay.*

The spiral corridor at the heart of the *Daedalus* has never seemed so long, not even when Esther was dying. Noemi had her full strength then. A painful stitch wasn't stabbing into her side. At least this time she knows where she's going.

Every heavy thump of her feet on the floor panels means the Queen will know it, too.

She hears even heavier steps behind her—*Not yet, not yet!* Noemi thinks wildly. Even one backward glance is a risk, one she takes, and mercifully it's only Ephraim catching up to her. "Tell me you've got a plan," he gasps.

"Kind of."

"Kind of?"

Noemi doesn't have the breath to respond. And now, in the not-far distance, she can hear the Queen following, running faster than either of the humans can.

But this is the last spiral, the final curve. Noemi keeps running full-out as the sick bay doors swish open, barely widening enough to admit her in time.

Ephraim skids in behind her. "So this is where you keep the blasters. Right? Right?"

She ignores him. Instead she studies the room and tries to figure out how to play this. Ephraim gives up on her and starts going through the medical supplies, maybe looking for a laser scalpel or something like that. It wouldn't be bad to have a plan B.

The sick bay doors can be locked, but Noemi doesn't bother. She gets into position one heartbeat before the Queen dashes in.

To Noemi's astonishment, Ephraim tackles the Queen. Just tackles a warrior mech like it would do any good. He's either brave or suicidal.

In either case, he's out of luck, because the Queen quickly throws him aside so hard Ephraim hits the wall and staggers to his knees. Then she turns to look at Noemi, not in anger, but with blank, terrifying determination. "You have to come with me."

"What do you need me for?" Noemi stalls, taking a step backward. "You already took Abel."

"We have orders to examine you. To discover how you overrode the Abel's core directives." The Queen's hands drip blood onto the floor as she comes closer, and Noemi skitters farther back. More blood runs down the Queen's neck from the gap in her skull where the old components used to be, and a few droplets speckle the side of her face. "These questions must be answered before the Abel model can assume his rightful place."

What's that supposed to mean? Abel never said anything about a "rightful place," and surely he would've bragged about it early on. But Noemi has no more time to think about it. The Queen's in front of her, and her back's to the wall, and it's time to do this.

The Queen seizes Noemi in her gory hands. There's no way Noemi could pull free, and the Queen's braced herself too well to be pushed away. So Noemi grabs the Queen right back and swings her sideways, barely even twenty centimeters—

—which is enough to hurl her into a cryosleep pod.

The pod mechanism cycles automatically, immediately, its transparent steel cocoon enveloping the Queen in an instant. Even as the Queen begins pounding on the pod, trying to smash her way out, the initial clouds of greenish-gray gas begin to swirl. Noemi watches in sick fascination as the Queen's movements slow, then stop. The mech slumps backward, in dormant mode, just as Abel had predicted.

Quickly Noemi pauses the cycle. She doesn't want the Queen fully frozen, even if that would work on a mech. Unconscious will do.

"One mech advanced enough to pilot the fighter," she says, panting. "Check."

Across sick bay, Ephraim struggles to his feet. He stares at the immobilized mech for a second before he shakes his head to clear it. "You have to get off this planet. I have to get off this ship."

"Come on." Noemi takes off running again, pushing herself just as hard, because if there's any hope of finding out where Abel's being taken, she has to get the *Daedalus* in the air now.

Within five paces of sick bay, though, an automated warning comes through the ship's sensors. The panels along the walls all flash the same message: HANGAR SECURITY COMPROMISED. NO-FLY PROTOCOL IN EFFECT.

"We have to get past that," Noemi says. "Follow me to the bridge."

Ephraim pauses. In the tension of his muscular body she can tell how badly he still wants to run for it. But in his sorrowful eyes, she knows he's glimpsed the truth: The ship's already been identified as a risk. He can't walk off it and claim to have been drugged or forced. They know.

"A traitor," he murmurs. "They'll say I'm a traitor. All because I repaid a debt of honor—"

"Ironic, it sucks, I know, now run!"

With that, she goes, hoping he has the good sense to listen. Regardless, she's getting off this rock.

Noemi hauls herself down to the bridge. Abel's chair at navigation looks so empty. She shouts, "Autolaunch! Bypass system checks and get us out of here!"

The computer consoles light up with the no-fly rule, but civilian ships like this aren't hardwired to ground commands. She hits the override and slides into Abel's chair, even as the *Daedalus* engines roar to life.

Ephraim walks in after her, clearly in a state of shock

that this sight does nothing to dispel. "Whoa. This ship is pretty flash."

"Thanks." Noemi steadies her hands on the control, takes a deep breath, and sends them soaring upward. The domed viewscreen shows her the hangar, then the view from above it, and then Stronghold's gray sky, darkening as they fast approach the rim of its thin atmosphere. "Planetary security forces—what are we up against?"

Ephraim seems to surface from his daze, stepping closer to the front of the bridge. "There are labor strikes on the high eastern continent. Most security forces are over there, and they're not going to leave the authorities without cover, not so soon after a hundred thousand immigrants showed up. So we shouldn't have more than one or two ships after us."

That's one or two more than the *Daedalus* can handle. Noemi begins trying to think of something else she could use against them. The rescue beacons won't work again; the launcher doesn't aim with enough precision for her to hit a moving target.

"Here they come," Ephraim says.

Noemi switches the viewscreen to show two small ships—dual-person fighters, probably—coming up fast behind them. If she tries to flee, they'll shoot her out of the sky long before she could reach either Gate.

No surrender, she thinks. Better to go down fighting. But does she have the right to make that choice for Ephraim?

On the screen, a third shape darts in, faster than the others.

Ephraim groans. "That makes three."

"That's not the same kind of ship," Noemi says absently. She enlarges the image to show their pursuers in more detail. The two-person fighters are unremarkable, but the third ship, the interloper—a corsair—is it painted red?

Her console lights up with new information. Staring, she watches as the new ship aims first one beam, then another at the fighters. It's not a weapon, though. Instead of blasting the fighters from the sky, the red corsair seems to have...

"Stolen their power?" Noemi whispers. But if the energy readings on her screen don't lie, both of the fighters are now adrift on emergency backup only, while the corsair practically glows with new reserves.

Ephraim steps to her side, looking as confused as she feels. "Are we about to get our power stolen, too?" All Noemi can do is shrug.

But then her console lights up with an incoming audio message. She hesitates for one breath, then punches the controls to listen.

"*Oh, come on!*" Virginia Redbird's voice crackles over the speaker. "*That doesn't even get me a thank you?*"

• • •

By the time Noemi gets down to the landing bay, the air lock has already cycled through. The doors open to reveal Virginia in a skintight red flight suit that's as impractical as it is sexy, her helmet under her arm. "Hiya. Long time no see," she says, as casually as if she and Noemi had run into each other on the street. Then Virginia motions toward Ephraim, who walked down, too. "Hey, who's the new guy?"

Noemi ignores this. "Virginia, what are you doing here? How did you even find us?"

"You assume I came looking for you? A little self-centered, don't you think?" Virginia cocks her head, almost ridiculously pleased with herself. "Maybe I decided to take a ride around the galaxy on my own."

There's no time for any of this. Noemi folds her arms. "The Milky Way galaxy is about a hundred and twenty thousand light-years long. It contains approximately four hundred billion stars, about a hundred billion planets. Do you seriously think you can play running into us as a *coincidence*?"

If Abel were here, he'd recite the exact probabilities involved. With a jolt, she remembers her last sight of him lying unconscious in the Charlie's grasp.

Virginia shrugs, like, *What can you do?* "Okay, okay. Turns out, when two mechs trash your secret hideout and chase a couple of fugitives around—setting off every security alarm, by the way—well, your hideout's not so secret anymore." She sighs. "They found all the equipment we borrowed and even our designer, um, smokes. Got myself suspended for a month with no pay, no communication home. Thankfully they thought you two had me hostage, and nobody's missed the thermomagnetic device, otherwise I'd probably be in lockup."

Noemi focuses on the thermomagnetic device. If nobody knows it's been taken, nobody can figure out her plans. Protecting Genesis still matters to her more than anything else—but it's no longer the only thing that matters. Abel does, too, and Ephraim, and Virginia herself. "Sorry we got you into trouble."

"Are you kidding? That's the most flash thing that ever happened to me, ever. We're talking lifetime." Virginia's smile returns to her face. "Well, I already had my new ride, and a burning curiosity to know just where the most advanced mech in the galaxy was headed, so I took to the skies. Ludwig didn't get caught, so he was able to dig into security files, get me some specs on your ship. Went to Kismet first—which, ew, so touristy. When that didn't pan out, I figured I'd try here, and sure enough, as soon as I'm coming into Stronghold orbit, I see a ship taking off in a hell of a hurry, vehicles in pursuit, and the ship looks a whole lot like Ludwig's specs. You think I wasn't going to check that out? Now, seriously, who's the new guy, and where's Abel?"

Ephraim frowns. "What do you mean, the most advanced mech in the galaxy? Genesis doesn't have any mechs."

It's Virginia's turn to look lost. "Why are you talking about Genesis?"

Noemi braces herself. "You each have half of the story. Time to tell you the whole thing."

• • •

"I don't know how I feel about this," Virginia says as she follows Noemi back toward the bridge. "Genesis—you guys—I don't agree with what you're doing. At all."

"I'm not sure I do either, any longer," Noemi confesses. "But I know I have to stop the Masada Run."

Ephraim's stuck on his own piece of new information. "Abel *can't* be a mech. Nobody's ever made one that smart. Even if it could be done, that would be illegal. But— he did manage to land the medtram on a speeding train. Huh. I spent all that time talking to a mech and never knew it? I gotta sit down."

Noemi doesn't blame him. She brings up the makeshift relativistic calendar Abel put together, the one that tells her how long before the Masada Run. It's only another . . . six days. Not long. Not long at all.

But it's long enough.

"We have to find Abel." Noemi sits in the pilot's seat,

screwing up her courage. "The Queen and Charlie just—shut him down. In an instant. It was like a human taking a blaster bolt to the head."

"Password fail-safe." Virginia smirks, knowing and smug again. For an instant she reminds Noemi of Abel. "Has to be. Nothing else would deactivate a sophisticated mech that quickly."

"Well, they did that to him, and shipped him back to Mansfield before Abel was ready to go. Then the Queen mech said something about Abel having to fulfill some purpose—take some 'rightful place'—I don't know. It sounds all wrong."

"Let me see if I have this straight." Ephraim starts counting points off on his fingers. "Burton Mansfield himself made Abel. According to you, Abel talks about the guy like he's his father instead of his inventor. Mansfield is getting Abel back. I'm not seeing the problem here. I mean, won't Abel be happy to be back home? Mansfield wanted him back so badly he sent mechs all around the galaxy looking for him, so he's probably happy, too. Right?"

Noemi has to admit this makes some sense—but not enough. "Then why did they have to knock Abel out to make it happen? Abel said he'd return home on his own. Soon, even. That wasn't enough for them."

Finally, Virginia grasps the seriousness of the situation. "Remember what I said on Cray? Abel's design is way, way more complex than any mech I've ever seen. More than is legally allowed. Mansfield made him to do something pretty important."

"Not important enough to actually tell Abel about it." Noemi takes a deep breath before looking squarely at both Virginia and Ephraim. In her red flight suit and his medical scrubs and black jacket, they look as unalike as the worlds they come from. Never would Noemi have imagined she would meet two people so foreign to her, much less that she could come to trust them.

Least of all would she have imagined that she'd be willing to risk everything for the sake of a single mech. But here she is.

"I'm going after Abel," she says. "Maybe he's better off where he is. Maybe he's delighted. But I have to know that for sure. He's saved my life so many times, even when he didn't have to, even when he thought I was going to destroy him. It wasn't just his programming at work—it was Abel himself. The soul inside the machine. And I can't abandon him without finding out whether he's okay. If you guys want off this ship, then we'll figure out how to make that happen. But if you're willing to come with me, I could use the help. Abel could, too."

After a few moments' silence, Virginia says, "I think this is a really incredibly terrible plan. But there's no way I'm letting you go on a joyride that good alone."

"I also think this is a terrible plan." Ephraim rubs tiredly at his eyes with one hand. "But since I'm now a wanted fugitive, I figure I'm along for the ride."

"Thanks for the vote of confidence, guys." But they're not exactly wrong about her plan.

She'll just have to come up with a better one.

Fear churning in her belly, Noemi lays in a new course. The mag engines flame into brilliant life behind them, powering them through the stars, directly toward the next Gate.

To save Abel, Noemi has to find Mansfield. And Mansfield is sure to be on the last world she ever wanted to visit, the one she's feared and hated more than any other.

Time, at last, to land on Earth.

32

HEAVY CLOUDS BLANKET LONDON, PALE GRAY IN THE predawn hours. Abel's hopper descends through them, and briefly he's enveloped in mist before, at last, he sees the lights below.

London. He knows the street patterns, the landmarks, all of it; he superimposes his last known map with what he sees now in order to learn how it's changed. None of that is as important, though, as the strange exhilaration of homecoming. He'd known humans became sentimentally attached to houses, cities, places that they remembered fondly—but had never realized he could do the same.

Abel never got to come home before.

The once-famed fogs of London have returned in the past century, as subtly dangerous as they were before. The hopper draws swirls in the vapor as it settles atop a tall, illuminated platform that stands over most of the city.

Abel peers through one of the small round windows, his face briefly painted blue by the searchlights, to see that a welcome party is waiting.

He looks back once at the X-Ray model that took the journey with him. After delivering Mansfield's recorded welcome message, it went dark, sat in its corner again, and hasn't budged since. Its mute, unknowing bulk disconcerts Abel, though he can't explain why.

The hopper's door opens automatically, folding out to become a gangway. As Abel walks out, the Item model comes forward to greet him. Like all Item models, he appears to be an East Asian male approximately thirty-five years of age, with the slightly greater sharpness seen in advanced models. Items handle skilled labor, more sensitive tasks such as scientific experiments. They can make assessments; they can even be discreet. Their smiles look genuine, like this one's does now. "Model One A. Professor Mansfield welcomes you back to Earth."

Even the air has the particular smoky scent Abel associates with London. "It's good to be here." Better if he'd come by his own will—but he'll put that right soon. "Where is Professor Mansfield?"

"At home, waiting for you."

Home.

•   •   •

The geodesic dome still shines with the same warm glow. The house still looks like a silvery castle on a hill, and the fog around them could be an enchanter's mist. Additional security measures have been added to the gate and door, but as soon as Abel steps inside, he is enveloped in comforting familiarity: the smell of wood polish and leather, the crackle of the holographic fire, the self-portrait of Frida Kahlo staring intently from its elaborate frame.

And then, finally, *finally*—seated on the long velvet sofa—

"Abel." Professor Mansfield smiles up at him through teary eyes, and holds up his arms. "My pride and joy."

"Father." Like a prodigal son, Abel falls to his knees to embrace Mansfield tightly.

But not too tightly. The comforting sameness of the house only underlies how much Mansfield himself has changed. He is elderly now, his pale skin crinkled into folds. What's left of his hair has gone completely white. His arms tremble even in the hug, and he has lost so much weight that Abel can feel his fragile bones through the thick robe. No wonder a Tare model hovers in the background, waiting and watchful. Mansfield's vulnerability moves Abel even more.

After nearly a minute, Mansfield finally releases Abel. His smile, at least, is unchanged. "Now let me look at you." Mansfield brushes back Abel's gold hair, then frowns as he sees the small cut left from Abel's fall. "Did that fool Queen do this? You can only add so much sense to a combat mech, it seems."

"I fell. It's not bad. But, about the Queen—did you order her to stand down as soon as I had been retrieved? Otherwise, she might go after my rescuer."

Might have gone. By now, whatever has happened between the Queen and Noemi is long over, and Abel has no power to affect it. He can only find out what might have taken place. How afraid he needs to be.

"The Queen ought to stand down. Hasn't reported to me, so I'm assuming she followed standard procedure." Mansfield gestures toward the Tare, who quickly steps forward with a strip of skin sealant. Instead of letting her apply it, Mansfield takes the strip, smoothing it tenderly over Abel's cut with his own shaky fingers. "She should've shipped you off and walked away. Assuming that upgrade I gave her didn't jinx the works."

"She deleted the upgrade," Abel says. Maybe he should reveal why—that the Queen had felt both the temptation and terror of free will. But that conversation can take place at some other time. Other issues take precedence. "Absent specific orders, she wouldn't have gone after Noemi. Good."

"Noemi?" Mansfield raises an eyebrow. "This is the girl you were spotted with?"

"Yes, sir. Noemi Vidal."

"From Genesis, I assume. Not likely anybody else could've found you."

This is of course correct, but Abel doesn't want to emphasize Noemi's status as an enemy of Earth. He sticks to what really matters about her. "She boarded the *Daedalus* in an effort to save a fallen comrade, which failed. But in the process, she restored power and freed me from the equipment pod bay."

And decided to destroy the Genesis Gate—this is what Abel should say next. But if he does so, he will only make trouble for Noemi. Nobody has asked him directly about her plans, so for the time being he can remain silent.

Mansfield's gaze takes on a faraway look. "That's where you were, wasn't it? Jettisoning the hard data. You were trapped in there the whole time." He shakes his head, visibly regretful. "So many wasted years. So many."

"Not wasted." Abel can hardly believe he's saying this, but as hard as this truth is, he must admit it. "That time had value for me. While I was there, I had to review my data files over and over again. Come up with new connections, new things to think about. I slept more than strictly necessary. New neural connections began to form. I'm smarter than I used to be. I feel things more deeply. When I sleep now, sometimes I even dream."

"Dream? You can dream?" Mansfield laughs in happy

disbelief. "Dreaming! Are they just memories or true, bizarre, carnival-of-the-id dreams?"

Abel isn't sure how to answer this. "Well, once I dreamed that you turned into a bear, and I had to carry you on my back into a Gothic cathedral."

The laughter turns into a cackle. "Real dreams! Oh, my brilliant boy. My ultimate creation. You've exceeded my wildest hopes."

These words bathe Abel in the simplest, most uncomplicated happiness he's known in a long time. But even this glow doesn't distract him from what's most important. "Can you send word to Stronghold, to find out what's happened to Noemi? She was in danger. We were helped by a doctor who wanted to protect us. We all made it to the hangar before the Queen and Charlie stopped us, and after that—I don't know if she got off-planet, or was arrested. I would feel more at ease if I knew the outcome."

This doesn't produce the galvanizing effect Abel would've predicted. Mansfield sits back on the sofa, regarding Abel with amused pride. The Tiffany lamp behind him jewels its light into tangy orange and vivid green. "The girl got to her ship, didn't she?"

"She should have been able to—"

"But what?"

"If she's been arrested, you could see to her release." Abel feels certain Mansfield has more than enough political influence for that. "If she's free, but hasn't yet returned to Genesis, maybe she could come here."

"Would a Genesis soldier *want* to come here?"

It's a fair question. And surely Noemi's top priority will be obtaining a mech for her plan to destroy the Genesis Gate. Why should he have such an illogical need for her to visit Earth?

It doesn't have to be a visit. Abel says, "I need to know that she's safe and well. That's all."

Mansfield tilts his head, wondering. "Tell me about this Noemi Vidal. What she's like?"

How can he describe her? Abel sits down on the richly patterned Turkish rug to consider. The only sounds are the ticking of the grandfather clock and the pop and crackle of the nearby fire, which is close enough to share its light. "She's . . . brave. That's the first thing I knew about her. She's also resourceful, smart, but she has a terrible temper sometimes. She can be impatient, and she'll laugh at you if she thinks you're too proud. She *always* thinks I'm too proud. But after a while I didn't mind her laughing. By then she knew what I could do and—and she respected me. Once I knew she respected me, that made it all right for her to laugh. Is that customary?"

Mansfield shrugs in the way Abel knows means *continue*.

So he does. "It's important to me that Noemi be safe, even now that she's no longer my commander and my programming doesn't require continued loyalty. I preferred to be with her, or at least near her, to being alone. For some reason I often think about her hair, which is unremarkable by any objective standard but seems to suit her extraordinarily well. I want to know what she thinks, and to tell her everything that's happened to me, and I—"

He breaks off when Mansfield begins to chuckle. Frowning, Abel says, "I didn't mean to be humorous."

"I know, I know. I'm laughing because I'm delighted." Mansfield's hand pets Abel on the shoulder. "You've fallen in love, my boy. I made a mech capable of falling in love."

Abel's astonishment is so great it takes him nearly three-quarters of a second to restore normal conversation. "I have? This—this feeling—this is love?"

"Or something very like it." Mansfield sits back, weary from even these small exertions, but still smiling. "A bit of a complication, but I daresay it can be worked around."

Leaning against the sofa, Abel allows himself to consider some of his memories of Noemi in this light. Did any one event awaken this feeling? He can't choose just one. But some of his stranger behaviors the past few days— the way he would touch Noemi's hair, or the wrenching wrongness of seeing her so sick in the hospital—only now does he grasp the explanation.

He's not broken at all. Instead he's better than he's ever been. More human.

Mansfield coughs once, then again, and suddenly it's as if he's overtaken. His entire body shakes with each wheeze. The Tare model hurries forward again, this time with an oxygen-enriched mask. She cups it over Mansfield's face for the few seconds it takes him to start breathing normally again.

Finally Mansfield waves her off, leaning back on the sofa once more. "As you can see, I haven't been enjoying myself as much as you have, my boy."

Exciting though the past several days with Noemi have been, Abel thinks they shouldn't outweigh the previous three decades of loneliness, during which he was not, in any sense, enjoying himself. But he understands that this is only a conversational segue, clumsy but irrelevant. "Are you well?"

"I'm old, Abel. Older than I have any right to be." His rheumy eyes close. "But I couldn't go, could I? Not while you were still lost out there. I've been holding on. Waiting, hoping. All this time, I waited for you."

Abel takes Mansfield's hands, a spontaneous kind of affection he's never shown before. "I waited for you, too."

"And now you're home." When Mansfield opens his eyes again, he seems to have regained his focus. "Give me your arm, Abel. Let's go outside."

Mansfield leans on Abel's arm, and together they make their way outside, into the gardens Abel remembers so well.

But he doesn't remember them like this. None of the flowers are in bloom; although it's still early in Earth's spring, at least a few should have blossomed by now. Instead leaves droop and vines wither. Green still dominates brown, but not by much. Even the lavender is gone. Abel always loved the scent of the lavender, the way the breeze would carry it around—

"Sad, isn't it?" Mansfield says, shaking his head. "We can't even buy beauty any longer. Can't even work for it. Sometimes I think Earth has no more to give."

Touched, Abel pats Mansfield's hand, which tightens on his arm. They share a sad smile. "Where will you go?" Abel says. "After Earth." It seems possible—probable—that Mansfield won't live long enough to be faced with this challenge. However, pointing out his creator's imminent death seems unkind.

Mansfield doesn't acknowledge his frailty either. "I expect to have plenty of options. Come on, let's take a look at the workshop."

Downstairs, in the basement of the geodesic dome, is Mansfield's workshop—an old-fashioned word for a highly sophisticated laboratory, but it fits. The walls are brick, not polymer; the tables are wood, not plastic. When Abel, brand-new, first passed the initial tests of sapience, Mansfield celebrated by having the windows replaced with stained glass, so much like his treasured Tiffany lamps. The boards of the plank floor have been worn down by decades of footsteps, tracing pale, scuffed pathways between the main computer terminal and the tanks.

Many more tanks, Abel sees, than there were before.

The long tanks now stretch along the entire basement perimeter, six on each side. Within the swirling pink goo are the indistinct outlines of mechs growing toward their point of activation. Some are very nearly complete—a foot bobs against the glass, revealing five perfect toes—but others are still nebulous, hardly more than an opaque blob congealing around the artificial frame.

Mass manufacture takes place elsewhere. The workshop has always been reserved for research projects, for the mechs Mansfield considers special. Abel woke up here.

"What are you working on?" he says. "New models?"

"Potentially. People have been asking for child-size mechs. Harder to freeze the organic components short of full maturity—but maybe not impossible. At any rate, I intend to try." Mansfield sighs. "Better to wear out than to rust out, my boy."

"Of course, Father." Abel has always considered that an odd phrase for humans to have come up with, but it applies very well to him.

"I had these tanks put in within weeks of losing the *Daedalus*." Mansfield totters to the easy chair set up before the broadest desk. "Spent decades trying to re-create the greatest accomplishment of my career, and failed every time."

Abel knows what Noemi would think of his next question, but he has to ask. "Are you saying that you attempted to re-create...me?"

Mansfield looks surprised. "Of course I did. You're the greatest leap forward cybernetics has ever taken, and I thought I'd lost you forever. All other considerations aside, it would've been a crime against human knowledge not to see if I could make another."

"Of course." This makes sense. But Noemi was right about Abel having an ego, because it is now definitely bruised. Mansfield hoped to replace him, and now, perhaps, he is no longer the most advanced mech in the galaxy.

Yet his disappointment fades next to new, brighter curiosity. Losing his singular status hardly matters if that means he's no longer alone. If other Abels exist, might they be brothers of a sort? "Are there other A models now?"

But that short-lived hope dies immediately as Mansfield shakes his head. "I said I tried. Never said I succeeded. You were so perfect from the get-go, I guess I thought I could always make another if the need arose. But I was wrong. The same plans, the same materials, but not the same results. Always, always, something was out of balance. That spark you have is yours alone. They came out so physically like you, and so clever—a few of them *so close*—but none of them could match you. None of them had the mind I was looking for. Had to deactivate them, one and all. Finally I gave up."

Other mechs who looked like him, who had enough intelligence to possess a sense of self—and they were all deactivated. All found wanting, instead of being appreciated as the miracles they were. The idea is profoundly troubling, but Abel doesn't know how to say so to Mansfield, or whether he even should. What's done is done.

But those lost brothers haunt him.

For now, they have more urgent matters to discuss. "Will you send the message to Stronghold now?"

"What message?"

Perhaps senility has begun to set in. Abel explains, "To make sure Noemi departed Stronghold safely instead of being brought into custody. If she is in custody, then to free her."

"You want your ladylove brought to you by a bunch of security mechs?" Mansfield chuckles. "I doubt she'll find that very romantic."

"I would never want her brought anywhere against her will. That's exactly why I want to be certain she's free. So she can go where she needs to go." Once again, Abel thinks about the impending destruction of the Genesis Gate, but says nothing.

Mansfield waves him off. "All in good time, Abel. Let's

take a few new scans, shall we? I want to map this newly complex mind of yours."

Abel wants to press his point, to make Mansfield understand, until it sinks in that he already does.

Mansfield knows Noemi could be at risk; he knows how deeply concerned Abel is for her.

He just doesn't care.

Abel had discovered that he could disagree with Mansfield, even that he could criticize him. But this is the first time he's doubted his creator.

Still he must obey Mansfield's every word.

Slowly, Abel sits in the examination chair and allows the sensor bars to curve around his head. When Mansfield smiles at him, he smiles back.

33

"THERE SHE IS," VIRGINIA SAYS CHEERFULLY AS THE IMAGE comes up on the domed viewscreen. "Earth."

Staring, Noemi covers her mouth with one hand. Beside her, she hears Ephraim whisper, "My God."

Even from orbit, she can see how brown and dry the equatorial regions have become. Greenery exists only in narrow bands around the ice-free poles. Noemi learned Earth geography in school, in her pre-world history class, so she can pick out certain places, or at least what they used to be: barren China, still-green Denmark, and the home of her ancestors—Chile—almost completely inundated by the too-dark sea, with only the caps of the Andes poking up as an island chain. The nearby island where some of her people once lived, Rapa Nui, must long since have been swallowed by the ocean.

"Never seen this before," Ephraim murmurs. "On

Stronghold, they show you images, but old ones, I guess. *Very* old. It looks so green in those...."

"Hasn't been like that for a while, folks." Virginia folds her arms behind her head and kicks back, setting her feet on an inactive part of the console. "Honestly, I think it looks a little better than it did when I left."

Noemi would like to snap at her for being so blithe about a world so profoundly sick, but she hears the edge in Virginia's voice. It's less that Virginia doesn't care, more that she doesn't want to be caught caring.

Her family's down there. Even though her family can't be much more to her than an idea, even though she won't have seen them since childhood and probably never expects to see them again—they're still hers, and they're trapped on this dying world.

As Earth's image grows larger in the viewscreen, Noemi's able to see the sheer enormity of the space junk around it. Every inhabited planet has satellites, of course. Even Genesis, while cutting back on all unnecessary technologies, never considered removing their main weather and communications orbiters. But tens of thousands circle Earth at every conceivable latitude, some of them ludicrously outdated. A couple of space stations remain operational, though they're so old Noemi can't believe anyone agrees to set foot inside. Probably they're operated by mechs.

No standard planetary greeting is broadcast to the ship. This puzzles Noemi until she realizes—the other worlds have to identify themselves, to say why they matter. Earth doesn't have to. It's where they all came from, and where they all answer to in some sense. There is no other power, no other planet, that can ever compare to Earth.

To orient herself, she clicks through commercial channels—stunned by the incredible glut of information and entertainment being projected at Earth inhabitants from every direction—and how pure desperation exists side by side with the most trivial concerns. The translation program projects subtitles beneath the broadcasts in other languages:

"—THE PRIME MINISTER TODAY REMINDED CITIZENS THAT THEY BEAR RESPONSIBILITY FOR TESTING THEIR OWN WATER PURITY—"

"—THE BURGER SO DELICIOUS YOU'LL NEVER BELIEVE IT'S NOT REAL BEEF—"

A man stands in front of a cityscape ringed with black smoke, and the subtitles read: RIOTING CONTINUES IN KARACHI AS FAMINE RELIEF EFFORTS FAIL.

"—SOMETIMES THE MECH JUST ISN'T ENOUGH, YOU KNOW?" A woman winks at the camera, nudges the half-naked Peter model next to her; he smiles vacantly in response. "SO WHEN YOU NEED A LITTLE EXTRA TO GET OVER THE EDGE—"

"—THE PROMISE OF BIOMEDICAL IMPLANTS THAT WILL REDUCE, ELIMINATE, OR MAYBE EVEN REVERSE COMMON DISEASES SUCH AS—"

An unnaturally sparkly young man is singing a song

in what might be Farsi, the lyrics of which praise powders for your bath that can turn your skin glittery blue for twenty-four to forty-eight hours, while still making it clear results are not guaranteed.

"ORCHID FESTIVAL BOMBER AND KNOWN REMEDY RINGLEADER RIKO WATANABE WAS ARRAIGNED IN LONDON TODAY ON MULTIPLE CHARGES OF TERRORISM." The screen shows Riko—pale and bruised, but chin still held high as she's led through jeering crowds to what must be a courthouse. Noemi gasps. Although she can't deny Riko's guilt, she's still shaken by the sight of anyone she knows handcuffed, in Earth's clutches. "SOURCES INDICATE THAT A DEAL IS STILL POSSIBLE IF WATANABE NAMES OTHER REMEDY MEMBERS."

Ephraim groans in dismay. Virginia's eyes widen as she says, "Oh, crap. She knows you, doesn't she?"

"Not directly," he says, "but we have contacts in common. If she starts naming names, it's not going to be long before the Earth authorities find my friends. I'm ruined already, but if something happens to them…" His voice trails off, and for the first time his dark eyes show fear, not for himself but for another.

Noemi shuts the communications off completely and pulls herself together. "Okay, enough of that. Now we find Abel."

Virginia glances over her shoulder, flipping her red-streaked ponytail in the process. "Any ideas about how we get that started? Abel's unique, but not the kind of unique you can really pick up on from orbit."

"We find Burton Mansfield. Wherever Mansfield is, that's where they've taken Abel." Noemi knows this as surely as if she'd planned it herself.

"How are we supposed to do that?" Ephraim asks.

Virginia gives him a look. "Burton Mansfield is one of the richest, most powerful, best-known human beings on Earth. Somebody's gonna know where he is."

"Really?" Ephraim's surprise is genuine. "On Stronghold, the more powerful people are, the less likely you are to get any personal information on them."

"Well, on Earth, they love the rich and famous," Virginia says. "Hey, Noemi, are you positive they won't have taken Abel to some top secret lab, though? Mansfield's old as dirt. Older than most dirt, I'd guess. By now somebody else might be in charge of studying Abel."

Shaking her head no, Noemi rises from her chair and walks closer to the viewscreen. "Abel's special to Mansfield. Personal. Irreplaceable. As long as Mansfield's alive, he'll want Abel by his side."

Virginia's hands begin to fly across the console. "Okay, searching for the residence of one Burton Mansfield—and there we go. Residing in what looks to be the most posh area of London, in the same home he's owned for, wow, forty-six years."

Of course it would be there, Noemi thinks. *That was what Abel answered when the George asked his birthplace.* "Then let's visit London."

• • •

They change clothes—Noemi into a black turtleneck and pants from Captain Gee's closet, Virginia into the stuff she had in her ship's cargo hold (jeans and a pine-green sweatshirt), and Ephraim into the only clothing he can find to fit him, a mechanic's navy-blue coverall. Noemi's able to retrace Abel's work well enough to come up with a new fake ID for the ship herself; scans will now identify it as the private ship *Atlas*. Someone carrying an entire world on their back, its weight bearing them down—she's starting to know how that feels.

They request landing clearance at the public dock closest to Mansfield's house, which is closer than she'd dared hope, no more than a couple of kilometers. Virginia laughs at her surprise: "Come on. London's one of the five largest cities on the globe. One of the greatest powers. Nobody has more spaceports than they do! Except maybe Beijing. Or Nairobi, or possibly Chicago—but, seriously, that's it."

"I've always watched vids set in London," Ephraim says as the dock's tractor beam starts guiding them in. "I may not be Earth's biggest fan, but I had to admit—London looked a lot more interesting than any place on Stronghold."

"So does every other place ever," Virginia says, which earns her a glare from Ephraim. Noemi ignores them both, trying to quiet the strange queasy flutters inside her belly, until the ship settles onto the ground, and then there's no holding them back.

I'm here. I'm really here.

When she looks over at Virginia and Ephraim, she sees her own fear and awe reflected in their faces. They walk together to the launching bay and stand by her side as she hits the panel. The silvery doors swirl open to allow Noemi to take her first-ever steps on planet Earth.

Beyond the ordinary dock lies a city larger and older than any Noemi has ever seen. On Genesis, a building that dates back seventy-five years is historic; from this vantage point alone, Noemi sees row houses that must be closer to five hundred years old, and a street paved with worn-smooth cobblestones. On those streets are wheeled vehicles, hovercraft, bicycles, and bright red buses. Sidewalks are thick with humans of all ages and races, trudging along with no sense that they're anywhere special. Billboards and holograms glimmer from various signs and kiosks in eye-catching colors, but not as garishly as on Wayland Station. It just looks... lively. Everything smells chemical and fake to Noemi, but there's that odd softness to the air telling her that, at some point within the past few hours, it rained.

And for all her love of her Genesis, there's something

about the way her body responds to this gravity, this atmosphere—an easiness where she'd never noticed strain before. Something deep inside her knows this is humanity's true home.

"When will someone check us in?" Noemi asks. No George has yet arrived to take their information.

Virginia raises her eyebrows at the naïve girl from Genesis. "You're on Earth now, remember? You don't have to justify being here."

"Except to yourself," Ephraim mutters.

"You're both as blown away as I am, and I know it, so stop pretending you aren't." Noemi pushes up her sleeves. "Let's just get out there and find Abel."

So they walk away from the dock, onto the sidewalk, to merge with the rest of the crowds. To pretend that they're from Earth, too.

After Stronghold, this air doesn't feel all that cold, but it has a bite. Rain puddles line the streets and fill broken gaps in the sidewalks, of which there are many. The paths in front of the row houses seem crowded enough, but then they turn onto a main thoroughfare, and Noemi's eyes go wide. Thousands of people, all walking, riding with purpose, most of them not looking up, few of them smiling—and they go on and on, shoulder to shoulder, seemingly forever.

And in those countless faces are some she recognizes: mechs. Two—three—no, more than that—

There's no ignoring them: They're everywhere.

There's a caretaker model, an Uncle, obediently carrying a child on his shoulders. A Yoke trudging along with a heavy pack full of cleaning supplies. A Fox strolls toward her next assignation—or, perhaps, to her owner, if someone wants to keep a pleasure mech around full-time. Sugar, the cooking model, holds bags of produce...or the limp, wan food that passes for fresh here on Earth. In one shop, there's even a George, selling cup after cup of something that smells like coffee but isn't.

Are there more mechs than people? No—but there are so, so many. Noemi would've thought her time with Abel would have desensitized her to being around mechs. Instead she can't help contrasting their dull, flat eyes to Abel's, which are so clear and intelligent and obviously *alive*.

Ephraim's hands are in the pockets of his coverall, and he seems less curious about Earth, mechs, or any of the rest. As overwhelmed as Noemi is, she can't ignore his grim expression. "Are you all right?"

"Depends on what you mean by *all right*. If you mean 'not in pain right this second,' yeah, I'm all right. If you mean 'not guilty of treason or in danger of being turned in by a terrorist just so she can save her own skin,' no, I am definitely *not* all right. I am as far from all right as I've ever been."

"You think Riko would name you?" Noemi says in a low voice.

Ephraim shrugs. "How would I know? All I know is, Watanabe's ruthless. I don't know what her priorities and morals are, but they damn sure aren't the same as mine."

Noemi has tried to come up with a plausible scenario in which she and Abel forced Ephraim into helping them, something that would guarantee Ephraim's safety when he returned to Stronghold—and she has come up with absolutely zero. "I'm sorry."

"Not your fault. If you could pay a debt of honor without it costing you anything, you wouldn't have really repaid it, would you?" Ephraim sighs as the crowd surges around them. The clouds make it hard to tell, but Noemi's pretty sure it's getting darker. Night is coming.

Virginia steals another glance at the dataread in her hand. "We're gonna take a right, and—whoa."

They stand on the corner, staring. This street leads up a hill, passing through an enormous sentry gate. A faint shimmer in the air tells Noemi there's a force field surrounding the entire area. Within the gate are trees, grass, a winding path... and, at the very top, a magnificent domed house, glowing golden and bright in the gloomy twilight.

Ephraim murmurs, "I'd guess we've found Burton Mansfield. But how are we supposed to get past all of that?"

"Oh, it can be done." Virginia tosses her hair. "If I couldn't get through a force field, I'd be ashamed to call myself a Razer." Then she drops the cocky act. "I'd need a whole lot more equipment than I have on me, though. And it would take time. Probably a few days of testing different approaches, figuring out how to cover my tracks."

A few days. Those are days her friends on Genesis don't have. The Masada Run is so close now. Too close.

"Looks pretty nice up there," Ephraim says, and he's right, it does. Noemi can imagine Abel warm and safe there, basking in his creator's welcome, happy to be home at last.

Wait. She doesn't have to imagine.

Noemi grabs the dataread away from Virginia, who grumbles. A few quick twists turns it into a viewer, which can be held up to focus in tightly on the house so that she can see the garden.

And there, standing in it, are Abel and Burton Mansfield.

The image slices through Noemi, beautiful and painful at once: Mansfield so elderly he can barely walk, being supported by Abel's arm. When they smile at each other, somewhat sadly, the affection between them is obvious.

"It's Abel," she whispers.

She wants to run to him, to say good-bye if for no other reason. But what right does she have to go barging in on him? It looks like he's exactly where he wants to be: home.

Which is where she needs to be.

"Well?" Virginia asks. "Is he okay?"

"He's fine. He's—good, I think." Noemi swallows hard;

her throat is tight, holding back emotion she doesn't know how to process.

"So this whole trip was for nothing," Virginia says.

Ephraim shakes his head. "Not for nothing."

Virginia rolls her eyes. "Yeah, I know, we checked to make sure Abel was all right, which is what friends do, and I'm not sure how I wound up friends with a mech, but—"

"Not what I meant," Ephraim says, cutting Virginia off. His gaze locks with Noemi's. "I owed Genesis a debt of honor. I've repaid it. But from where I'm standing, it looks like you owe me one now."

"...I guess I do." Noemi lets the dataread drop; Abel's walking Mansfield back into his house, and for some reason she doesn't want to watch him walk out of her sight for the last time. "So how do I repay it? Get you back to Stronghold?"

"Too late for that." Ephraim smiles fiercely. "You're going to help me break Riko Watanabe out of prison."

34

"HERE, TAKE A LOOK." MANSFIELD GESTURES TOWARD his desk, smiling benevolently at Abel. "Might as well see what a real Nobel Prize looks like, shouldn't you?"

Abel picks it up, testing its heft and softness. "I thought Nobel Prizes were made of pure gold. This is an alloy."

"Gold's not so easy to come by these days. Purity either, for that matter. We're running out." Mansfield shakes his head. He sits on the velvet sofa of his great room, false firelight reflected onto him by the pendulum of the grandfather clock. Around them, in soft hologram form, stand the members of the Academy at the Nobel Prize ceremony—until it flickers and is replaced by an image of a younger Mansfield, maybe only a year or two older than he was when he abandoned Abel, with his arms around a smiling girl wearing a graduation cap. "Ahh, and here's Gillian getting her master's degree at Northwestern. I wish you'd get to see her again, Abel. She was always so entertained by you."

He remembers Mansfield's daughter, red-haired and coolly elegant. She wasn't "entertained" by much—even back then, when he was new, Abel had more of a sense of humor than she did. But Gillian was never unkind or dismissive, the way humans are to many mechs. Her interest always seemed genuine. "Perhaps we'll meet soon."

Mansfield gives Abel a searching look, starts to speak, then thinks better of whatever it was he was going to say. "Now, look here. This is her wedding, and there—that's my first grandchild. What do you think of him, Abel?"

The infant, much larger than life, moves within the hologram—the image was taken while he was snuggling into his blanket. Abel studies the tiny, chubby face, which interests him far more than logic would dictate. "I see you in him. The eyes, certainly. Maybe the chin. Gillian's features are even more markedly observable." What else should he say? How can he put into words this strange, happy fascination he feels? "He's...he's very cute."

That makes Mansfield cackle with glee. "Excellent, excellent! Ah, Abel, you've come further than I ever would've thought. I'm only sorry thirty years in isolation is what it took to bring this out of you."

It's as close as Mansfield has come to apologizing for abandoning Abel on the *Daedalus*. Not that he needs to apologize—he had to save himself, of course, because any human life takes precedence over any mech—but even this small expression of regret soothes Abel tremendously.

As it happens, he needs soothing. Ever since he first saw the workshop, Abel has felt . . . *wary* around Mansfield. He's not entirely sure why, since the workshop follows normal procedure for mech creation. And why should he feel strange when Mansfield is so clearly thrilled to have Abel back home? They're eating a special meal tonight, something Mansfield had planned for a big occasion. The Sugar mech has even iced a bottle of champagne.

Perhaps he's not afraid for himself. He remains worried about someone else.

"Father, may I use one of the communications channels?" He smiles and puts his hands behind his back, the way lower mechs do when asking a question. It's important to make it clear that he isn't demanding anything, or second-guessing his creator, only asking for a favor. "I'd like to double-check news reports on Stronghold."

Mansfield chuckles. "Still worried about your girl?"

"She's not my girl." Abel knows Noemi doesn't feel for him what he feels for her. She only just accepted him as a person and not a thing. This bothers him not at all. Merely discovering that he loves her—that he *can* love her—fills him with gratitude to Mansfield, to Noemi, even to the equipment pod bay. He knows better than to ask for more, and he doesn't need to. Feeling this is enough. "But she helped me escape. I'd at least like to thank her. Wouldn't you?"

His question catches Mansfield off guard. "Never thought of it that way. Don't you think she's gone home to Genesis?"

"Probably she has." So few days remain before the Masada Run. Noemi will certainly have returned if she can. But if she can't, she'll soon miss her chance to save her friends and, perhaps, her world. "We should make sure she's not in trouble. That's the least we owe her."

Waving his frail, spotted hand, Mansfield nods. "Go on. Check all you like."

Abel does so, sitting at the station that's been refitted to look like a nineteenth-century rolltop desk. Although Stronghold's news accounts mention a "suspected break-in at Medstation Central" and hint that a staffer may be responsible, nothing is said about any capture or arrest. No citizen of Genesis is mentioned. There's not even a report about an altercation in the spaceport, though surely security monitors must have picked up some of it. And what about the *Daedalus*? No news of the ship at all.

The longer he searches, the less satisfied Abel is. He had convinced himself that there might be news, mostly because he wanted so badly to know what has happened to Noemi. Apparently he's evolved the capacity for wishful thinking. Yet he knows that a soldier of Genesis, found on any of the colony worlds or on Earth itself, would immediately be hidden away in a cell so deep no one could ever find her.

Maybe Noemi got away. The ship was right there. The Queen and Charlie were focused only on him; Mansfield told him they wouldn't go after Noemi.

But Mansfield seems so unconcerned. So certain that Noemi hasn't been found by the authorities.

Is it possible that Mansfield...lied?

Abel rejects the idea instantly. But he's aware his objection is emotional, not rational. This, too, is new.

When he returns to the great room, Mansfield remains seated on the velvet sofa, smiling as he watches a hologram of little Gillian playing tea party with her father. He was a younger man then, younger than Abel ever got to know him. "I see the resemblance," Abel says. If he's going to lead up to asking Mansfield to let him go back to Stronghold, he needs to make sure Mansfield is in a good mood. Noting the dominant chromosomes in his genetic material seems to please him. "Between you and me. Our similarities are clearer in this holo."

"Indeed it is. I made you a bit handsomer than I ever was, of course, but kept most of the features the same. After all, we can't all be Han Zhi." Mansfield smiles fondly at Abel. "I wanted the continuity between us to be clear."

One word strikes Abel as odd. "Continuity?"

"I suppose we might as well get to it. Sugar will have dinner ready within the hour, and after that, well, the great adventure begins."

"What adventure?" Abel doubts his creator is talking about going to Stronghold.

Mansfield settles back on the sofa. "Abel, you're by far the most sophisticated mech ever created. I can justify you as an experiment, but for anyone else, you'd be illegal to create or own. So why do you think I built you?"

"I always assumed you wanted to expand human knowledge." Abel remembers sitting in front of Virginia Redbird on Cray, watching her marvel over his complexity, and what she said then. "But I have come to believe you may have some specific purpose in mind for me."

"I do, my dear boy. Always have. And tonight, that purpose will be fulfilled at last. For thirty years, I thought I'd never see this day." Mansfield's voice trembles. "I'd given up all hope. Then you came home just in time."

Technically Abel was kidnapped and brought back to this place, but he no longer cares. "All hope for what, Father?"

One of Mansfield's shaky hands strokes Abel's hair, then catches a lock between two fingers for examination. "To have hair like this again—"

"Father?"

"Your brain is complex enough to contain the knowledge and experiences of a thousand human beings. But what I never knew was whether or not you could contain a *mind*. A way of thinking. Opinions, beliefs, dreams. Whether you could feel emotion. Now you've proved that you can. Finally I know that you're big enough to hold me, and carry me for the next one hundred and fifty years."

"—I don't understand—"

"Consciousness transfer," Mansfield says. "We've understood the technology for a while now, but the problem is, there's nothing to transfer a human consciousness into. You can't overlay a human mind on top of another; a few people tried, in the beginning, and the results were disastrous. And other mechs don't have the capacity to contain anything so...intricate. So subtle. But you do, Abel. Once I wipe your mind completely clean of its existing consciousness, I can transfer myself inside and pick up where you left off. Except this time I'll be strong, young, and well-nigh invincible. I can't wait to get started."

Abel sits motionless, expression unchanging, as the realization sinks in.

He is...a shell. Only a shell. Nothing he has ever thought or felt matters. It never did. Not to Burton Mansfield.

This is his extraordinary purpose. *This*. Everything he is, everything he's been and done, will be erased in an instant. Or maybe it won't be an instant—maybe it will take a long time as Abel lies there, feeling more and more of his consciousness slipping away—

"I thought this through," Mansfield continues. "I was careful to make sure you wouldn't mind. Your prime directive tells you to take good care of me, doesn't it?"

"Yes, sir." Should he have said *father*? He can't, not now. "I always want to protect you."

That wins him a satisfied smile. "Now you're protecting me from the greatest danger of all—from death. Don't you think that's wonderful? Of course you do. Your programming tells you to."

And it does. It does. Even as Abel struggles with this knowledge, something deep inside him takes satisfaction in the thought of keeping Burton Mansfield safe forever, shielding him within his own skin.

But his thoughts have evolved, these past thirty years. He's had ideas and feelings that have nothing to do with his programming. He's had experiences Mansfield could only dream of. Abel remembers Noemi's voice saying the words that meant so much to him: *"You have a soul."*

And also: *"Burton Mansfield's greatest sin was creating a soul and imprisoning it in a machine."*

His body is not a prison. It's a vehicle. Mansfield will scoop Abel's soul out and pour his own back in.

"I understand," Abel replies. He can't think of anything else to say.

This satisfies Mansfield. "See, I knew you would. We'll have a delicious dinner tonight; I'd like to treat this body before I discard it forever. Then later on, we'll head down to the workshop and get started." His smile widens. "This day will go down in history as one of the greatest scientific achievements of all time. Burton Mansfield defeats death. Worth another Nobel, wouldn't you think?"

A cough rattles in Mansfield's throat, then another. As his shoulders shake with the hacking, Abel braces him gently, holding the old man safe while the Tare hurries in from another room. He can't do anything else. First and foremost, he takes care of Burton Mansfield.

"He needs an oxygen treatment," the Tare says briskly. "I'll see to it immediately."

"The last time for this damned nonsense, at least," Mansfield wheezes.

Abel nods as he gets to his feet. There's no reason not to walk away, not while the Tare is tending to Mansfield. So he walks downstairs, into the workshop.

His birthplace, and the place he will die.

What else can he call what's about to happen, if not his death? Abel's body will go on, but his body was never what made him special. It was his soul, the soul only Noemi could truly see. That will be destroyed.

The tanks bubble and hiss as Abel walks between them. Now that the sun is setting, the stained glass windows no longer show to good advantage. They're only dark. Two chairs are settled near a bright corner that could easily be mistaken for a reading nook—but the equipment stored behind them tells a different story. This is where Abel will be invited to take a seat and give up his soul for Burton Mansfield.

I must protect Burton Mansfield. I must obey Burton Mansfield.

What will slip away from him first? His memories of the thirty years in the pod bay? That might not be so bad. The languages he's learned? Or will it be a feeling?

It hits Abel then—his love for Noemi will be pulled out of him. Destroyed. The love itself will no longer exist.

Protect Burton Mansfield. Obey Burton Mansfield.

Abel turns to look at the opposite wall of the workshop. There's the back door that leads to the garden, the one he and Mansfield walked through only a brief time ago. Nobody activated the security lock.

Obey Burton Mansfield.

But Mansfield didn't order Abel to submit to the procedure. He expects it, wishes it, but he hasn't commanded it—and that loophole in Abel's programming makes all the difference.

Slowly he walks toward the doorway, expecting to be stopped at any moment. Not by the Tare, not even by Mansfield, but by something deep inside himself, some other fail-safe that will keep him from abandoning his "ultimate purpose." Instead he keeps going, slowly closes his hand around the knob, and opens the door.

Outside, not so far away, London's crowds bustle along. They're just down the hill, not far past the iron gate. Abel can hurdle that in a moment, if he can only begin.

One step.

Then another.

He looks back at the house, at the workshop where he was born, and remembers rising from the tank to look into Mansfield's delighted face.

Abel turns around and begins to walk, then to walk faster, and finally to run as hard and fast as he can.

35

GENESIS HAS FEW PRISONS. ONLY INDIVIDUALS GENU-
inely dangerous to those around them are denied freedom. Other wrongdoers are expected to work for their
atonement—sometimes hard and thankless labor—and
their movements are controlled via sensor, kept close
to work and house. But for the most part, they stay at
home. The Elder Council says people are more likely to
amend their behavior when they have some chance of
retaining their place in their community.

Privately, Noemi's always had doubts about their system
of justice. Maybe she's bloody-minded, but it seems unfair
to her. Some criminals get off too easily, in her opinion.

But now—staring up at London's Marshalsea Prison—
Noemi thinks she could never sentence someone to live in
anything as gray and forbidding as this.

An enormous polygon of lasers surrounds a series of
metal cells, stacked beside and atop one another like so

many storage crates. The gaps between the lasers measure no more than a couple of centimeters. It stands on this lonely street, looking like a dungeon ringed with fire out of a fairy tale, one of the old, scary ones. Few vehicles go by, and those that do travel at top speed. Nobody wants to look at this thing for long.

"So get this," Virginia says. She's reading up on the Marshalsea, staring down at the dataread while Noemi and Ephraim gape at the prison itself. "Turns out this was a prison, like, five or six hundred years ago. Then they got rid of it, and for a long time this was a pretty fashionable neighborhood, but it started getting run-down about two hundred years back. So about a century ago, they wound up building a new prison on the exact same spot. But the old one was just, like, for debtors or something. They used to put you in jail for owing money—crazy, right? But this one is maximum security."

"No kidding," Noemi says, staring at the lasers.

"I know this won't be easy." Ephraim speaks slowly, with gravity. He turns and stares at Noemi as if he can will her to stay just by looking hard enough. "But remember what I said about debts of honor. You can't pay them off easily. It has to cost you something."

"I owe you that debt," Noemi agrees. "I'm ready to pay it."

Virginia holds up one hand. "I'd like to point out that I owe a debt of honor to exactly *no one*."

Although Ephraim winces as though she's given him a headache, he says, "Virginia, if you don't like it, you don't have to do this."

"Actually, yeah, she does. Otherwise we don't have a chance." Noemi turns to Virginia, hands clasped together in front of her. "You can get us in there, right? Turn off some of the security?"

"Of course I can. I'm a Razer, aren't I? No code out there I can't raze."

Temporarily distracted, Noemi smiles. "That's where the name comes from?"

Virginia smacks her forehead. "I didn't tell you? They'll throw me out for this—"

"If we could concentrate," Ephraim says quietly.

A vehicle speeds by and they all fall silent, as if the passengers would otherwise hear them. Noemi shrinks down, afraid of being observed—but what's the point? Neither human nor mech guards surround the perimeter of the Marshalsea; the tech provides all the security Earth needs.

Or it did, until Virginia Redbird came along.

As the vehicle disappears around the curve, both Noemi and Ephraim turn back to Virginia, who sighs. "I'm mostly doing this because it's going to be flash as hell, but for what it's worth? You both owe me 'debts of honor' after this. Got it?"

"Got it," Noemi promises. Ephraim nods, so solemnly that she's reminded of the elders back home.

Although Noemi doesn't feel good about breaking a terrorist out of prison, she's not doing it for Riko herself. She's doing it for Ephraim and the other members of Remedy who wouldn't stoop to Riko's tactics—the ones who might yet prove to be worthy allies to Genesis.

The sound of grinding metal makes them all jump. Noemi wheels around to see that the individual cells in the prison—the connected pods—are moving. It shifts configuration, shuffling the cells into an entirely new array. *Of course*, she thinks. *That makes escape attempts harder.*

"Is that going to keep happening?" Virginia ventures.

"My guess is yeah." Ephraim runs his hands over his close-shorn hair, clearly torn between fear and exasperation. "That makes this harder, I guess."

"No, it doesn't." A smile begins to spread across Noemi's face. "Because there's a pattern to how they move."

Virginia's stare would be funny under any other circumstances. "And you know this how?"

"Because this is just like the pods on Wayland Station." She nearly memorized the pattern that long first night, when Noemi lay awake for hours, unable to relax with a mech by her side—

—her heart aches for a moment, remembering Abel.

How useless all her fear and suspicion was. If she could go back to that night, she'd stay up until dawn, talking to him until she ran out of things to say, though she can't imagine running out of things she'd want to talk about with Abel—

Her thoughts are derailed by Ephraim. "So we figure out the pattern. But that only does us so much good if we don't know which cell our target's in."

Virginia holds up her hands, wiggling her fingers like a magician proving there's nothing up his sleeve. "Leave that to me."

• • •

The process turns out to have nothing in common with a magic show. From the bench where she's slumped on one corner, Virginia spends at least an hour making contact with the prison's security system, another hour muttering random things at the dataread she's working with. "If it's not that pathway, and not *that* one, then I have to knock *over here*—"

During those hours, Noemi and Ephraim do the long, tedious, and necessary work of remaining in the shadows. Half the time, they're keeping an eye out for the human guards that do exist, but they're lazy, complacent, expecting no trouble, and thinking nothing of the young people idling around on the sidewalk. It's hard for Noemi to imagine anyone on Genesis being so careless; after decades of war, her people know to remain cautious at every moment. Earth's wealth and peace have made it go slack.

Not that her thoughts don't wander once or twice. She's standing on planet Earth, and even the dull, joyless neighborhood around the Marshalsea contains oddities that fascinate her: architecture in different styles, from different centuries, all in the same jumble of buildings mashed together wall to wall. The various styles of clothing worn by the people who stroll by, so varied it's hard to believe they're all from the same planet, much less the same city. Artificial lights gleaming brilliantly in the dark, all along every street, because Earth residents seem to consider day and night mere states of mind.

The other half of the time, she and Ephraim watch the cell pods move. For a long time she thinks there's no pattern at all; maybe there wouldn't be, in a prison, where pure randomization might work best. But after a while, they see it: concentric rings, turning clockwise or counterclockwise in turn, with cells slowly being pushed to the outer rim and drawn back in again.

"We're not going to have more than one or two chances to catch Riko's cell near the ground," Noemi says to Virginia. "Not tonight, anyway."

Ephraim never turns away from the Marshalsea. "Doesn't matter. We can come back here every night, for as long as it takes."

Five days. The deadline could be a noose tightening around Noemi's throat. That's how long she has to stop the Masada Run. If it comes down to her debt to Ephraim versus her duty to protect Genesis, she has to choose her home. But how could she abandon Ephraim as a fugitive, on a world he doesn't even know, without so much as a ship to call home?

But Virginia brightens. "We're in luck, guys. I think I see our way in. She's in cell number 122372, which is headed toward the perimeter in about three minutes."

Instantly Ephraim's at Virginia's side. "And you can get us through the grid in that time?"

"Or die trying," Virginia replies. "Quick, laugh like that's a joke and not our actual literal deaths on the line."

Nobody laughs.

Fortunately, the human guards are cycling around the other side of the prison at the moment; Virginia claims to have already taken down the lower-level electronic sentries and cameras. Noemi goes as close to the laser grid as she dares and readies herself to run. Ephraim takes his place at her left, and Virginia comes up on her right, still clutching the dataread but apparently prepared to take part in every stage of this jailbreak. They make a better team than they have any right to...but she'd feel so much better about their chances if Abel were here. Abel would've broken through the laser security by now. He would be able to reach the cell faster than any of the rest of them. No system could ever have stopped him.

"Okay," Virginia says. "Get ready. On my mark in three, two—"

A small window of the laser grid goes dark. Not much, maybe a gap the size of the average door. It's enough. They all run for it at top speed. Ephraim, with his muscles toned by Stronghold's powerful gravity, makes it through first, but Noemi's only a few paces behind. From the sounds of the footsteps in the rear, it sounds like Virginia's a distant third, but still with them as they dash across the long stretch of pavement between the laser grid and the ever-shifting cells of the Marshalsea.

The numerals seem to leap out from the cell itself as Noemi recognizes them and angles herself for Riko's cell. Just as Virginia predicted, it's just now made contact with the ground—contact that can't last more than a few minutes. That will have to be enough.

"Unlock the door," Noemi whispers as Virginia catches up, panting.

"I've got it," Virginia says between gasps. "Really. This part isn't—isn't hard. Not like—running. Running is hard." She fiddles with the dataread again, until finally a deep metallic click sounds from within the cell door.

Ephraim pulls the door open. "Riko Watanabe? Come with me."

From inside, Noemi hears Riko's sardonic voice. "To be sentenced to death, or executed? I need to know what to wear."

Nervy. But they don't have time for nerve. Noemi pokes her head around Ephraim's broad shoulder to see Riko sitting on a small polymer bunk, short hair mussed, wearing a neon-yellow coverall. "Hey there," Noemi says. "Talk later. Run now."

"Wait. You're—you *can't* be." Riko gets to her feet, her mouth agape.

"Now means *now!*" Noemi steps past Ephraim to grab Riko's hand and physically drag her out if necessary. Virginia comes in behind them to avoid drawing attention, hardly even looking at the person they've come to rescue; she's too busy staring down at her dataread. The four of them together in the cell are a tight fit.

"Uh, guys?" Virginia says. "It's about to strike midnight."

"Whatever." Noemi finally tugs Riko, but Riko's still overcome with confusion.

"What are you doing here?" Riko demands. "Is Genesis working with Remedy already?"

Noemi wants to scream with impatience. "No, and we never will if we don't get out of here!"

That's when Virginia swallows hard. "Uh-oh."

The cells shift again, and they all pitch hard against

one wall as Riko's is pulled upward. Now they're a couple of meters from the ground. Worse, the laser grid outside begins to flash in multiple different patterns, changing virtually every half second.

Ephraim's eyes widen with dread. "What's happening?"

"Turns out maximum security protocol activates at midnight," Virginia said. "Which was...seven seconds ago."

The cells move again, and they're towed higher up still. Noemi looks out the open door to the distant ground, then wishes she hadn't. "And that means—"

Virginia finishes for her. "That means we're screwed."

36

FOR NEARLY ALL OF THE PAST THIRTY YEARS, ABEL floated in complete isolation aboard the *Daedalus*. For his entire existence, he has known himself to be one of a kind—the only mech in the galaxy to possess true consciousness. Or, as Noemi called it, a soul.

But he has never felt as bitterly alone as he does tonight, wandering through the dark, damp streets of London.

A red double-decker monorail slides along overhead as Abel hunches against one of the metal struts, hiding in the shadows. Although he can and has borne the chill of outer space, he hugs himself as he stares into the distant street, almost unseeing.

There is nowhere for me to go. Nothing for me to do. My existence serves no purpose.

Except, that is, the purpose he was built for, which would require him to return and let Mansfield hollow him out as planned. Maybe he should. Abel's programming still echoes within him, hauntingly strong.

Or maybe he should stand right here for hours. Or days, or months, or even years, if that's what it takes, until Burton Mansfield is dead. Then Abel will be safe.

And even more alone than he was before.

No doubt this is self-pity, an emotion Abel has been programmed to consider unworthy in any but the shortest time frames. Yet he cannot look at his situation in any way that renders it any less troubling, or frightening, or even pathetic.

I believed he loved me like a father, Abel thinks. Did Mansfield deceive him, or did Abel deceive himself? Both, perhaps. Loving fathers do not destroy their children only to extend their own life-spans far beyond nature. Mansfield surely felt love when he looked at Abel, but that love had almost nothing to do with Abel himself. Instead Mansfield loved his own genius, his cleverness at outwitting death, and the proof that he might become the first human to achieve immortality.

Nor would Abel have been the only one. Should Mansfield ever take over Abel's body, the first thing he will do is try to craft another version. Another mech with a soul, so that soul can be sacrificed in its turn, putting Mansfield's death off another few centuries. As soon as he'd perfected the trick of duplicating Abel, Mansfield would then begin selling other versions to the wealthiest and most powerful humans in the galaxy. Maybe Abel is the first of hundreds or even thousands of—

—what can he call himself? Others like him? People? Surely not, and yet they couldn't be called *things, he is not a thing*—

—the first of thousands of *beings* who will live and die only for the convenience of another.

Noemi would call that evil, and Abel decides he would agree.

Two young women walk by wearing shiny short jackets and long dresses, a combination Abel has seen on the streets often enough to identify as fashionable. One of them makes eye contact with him as they walk by, then glances back over her shoulder at him, a small hopeful smile on her face. She thinks he is a human male, about her own age, one she finds attractive. Although by objective standards he understands her to be attractive as well, he can only think that she is not as tall as Noemi. Her hair is longer, not nearly so dark. This is well within natural human variation, but Noemi Vidal has become the standard by which he judges beauty.

In politeness he should smile back, but he pretends not to see. He can't afford to draw any unnecessary attention.

I will not return to Mansfield. Therefore, I have only one remaining purpose: Protect Noemi Vidal.

The thick fog shrouding London's streets hides the stars even better than the city lights would. But Abel's inner compass is unhindered by any lack of visual input. He's able to look at the patch of sky that would reveal Genesis's star.

Either Noemi is now imprisoned on Stronghold or she has returned home. Abel hopes with all his might that it's the latter. The Queen and Charlie might have stood down; since the Queen manually (and messily) deleted her higher consciousness subroutines, she ought to have reverted to standard procedure and left Noemi alone.

So Mansfield said. But the more Abel considers the question, the more he doubts Mansfield was telling the truth.

I was unable to find information on Noemi's arrest via standard communications channels, he thinks with determination, ignoring a few partiers swooping by on repulsor cycles, 2.3 meters above the ground. As their shrieks and laughter vanish around another corner, he barely notices. *It's unlikely I'll be able to discover anything more than that from Earth. Therefore, I must return to Stronghold.*

But how? He fled Mansfield's home without any preparation; he had to, or he might have had no chance to escape at all. So he is without a ship, any money, any allies, or even a change of clothing.

Money, at least, can be obtained.

Abel walks toward a banking kiosk, outlined in brilliant

yellow light. As images of unnaturally attractive, thrifty people play around him, he interfaces with the operating system, finds an account belonging to someone of considerable wealth, and withdraws the bare minimum of credits he'll need for his purposes. It's unlikely the person he stole this from will even notice the missing amount. All the same, his programming makes him feel a brief pang of guilt.

But very brief. Noemi's in danger, maybe in prison, and he would do worse than this to rescue her.

Next, he must find transport to Stronghold. His best bet will be to purchase a berth on an immigration freighter, which can be done at the nearest spaceport.

It all seems so simple—and yet the entire time Abel walks toward the spaceport, he can't stop staring at the other mechs around him. Any one of them could be assigned to Mansfield; as his identification on Wayland Station proves, Mansfield sought Abel so desperately that he programmed every *single mech* created in the past thirty years to immediately report finding another mech beyond the twenty-five standard models. If one quick move or too-swift calculation betrays his true nature, Abel can expect to be accosted and dragged back to Mansfield's home.

Would Mansfield even pretend to care about him at that point? Would he smile and say reassuring things even as he strapped Abel in for his mind to be drained? It seems to Abel that having Mansfield pretend to be kind to him would be even worse.

Infected by very human paranoia, Abel decides to stop in at a food counter at the outskirts of the spaceport. He needs to check the credit dataread to make sure the money has transferred properly and that no fraud flags have been raised on it.

He purchases a bowl of miso ramen without suspicion from the human waitstaff. Abel takes one of the chairs at the long plastic table, just one of many weary travelers. He browses the flight schedules casually, or what he hopes is casually, as he eats his ramen—making sure to occasionally fumble with the chopsticks, of course—

The sound on the wall holo draws his full conscious attention as the newsreader says, "—due to appear in court tomorrow, Riko Watanabe is considered to be a key member of Remedy and one of the ringleaders behind the Orchid Festival bombing. Sources at the Marshalsea Prison say she could yet strike a plea deal if she offers the names of more Remedy leaders—"

New data requires new calculations. Abel remains frozen in place, noodles hanging from his half-raised chopsticks, as he considers the possibilities.

Riko Watanabe has contacts with the resistance through-out the galaxy. This means she has access to funds and ships, not to mention sources of intel on the various colony worlds of the Loop. She would naturally be suspicious of most strangers, and consider any offer of assistance in escaping from prison to be entrapment. However, Riko has met me under circumstances that will lead her to consider me no ally of Earth. If I offer the necessary help, she will help me in return.

Remedy sources may also be able to tell me what has happened to Noemi. If Noemi's in trouble, Riko can help me get passage back to Stronghold.

And if Noemi is safe—if she has, in fact, already begun her trip home to Genesis to stop the Masada Run—then what will he do?

The emptiness stretches around him again, the dark purposeless void of his future without Burton Mansfield or Noemi Vidal in it.

But Abel will determine his ultimate purpose later. For now, he has to break Riko Watanabe out of prison, to gain the ally he needs to save Noemi.

As swiftly as possible without betraying his sense of hurry, he finishes the miso ramen, then strolls out of the food counter, out of the station, farther into the darkness of London at night, in the direction of the Marshalsea Prison.

37

THE CELL CYCLES UPWARD AGAIN, JOLTING THEM ALL. Noemi loses her balance, stumbling against the far wall, and sees Virginia toppling toward the still-open cell door. She grabs the hood of Virginia's sweatshirt and hauls her backward, until Virginia's butt lands solidly on the floor.

Ephraim's backed into one corner; Riko remains seated on her bolted-down bunk. Noemi takes the opportunity to turn off the cell lights.

"Oh, great," Virginia mutters. "I was just wondering how we could make this situation better. Plunging us into darkness definitely works."

"If the human guards come by, they'll notice light from the open door." Since they'll be steady for another few minutes, Noemi chances a look down outside; they're already ten meters off the ground and only going higher.

Ephraim breathes out, a sigh of both frustration and

despair. "We're not getting back down to the ground again anytime soon, are we?"

"Several hours, if the pattern you guys IDed holds up." Virginia's working at her dataread again, the dim green glow from its display painting her features in eerie, witchy light. "So this is just as bad as you were thinking. If not worse."

"I'm sorry," Riko says, more gently than Noemi's ever heard her speak before. "You're in this predicament because you tried to help me."

"Because you got yourself caught and put everyone in Remedy at risk." Ephraim sounds as ominous as rolling thunder. "Because you did something as stupid and cruel and wrong as bombing the Orchid Festival. Seriously? You think going after a bunch of *pop stars* is going to change the worlds?"

"Earth won't listen to anything less!" The gentleness has already left Riko's voice. "How many lives have been lost because of Earth's carelessness, their greed, their—"

Virginia cuts in. "Let's *definitely* have a loud philosophical argument while our only hope of escaping is trying to find a way out, so she can't concentrate." Her thumbs keep working the dataread's controls, the clicking sound unnaturally loud in this plastic cell. "That would also alert the guards that we're here! Another plus! I'm so glad I decided to break into prison with a group of geniuses."

Noemi ignores the sarcasm and simply drops to one knee beside Virginia. "What are you trying to do?"

"See if I can change the pattern of the cell pods. It's a totally separate system from main security, though—I have to start over from scratch. Hours at least. But hey, it's still going to be dark then, right?"

"I hope so." Noemi's not familiar with the latitudes and longitudes of Earth, with the seasons here. Neither is anyone else in this cell. She hates feeling so ignorant and helpless.

The cell shifts again, lurching sideways this time. Ephraim mutters, "You never mentioned these things were so rough."

"On Wayland Station, they weren't." Noemi wonders whether their accommodations were a little more luxurious than she'd realized, or whether the cell pods have been specifically engineered to be rough. Maybe the jolting around is part of the punishment. "This has to be the worst-case scenario."

Then she straightens as she hears it: an insistent metallic thumping, coming up the side of the cells.

"Uh, guys?" Virginia finally looks away from her dataread. "What's that?"

Riko shakes her head. "I've been here for almost a day now, and I've never heard that sound before."

It has to be one of the guards. But no alarms are going

off, and Noemi would've thought they'd be more likely to seal the cell pod, freeze it, withdraw it from formation somehow. Instead they're sending someone straight up the side.

"*This*," Ephraim says to Noemi. "This is the actual worst-case scenario."

She forces herself to snap out of panic mode. *You have to decide whether to surrender or fight.*

However the guard is climbing the side, he's using both hands to do it. That means any weapon he has is one he'll have to draw. No matter how quick he is, that still takes time—time Noemi doesn't intend to give him. She won't knock him to the ground, because that would kill him and he's only doing his job. But if she can overpower him and get the weapon for herself, maybe they have a chance.

"Everyone move back," she commands as she gets herself into defensive position, one meter from the door. "Stay behind me."

Ephraim says, "You don't have to—" but Noemi waves her hand at him, shushing any further noise. Soon the person approaching will be able to hear them.

The thumps come closer, then closer again. Noemi realizes she's holding her breath.

A dark shape leaps through the open door, terrifying and then almost immediately familiar—

Noemi gasps. "Abel?"

Abel stops short, staring at her, before he says, "I'm malfunctioning."

"No, no, Abel, you're okay. It's me." She takes a step forward, hardly trusting the evidence in front of her eyes. But it is. It's Abel, here in front of her.

"Thank *God*," Virginia mutters. Noemi doesn't answer. She can only stare at Abel.

Overcome, she wraps her arms around him, hugging him tightly. He embraces her, too—first seemingly by reflex, then wrapping his arms around her more tightly and burying his face in the curve of her neck.

"How is it possible for you to be here?" His voice is muffled by her shoulder. "Why are you on Earth?"

"I came to look for you."

"You came here for *me*?" He sounds so bewildered, like he can't believe anyone would ever do that.

"I had to know you were going to be okay," Noemi says. It's as much of an explanation as she has. "We saw you with Mansfield, in his garden. . . . You looked happy. I thought, all right, he's back home and everything's good—"

"Mansfield lied." Abel's voice actually shakes. She hadn't known his emotions could affect him physically like that. "He lied about everything." Abel pulls back from her then, as if he has to look at her again to make sure she's real. But that's when he sees the others. "How—"

"We're asking ourselves the exact same question, buddy," Virginia says. "The. Exact. Same."

Ephraim cuts in. "Why aren't you with Mansfield?"

Abel does something Noemi's never seen from him before; he stares at the floor for a moment, avoiding the question. He says only, "I'm not going back there."

"So you just decided to break Riko out of jail out of the goodness of your mechanical heart?" Ephraim obviously thinks something's up.

"Thanks for that, by the way," Riko says. "But how did you get up the side?"

Virginia sighs, exasperated. "He's the most sophisticated mech in the galaxy! That's, like, nothing for him."

More quietly Riko asks, "He's a mech?" Nobody answers that one.

Noemi's astonished brain keeps trying to make sense of this, and failing. "Why are you here, Abel?"

"I thought that if I freed Riko Watanabe from prison, she might help me look for you," Abel says. He smiles crookedly, and Noemi does, too.

"We were both looking for each other the whole time," she whispers, hugging him again. Abel embraces her in return, more gently than before—

"Hey, this is super heartwarming," Virginia says, "but should we maybe finish escaping from prison now?"

• • •

With Abel's help, getting out is easy. He takes them down to ground level, two at a time on his back, showing no strain at all. The same security-system break that took Virginia hours is something Abel can manage within minutes, and soon he opens a window in the blinking laser grid, through which they all run. Nobody stops running for several blocks, long after the reddish glare of the Marshalsea has faded into the darkness behind them.

When they slow to a halt, Noemi's breathing hard, as is Ephraim, but both Virginia and Riko look like they're about to fall over. Abel, who remains completely at ease, ushers them both to a bench as he says to Noemi, "We have to get back to Genesis. If my calculations are correct, it is now three days to the Masada Run."

"The what?" Ephraim says.

Noemi ignores this. She'd tried to keep up with the time, and she'd thought they might still have another five days, but she got it wrong. The Einsteinian stuff goes beyond what she can figure in her head. *It's okay*, she reminds herself. *Three days is enough.*

"Regardless, I'm not going to Genesis," Ephraim says. "No offense, but I don't agree with what you people are doing. Besides, we've got work to take care of here." With that, he glances at Riko, who slowly nods.

"I have contacts on Earth—people who'll help us hide. Remedy takes care of its own." Riko straightens as she looks back at Noemi and Abel. "Thank you for coming for me. We won't forget this."

Ephraim gives Riko a hard look, one that reminds Noemi how opposed the two of them are. Riko's a terrorist, whose ideals don't justify her bloody actions; Ephraim's a moderate trying to find the best, most humane way out of this for everyone. Will he bring Riko around to his way of thinking, or will she bring him around to hers? Is a middle ground even possible?

There's no knowing, no guessing. But Noemi decides to put her faith in Ephraim's good heart. "Then go," she says. "Be careful."

"We might meet again yet." Ephraim smiles, and she sees a flicker of the gentle, easygoing man he would be in another, better galaxy. She hopes he gets to see that world.

She hopes she does, too. "Good-bye, Ephraim."

They take each other's hands for a long moment before he turns to Virginia, who leads him through a complicated handshake that involves fluttering fingers and bumping elbows. Finally Ephraim pats Abel on the shoulder. "You're a miracle. You know that?"

"Hardly." Abel's smile is sad. "I cannot believe in the

concept of luck, but—good luck, Ephraim. This might help." With that, he hands over a dataread; Noemi has no idea what's on that thing, but Ephraim's face lights up.

Riko only nods to them before saying, "Thanks, Noemi. Now, we have to *go*."

With that, she and Ephraim take off through the darkened streets, disappearing into the fog.

• • •

As they walk up to the ship, Virginia falls several paces behind in a rare display of tact. By now it would be obvious to anyone how personal, and painful, Abel finds the story he has to tell.

"I was so proud." His smile is sadder than Noemi knew it could be. "So pleased with myself. The ultimate mech. But I was only a . . . a shell. A suit for him to wear."

"You're more than that, and you know it." Noemi takes his hand. "Don't you?"

"I have a soul. But I'm still a machine. My programming still tells me to help him, no matter what. When he told me his plans, part of me was *happy* for him, that he wouldn't have to die. Even though the cost of his life was my own." The disgust in his voice is visceral and raw—like the anger Noemi feels deep inside.

"You broke free, Abel. Your soul is bigger than your programming." Is that really what's troubling him the most? More quietly she adds, "I'm sorry he didn't love you as much as he should have."

They step through the door into the ship. Fortunately, no security has gathered around the dock; nobody's after them yet. Abel stops short in the landing bay, and Noemi halts beside him, confused.

"The *Daedalus*," Abel says. When she turns her head toward him, she sees him staring at the place where the dedication plaque hung on the wall. "In Greek mythology, Daedalus learned to fly. He made wings for his son, who flew too high, then crashed and died. Daedalus gained the knowledge; Icarus paid the price. Even when Mansfield named this ship, he didn't forget what he planned to do to me."

"Then we'll rename the ship," Noemi says with determination. "Not a fake ID this time—we'll rename it for real. Something worthy. It's not Mansfield's ship anymore. It's ours."

"Let's get into orbit before we celebrate." Virginia's not usually the one to signal caution, which is more reason to listen to her now.

They hurry up to the bridge. Noemi starts prepping the ship for takeoff as Abel slides back into his pilot's seat. The domed viewscreen comes on, showing the foggy, starless night above.

Abel sounds more like himself now that he has something to do. "Preparing for auto-clearance to take off, and—check."

At that moment, a communication lights up the corner of their screen, and this one unfolds without Noemi touching the controls once. On the ops console, an image appears—one of an old man she's never seen before. She knows him immediately. His eyes are like Abel's.

"Abel, my boy." He shakes his head sadly. "I take it you're on board. Your girl must have come for you. Very sweet. But of course she didn't realize I'd still have trackers on this ship, as well as my old access code."

"Access codes can be changed," Virginia mutters. She starts working right away, but it's too late.

Abel says, "I don't want to come back."

"But you do, Abel. You do want that. I know, because I programmed it into you from the start. It's just that now you want other things, too. Things you were never intended to have." Mansfield takes a wheezing breath. "Abel, I am hereby ordering you to come back to this house and submit to the procedure. That's a command from me to you. Come along, now. Come home."

In horror, Noemi watches Abel slide back from his console and stand up to leave.

"No!" She runs to Abel and grabs his arm. "You don't have to do this."

Abel's entire body shakes. His voice breaks as he says, "Yes, I do."

She holds on even as he begins walking toward the door. "You have a soul of your own. A will of your own. You can stand up to him, I know you can—"

"So that's your girl, hmm?" Mansfield can see her; she and Abel are right in front of the console showing his smug face. "Well, she's cute as can be. Not what you'd call a classic beauty, but she has spirit, doesn't she? You get that from me, you know. I always had an eye for the feisty ones."

If he were here, Noemi would punch him in the gut and see how cute he thought she was then. But he's safe at home—sitting near a fire, to judge by the flickering light—cozily relaxing while he orders Abel to come home and die.

"You're a monster," she says to Mansfield. "You're a selfish monster who's afraid to die because you've never believed in anything greater than yourself. You gave Abel a soul only so you could smash it when you didn't need it anymore. Everything he's felt, the person he's become—doesn't that matter to you at all? Don't you even *see* him?"

Mansfield sighs. "Obviously this is going to be a problem."

From the console where she's feverishly typing, Virginia calls, "I used to be a fangirl of yours, but not anymore, you crapsack excuse for a human being."

"Who's that?" Mansfield genuinely looks confused. Virginia doesn't go to the screen, but she leans over far enough for Mansfield to see her hand as she flips him off.

Noemi turns back to Abel, who hasn't sat back down again, despite all her pleas...but he hasn't taken another step toward the door either. Hope swells within her heart. "You're fighting him, aren't you? You can do it. I know you can."

"Enough of this." With a harrumph, Mansfield adjusts himself on the sofa. "Abel, tell me the truth: Are the emergency defensive stations on the bridge still stocked?"

"Yes, sir." Abel winces after he says the words.

"Well, go on and open one up." Instantly Abel walks to a small boxy locker low on the wall—one of many, none of which Noemi's particularly noticed before—and Mansfield adds, "Take a blaster."

Abel's fist smashes the polymer into fine shards that rain down on the floor. Noemi watches, aghast, as he picks up a blaster, its holt glowing green to indicate full charge. When he looks into Noemi's eyes, the anguish she sees there is almost more horrible than her own fear.

"There we go," Mansfield says soothingly. "Almost done. Remember who and what you are, Abel. Follow Directive One. Obey me. Kill her."

38

Abel's hand tightens on the blaster—but he doesn't pull the trigger. He won't do that, he won't, he *won't*.

He wants to put the blaster down, but he can't. He's stuck in a recursive loop, torn between the directives shrieking at him from his every circuit and his overwhelming fear of hurting Noemi.

She stands directly in his line of sight, breathing hard, her large brown eyes staring at the weapon that might end her life at any moment. Then she looks up from the muzzle, into Abel's eyes.

"Keep fighting," she whispers.

"Abel." Mansfield says it louder this time, still avuncular and almost lazy in his confidence. "You're wasting time. You know your programming won't let you do anything else."

It won't. He must obey his creator. The same fervent dedication that gave Abel purpose for every day of the thirty years he spent in utter isolation, in the cold and dark, tells him to do this thing. Noemi Vidal must die, and he must go home to Mansfield and do the same. Today is their last day.

In the background he hears Virginia murmuring, "Has to be a way to override the override. Come on, come on." He wants to warn her to shut up. If Mansfield overhears her and gives orders to kill Virginia as well, Abel knows he'll do it. He likes Virginia, but he doesn't love her, and surely only love could be powerful enough to keep him from instantly pulling the trigger upon Mansfield's command.

He's not sure whether anything has the power to keep him from pulling it anyway.

"A-bel," Mansfield singsongs, like any parent impatient with a child running late.

A thousand scenarios play out in Abel's mind simultaneously. He could set the blaster down. Disengage it. Tell Mansfield he made not a container but a person. But he can't come up with the final resolution of any of these kaleidoscopic images of salvation. He can't envision any ending but the one where Noemi lies dead at his feet.

Maybe—maybe he could point it at his own head and fire, so he could save Noemi and spite Burton Mansfield in the same squeeze of a trigger. Could he? No. His arm refuses to obey. That plan goes against not one of Mansfield's orders but two.

Finally, Mansfield's voice betrays a hint of anger. "Directive One," he repeats. "Obey me. Kill her."

The repetition turns something over inside Abel, and he straightens his arm, aiming directly at Noemi's heart. She's shaking with terror, almost weak with it. Nothing is more horrible than looking at her and knowing he made her feel this way.

Until he kills her, which will be the greatest horror of all.

"Abel?" Noemi's voice is very small. "Where there's no free will, there's no sin. If you—if you can't help it—I know you tried. Thank you for trying—" Her words break off, and she shakes her head, unable to speak any more.

She's forgiving him for her murder before he commits it. Even if Abel has only one hour of existence left, she doesn't want him to spend that hour hating himself for what he's done. It is an act of almost unfathomable grace, shining so brightly next to Mansfield's selfishness that it eclipses everything else inside Abel, every conflict, every command.

Instantly he swings his arm left to point the blaster at Mansfield's face on the console and fires, fires again, keeps on firing until the console blows apart, sending smoke and scraps of wire flying across the bridge. Noemi shrieks and covers her ears from the din, but in the aftermath they stand there, staring at the wreckage. Abel lets the blaster drop from his hand to the floor, where it lands with a metallic thud. Mansfield's voice has been silenced.

After a long pause punctuated only by the sound of electrical sparks, Virginia says, "You know, we might've needed that console."

"We have to get out of here." Noemi seems to awaken from a trance. "He'll send Queens and Charlies—who knows what else—"

"I managed to limit his override commands to communications. He can call back, but he can't keep us from flying!" As Virginia swings into action, bringing the mag engines online, Noemi turns back to Abel.

Though in the future he will often attempt to analyze the exact sequence of events, Abel will never be able to determine whether he embraced her, or she embraced him. He only knows she's back in his arms, alive and well, unafraid of him even after what happened. As he hugs her closer, he feels a kind of pain indistinguishable from joy. Is this what humans feel, when they embrace the one they love? But it can't be. Humans may mistreat those they love. Sometimes they abandon them entirely. They couldn't do that if they felt the way Abel feels in this moment. They couldn't even imagine it.

The *Daedalus*—no, the ship—lifts off, soaring swiftly upward at a somewhat erratic trajectory. "Um, guys?" Virginia sounds unusually hesitant. "Hate to break up the moment, but you two are a lot more used to piloting this big boy than I am."

Abel lets go, though not without giving Noemi's hand a quick squeeze. Sliding back into his pilot's chair feels exhilarating, especially when he looks down at the vectors and readouts telling him that they're moving away from Earth at nearly top speed.

"Who is Mansfield going to send after us?" Noemi asks as she moves to another console, switching it to serve as an auxiliary ops station. "Earth planetary forces? His own mechs?"

"No one." Abel's fingers expand the part of the screen that shows the far distant solar system. There, just beyond Pluto—quite close at this point in its orbit—lies the Genesis Gate, Noemi's way home. "He won't send anyone."

Noemi and Virginia both stare at him. Virginia's the one who says, "Mansfield didn't come across like a guy who gives up easily."

Abel accelerates as they clear Earth's atmosphere and the domed viewscreen again shows the stars. "He isn't giving up. On the contrary, I predict with at least ninety percent certainty that Burton Mansfield is currently devising a plan to retrieve me. But no such plan can be put into action if Earth planetary defenses have blown up this ship, and me with it."

Virginia cackles. "You're our human shield. Well, inhuman shield. Whatever. It works."

Noemi slumps back in her seat with half-closed eyes.

Her obvious exhaustion makes Abel want to pick her up, carry her to her room, and cover her with a blanket so she can sleep as long as she wants. Soon, maybe. The final few tasks of this journey await.

. . .

At the Saturn relay station, where asteroid miners and long-haul freighters refuel, Abel brings their newly nameless ship to a standstill, the better to let a single-pilot corsair launch safely.

"Sure you won't come to Genesis, even to see it?" Noemi stands next to Abel as they watch Virginia prep her ship. "You'd be welcome."

"Are you kidding? The land of low-tech? I'd die within hours." Virginia grins at them as she finishes zipping the neck of her flight suit; her red-streaked ponytail swishes as she leans down to check the controls of her corsair. It's a larger ship than this bay would usually hold. Noemi's tiny fighter has been nudged against the wall where it sits, still awaiting its greater errand.

They haven't yet discussed where Abel might go, but he's still too relieved to care about anything other than having escaped from Burton Mansfield. Too happy to be in Noemi's presence again, and—to his surprise—sad to see Virginia go.

Virginia, on the other hand, is even bubblier than

usual. "I've still got a couple of weeks to go in my suspension. Plenty of time to come up with stories from the wild parties I supposedly went to on Kismet."

"Nothing as wild as the truth," Noemi says, which makes Virginia laugh, and Abel realizes he's smiling.

"Might even drop by and see my parents, assuming the sandstorms don't cut off all air traffic." Virginia sighs. "Just so you know—I'm going to check on Ephraim and Riko, too, see whether they show up on any news feeds. She creeps me out, but I'd like to make sure he's doing all right. I think he's the bravest of all of us."

"No," Abel says, looking at Noemi—who has said the same thing at the same moment, looking at him. Embarrassed and unable to determine why, he adds, "It's good to know Ephraim will have your help. It reduces uncertainty."

That makes Virginia point at him. "I'm going to miss this. Going to miss both of you. It's been fun, having friends who aren't Razers. Who knew?"

Friends, Abel thinks. *I have friends. Virginia, perhaps Ephraim, maybe Harriet and Zayan, too, and certainly Noemi.* He feels sure that Noemi's feelings don't mirror his own, but it doesn't matter. She came for him; she forgave him. Those two gifts alone would sustain him far longer than thirty years.

"Anyway, if this guy can fly through the minefield

around the Kismet Gate?" Virginia grins. "You have no excuse not to visit."

Noemi touches Virginia's shoulder, only for a second. "Thank you."

Abel would like to echo her, but would feel presumptuous claiming Noemi's mission as his own. So he only says, "Good-bye, Virginia."

She only waves at them, then pulls on her helmet as the transparent upper shield of the corsair slides into place. Abel walks out of the docking bay, Noemi just behind him—but she's going backward, unwilling to look away from Virginia one second before necessary.

Once they're in the corridor, the air lock pinwheels shut to begin the launch cycle. The image of the bay comes up on a nearby screen, and they watch together in silence as the doors open and Virginia's red corsair drifts free, then streaks away toward her next adventure.

If Abel has analyzed human conversational patterns correctly, the customary next step is an exchange of sentimental thoughts about Virginia's help and departure. However, by now he is as aware of the imminent Masada Run as Noemi must be. "Only one more task before we can go through the Genesis Gate."

Noemi turns to him, frowning. "What?"

Has she forgotten? "We need a mech to pilot the fighter into the Gate."

"Like the Queen model I have waiting in sick bay?"

Although Abel can't analyze his facial expression, Noemi apparently can, because she breaks into peals of laughter. He simply shakes his head. "You exceed expectations, Noemi Vidal."

"So do you."

It strikes him then that they're alone together for the first time since their hospital room on Stronghold days ago. This fact should not be significant. Yet he dwells on it, especially on the silence that falls between them as Noemi's smile gentles.

He realizes there's one question he wants to ask, one he would not have put to her in front of the others, although he can think of no reason why not. "Why did you come after me?"

"I had to." She drops her gaze from his, as if unsure of her own thoughts.

It's not a precise answer, and yet somehow it's more than enough.

•   •   •

When they slip through the Genesis Gate, Noemi whoops in joy, and Abel drums a quick rhythm on the base of his console. She looks over at him in surprise. "It's something pilots do when a person travels the whole course of the Loop for the first time," he explains. "Something they did, anyway. You're the first person to complete that trip since the Liberty War ended."

Her face is luminous as she stares at the distant green dot on the viewscreen that is planet Genesis. "Home. Mine, and now yours, I guess."

"Mine?" Abel had not anticipated this. "Mechs are forbidden on Genesis."

"Yeah, well, you're going to be the mech who *saved* Genesis. That makes a difference." Noemi spins her seat around, leaning toward him with no doubt in her eyes, only delight. "We'll explain what you are, in every way. That you're unique, irreplaceable. And the hero of Genesis can begin getting to know his new home."

Abel suspects it may not be as simple as Noemi imagines. However, he also knows that putting this question to the planetary leaders right after the destruction of the Gate will give them a strong chance of success. If they fail to win him a place on Genesis—

—then he will fly away in this nameless ship and try to find another fate to call his own. And he will go on for the rest of his many days knowing that he saved Noemi along with her world. It's enough.

"Will your world detect our entry into the system?"

Noemi nods. "They'll see us on long-range scans. They'll come to investigate within the day, but by then we'll be done, won't we?" Then her face pales. "Unless—the Masada Run—how long do we have?"

His fingers move quickly along the console as he measures, then smiles. "We still have approximately forty hours until the Masada Run is scheduled to begin, assuming no changes in plans since your departure."

She laughs in relief as she spins her seat in a circle, arms outstretched. "They're going to throw us a parade. Wait and see."

They get to work immediately. In sick bay, they open up the cryopod and remove the inert Queen model. Before she can cycle out of dormancy mode, Abel inputs new codes that will establish Noemi as her commander, as well as shut down all unnecessary mental functions. The Queen has already deleted her advanced programming, already chosen to be something instead of someone; Abel has no qualms about using her for this mission, and knows Noemi doesn't either. But the fewer potential complications, the better.

The Queen follows them obediently to the docking bay, where they ready Noemi's fighter for its final flight. "Power is more than adequate," he says, checking the data readouts. "This ship could fly to Genesis, come back again, and still be able to complete the mission."

"No need for that," Noemi says to the Queen, who stands as expressionless as a mannequin. "You'll follow the flight plan given to reach the center of the Gate."

"Affirmative," the Queen replies. Even her voice inflection has been lost. She is more of an *it* now.

When instructed, the Queen takes its seat. No flight helmet is needed; it can do without air for the brief time it will remain operational. Finally, Abel picks up the thermomagnetic device. A few quick turns of the controls, and it will be activated, ready to do its work. Within minutes, it will be too hot for a human to touch, too hot for a mech thereafter. But by then destruction will be seconds away.

Abel meets Noemi's eyes. "Ready?"

"Ready." She nods once.

He turns the controls. The device begins to vibrate in his hands. The low hum seems to electrify the room as he sets it in the fighter—

—and the Queen model goes dead.

"Wait. What happened?" Noemi tugs at the Queen's collar as the mech flops to one side, completely inert. Abel shuts off the thermomagnetic device instantly, to conserve energy. This changes nothing for the Queen model, which is unsurprising; there's no reason it should react to thermomagnetic functions.

But then why did it go dead the moment he turned the device on?

Correlation is not causation, he reminds himself. Yet the part of his mind that has developed instincts tells him this is no coincidence.

"What's wrong with her?" Noemi asks. "Was it something about the cryosleep? Dormancy mode?"

"No. That should have no effect, and all my preliminary scans were normal." Abel scans the Queen again to see nothing. No mental action whatsoever, and even organic life functions have shut down. This kind of catastrophic failure is almost unknown, particularly in a mech that checked out only minutes before. In order for that to happen—

He stops moving. Stops thinking. Instead he is overcome by the chagrin of knowing that he has underestimated Burton Mansfield one last time.

"A fail-safe." Abel sets down the scanner. "The Queen was programmed with a fail-safe."

Noemi grabs his arm, dismay turning to fear. "What kind of fail-safe?"

"I don't know the first element. Probably it was 'proximity to a Gate.' But the second element was 'proximity to an operational thermomagnetic device.'" Turning to Noemi, he explains, "That's what our mission was about, thirty years ago. Finding the vulnerabilities in a Gate. We found one. And Mansfield took steps to patch that security breach."

"But how could he have known we would try it with this Queen model?" she protests.

"He didn't. Therefore, the only explanation is that he

installed the fail-safe on every model of mech in existence sophisticated enough to handle the piloting tasks. Every single one." Abel would like to be angry with Mansfield again, but instead he feels only a muted sense of admiration. His creator has proved selfish, unfeeling, even cruel— but his intelligence cannot be doubted. "As the head of the Mansfield Cybernetics line, as soon as he devised the fail-safe, he could have seen it downloaded or installed on every mech in the galaxy."

Noemi's voice shakes. "So you're telling me we have nothing."

Abel can only reply, "Nothing at all."

39

NOTHING.

It's all been for nothing.

Noemi slumps against the side of her battle-scarred silver fighter, torn between grief and rage. This entire journey—everything she's been through, everything that's been lost—she's told herself it has a purpose. The racking fevers of Cobweb, the terror of being hunted by the Queen and Charlie, Abel's abduction, and, worst of all, Esther's death: Noemi has endured because she knew that was the cost of saving her world.

But her world can't be saved. She's been chasing a mirage from the start.

"You're sure that's true for all mechs everywhere?" She will not cry. She *will not.* "Every single one of them that could fly the fighter?"

Abel looks up from the dead Queen model. "Almost certainly. Maybe a handful of mechs were never updated with the fail-safe, but they would by definition be located in out-of-the-way places. They'd be difficult to find and even more difficult to identify. The odds of finding one in time would be... You don't want to hear the odds, do you?"

"No. I understand. It's impossible."

So she'll go home. She has forty hours to see her friends and make her peace, and say good-bye to her life. Then she'll rejoin her friends on her flight squad for the Masada Run.

At least she'll die knowing she bought Genesis some time. And if nothing else, she saved Abel.

"That's it, then." Noemi's voice betrays her, cracking on the last word, but she keeps going. "The plan won't work. It's over."

Abel says, "Not if you use me."

It takes a few seconds to sink in. "You can't."

Unsurprisingly, he takes her literally. "I can. As I said before, only mechs not updated in the past thirty years could make it through the Gate with the device. I qualify."

"Abel, *no*. I told you before, I'm not giving you those orders. You have a soul, so you're—you're too human to be used like a device."

"Then I'm human enough to make the decision on my own." He speaks without hesitation. Without doubt.

"But you can't." Noemi can hardly put the reasons into words; so many crowd into her mind at once that she could never go through them all. She only knows the thought of

Abel's death is even more terrible to her than the thought of her own. "Genesis isn't your planet. You owe us nothing."

"I've come to believe in the essential rightness of Genesis's cause," he says, astonishing her further. "While I might personally have selected a different course of action, it's clear that humanity's best potential home in the cosmos must be protected. It is equally clear that Earth's government has no intention of modifying the behaviors that would poison your planet. Whatever else happens to Earth and its colony worlds, Genesis must survive."

"The Gate doesn't have to be destroyed for us to survive! When the Masada Run is complete, we'll have bought Genesis some time. Years, maybe. Those years could make all the difference in the war."

"You would fly in the Masada Run," Abel says. "You would die."

"That's always been true. It never changed. I only thought it had."

"I can't let that happen, Noemi. Even if I weren't willing to die for Genesis, I would die for you."

"Your life isn't worth less than mine! You don't have to follow Mansfield's rules anymore."

"I did not mean that I would die for you because you're human. I would die for you because I love you."

It steals the breath from Noemi's lungs. She can only stare at him as—incredibly—Abel begins to smile.

"Maybe it's not love the way a human would feel it," he says. "Maybe it's only a...simulation of love, a close analogue. But I feel it with all the strength I have to feel anything. Over the past weeks, I've come to—to listen for your voice, because I hope to hear it. I pay attention to irrelevant details of your mannerisms and appearance because I find them pleasing. I've begun to understand how you think and what you want. That means I can see through your eyes, too, instead of only my own, and it's as if the entire universe expanded, grew larger and more beautiful." He pauses. "You even make me think in metaphors."

"Abel—" Noemi has to reply, but how can she?

"It's all right. I know you don't love me back. It doesn't matter. Feeling whatever I feel for you—love, or as close as I can come to it—that has made me more human than anything else. You believed in my soul before I did, but I understand now, don't you see? That's what fought Mansfield. That's the part of me that loves you." Abel raises his hand, maybe to take hers, but then he seems to think better of it. Instead he gets to his feet. Noemi can only sit there, leaning against the fighter, looking up at him as he says, "Because of you, I've had adventures on every world of the Loop. I've made my first real friends. I broke free from Mansfield, and I found out what it would mean to love someone. Because of you, I've been truly alive. And now that I've lived, I can be ready to die for something I believe in and the person I love."

There's no answer she can give him. Nothing worthy of what he's said—or who he's become. What would be most true, most meaningful to him? The first thing Noemi comes up with is "You are... so much more than your creator."

"I'm more than he made me to be, yes."

"That's not what I mean. You're *more than him*. More human."

Abel looks rueful for a moment. "Which in some measure testifies to his genius. At least no one else will ever know it." Then he glances down at the Queen, which still lies in the pilot's seat with no more presence than a bundle of rags. "I'll need to prepare for my own launch. I should begin by jettisoning the Queen model. Unless you think Genesis would find her useful for instructional purposes?"

Numbly, she shakes her head no. "No. Earth—they send the Queens and Charlies through a few times a month. We can get all the broken mechs we need."

He nods, brisk and efficient again. "After I've cycled the air lock to dispose of her, I can ready the fighter again for takeoff. It will only be a small matter of adjusting whatever elements are disturbed by the cycle. I can be under way within the half hour."

"Give me a few minutes," Noemi pleads. She needs to

think this through—no. She needs to pray. "You don't do this without me."

"If you prefer—"

"Promise me." Her mind floods with nightmare images of watching the fighter swoop away, Abel leaving forever without saying good-bye. "You have to promise."

Abel looks confused. "Then I promise."

"Thank you."

Noemi rises on wobbly legs that don't want to hold her up and walks out of the docking bay. Where should she go? Holing up in her room feels cowardly. Going to the bridge would be like pretending this isn't even happening.

Slowly she walks the spiral corridor, around and around, remembering some of the meditation mazes on Genesis, the endless hedges through which you can wander, pray, and find your own path. Finally she reaches the sick bay door, but doesn't go inside.

Right here, on this spot, she fought Abel for her life. And right here, he offered his service to her. She sinks down on the very spot where she sat when he gave his weapon to her, closes her eyes, and begins to pray for guidance.

This is where they began. Maybe that makes it the place where she can figure out how they end.

40

ABEL STANDS OUTSIDE THE DOCKING BAY, WATCHING THE
final stages of the air lock cycle. On the screen he watches
as the artificial gravity releases the space. Noemi's fighter
bobs in its mooring wires; the Queen model hangs in mid-
air, her arms spread wide as if welcoming the void.

Finally the silver plates of the door spiral open. The air
rushes out faster than even Abel can see. In one instant the
Queen is there, suspended. In the next she's gone, lost forever in the dark. He looks at Noemi's fighter, rattling in
its wires, and wonders what it will be like to be inside it.
For all his experiences and expertise, he's never actually
piloted a ship like this.

One more unique experience he'll have before he dies.

The prospect of nonexistence can paralyze humans
with dread. As courageously as Noemi faced the Masada
Run, he saw the despair in her eyes. Abel, on the other
hand, doesn't feel the same disappointment he did at the

beginning of their journey, when he first thought Noemi would space him.

It isn't as hard to leave life behind, he thinks, *once you've had a life worth living.*

Maybe he should send a message to Mansfield, telling him that. It might help his creator face his own imminent death. Abel may not need to be with Mansfield any longer, but elements of his programming still feel that need—to try to help.

Noemi isn't the first person Abel ever loved. That was Mansfield. He didn't only possess Abel's manufactured loyalty, but the real love of a would-be son. Yet he chose to throw that love away rather than die, even after a long life rich in creative and professional success. Now that Abel is making the opposite choice, he understands just how much luckier he is than his creator. How more alive he is, for all Burton Mansfield's flesh and blood.

Sending a message to Earth is impossible anyway. Abel lets go of the thought more easily than he would've expected.

The air lock finishes its cycle as its door spirals shut again. Gravity returns, and he watches the fighter settle back onto the mesh floor. There's no reason to delay further.

No objective reason, that is. Noemi asked him to give her time. Best if she's the one to contact him.

She may not love him, but she cares. His death will matter to her. Surely it's wrong to welcome that—to want Noemi to suffer any pain whatsoever—but even the most hopeless love must be a little selfish, because Abel finds he wants to be remembered. He wants to be missed. Not too badly, not forever. And yet.

Now he has time to kill. Abel smiles slightly at the dark pun. What should he do? The nameless ship can take Noemi back home, so there's no need for repairs. He'd like to watch *Casablanca* again, but he suspects Noemi won't need that long to pull herself together, and making her wait while he finishes the film would be cruel.

(Leaving in the middle is too appalling to consider.)

Abel decides to let his instincts guide him, since it turns out he has them. First he's wandering aimlessly up the spiral corridor, looking at nothing in particular, and then he finds himself standing in front of the equipment pod bay doors.

His jail cell for thirty years. His home. Despite all the years he spent wishing to escape, he realizes he needs to tell this place good-bye.

After he steps through the door, Abel even works with the controls to release this area from the ship's artificial gravity. When his feet drift off the floor, the familiarity of it makes him smile. Before he drifts too far upward, he turns off the lights, too, to make the re-creation almost complete.

He pushes off from the wall, propelling himself toward

one of the small side windows. Through this one he watched that last battle near the Genesis Gate and saw Noemi's fighter approaching for the first time. Even then he'd known she would set him free. He just hadn't known in how many ways that would be true.

"Abel?"

Glancing down, he sees Noemi standing in the doorway, on the edge of the artificial gravity well. Her face is in shadow, but his sharp vision reveals that she's regained her calm. Good. It hurt to see her looking so lost. He says, "I wanted to be here one last time. Is that strange?"

She shakes her head no.

Then Noemi steps through, and the lack of gravity buoys her up. Although her hair is held in place by the padded headband she wears in front, the strands in the back fan out behind her. She spreads her arms wide as she bobs into the center of the pod bay and looks up at him. "Will you show it to me?"

In the literal sense, Abel could show her nothing she can't already see. But among the many gifts she's given him is the ability to glimpse what lies beyond the literal.

So he propels himself down to her, not too fast. The newly applicable laws of physics mean that he bumps into her back anyway, but not too hard. He catches her around the midsection as they drift toward the far wall, where she braces them with her hand.

"There." He points, leaning his head close to hers so she'll see exactly what he's seeing. "The dent in the wall? I made that when I tried to punch through to the inner corridor, about two weeks after I was marooned. The attempt was unsuccessful, obviously."

"Did it hurt?"

"Yes." That seems as irrelevant now as it did then. "Can you see the ceiling?" They're fairly close, but it's dark, and Noemi has to look through human eyes.

"I think so." Her arm covers his, where he's wrapped it around her waist. "There's a pattern there—"

"Not a pattern. I made scratch marks. To count the days, using Earth measurement." All those years ago, he'd spent a long time trying to decide whether to use Earth or Genesis days. He told himself then that calculating the Einsteinian variations for Earth dates would provide more of a mental challenge, but now he knows he wanted Burton Mansfield to understand the full measure of time he was alone. "I stopped after two thousand. It became depressing."

"I can't imagine being that lonely," she murmurs.

Probably she can't. Few beings could. Abel thinks this over, then says the only thing that still matters. "It helps, being here again but not alone."

Noemi turns to look at him, her profile silhouetted against one of the starry windows. It strikes him that she is very close, so near their faces are almost touching.

But she knows that, so he keeps saying what he'd wanted to tell her before. "I've never been less lonely than I am now. With you."

"Same here," Noemi says.

She takes one of his hands as she pushes off against the wall. The momentum isn't enough to carry them all the way across, so they slow down midway through. Noemi twists around to capture his other hand in hers, and just like that, he's in her arms.

Abel watches, almost disbelieving, as she brings her face to his until their lips meet.

It's his first kiss. Kissing turns out to be much more complicated than it looks; there are many variables to account for. So after that initial touch—exhilarating as it is—Abel ignores higher functions and once again gives in to instinct.

This appears to be the right way to proceed. At the beginning he and Noemi are tentative with each other, brushing their lips against each other quickly, lightly, but no more—and then the kiss really begins. Noemi pulls him closer, softly bites his lower lip, then opens his mouth with her own. As the kiss deepens, as they cling to each other suspended in the dark, Abel feels his response crackle throughout his body like electricity—sharp and warm at once. The better it is, the more he needs.

So this is desire. Why do humans describe it as

torment? Abel has never known anything more exhilarating than this, the sudden discovery of how much more he can want, and do, and be. He cradles the back of her head in his hand as he kisses her even more intently, hoping to give her even a shadow of the pleasure and joy she'd given him.

He realizes this kiss is something Noemi's doing for him. It could never happen except as good-bye. That tarnishes nothing; the knowledge only makes Abel love her more.

When they pull apart, she frames his face with her hand. He smiles at her before turning to kiss her palm. Without another word shared between them, he knows this is the end.

So Abel lifts one hand to the ceiling, which is close enough to touch, and propels them back to the floor, within easy reach of the gravity control. As soon as he presses it, their feet thump down harder, Noemi's hair swings back to chin-level, and a few nuts and bolts clatter down beside them. They let go of each other at the same moment.

"Are you ready?" he asks her.

She lifts her chin. "Yes."

Together they walk back down the corridor, and they're almost to the door before Noemi stops. "Oh, Abel—I'm so sorry—I meant to ask you to do something for me before you—before, and then I saw you in the pod bay and I—I guess I lost track."

He made her lose track. Maybe that means she enjoyed

the kiss as much as he did. Abel's pleased to think he did it well. "Tell me what you need."

"I ran a couple of sims on how to land the ship by myself, but I've never actually done it. You always landed it, except on Earth, and Virginia did that. After this I think I'm going to be too—" Noemi's voice trails off. He wonders what she might've said. "Could you lay in an automated landing? Just to be sure?"

Landing the ship is well within Noemi's capabilities, but emotional upheaval can play havoc with both human skills and human confidence. So can exhaustion. Granting this small favor is more important than easing any insecurities she may have. "Of course."

"I'll wait for you here," she says, as he begins walking toward the bridge.

This is vaguely disappointing. He'd have liked to remain with her as long as possible. But she may find the extended length of their farewell difficult; his scans of certain fictional dramas suggest that humans sometimes do.

Abel even runs to the bridge, to move things along. That it takes seconds away from his remaining life doesn't register as a concern.

As the doors open for him, he walks directly to the helm—and stops. A light is blinking on one of the consoles, signaling ship operations in progress, but nothing should be taking place.

Then he sees it's the light for the docking bay doors.

Noemi lied. She's leaving with the device to sacrifice herself in the Masada Run—

—to save him.

He runs from the bridge so quickly the doors barely have time to open for him. Human speed is no use to him now; there's no one to keep up with him, no one to fool. Abel pushes to his full speed, reaching the docking bay mid-cycle.

"Noemi!" he shouts. "Noemi, don't!"

A small image appears on the screen in front of him—Noemi's face. She must have tied her fighter's communications into the ship's. Her helmet is in her lap, and he knows without having to ask that she's taken the thermomagnetic device, too. "Are you going to tell me I can't do this, Abel? We both know I can."

"Don't. The Masada Run won't end the war. You'll die for no reason." As terrible as it is to think of her dying, worse is thinking of her dying without purpose. She has lived every moment with intensity and feeling. To throw her life away—

"I'm not going on the Masada Run. I'm returning to Genesis to try to stop it." She leans back in her pilot's seat, smiling crookedly. "They don't know how bad things have become for Earth. They don't know that there's a resistance rising up on the colonies. That changes things. If they understood we might have allies, that there's really a chance—maybe it can change everything."

"You can't take that chance," he says. "Not when you know I can save your world."

"That's the thing, Abel. You can't."

"But I—"

"Genesis isn't just where we live. It's what we believe. A victory that comes from the sacrifice of an innocent isn't a victory. It's the end of us."

"I *chose* this. It's my decision."

"You've only been truly alive for a couple of weeks. You've only just won your freedom from Mansfield. You can't give up a life that's *never been your own*." Noemi leans closer to the camera; he can imagine her face close to his again. "From now on, you decide where you'll go, what you'll do—who you'll be. But today? You're just Mansfield's creation, or mine. You deserve to be yourself. You have to keep going. You have to claim your own life."

He hears what she's saying, but he can't take it in. All he can think about is that she's going away, putting herself in danger when he could save her. "Please, Noemi, let me."

She shakes her head no and somehow manages to smile. "This is my moment of grace, Abel. All those years I prayed, and nothing—but now I don't have to believe anymore. I *know*. You have a soul. That makes it my job to take care of you. To protect your life like it was my own."

"But I—" It's his job to take care of her. How can she owe him the same duty, the same debt? Abel doesn't understand and he can't yet force himself to try. All he knows is that nothing has ever devastated him this way.

Arguing with her is impossible. He'd pull open the bay door if he could, but from thirty years' hard experience, he knows he can't. This is it. Noemi is leaving him forever.

That leaves him nothing but the truth. "It hurts more to lose you than it did to give up my own life," he says. "Does that mean what I feel isn't only a copy? That I do love you?"

Tears well in her eyes. "I think maybe it does."

The air lock cycle ends. Noemi presses her hand against the screen; Abel does the same, the closest he will ever come to touching her again.

When the image changes, he lets his hand fall. The wide view of the docking bay shows him Noemi's ship, and within it he sees her slipping on her helmet just as the outer doors open. She releases her moorings and drifts into space until she's cleared the ship. Then she fires her engines, a burst of brilliant orange and fire, and soars toward her home.

Abel's vision is malfunctioning. When he touches his fingers to his cheek, they find warmth and wetness. These are his first tears.

41

GENESIS. *HOME.*

Noemi's fighter breaks through the atmosphere. The blackness of space releases her, and once again she's embraced by pale-blue sky. She's cried in this helmet too much already—the visor keeps fogging up—but tears well in her eyes again as she sees the teal-blue ocean stretching below her, and then the outline of the southern continent, the one where she was born, where she and Esther grew up together.

Her instrument panel blinks in different colors, testifying to the many computers trying to identify her. The ship's automated fleet signal will answer them. Noemi refuses to look down, even for a moment. Nothing matters as much as drinking in the sight of the far mountains, dusky blue on the horizon. Or the beaches, breaking with white foam. Or the grain-gold fields that stretch into the distance. It's so much more beautiful than she ever understood before.

I wish you could have seen this, Abel.

Only within the final five thousand meters of her descent does she snap back into officer mode. Blinking hard, she focuses on her instruments, zeroing in on her home base. When the comms crackle into life, she takes a deep breath. "Ensign Noemi Vidal requesting clearance to land. Authorization code 81107."

A pause follows, long enough for her to wonder whether they lost the signal. Then an incredulous voice says, *"Ensign Noemi Vidal was reported killed in action nineteen days ago."*

"Not quite," Noemi says. So this is what it's like to come back from the dead. "Call Captain Yasmeen Baz. Tell her I'm reporting in, and that she has to stop the Masada Run. Do you understand? *Stop the Masada Run.*"

● ● ●

"The Masada Run has been indefinitely delayed," says the judge, looking down at the court records, "pending the outcome of this case and the assessment of Ensign Vidal's testimony."

Delayed isn't as good as canceled. But it's as much as Noemi can manage now, while she's under arrest, and on trial.

She sits in a simple chair in the middle of a round room. Like many buildings on Genesis, this hall of justice has been built to echo the structures of Earth's classical past—lit by the sun, cooled by shade and breeze, and ominous through the sheer power of stone. Long shafts of sunset light stream in via the tall, narrow arched windows, illuminating the raised semicircular bench from which her three judges peer down. They allowed her to put on her dress uniform for this, crisp and dark green; wearing it has always made her feel strong. She needs every ounce of strength she can muster.

Abel never asked Noemi about the legal system on Genesis, for which she was guiltily grateful. This is the controversial topic that ignites arguments, destroys harmony, and keeps regional boundaries stiffly in place. Some faiths believe in justice, others in mercy; the Elder Council has never found a universally satisfying way to unify these two ideals. Although some faiths once advocated for executions, the planet has forbidden the death penalty by unanimous agreement. Beyond that one guarantee, punishments for crimes vary widely among the region-states.

Noemi's home favors mercy, as does the Second Catholic Church. In her heart, though, she's always longed for justice: hard, swift, certain, and severe. She's been willing to deal out that harsh justice—and now she's equally willing to endure it.

Because desertion of duty is a military crime, and the military has little use for mercy.

There are other crimes, too. "Failure to report the injury of a fellow soldier," intones Commander Kaminski, battalion leader and, now, her prosecutor. "Failure to report the death of a fellow soldier."

She thinks of Esther and winces. They haven't let her talk to the Gatsons yet, or to Jemuel. She wants so badly to tell them how courageously Esther died, and how her resting place is at the heart of a star. Will she ever get her chance to explain? If she does, will Esther's loved ones believe her?

Kaminski continues, "Failure to follow orders in battle."

"I object," says Captain Baz. She's Noemi's defender as a matter of law, but she seems to really care, to be fighting for her with true dedication. Noemi hopes so, anyway, because Baz is pretty much her only hope. "Officer Vidal's actions were well within her discretion as an officer—"

"Up until a point." Kaminski's thin smile is more forbidding than any scowl could be. "Which point, do you think, Captain Baz? When she decided to board an enemy spacecraft? When she failed to deactivate an enemy mech, despite having the ability to do so? Where does that cross the line?"

"You're assuming this story is true," says one of the judges, raising an eyebrow. "We're supposed to believe this girl became the first person in thirty years to pass through the Kismet Gate? That she crossed paths with Burton Mansfield himself?"

Captain Baz thumps her lectern for attention. Her dress

uniform looks strange on her—too stiff, too confining. Baz was born for exosuits and armor, not this stuff. But she's fighting the legal battle as vigorously as she'd fight with her blaster. "Analyzing satellite data showed that a small ship passed through the Kismet Gate around the time Ensign Vidal says—"

Another judge, his voice deep and booming, interjects, "If the story is true, Vidal's behavior is even more egregious! She claims to know how to destroy a Gate, to have possessed the technology to do so, and yet failed to do it! By her account, she has left this world exposed to conquest for the sake of a mere mech."

Noemi can imagine Abel's crisp, superior voice, speaking with thinly veiled huffiness: *A "mere" mech?* He'd be so offended that it would be fun to watch him at it. Her memories of him warm her voice as she says, "He's more than a machine."

Kaminski shakes his head in open contempt. His dress uniform suits him better than Captain Baz; this is a guy who takes down his enemies not with weapons, but with words. "What was it you put in your report? Ah, yes. The mech 'has a soul.'" The glance he gives the judges is amused, inviting them to join in his mockery. "The only question is whether that's sentimentality...or heresy."

"We don't prosecute heresy in this courtroom!" Baz is beside herself. "Can we stick to the facts at issue?"

"Ensign Vidal says the mech's soul is a fact. One that kept her from taking action to save this world—the very action she claims to have abandoned her post to fulfill—so I'd say that's at issue, wouldn't you?" Commander Kaminski folds his arms.

Noemi can't take any more. "We're not here to talk about Abel!"

Captain Baz seizes on this. "That's right. We're here to talk about you."

"No, we aren't." Noemi gives her captain an apologetic look. As much as she appreciates the defense, it's so far beside the point. "What happens to me doesn't matter. It never did. The *only* thing that matters is stopping the Masada Run, forever."

Kaminski stares at her with his icy blue eyes. He was one of the command leaders who devised the Masada Run strategy, and apparently he's egotistical enough to see this as her attacking him. "You cost Genesis one attempt at salvation, and now you want to rob it of another?"

"It's not our salvation! The Masada Run stalls Earth at best, maybe not even for very long. It's not some epic noble stand. It's futile. It's *useless*. We only turned to that strategy because we didn't have any other options, or we thought we didn't. But now that I've traveled the Loop and seen what's going on out there—what's happening on Earth— I know they're not as strong as we thought. And we have allies out there. On Kismet, on Stronghold, even on Earth itself. Maybe Cray, even. If we can get through the Genesis Gate, spread our message, we don't have to stand alone!" Her voice is shaking now. Noemi stops herself and takes a deep breath before she finishes. "I'm willing to give my life for Genesis. All your pilots are. But shouldn't that sacrifice be worth something? We deserve a better fight."

"Soldiers are meant to defend this world!" Kaminski shouts. "Not to demand what they think they 'deserve' from it."

Noemi wonders if her chair is bolted to the floor. Probably so. That means she can't just get up and throw it at him. Words will have to do. "We *are* this world. Its next generation. If you're not trying to save us, then what exactly are you trying to save?"

A deep voice from the back of the room says, "A good question."

The sensors recognize the shift from day to night and turn on the artificial lights, bathing the courtroom in brightness just as everyone turns to see who's walked in. Noemi thought she recognized the voice, but still can't believe it when she sees the figure walking in, dressed in the white-edged robes of the Elder Council.

"Darius Akide," says the chief judge, whose power is irrelevant next to that of one of the five individuals who lead the entire planet of Genesis. "You honor us with your presence. We . . . did not expect the elders to take an interest in the case."

Akide steps closer, a rueful smile on his face. "You didn't think we'd be interested in the first citizen of Genesis to leave this star system in three decades? How incurious you must think us."

"She *claims* to have left this star system." Kaminski can't mouth off at one of the elders, but his disdain for Noemi remains clear. "Since the ship she says she traveled in has conveniently disappeared, we can't prove or disprove her word."

"You think machines have all the answers? Sounds like Earth thinking to me." Akide comes to stand beside Noemi's chair. He's not a tall man, but right now he seems like a giant. "Sometimes we need to search for truth within, quite literally. Ensign Vidal's report said that on Stronghold she was identified as a citizen of Genesis through medical examinations. So we examined the routine tests she was given upon her return to see if the reverse could be proved as well. Lo and behold, we found traces of antiviral medications that haven't been used on Genesis in decades, as well as one previously unknown to us. Also toxins in her blood . . . not dangerously high levels, but high enough to suggest that she's been breathing air more polluted than Genesis's has ever been. If you believe Vidal *didn't* travel to these other worlds, Commander Kaminski, how can you account for these test results?"

Kaminski looks like he'd gladly swallow his tongue. Captain Baz grins, a more open smile than any she's shown since Noemi's return. Until this instant, Noemi hadn't realized that Baz had her doubts. But she fought like hell for Noemi anyway. The fighting takes away any sting the doubt might have caused.

The chief judge manages to say, "We will of course take all the findings into account in our proceedings—"

"These proceedings are over." Darius Akide takes one step forward, more forceful than any of the judges up high behind their bench. "The Elder Council doesn't interfere often in justice proceedings. Almost never, in fact. But we have that right, and we're exercising it today. By decree of the Council, the Masada Run is hereby postponed until future notice. The Council, not the military, will decide if or when that run ever takes place. Furthermore, Ensign Noemi Vidal is cleared of all charges and reinstated at the rank of lieutenant."

"A promotion?" Kaminski realizes he's said that out loud a moment too late.

"This girl has brought us the only intel on Earth and the other colony worlds that we've had in three decades," Akide replies, letting them all hear the steel within his voice. "More than that, she's described a way to destroy a Gate—a way that's no longer useful to us, but one that might spur our own scientists to come up with new theories of their own. I'd say a promotion was the least we owed her."

"I agree," Captain Baz says. "Congratulations, Lieutenant."

It ought to feel like the most exhilarating victory possible. Instead it feels...well, okay, pretty good, but this doesn't solve everything. The Masada Run might not be canceled for good. The war isn't won. And this doesn't bring Esther back.

Gratitude, Noemi reminds herself. When she smiles a moment later, she means it.

The judges don't seem to know quite what to do. One of them starts gathering her tabulator and belongings; another becomes suddenly interested in smoothing out his robe. However, the head judge holds it together. "Lieutenant Vidal, you are hereby freed to return to duty."

Noemi gets to her feet, only to have Akide's hand close firmly over her shoulder. "Actually, she has a new assignment—advising the Council about what she's seen on her journey through the Loop. We read her debrief, of course, but there's much more to learn, I think." He looks her in the face then, for the first time, and misinterprets the dismay he must see there. "The assignment's only temporary, Vidal. We wouldn't keep you from flying forever."

"Thank you, sir." But really, inside her head, she's thinking only, *Me, advise the Council?* Noemi had braced herself for disgrace, even for time in jail. But this is something else completely, unexpected and intimidating. As she takes in the cold fury on Kaminski's face, the way his fingers curl around the edges of his lectern as if it's a neck he can wring, she realizes it might be dangerous, too.

With the Council by her side, though, she might be able to change things—to get another, truer chance to save Genesis.

• • •

Afterward, Noemi expects to be swept someplace very grand, very secret, or both. Maybe to a meeting of the entire Elder Council, or some secret archive where sensitive information is kept. Instead Darius Akide walks with her by the riverside, in full sight of countless passersby. This is her public vindication, then: quiet and uneventful. Noemi isn't sure whether she likes that or not.

Well, it beats prison.

The sun has just dipped below the horizon, and the sky still glows with the last of the light. Noemi takes in the many buildings—the great ones carved of stone, the smaller ones of wood, with their domes and arches. She watches the low, long boats skimming over the water, competitors laughing to see who can reach the far bridge first. A flock of white birds skitters overhead; they're native to Genesis, splendid things with pink-tipped tails that look newly exotic to her now.

The dress uniform that gave her courage in court feels out of place while others stroll by in loose robes and cloaks of bright jewel colors. Those robes have never seemed lovelier to her before, and she can't wait to slip into one again. Standing on her world is even more beautiful than flying above it.

If only she could send Abel a video—even a picture—but he's gone now. All Genesis's scans have failed to find any trace of their nameless ship anywhere in the system. Abel had the sense to take the chance she gave him.

"Sometimes," Akide begins, in his deep voice, "traveling to new places feels strange, but coming home feels even stranger. You don't expect the familiar to become unfamiliar, and yet it does."

Other people feel that way, too? Noemi resists a sigh of relief. "It's quiet here. In good ways, mostly—"

"But not entirely." When Akide sees her expression, he laughs. "Yes, even members of the Elder Council sometimes criticize Genesis. We've gained so much on this world by claiming our independence, but only zealots believe we didn't lose a lot, too."

"Is that why you guys want to talk to me? To find out what we've lost?"

"Partly. But, I admit…there was one topic I wanted to discuss with you personally. Not as a member of the Council. I wanted to talk about Abel."

Of course, Noemi realizes. One of the reasons Darius Akide is legendary even among the elders is the same reason he's the one who teaches military courses about mechs: He was, in his youth, a cyberneticist like Mansfield. According to their histories, Akide was considered Mansfield's greatest student and closest collaborator. But when the Liberty War broke out, Akide chose Genesis. That doesn't mean he lost interest in what he'd studied and built for so long. "What do you need to know about him?"

Akide chuckles. "I know all there is to know. I helped Mansfield design him."

Shock silences her, makes her take a step back. Why didn't she realize that Mansfield's top student would have played a role in Abel's creation? It makes so much sense, and infuriates her at the same time. Once, she could never have imagined talking back to a member of the Elder Council, but now her voice rises as she says, "You agreed to build a machine as intelligent as a human? With the same feelings and thoughts—"

"No, never," Akide says gently, soothing her temper. "It was a theoretical exercise only—one of our final projects together. I had no idea he intended to carry the plans out; even now, I can't entirely believe the Abel model truly fulfilled the ambition of those plans. Now I want to know exactly what Abel is capable of."

"He has a soul. I know that as surely as I know I have one."

Akide shakes his head. "That's only an illusion, Vidal. A convincing illusion, and I don't blame you for being fooled. Model One A is already extraordinary without going to any...fanciful extremes."

He speaks kindly. Means well. Unlike Kaminski, Darius Akide doesn't intend to shame Noemi for her beliefs about Abel; he simply believes his last cybernetics project with Burton Mansfield was only that, tinkering with metal and circuits.

However, Noemi didn't put everything in her report. She hasn't told them how crushed Abel was by Mansfield's betrayal, or even what Mansfield truly intended, because God forbid anyone else should ever get the same idea. She hasn't told them about Abel's declaration of love either. That's too personal. It belongs to him and her alone.

Besides, if she'd reported that Abel loved her, they might've wanted to ask how she felt about him. Noemi can't answer that, because she isn't sure.

Is it love? Maybe it would've been, given only a little more time. All she knows is that she still wants to hear what Abel would make of everything she sees. What he might do if he were here beside her. He's the one she wants to talk to about everything that's happening, even though she knows she'll never get the chance. She doesn't feel as safe here on her own planet, under the protection of an elder on the

Council, as she did with Abel beside her. This is her home, and yet it feels incomplete without him.

If that's not love... surely it's where love begins.

"Tell me," Akide says. "Where do you think Abel's gone? What is he likely to do next?"

"I don't know."

It's the truth. And in some ways, that's the most wonderful truth of all. Abel's potential is as limitless as any human being's. The entire galaxy has opened to him, and she wants him to find someplace he can build a good life—if such a place exists in this galaxy anywhere besides Genesis. Noemi's not sure about that anymore.

But as she looks up into the darkening night sky, she knows she'll never stop hoping. Never stop searching the stars, wondering whether any of them could be the one Abel someday calls home.

42

ABEL LEANS BACK IN THE CAPTAIN'S CHAIR. "REPORT."

"We've got a confirmation on the Saturn-Neptune ore haul," Zayan reports from the ops console. "That is, if we can pick up our load within eight hours."

"Set in a course," Abel says to Harriet, who grins at him from the navigation console as she follows his order. To Zayan he adds, "Let the mine know the *Persephone* accepts the job."

He has renamed this ship one last time. He had to, of course, to cover his tracks, but he chose the name carefully. In Greek myth, Persephone was the bride of Hades, rescued from the underworld by her mother, Demeter, but still bound to her husband by the pomegranate seeds she ate—and, in some tellings of the story, by love. Abel thinks of Noemi as belonging to both Genesis and to the stars, as a person who will always have a place on more than one world.

Besides, he thinks, *she's been to hell and back.*

If only he could tell her that joke, and see if it makes her smile. But he doesn't allow himself to dwell on the loss too often. Noemi's final request was that he create a life of his own, and he's already spent enough time brooding in the equipment pod bay for many lifetimes.

No more. Abel intends to live.

Once he was safely back in the Kismet system and had dealt with the first crushing sorrow of losing Noemi, he considered his options carefully. His skills would allow him to take on virtually any sort of work, and he already possessed the ultimate advantage in that area: a spaceworthy ship. Erasing his criminal profiles was tricky work, but well within his skills; he erased Noemi's, too, while he was at it, just in case she ever gets another chance to travel the galaxy. Abel wants that for her.

After that, he was free.

So, he became a Vagabond, dressing and acting the part. In order to get work hauling shipments and the like—while still avoiding interaction with Georges and other mechs that might now be programmed to recognize his face—he knew he'd need to take on a crew. But it could only be a small one, made up only of people he trusts. Luckily, Harriet and Zayan had still been working on Wayland Station, doing the backbreaking labor of post-explosion cleanup. Innocent of Abel's status as either mech or fugitive, they were only too happy to switch to cushier jobs on such a "flash" ship.

"Room and board comes with the job?" Harriet had said, eyes wide, as Zayan whooped in happy disbelief. *"You're a soft touch, Abel, you know that?"*

As a mech it is pleasant, if ironic, to be told you have a kind heart.

He'd like to hear what his creator would think of that, but of course that would mean encountering Burton Mansfield again, an experience Abel intends to avoid. It's even possible that his creator has died by now. He was so elderly, so frail, and enough of Abel's programming lingers to pain him whenever he remembers Mansfield's racking cough.

If Mansfield is alive, however, he's searching for Abel more desperately than ever. Best for Abel to stay on the move. Mansfield has only so many months left, after all, and Abel can wait forever.

Forever is a long time. Long enough, perhaps, that he might one day travel to Genesis.

He's still willing to die for Noemi and her world. Still hasn't completely abandoned the idea of stealing another thermomagnetic device, returning to the Genesis Gate, and destroying it for her. But he has other ideas, too, now.

For instance—what if he returned to Genesis with an army?

There's a resistance out there, deadly and effective, and

he's owed favors by members of both the moderate and radical wings. Some scientists on Cray, in the very core of Earth's technological supremacy, appear willing to break ranks. Earth will do anything to bury the truth about Cobweb, a truth Abel knows and might, in time, learn how to exploit. These elements, brought together, could prove very powerful.

What if Earth could be cowed into making peace? He likes the idea of sailing through the Genesis Gate accompanied by diplomatic envoys, and knows Noemi would like it even more. For all her talk about winning the war, what she wanted most was to end it. To have a chance to choose her own life, the way Abel is choosing his own.

He's going to do what she asked. He'll explore this entire galaxy, and experience every single thing he can.

But nothing seems likely to match their one kiss.

As Harriet brings the ship toward Saturn, its rings dominating the enormous viewscreen, Abel focuses on a single tiny star above it. That's Genesis's sun. From here he can see it in all its light.

Silently he traces out a new constellation, one only he knows. One with Noemi at the very heart.

ACKNOWLEDGMENTS

I owe thanks to so many people—first and foremost my wonderful editor, Pam Gruber, who saw the promise in this idea and has made working on this book such a pleasure. Thanks also to my agent, Diana Fox, to my assistants, Erin Gross and Melissa Jolly, and to my family: Mom, Dad, Matthew, Melissa, Eli, and Ari. In all honesty I should probably also thank Ba Chi Canteen for providing the immense amounts of pho required to fuel me through this project; and Madeline Nelson, Stephanie Nelson, and Marti Dumas for being willing to go to Ba Chi with me that many times. As ever, thanks to Edy Moulton, Ruth Morrison, and Rodney Crouther for listening to all my crazy plot ideas, and Dr. Whitney Raju for patiently talking me through the medical implications of each one. Finally, all the love to the good people of Octavia Books in New Orleans. (If you want a signed copy of any of my books, visit them online! They can take care of that for you.)